MY
POOR
PIRATE

A novel by Jurģis Liepnieks

Dedicated to my dear wife Ilze Elizabete, whom I've never intended to kill. Without her love and support, this book would never have existed.

PART 1.
Best For Everyone

CHAPTER 1

Marat grinned, watching Dimitri approach him along the park walkway with his distinctive stride. He waddled as he walked. The only other people who walked like that were beefy bodybuilders: setting their feet a little wider than everyone else, shifting their weight from one foot to the other – as though they had to be careful, lest the ground rock like a ship in a storm, causing them and their top-heavy body to tumble. But, unlike bodybuilders, Dimitri didn't stick his chest out when he walked. Quite the opposite, in fact. His shoulders were slouched forward ever so slightly, making his arms more prominent and his posture more stable. Dimitri didn't hold his head up, either; his chin was almost pressed into his neck, making it seem as though he were watching the world through his forehead. That's how all Greco-Roman wrestlers or Judo athletes (Dimitri having been both of these) tended to walk – always on the lookout for a sudden, incoming move, so that they could maintain their balance and combat any jerking or pulling.

"You look more like a bouncer than a banker," Marat said when Dimitri had finally come close enough, "is this how you walk around the bank, too? And wearing the same expression?"

"I'm not a banker. I'm a mathematician," Dimitri grunted as they shook hands. "And you look more like a sales assistant in a suit shop," he shot back, assessing his friend with contempt. "I can't decide what's more annoying – your stripey suit, or that pretentious little handkerchief in your pocket." Continuous mocking was a cornerstone of their friendship.

"Oh, getting serious now... For a man who actually knows how to dress, there's nothing worse than being compared to a suit salesman," Marat replied, with mock bitterness in his voice.

But Dimitri didn't relent.

"That handkerchief in your pocket, though. Total overkill."

"What? I'd say I look like a man who's climbed Everest," replied Marat, "I mean, a man who's capable of achieving the goals he's set for himself. You, on the other hand... If the old-timers saw the shady character who was modelling their pension plans, they'd demand your resignation immediately."

"They can't fire me. I'm untouchable. I'm a numbers genius," Dimitri shot back. "Insurers and fund managers are willing to queue for hours just to see me. Because none of them know what maths is, let alone how to use it."

"And also because they love how humble you are," said Marat, perpetuating the friendly sarcasm.

"That too," Dimitri agreed. "Imagine what would happen if *I* started going around, telling everyone that *I'd* climbed Everest any chance I got?"

"I don't know how or when," said Marat, "but one day fate will make you pay for being such an arrogant prick. People don't like it when others go about flaunting their supremacy. They always find some way to take their revenge for the embarrassment it causes them to feel." Marat unbuttoned his suit jacket and spread himself on the park bench.

"Right." Dimitri smirked. "And that's coming from one of the richest and most public figures in town. The famous 'conqueror of Everest', with the pictures of said conquest forced upon anyone in this city who has access to the internet or the tabloids."

"You're right," conceded Marat. "I'm probably not the best example. Speaking of which, I'm planning to write a book. I'm going to call it *The Code of Success*."

"Of course. Where would we be without your book?" Dimitri's tone was again one of ridicule.

"Yeah. It will be a manual for reaching any summit. The main point being that three things determine success – proper research and careful planning, strict discipline, and teamwork."

"Erm, I'm pretty sure that's four things," Dimitri corrected him.

"And hard work, of course."

"Of course. Where would you be without hard work?!" Dimitri made no attempt to hide the incredulity in his voice.

"You know, I ran over a bird today," said Marat, changing the subject suddenly, "a pigeon, I think. Probably sick or injured. It was crossing the road, and by the time I realised that it wouldn't be taking flight it was too late. I feel kinda bad about it. Maybe I should have stopped after I—"

"Shouldn't we get going?" interrupted Dimitri. "I don't like being late. I'm a banker after all," he added, sarcastically, paying no attention to the tale about the pigeon.

"No. The sommelier called me to say there's no need to rush. They've had a fire in the kitchen and they need to air out the rooms – or something like that. He asked if we could come an hour later." Marat crossed his legs, making himself more comfortable on the bench.

"A fire?" Dimitri didn't hide his discontent. "What are we going to do for a whole hour?"

"Well, that's just life." In contrast to his friend, Marat looked very relaxed about everything. "You can't predict anything. And the worst thing is, you can't even predict that everything will happen unpredictably – because things can go smoothly, too: just as you had planned them, without the slightest hiccup."

Dimitri looked annoyed, but he didn't say anything.

"Oh, come on! Let's just sit here in the park for a bit. Look at the gorgeous weather! It's not often you get a chance to just sit on a bench and ponder how wonderful everything is." Marat stretched out his legs; his leather shoes glistening with their recently purchased, fresh-from-the-shop shine.

Dimitri sighed.

4

"I mean, look, it's spring!" Marat was showing no sign of stopping. "A perfect Wednesday afternoon! The sun is glistening on all the windows, people have disappeared off somewhere, and the linden trees smell delightful. The Easter weekend is coming up, and everything is just so perfect and peaceful." Marat sent his satisfied gaze across the park. "And, by the way, I've decided to kill Twinka," he added in passing, as though having just remembered some insignificant piece of news that was only worth mentioning because they had an hour to kill.

"To kill her, is it?" Dimitri repeated, sure that this was another witty remark from his friend.

"Yes. I intend to murder her," Marat confirmed with a straight face. "Don't act surprised – every other husband longs to kill his wife. And don't tell me that you've never felt like murdering your ex."

"But you've always insisted that you don't want to divorce her?" Dimitri was baffled.

"Yeah, that's right. I don't want to divorce her. I want to kill her."

Dimitri didn't reply, and instead waited to see which direction his friend's new thread would take.

Meanwhile, a self-satisfied Marat, who had practically splayed himself across the park bench and now tossed his left leg over his right, continued:

"Divorce, you see... it's such a mess; so many negative emotions involved; a massive trauma for the children. It turns childcare into total chaos; into a wound that will never heal. Ronia is fourteen now, and she just won't understand. She'll blame and judge me for it, and eventually we'll lose touch. Meanwhile I'll be forced to watch Twinka's demise: to look at the shambles of her broken life and feel guilty about it. It's one thing to break someone's heart when they're twenty; it's something else entirely to break a forty-year-old woman's life. I mean, I'll obviously find another woman and feel happy again. I'll fall in love; go to Venice, Kyoto, Bora Bora; and my younger – and probably less intelligent – new girlfriend will publish everything on her Instagram. And who will have the heart to stop her? Because these new, amazing experiences would be her *real life*. And everyone will see just how happy we are together, how radiant, our love blossoming... But I won't be able to fully enjoy it, because, regardless of whether I want to or not, I'll be wondering how Twinka's feeling. And I know exactly how she'll be feeling. My new happiness will become a painful, chronic illness for her, and I'll feel guilty of course. I'm not some heartless monster, you know. That guilt will then stay with me. It will poison all my new pleasures. And, honestly, who needs all that?"

Dimitri laughed to himself, but said nothing further than "Hmm..."

Marat wasn't finished.

"Not to mention how much I'll have to change my life. I'll need a new house, I'll have to argue and testify in court, split our assets, and redefine my relationship with so many people – all our mutual friends and acquaintances. And they'll all feel terrible about it. They'll want to carry on their relationship with both of us, but that will become so complicated. Everyone will have questions: they'll want to know what happened, and why, and who's to blame for it. It would be a complete nightmare. And it would all carry on like that for years. I mean, it would be a total disaster. Absolutely everything about that scenario feels rotten to me," Marat said, ahead of then leaning in closer to Dimitri. "On the other hand – if my wife were to... oh, I don't know... die in some horrid accident, then all I'd need to do is arrange the funeral, and that's it. Everyone would carry on living just like before. In fact, they might even become friendlier and emotionally closer to one another. I already have a good connection with Ronia, but it could be a lot tighter. I think she maybe respects me too much? It just feels like she never fully opens up and reveals herself. The most sincere and significant conversations are always between her and her mum. If we were to go down the road of divorce, then there's absolutely no chance that my relationship with Ronia would ever improve. If Twinka were to die, though, it would be an entirely different matter. We'd be closer than ever. Because there simply would be no other option. And no one would have to move out. We wouldn't have to divide things between us or change anything in our lives. I mean, sure – we'd grieve for a bit – but that's it. Life would go on. Doesn't that sound a million times better to you?"

"Well, I mean, divorce is a huge mess and certainly traumatic for a child," Dimitri began, before succumbing to laughter, "...but I can only imagine the trauma Ronia would suffer when she eventually found out that you killed her mother, because you thought that getting a divorce would be messier."

"Touch wood." Marat tapped on the park bench. "The devil is in the detail, which is why everything needs careful planning."

"So, you've decided to... ?"

"Poisoning. I'd like to do it by poisoning. I don't want her to suffer," Marat said, pulling out a flashy leather cigar case from his inner jacket pocket. Inside it were two Cubans, and he offered one to Dimitri.

"No, thank you." Dimitri scrunched his face in disgust.

"Suit yourself," Marat said, before leaning back. "Now, the best option would be cyanide, of course. It's a classic, very elegant, type of poison. Cyanide is like... a Porsche 911, or Leica, or Patek Philippe," he continued, searching his other pockets for a knife and a lighter. "Look, imagine it's the year 1945, April, and Russians are encroaching on Berlin. Everyone there knows that they've lost the war. Berlin Philharmonic is playing their last concert, and everyone knows that this one truly will be their last. The Third Reich has fallen, and – any minute now – the biggest war in human history will end. The mood in the city couldn't be more grim. But despite this, they're all wearing smoking jackets, uniforms covered in war medals, evening dresses, tuxedos and tailcoats. Then, during the intermission, teenagers from the Hitler Youth start bringing out these massive, beautiful, ornate silver platters and distributing capsules of cyanide. Imagine how saturated that moment must have been. Now, that's life! Real living. And many of them did make use of those capsules."

"How can you smoke that shit? The stench is horrible." The disgust on Dimitri's face could also be described as saturated.

Marat ignored Dimitri's remark. "Arsenic. That's another classic poison. The most popular method of assassination among European upper and middle classes, all throughout the nineteenth century. It's hard to find traces of it because the effect isn't immediate. But, unfortunately, death from arsenic is absolutely horrific. In fact, Flaubert described it really well in his *Madame Bovary*. No, that won't work; I don't want Twinka to suffer."

"Sounds like you've really made a head start on this thing," Dimitri concluded.

"Strychnine. Another poison, from Agatha Christie's novels. But it's no good either. For the same reason as arsenic, plus it's almost impossible to get hold of. You know, I think the best thing would be to use something that comes from Mother Nature. Did you know that the poison in the cup that Socrates was forced to drink was made of hemlock root? It grows in these parts, too."

"You do realise that the husband is always the first suspect whenever a wife gets murdered? You'll be taken into custody

8

immediately. What will you do then?" Dimitri had butted in, without realising that he was now discussing Twinka's murder as a very real possibility.

Marat didn't listen. "Mushrooms – that's why mushrooms are the best. The death cap, incredibly poisonous, also grows in our neck of woods. You just need half a cap; a few grams should do it. What's more, you can actually boil it, fry it, freeze it or dry it, and it will still remain poisonous. And apparently it tastes great!"

"If it's so poisonous, how could anyone tell you that it tasted great?" Dimitri always demanded precision in people's words and thoughts, and Marat loved him for it.

"Hmm yeah, you're right." Though the expression on Marat's face signalled that he himself had already considered this. "There are a few survivors, which worries me – I was researching the statistics. A couple of years ago two people died of the less-poisonous 'destroying angel', and another two survived the following year. That's the problem with these mediaeval poisons – modern medicine knows how to pull you through it. In the olden days, you could just make a separate mushroom sauce for your spouse, have them wash it down with a good Bordeaux, and the deed was done. Nowadays, the ambulance arrives in minutes. Resuscitation, medication, and *voilà* – a week later, you're back on your feet, walking around as though nothing ever happened," Marat reasoned, disgruntled.

"Sounds to me like your grand plan isn't quite hatched yet," said Dimitri.

"No, not yet," Marat confessed.

"I just don't get your thinking. You've always had so many interests, hobbies, and your work. Meanwhile, your daughter is being fed, cared for and looked after, taken to all those afterschool clubs. What will you gain by killing Twinka? You'll have to raise Ronia all by yourself: sort out her clothes, her hair bands, homework, sanitary products, take care of her pimples, and a thousand other little details, which you probably haven't even pictured yet. Why do you need all that? Get yourself a lover, go to Venice or Kyoto – and wherever the hell else you said you wanted to go – and calm down. You're not the first one to find yourself in this situation, and you certainly won't be the last."

"No, that won't work. That's not it," Marat objected categorically. "First of all, I don't want to hide and sneak around. Secondly, what do you think is best for Twinka? To see me with a new lover, or to be dead before we even get to that?"

"Well, I think if we asked her, she'd probably take the lover option." Dimitri chuckled.

While they'd been chatting, Marat had managed to turn half of his cigar into a column of ash. He held the remainder carefully in his stretched-out hand, making sure the column didn't collapse.

"It drives me insane," Marat continued, gloomy and serious now, "completely mad. Listen to this – she drinks wine in the evenings. Actually, she gets started in the afternoons, but she manages to somehow keep herself together until our daughter's bedtime. Then, around nine, when Ronia is put to bed, the gloves come off. By eleven, twelve o'clock, she's completely wasted. And then she goes to the garage to have a smoke – because, God forbid, if Ronia was ever to find out that she's smoking! But you know what annoys me the most? She has this habit of leaving the cork in the bottle opener. Do you know what that means? She takes a fresh bottle of wine, pulls out the cork, then leaves the cork stuck on the fucking bottle opener. When she inevitably feels the need to open another bottle, she just goes and finds a new opener – pulls the cork out and, once again, leaves it there. The entire house, all our drawers, are packed full of bottle openers with corks still stuck on them! Sometimes I think she's buying a new bottle opener every time she buys a bottle of wine." Marat was on a roll. "I used to remove those corks in the mornings, but then one evening I decided to watch her. At this point she is on her third bottle that evening. *Is she going to open another or not?* is the question being begged. So, she's looking around, and I realise that she's looking for a bottle opener, but they've all still got the bloody corks stuck on them, so she obviously can't use any of them. She sighs, puts the bottle down, and decides to go to bed. From that day on I stopped rescuing the corks. I only do it when I need one myself. At least she's drinking a little less because of that, even though it doesn't help much. When our cleaner comes round twice a week to make the place look tidy, she removes all the corks again..."

Dimitri didn't say anything. He imagined what would happen if Marat raised the cigar to his lips. Most likely, the ash column would fall on his lap and ruin his fine striped suit.

"They're just little things, of course, so I don't say anything. It's not like it affects me, but I mean... what the hell?! How hard can it be to remove a cork from a bottle opener?"

"I don't want to interfere in your affairs, of course, but I have to say that people have bigger problems than that," Dimitri objected with a warm laugh.

"I hate it." Marat tipped the column of ash by his feet.

"How long has this been going on for? I mean, you used to love her, didn't you?"

"I don't know... Things just built up, I guess. All marriages wilt eventually, even the best ones. But she wasn't always an alcoholic. And her Christianity on top of it all. It didn't bother me before, it sort of amused me, but now it's proper grating on me. And the whole house is full of bottles – empty ones, half-empty ones, full ones. She always has two on the go, because she – you see – doesn't *actually* drink; she's just tasting the wine, comparing it, researching... do you get it? She'll open a bottle and then open another one from the same year, but from a different winery. Or she'll open one from the same winery but from a different year. Or one from a different grape, but the same year. Or the same grape but from a different country; and so on and so forth... and then she'll compare them all – 'Which one's better?'" Marat winced. "And, naturally, one is always worse than the other, or maybe just shit, so she doesn't finish it, and starts a new one instead, until she's got three bottles on the go. Eventually, though, she'll finish the bad one, too. And you can't throw the bottles away – oh, *no* – so as not to forget which wine was good, and which one wasn't. Or one of them might have a pretty label, so you can't throw that one out; or another might have an unusual label. Others are very expensive or very old, so you can't chuck those either. As a result, there are bottles absolutely everywhere."

Dimitri didn't hide his astonishment, and interrupted. "Does she drink on her own though? I mean, you usually have a drink together, don't you?"

"Well, I drink a lot less than her," Marat grunted back.

"But you're the one who taught her to drink; you led her into the 'world of fine wine', so to speak. I mean, all that tasting, comparing, savouring and describing different flavours – she picked all that up from you, didn't she?" Dimitri's confusion was palpable.

"And we barely have sex –" Marat had ignored his friend's question – "she's just too drunk in the evenings. She seems to think that a trolleyed woman, reeking of fags, is very sexy. I'd like to do it in the mornings but she usually gets Ronia ready for school and goes for a nap until noon. Then she gets up and drinks coffee until one or two in the afternoon. I mean, I can't wait that long – I'm working," Marat continued to complain. "On weekends there's always something that involves Ronia. Either her friends are staying over, or we're going out somewhere."

12

"Forgive me," Dimitri chimed in, "but what you're describing here sounds like the most typical scenes from a married life. I'd say it's a good, normal marriage; to be honest, I don't even see a good reason for getting divorced, let alone..."

"No, trust me, it would be much better for her if I just killed her. It would be far better for her than getting divorced."

"It would be better for her if you killed her?" Dimitri repeated, his eyebrows raised.

"Well, of course." Marat had started blowing smoke rings. He managed to blow two at once. "Think about it. A thirty-eight-year-old woman, a divorced woman, and – let's be honest – an alcoholic woman, who doesn't have a real profession. I mean, Portuguese language and literature hardly constitutes a vocation. She's never worked a day in her life. What would she have to look forward to? Is she going to find another man? Being forty for a woman is like being eighty for a man. Who needs a woman in her forties? Only some loser, alcoholic or druggie; a mediocrity at best. And it would be very difficult for Twinka to lower the bar after being with me. I'd say impossible. It would have been different if she'd never lived with a decent guy, but now... No, it's obvious that the 'classic' problems will start. She'll demand that Ronia feel sorry for her; she'll blame me for ruining her life; she'll be angry at me and everyone else; she'll fall into self-pity, depression, alcoholism. She'll probably start taking all sorts of pills, too; then she'll put on weight, fall into an even deeper depression, consume even more alcohol and drugs. Then, to top it all off, she'll hit her menopause. It's a clear downward spiral. She's got forty years of suffering and unhappiness ahead of her. Meanwhile, I'll have to spend those four decades feeling guilty, thinking that it's all my fault: that I'm to blame for her alcoholism and depression, and her wasted, unhappy life."

"Oh, come on, you're exaggerating now!" Dimitri interjected passionately. "Twinka looks great! She's a stunner, you could easily figure her for thirty. She's fit, good-looking and intelligent. You just don't see it anymore. She'd have no trouble finding another man," he argued.

But Marat had stopped listening.

"The world is cruel. It's not my fault that nowadays a decent bloke is at the pinnacle of his life even at the age of forty-nine or fifty-nine. He's mature, self-actualized, rich and stable, but still full of energy and the zest for life. That kind of man would make a great match for any woman. I could marry a woman in her twenties or thirties. Basically, the world is my oyster! But for a lonely, alcoholic woman who's approaching her forties... that's it. Game over! And – let me tell you something else – it's not only better for her, but also better for Ronia, if I murdered her."

Dimitri shook his head in genuine bafflement. Marat had always excelled with his out-of-the-box thinking – that's what made him Marat! – but this was just too crazy, even for him.

"Undoubtedly, her mother's death would be very traumatic for Ronia. But less traumatic than a divorce. Lots of studies – very serious studies – have shown that kids whose parents had got divorced do worse in school than those whose parent had died." Marat released two further smoke rings. They looked to Dimitri like doughnuts.

"And you honestly think that your daughter will be better off if you just killed Twinka?"

"But there's nothing to think about! It's simply a fact. She'll suffer her mother's death, but at least no one will yank her between two homes, or try to get her on their side. No one's going to try and convince her of their version of the truth. She won't have to watch an unhappy, self-destructive alcoholic mother go into decline for the rest of her life, thinking that her suffering was all Dad's fault. However, if Twinka were to die, Ronia would always have nice memories to cherish – about her wonderful mother who was beautiful, loving and caring – *and* she'll get to keep her family."

"By 'her family', you mean you and your new girlfriend? And you truly believe that this would be better for her?"

"But if we get divorced..." Marat paid no heed to Dimitri's questions, "...it could be even worse, you know. I mean, Ronia isn't stupid – she'll notice things and, eventually, understand everything. She won't blame me, because she'll be forced to watch her alcoholic mother drink herself to death. What will probably happen is that she'll turn away from her and choose me; she'll choose to get close to me. Can you imagine how painful that would be for Twinka? No, either way you look at it, a divorce would most definitely be the worst option for Twinka."

"So, let me get this straight... You don't want to cause any pain or suffering for anyone, which is why you've decided to murder your wife?"

"That's right. I want to do the right thing. And that would, very clearly, be the right thing to do."

"Are you actually serious?"

"Yeah."

"And you don't get the sense that breaking all possible laws – God-made and man-made – might be the *wrong* thing to do?"

"Ahhh." Marat sighed. "You mathematicians and your laws. You're the one who said that the husband is always the first suspect. Why do you think that is?" He gestured as he spoke. "Because every other husband is thinking exactly what I'm thinking now, except they lack the courage to actually do something about it. Mediocrities are never capable of following through with plans, so they don't even try. They're soft, frightened and completely incapable."

There was barely anything left of the cigar. Marat didn't usually smoke them all the way to the butt. For reasons still unclear even to himself, he wasn't ready to reveal to his friend that he knew that his wife had a lover. Maybe he was ashamed, or maybe it was just too painful to admit. In any case, he didn't want to discuss it. At least not today.

With a powerful flick, Marat flipped the remains of the cigar across the pavement and onto the grass.

"What an elegant gesture," Dimitri commented quietly with a smirk.

"For compost," Marat replied, wincing.

CHAPTER 2

Twinka called him Cat, and she remembered very clearly how it had all started.

He was an attractive man – tall, dark-haired, smart, confident and stoic. Twinka knew that women fancied him, and she also suspected that he was taking advantage of this, but she had never imagined anything remotely erotic or sexual between them. She simply didn't think about men on those terms anymore. She didn't allow herself to. Twinka had been, and had been, a loyal wife to her husband. And, for sixteen years of her married life, she had succeeded. Over the past few years their marriage hadn't been perfect – but wasn't that the norm? Wasn't a perfect marriage more of an illusion: a dream, or a myth, that had succeeded in ruining so many wonderful families? This eternal striving; this insatiable desire for something that only existed in movies, novels and fairy-tales; and which degraded the simple and ordinary everyday relationships between two people who loved each other, with all the hardships and daily routines that co-habitation brought with it.

No, Twinka loved Marat and she loved Ronia. Of course, Marat was no angel; he could sometimes be harsh, he could go without speaking to her for days – not because he was upset or passive aggressive, but simply because his mind was preoccupied with various projects, work and other things, all of which had become more important to him than family. But that's just who he was, and if he did manage to find some time for his family, he would spend it all on Ronia, not her.

Twinka had told herself that this was perfectly normal – Ronia was her priority, too – and yet you couldn't fail to notice that something in their relationship had died. Twinka felt like something was dying inside her, too. Despite the fact that their marriage was no longer at the centre of his world, Marat seemed to be leading a relatively wholesome life. He never treated Twinka badly, and Twinka was convinced that he still loved her. Not like he used to, of course – he loved her differently – but nonetheless, he did still love her.

Twinka wanted to have another child. She thought that it could, at least, bring back those times when Ronia was a toddler – which, in retrospect, seemed like the happiest of her life. But Marat was categorically against it and made Twinka take the pill.

Yes, they'd grown apart over the years; they'd started sleeping in separate bedrooms – but only because it was more convenient. Their passion (and, consequently, sex) had almost disappeared. On its own accord, their life had turned out completely different to how it used to be, but they still got on really well, and never usually had a fight. In short, they lived well.

And yet something suppressed – something important – had let, or had *made*, things happen in a way that surprised Twinka. She had always thought of herself as a woman who wasn't capable of something like that.

It had all started last summer, at a dinner party in their home on Button Street. It was a proper party: one of those crazy ones where everyone gets drunk very quickly and before long start to dance; where alcohol is flowing and soon enough cocaine follows – appearing out of nowhere – followed in turn by colourful pills; and where everything becomes wild and untameable.

It was a warm summer's night. The doors and windows to the garden were wide open, and the air smelled of linden trees. A group of people were dancing the foxtrot. Twinka was dressed in a light skirt and an open-backed top. As she twirled, she suddenly realised that her skirt was floating upwards elegantly, revealing more of her legs – which still looked stunning at her age – and perhaps something else a little higher up... That's when she first felt Cat's stare... and so twirled even more. She laughed, with both of her arms flung in the air, then stopped for a moment, feeling dizzy, and, with her eyes closed, started spinning in the opposite direction. She felt Cat's eyes, as though they were glued to her ass, and then she felt his arms. He had stopped Twinka mid-twirl: pressing her close up against himself, his hand wandering beneath her skirt. It happened right in the middle of the room. Anyone could have seen it. But no one seemed to have noticed, because they were all just as wasted as she was.

Everything had happened as if by its own accord. At least, Twinka couldn't recall deciding whether to do it or not, or even having time to consider it. No – but, all of a sudden, they had been kissing. It wasn't like he'd kissed her first – both of them were suddenly making out in the little corridor between the two rooms. They hadn't even attempted to hide it, even though anyone could have caught them in the act. They pulled away from each other for a moment, then resumed kissing with even greater passion, and Twinka had felt these strange, strong, unfamiliar, shameless and coarse hands touching her all over, and she hadn't found it repulsive. She'd felt something special all of a sudden, and it wasn't clear to her whether it was the alcohol or the cocaine, or something long-forgotten; something she'd been unknowingly yearning for all these years.

And that's how it had all began. Nothing more happened that night, but it was clear the plane's engine was ignited and it was building speed on the runway. Yet wasn't too late to stop: to slow down and reduce the speed, or even to bring the aircraft back to the hangar and continue to live her life as though nothing had ever happened.

When Cat called her the next day, she thought it was perhaps to explain himself; or for them to mutually agree that each had been completely wasted, drugged-up, and they couldn't remember anything that happened. But somehow, on its own accord, that conversation took a different turn. First, they had agreed to meet for a coffee, and following that twist they started discussing things that would have been better left alone. They hadn't put an end to it there and then, and buried what had happened somewhere deep inside 'the naughty memory box', as Twinka had thought and intended.

CHAPTER 3

The afternoon sun had disappeared from the windows. A tranquil and, in some sense, happy evening was dawning in the park. Considering it was Easter week, the weather was exceedingly warm. Murmur was coming in from the outdoor terraces of the cafes, where skilled waiters were rushed off their feet, manoeuvring between packed tables, trying to cope with the sudden influx of people. It was difficult to find a free bench in the park as well. The entire city seemed to have come out to enjoy the warm spring evening.

"Breathe in," Marat said. As though Dimitri didn't know how to do it, he demonstrated by inhaling deeply and then slowly exhaling, his eyes half closed. "Remember this moment. This is how I'd like to remember life. What aromas can you identify? The smell of water from that pond behind us? Can you sense how fragrant the concrete pavement is, and the grass, and this wooden bench over here..."

"All I can smell is your disgusting cigar," Dimitri grunted.

"It's Cohiba. A classic," Marat said, without any attempt to hide his self-satisfaction.

"Just like cyanide?"

"Yeah." Marat laughed. "Or like cashmere. Or a good suit."

"Or like a murder?"

"Well, I hadn't thought of it that way." Dimitri hadn't succeeded in wiping the smugness from Marat's face. "But if you say so..."

"I have a feeling that you're just looking to raise your hedonism to a new level by experiencing what it's like to kill someone and get away with it."

"No, not at all," Marat objected excitedly, "it's not like that. If I wanted to kill someone for some obscure pleasure that killing might offer – and I'm not saying it couldn't – I would have chosen to take the life of someone I really hate. An enemy, a traitor, a bastard, a true degenerate: someone you wouldn't just enjoy killing, but you'd enjoy torturing. The thing is, I don't hate Twinka; I still love her. I simply don't want her in my life anymore."

"Yeah, I get it, you want to kill her because it will be much better for her," Dimitri said with a healthy helping of irony.

"Yeah, that's right. For her and Ronia. And for me, of course."

"Killing is a sin. Do you realise that? A *sssss-in*," Dimitri stressed. "And you're talking about it as though it's some insignificant detail. But it will change your soul forever."

"My *sssss-oul*," Marat parroted him. "Did you know that the soul resides in the blood? No? It's written in the third book of Moses. That's why Jews aren't supposed to eat anything that still has a drop of blood in it. You, on the other hand, never say no to a bloodied steak. You're happy to stuff yourself with the soul of the bull, smacking and licking your lips."

"I'm not Jewish," Dimitri said, as though trying to justify himself.

"So are you saying that you're not talking about the soul from the Bible, but some other version? Please enlighten me as to what kind of a soul is it, and where it lives, because I've heard different concepts," provoked Marat.

"Remember Kant, who was baffled only by two things: the starry heavens above him and the moral law within his own heart. So, there you go – the soul is the moral law within your heart."

"Nah, that won't do, because Kant didn't say *that* – Kant said that two things fill the mind with admiration and awe: the starry heavens above us and the moral law within. He said nothing about the heart or the soul."

It seemed that, any minute now, Marat would positively burst from self-satisfaction.

"All I meant was that killing is a sin; that you shouldn't kill, and such things are never without their consequences. Any murder disrupts and destroys the natural order of things. It creates chaos. It's just too serious."

"Yes, of course it's serious. I'm not arguing against that. I'm simply arguing against the cliché that killing is always bad and inexcusable, because it's not true. I mean, it's okay to kill a terrorist, or a murderer who's attacked you or someone else. Then it's no longer considered to be evil. Quite the opposite in fact – then it becomes something good, right? It's the motivation and goal that differentiates whether a particular murder is good or evil. Let me offer another version to you, as a Christian. I am going to murder Twinka, so that she can meet Christ as soon as possible, which is what every Christian dreams of, because life over there is apparently much better than here. I'm going to become an altruist and, for my beloved's sake, I shall take upon myself the biggest sacrifice there could ever be. Namely, I'll roast in hell's flames forever, so that she, my angel, can reach the gates of Paradise sooner. I'll practically be leading her straight to Paradise. Isn't that the best thing you can do for a Christian? But I'm happy to do it, even if I have to burn in hell for an eternity. I'd be ready to bear such a sacrifice. Can you think of a bigger sacrifice than that? You know Twinka: she's an angel, the very personification of unconditional love, goodness and kindness, so she'll definitely get into Paradise. And Paradise will definitely be better for her than becoming a drunkard on Earth."

"I didn't know that you believed in hell and Paradise."

"I don't. But she does, and so do you, so I'm offering you an unbeatable argument – in your world, that is."

"There are simply some things you cannot do, whatever the goal or circumstances. You just can't. Because that's evil." Dimitri had started to resent their conversation, while it seemed to be having the exact opposite effect on Marat.

"No, that's not true." Not only was Marat enjoying it, he was just getting going. "Was it the right thing to kill Osama bin Laden, was that allowed? I'll spare you the thinking and just tell you that it was. One man, the President of the United States, made the right decision. Sent his people to a foreign country where they broke all the laws of that country and shot bin Laden, his son, his brother and whatnot."

"What a comparison." Dimitri looked at Marat with a perplexed gaze. "Osama bin Laden was a terrorist and a mass murderer. But you want to kill your own wife because she can't be bothered to remove corks from the bottle openers."

"Fine. But don't tell me that murder is some sort of evil, per se, prohibited under all circumstances. Murder is always one of the options. Always. And oftentimes it's justified. In fact, sometimes it's necessary in order to stop some bigger evil – or to stop evil altogether. They had to kill Hitler to put an end to it. And if they had killed Stalin in the early thirties, then millions of people would have been rescued from torture and dying a horrible death. Sometimes killing is necessary. Why did they kill Osama bin Laden? They could have got him alive and put him on trial. And what had the members of his family done that meant they deserved to be shot along with him? Their murderers could have instead organised a trial, gone over the evidence, assessed what the lawyers had to say, decided who was guilty of what and how long their sentences should be. But we know that all of that would have been bullshit: a completely pointless spectacle that didn't gain anything. And that's not the only case in history when the citadel of democracy has sent a drone or a rocket to kill an entire family. Whether you can or cannot murder someone always depends on what the ruler or the majority of that society feels is right in any given situation, not on some innate or God-given law. We all believe that it's okay to gun down a plane, if it's been hijacked by terrorists. All civilised nations have such laws. Agree?"

"Those are very exceptional situations in life. Our everyday moral norms don't apply in those cases," Dimitri objected. Marat, he thought, was really running away with himself.

"Oh yeah? So you admit that there are situations when one can stop obeying these God-given laws? Thank you, we're on the same page then. I couldn't agree more. Such situations *do exist.*"

"Don't be a demagogue. You can't possibly justify murdering your wife by comparing it to killing a terrorist."

"Look..." Marat showed no signs of slowing, "...all I'm saying is that there is no universal morality, no matter how much the church would like to convince us that there is. The only way is to put our trust in someone smart and competent, who can decide what's best in any given situation. When you've got a hospital full of patients, and you have to decide who to put in the ICU and who will need to wait, you should trust that decision to your most intelligent doctor. They would simply decide in every situation. In the same way, let's hope that we get a competent president who can decide whether we have the right to shoot down a plane or not. Only a moral person can say what is or isn't morally acceptable. There is no other way. It doesn't work like that in life, of course, because everyone is terrified of being sent to court and judged, then torn apart – that's why people crave regulations, instructions, the law. But it's very hard to write it in a way to make it apply to all situations in life. I would trust someone if they were a Brahman, of course..."

"A Brahman?" Dimitri was baffled.

"Well, if he had an innate intellect that had been nurtured and developed over decades. Because, naturally, an idiot shouldn't get to decide who gets to live or not."

"You're twisting everything – I mean, one doesn't have to prove that murder is the biggest possible evil," Dimitri replied, very seriously.

"What do you mean?" Marat was surprised. "Why not?" He was getting fired up again. "I shouldn't attempt to disprove it because you've chosen to believe in the fairy story of a miraculously conceived man who was some god's son or other, and who lived, died, and then rose from the dead? Or is it because you, as a mathematician, believe that your game theory proves that morality has some rational basis? Which of these two stories do you want me to disprove?!"

"You can't disprove either of them," Dimitri objected wearily.

"Oh, really?"

"One thing is clear from game theory – cooperation, collaboration, and, consequently, abiding by moral laws, is always best for everyone," Dimitri continued reluctantly, quietly hoping that they wouldn't start an argument about the existence of God. That was the only subject on which their opinions clashed, and Dimitri didn't like the way Marat talked about God.

"What about the laws set by God? *Thou shalt not kill*, for example." It was Dimitri's turn to interrupt Marat's impassioned speech.

"God's laws? Do you mean those laws that tell women to wear a black sack with two holes for their eyes?" Marat's tone had changed from ironic to scathing.

"No! I mean laws that go like: Thou shalt not kill, Thou shalt not steal, Thou shalt not—"

"Oh, you mean that list where committing murder is seen as less important than observing the Sabbath?" Marat continued sarcastically.

"You may not like Christianity, but the banning of murder is evident in all religions and all systems of morality that are known to man."

"That's true, and I fully support that we must get by somehow." Marat snickered. "But let's be honest – people's objectives can be different. If your IQ is only eighty, it will be very hard for you to follow an instruction manual and you'll probably struggle to complete basic tasks. You need simple rules – don't kill, don't lie, don't covet your neighbour's wife – and a very simple explanation as to why these laws should be observed. Because if you don't, you'll be in big trouble and burn in hell. Everything is simple and straightforward. Christianity does the job, provides a mechanism for controlling the dark, uneducated masses of people with a low IQ. But if you're Napoleon, Obama, the Roman Emperor, or the Pope, and you're exposed to situations where everything is a little bit more complicated than that, you'll need a different set of morals."

"No, I don't agree. Good and evil is universal. That's why we call it God's law." Dimitri wasn't prepared to budge.

"Just because you repeat the phrase won't make it any more true. The so-called 'God's law' was invented by people who wrote it down, broke it, then rewrote it again. And the fact that there are some patterns of morality repeated across all ages and religions – oh, I don't know, like women being subhuman people who need to know their place – it doesn't mean that it's been prescribed by some god. There are about two thousand gods known to humanity, and you, devoted Christian, are an atheist towards one thousand nine hundred and ninety-nine of them. By comparison, I'm simply an atheist towards one more god than you. Have you ever wondered what makes your imaginary friend different to all the others?

"That only proves that God is real, and reveals himself differently to everyone."

"Ha!" Marat exclaimed triumphantly. "So, your Jesus is no different from Marduk

or Huitzilopochtli? Yeah, I can agree with that. In fact, there's nothing left for me to prove in these debates."

Here we go, Dimitri thought to himself. It had become almost impossible to escape debating this topic. Marat seemed to enjoy it, but Dimitri didn't feel like it added anything to their friendship. It felt more like an argument than a debate; and, for some reason, they seemed to return to it again and again.

CHAPTER 4

Marat's birthday was coming up, which caused a problem for Dimitri: that of, what do you give to someone who's already got it all? On other such occasions Dimitri usually followed the principle of gifting something that cost more than any reasonable person would ever permit themselves to spend, but which they themselves would be very happy to receive as a present. It could be something ostensibly simple – like glasses, vases, belts, gloves, cufflinks – yet insanely expensive and over-the-top. This approach worked perfectly on most occasions, except for when it came to Marat.

Firstly, Marat wasn't the sort of person who paid attention to how much something cost. If he wanted something, he simply bought it, without even considering how much it might set him back. Secondly, Marat probably wouldn't even comprehend that the present was expensive – not from his perspective, anyway. (All he would see was that he was being given a tie, when his wardrobe was already packed with similar ones.)

Still, a fiftieth birthday called for something special. Dimitri was painfully short on ideas and, if he was being honest, he wasn't all too happy about the upcoming expense. Dimitri was trying to sort out his finances – so that he could start repaying the loan he'd got from Marat for his house, at least in instalments – but until now he'd not had much success.

At first, he'd needed to get some furniture for the empty house; then he needed to settle in; then God-knows-what else. Five years had gone by and Dimitri hadn't repaid a single cent. Marat never reminded him, of course. Quite the opposite – he always stressed that the contract between them was just a formality; that there was no need to worry; that he knew Dimitri would pay him back someday. However, Dimitri felt uncomfortable just thinking about it. And now Marat's fiftieth birthday would deal another heavy blow to the savings he'd only just started to scrape together.

The only way to surprise Marat was by giving him something truly special; something unique and select; something one-of-a-kind; something that had an added value besides the price. And yet art wasn't on Dimitri's list. Established pieces were well beyond his price range, and he didn't possess the talent nor ambition necessary to search out and discover, from the work of emerging or unknown artists, something no one had appreciated until now. So his only option was to head to the antique shop in the hope of finding an historic object, or something that had a clever and unique design that would constitute it being more than just a piece of old junk.

The respectable antiquarian Mark Lyevovich Tsimber, who endearingly called Dimitri 'Mitya', had already helped him out on a few such occasions. His shop, located on an enormous ex-factory site in the suburbs of the city, was stocked with the most unimaginable things: everything from furniture to road signs, old billboards, taxidermy mounts, children's toys, lamps, items that looked like industrial work tables, ancient boxes, buckets, neon signs, mirrors. There had to be something here that would make a good present for Marat. Something original, cool – and affordable.

As he approached Tsimber, Dimitri thought back on his and Marat's conversation in the park. His mind kept looping on it, and, having repeatedly recounted the details, he finally concluded that Twinka wasn't in any immediate danger. Marat didn't have a solid plan; and all that talk about different poisons seemed so far removed from reality.

However, there was something about their exchange that left him feeling uneasy.

While he didn't have a clear strategy, it was also obvious that Marat wasn't just joking around. He had seriously contemplated murder. He'd considered it from all angles – from the practical and the philosophical point of view alike. Marat was clear on his own goals and motivations, and it seemed he was relatively close to making a decision. Most likely, whether Marat had planned it consciously or not, he had needed that conversation with Dimitri: so that he could, by voicing them out loud, listen to his own arguments while simultaneously subjecting them to external scrutiny. Like a writer reading out loud what they'd written; or an architect or an artist needing to jot their ideas down somewhere, even if just on a napkin, so that they could look at their sketch, assess it and improve it.

Marat seemed grateful for the opportunity to hear Dimitri's counterarguments – but it was also clear that he expected his friend's full support, whatever his final decision. It was almost like Marat wanted Dimitri to be his accomplice. And Dimitri wasn't sure if he had ever agreed to friendship terms that would permit Marat to expect something like this.

Yes, he owed a lot to Marat; as Marat was the one who'd established Dimitri in the finance sector and made him, if not rich, then prosperous. And it had all happened at a time when Dimitri's life had been turned upside down. Dimitri had been in conflict with his ex-wife over the rights to see his son, and, overcome by anger, had punched her new boyfriend, who had regrettably got involved in one of their arguments and attempted to reprimand Dimitri. Dimitri had punched him: not once, not twice, not three times... In fact, he'd beat him up pretty bad. Dimitri had a heavy hand, having been a wrestler, and he ended up breaking his wife's new boyfriend's nose, cheekbones and two of his ribs. Naturally, his wife had called the police. They defined the harm as "moderate injuries". It was only thanks to Marat and his lawyers that Dimitri escaped a prison sentence, though he did lose his job at the university, which sank him into a deep depression.

For weeks on end, Dimitri didn't leave the house. He could spend days just in his bedroom. He stopped shaving to the point of resembling a homeless man. He just couldn't see a purpose or a meaning to anything anymore; he despised himself, and couldn't muster the strength nor the motivation to do something about it. And this manically depressed criminal was the same man Marat had set up with a job, in a bank where he was one of the partners. Marat helped Dimitri believe in himself again; allowing him to regain a sense of inner peace and providing him with a new, solid foundation on which to stand. He signed Dimitri up with a well-known psychiatrist; suggested a counsellor, too; pretty much found a new house for him; and lent him a lump sum on exceptionally favourable terms. Whichever way you looked at it, Marat had pulled Dimitri out of the deepest pit, given him back his life, and become his best friend. Naturally, Dimitri felt incredibly grateful to Marat for everything he had done for him... and yet – wasn't it *still* a tad much, asking him to become an accomplice in a murder?!

Tsimber saw Dimitri wandering around the warehouse, looking confused and lost in thought. He approached him to offer help.

"So, you're looking for a present?"

"Yeah. It's a present for a man who already has everything."

"Right, I see..." Tsimber muttered to himself. "Those who have everything always desire more," he meditated. "We'll find something, Mitya, don't you worry – we'll definitely find something..."

"I don't even know where to begin."

"Has he got a big house?"

"Two."

"And a garden?"

"Yeah. The one in the suburbs, on Button Street, that one has a garden."

"Right, I see... We'll find just the thing, Mitya, trust me..." Tsimber indicated for Dimitri to follow him. "Look over here, we have some Fase desk lamps. An iconic twentieth-century design from Spain. This one here is called Presidente because it used to sit on General Franco's office desk. It would do well in any home."

"Iconic?"

"This one, Boomerang 2000 – also a Fase – is very valuable," Tsimber pointed at a similar lamp in a smaller size, "but I'd personally recommend the Presidente as a present."

"That could do," Dimitri said, though he didn't sound convinced.

"Okay, so furniture is out of the question." Tsimber's seasoned ear had assessed the buyer's mood perfectly. "You can't give him a wardrobe now, can you, Mityenka? So, we need to look for some decorative objects. Let's go over there –" Tsimber pointed to a space filled with sculptures – "just look at these beauties." He gestured at two identical bronze dog statues, sitting stately. "They're from France. The eighteenth century." There was pride in the antiquarian's voice. "They'd look stunning by the entrance door, for example, or placed in a garden. And if the house is big enough, they could also work indoors."

"I'm not sure." Dimitri sounded even less convinced than earlier. "Hang on –" his attention had suddenly been caught by an ancient, tattered sculpture the size of an armchair – "what's that?"

"Oh, Mitya, Mitya..." Tsimber scolded Dimitri's ignorance in a warm, fatherly manner. "That's Michelangelo's *Pietà*. His most famous sculpture. Only David is more famous than this beauty here. It's the Virgin Mary, holding Christ in her arms just after he's been taken down from the cross. It's smaller than the original; a replica, of course. The original sculpture is housed in

St. Peter's Basilica in Vatican City. This one is a high-quality bronze replica from Italy."

Dimitri couldn't quite put it into words, but something about the sculpture seemed to speak to him.

"It's symbolically heavy, if one is permitted to say so," Tsimber continued, wiping dust from the sculpture with a handkerchief. "Christ has just died, he's just been taken down from the cross. But Michelangelo didn't want to draw attention to his wounds, so they're almost unnoticeable. Just look at Christ's face! It's so beautiful and at peace; not a trace of pain or suffering. Quite the opposite. And it's the same with Mary's face. It's like they understood that sacrifice was the only path available. And now that the path is complete, despite how full of suffering and hardship it has been, real life can finally begin. Some would say that this sculpture contains the entire meaning of crucifixion. Or at least makes us consider it."

Tsimber could see that he'd finally managed to capture Dimitri's interest, so he brought the item out and away from clutter, allowing the potential buyer to assess it from all angles. The sculpture really was heavy.

But Dimitri wasn't convinced. He decided to wander around the massive store for a bit longer. Perhaps his eye would catch something else. Something cheaper.

CHAPTER 5

After the fateful party on Button Street they had agreed to meet up in town, choosing a stylish place called Louis XVII Boulangerie. It had only recently opened, but people were already starting to refer to it as 'Louie's'. It was lauded for its fresh bread, homemade cakes, and the excellent – albeit expensive – wine and coffee. But Louie's' trump card was its location: at the end of the city's promenade, right where the beach started. Sitting on the cafe's terrace, one could enjoy a spot of people-watching, feeling as though they had one foot in an elegant city cafe and the other on the beach. In terms of the latter, there were tourists in swimsuits, groups of families and friends, little kids playing in the shallows and, from time to time, an adult who would wade to deeper waters for a swim. This part of the beach was predominantly used by the city's less wealthy. Louie's, however, was frequented by a more affluent set, and this juxtaposition created a wonderful holiday atmosphere. At least, Twinka was enjoying it.

"What was it? That thing that happened on Friday?" she had asked Cat, without preamble.

"I don't know, but I enjoyed it," Cat had replied with a warm smile.

Twinka was quiet, but her downcast gaze and slight upturn of her mouth betrayed that she felt the same way. "But what if someone had seen us?" she asked.

"Well, that wouldn't have been good."

"We were acting totally crazy!" Twinka had exclaimed: her subsequent laugh mischievous and the expression accompanying it one of mock horror. She had then covered her head with both hands, staring directly into his eyes through the gaps between her fingers, as though posing the question 'How could we?'.

"Well, I enjoyed it," he repeated.

"Were you always cheating on your wife while you were married?" was Twinka's next question.

"Once," he lied, worried that if he admitted to any more he'd look like a bad person. (Yet equally knowing that if he'd said 'Never', then it would have put an undue weight on their conversation and its ultimate destination.)

"I have never," had been Twinka's proud reply.

Cat hadn't responded to this, though he had continued to shoot her an impish, defiant look.

"But I think I could," Twinka had admitted, before then correcting herself quickly. "Well, maybe, only maybe."

"I would really like you to."

Twinka had noticed that her cheeks were hot. Dear God – that meant she was blushing! When was the last time she had blushed?

"So, how does it usually happen?" she then asked. "Tell me, since you're clearly more experienced than me."

"Why do you think I'm more experienced?"

"You just said it yourself. And you look the type." Twinka smiled. The tone of their conversation was light and playful.

Cat had smiled and looked dead into her eyes.

"For sixteen years," continued Twinka, "no one, except my husband, had ever touched me."

"I think we could agree to meet in a hotel next time, and then we'll both find out how exactly it happens," had been Cat's eventual response.

"But I'm scared. Look, I'm already blushing just thinking about what happened on Friday."

"I am also worried. It's normal! And isn't this exactly what we've both been longing for? This uncertainty, fear, worry, desire – a sense of foreboding before a new experience?"

36

"I'm not even sure if I like you enough in that way," Twinka had said, assessing him with a critical eye.

"Well, I know that I fancy you, because you're so gorgeous."

"Of course you'd say that, but it doesn't mean anything." Twinka hadn't hid her scepticism, though her tone remained playful.

"Either way, we won't find out by simply talking." Cat had sensed Twinka needed a decisive push. "Can you make it this evening, or tomorrow?"

"What? Right now?!"

"It's not that sudden. I mean, we've known each other for years, and we know how attracted we are to one another. There's only one way to get rid of the awkwardness, insecurity and agitation that this situation has created."

"Marat and I are going out this evening. I could maybe make it the day after tomorrow, only during the day..."

"Excellent. It's settled then – the day after tomorrow. I'll organise a hotel and let you know."

"Oh, I don't know... I need to think it all over." Twinka had found herself struggling to decide.

"Are you sure you need to think about it? I think that deep down you already know that you want it." Cat's tone had become serious.

"Yeah, maybe I do want it, but I fear my conscience and the guilt that might consume me afterwards. I don't know how I'm going to feel once it happens." Twinka too had stopped flirting, deep in thought instead.

"You'll never find out unless you try it. And yes, maybe you won't like it. You might realise that it's not for you. But you can only find out by trying it. If you walk away now because you're too afraid, you'll regret it for years, thinking that perhaps you should have tried that time." Cat had sounded very convincing.

And right then a thought had flushed through his mind. That he would never want someone else to seduce, so incessantly, a woman who mattered to him – be it his lover, wife, daughter or sister.

But he hadn't allowed the thought to fester.

"Yeah, but I don't know how I'll feel afterwards. Will I even be able to live with myself?" Twinka was looking at Cat with pleading eyes "Do you understand what I mean?"

"There's no need to be so serious about it, or to torture ourselves. We're talking purely about sex here."

"It's all so simple for you, men. It's all just sex! Whereas, I don't know, I'm bewildered by it all; I have so many questions going round my head." Twinka had pushed the plate with the half-eaten cake away from her, in preparation to leave.

Cat had then stopped her.

"What questions? Go on."

"Well... Am I just going to go to the hotel and get naked in front of you? Just like that?"

"Okay. Fine. I'll tell you what I think will happen. Yes, we'll both be incredibly nervous the first time. It will probably feel like we're losing our virginity all over again, but I'll try and help you any way I can. The sex won't be amazing and you probably won't reach an orgasm, but even so it will still be very, very good, because there will come a moment when our nerves will disappear and relief, excitement and comfort will wash over you. And all the following times too, as we start to get to know each other and work out how to get pleasure from each other – more and more pleasure..."

Cat had been making every effort to convince her.

"Oh, I don't know... I mean, it sounds great... the thought alone gives me butterflies, but I don't want you to set any expectations. I don't know if I'll be able to really let go and..."

"It will all be okay, I promise."

"I would love to, but I'm scared. I don't know. Do you understand what I'm trying to say?"

At this point the conversation had started to grate on Cat.

"What time can you make it? The day after tomorrow, I mean?"

If the conversation continued, he figured, then nothing would probably come of this. So he had decided to cut it short, pretending that the decision was already made.

"I'm scared."

"That's normal," Cat had replied, almost formally, before asking for the bill.

"Okay, I... I just need a day to get properly acquainted. Give me one day where I can get used to it. Take me out somewhere," Twinka suddenly found herself saying, as though she too had finally decided. "Let's go somewhere together."

"Go somewhere?" Cat hadn't quite twigged.

"Yeah, let's go somewhere without spending the night."

"But we've known each other for ages!"

"Yeah, but not like this..."

"Okay. I mean, I won't pretend to understand what's going on... But why not. Let's go somewhere, I'm up for it."

CHAPTER 6

Wandering through the overloaded labyrinths of Tsimber's shop, Dimitri remembered another long discussion with Marat, in which they had discussed friendships between men. Women's friendships were completely different, and the relationship between a woman and a man was another topic altogether – but, in the context of a friendship between two heterosexual males, the conversations between them (which went on for several evenings) resulted in the conclusion that a man can have five categories of friends.

One of them was a friend/competitor. This was a friend with whom you spent your entire life measuring up to and competing against. It could be toxic; but it could also drive you forth, motivating and inspiring you. The competitiveness could be unhealthy, or even border on a nasty kind of envy, but this type of friendship also presented the opportunity to gauge your opponent close up: to discover his secrets, and to learn and eventually quietly enjoy your superiority – if it ever got to that point. Such friends could easily become your best enemies, but they could also remain your competitors in a friendly race that lasted a lifetime. Such friendships could survive a lot, except, of course, the moment when one of the friends eventually gained the upper hand. Then the entire basis of the friendship was gone: as it was no longer exciting or useful for either party, and just too painful to bear for the loser.

The second category concerned friends/partners. These men would have become friends by working together, and by striving towards a shared goal. They were united by a mutual love of money or success, and enriched each other perfectly, without competing. The people in this category could have very different characters, personal qualities, skills or knowledge, as long as they made a powerful team when joining forces. It was the type of union whereby one plus one equalled five, yielding incredible results that neither of the friends could have dreamed of had they been operating alone. They knew this, and that realisation was the force that kept them together. But these sorts of friendships usually dissipated as soon as the rational basis for them was gone.

The third category was useful friends. These people often formed the basic structure of one's social circle, though there was usually no vulnerability or attachment in these types of friendships. Perhaps even the word 'friend' was over the top. They were essentially good acquaintances. It could be someone who knew the latest drugs and how to get them; or maybe someone who knew the best chiropractor in the city, or a journalist, or maybe a prosecutor. These people could fill you in on the latest news, which wasn't yet public knowledge, and/or help you to establish connections and gather information. Such relationships were quite shallow, comprising a lot of politeness, the exchange of services and, every now and then, a nice evening spent together. The basis of this friendship was mutual trust, in the sense that you'd always get help or a service in a certain area, but there was very little honesty or openness. Still, these kinds of relationships were pleasant, useful, interesting, and could endure for decades.

The fourth category was quite special – these were your old friends. They could be childhood friends, schoolmates or university friends. Your bond with them may not be overly tight; an outsider might even wonder what you have in common with these people, or what unites you as a group. It could be shared memories, although you wouldn't necessarily indulge in reminiscing very often. Of course, you'd have a lot of common experiences and mutual friends, but none of these topics came up very often either. And yet your old friends always took part in all your celebrations – sharing in your joys and sorrows, your big life events – and their names were never forgotten when a guest list was being drawn up, even if it didn't always result in an invitation ('Say, here's my old chum – but how will he fit in with my useful friends or my friends/competitors?'). Likewise, it was nice to see an old friend every now and then, but not too often. This was a low-maintenance, long-term relationship.

And then, last but not least, there was category number five – the most important category in the list – which could only ever hold one person. This was a true friend. Marat and Dimitri were in agreement that this was one of the most beautiful and important things that could happen to a man in his lifetime. A true friend was like true love without the erotic component. Every minute spent in the company of a true friend was filled with happiness and pleasure. Every joy in life was only half a joy if it wasn't shared with this friend, and every sorrow only half a sorrow if he was beside you. It was someone whose house you could crash at any time of day, and stay there as long as you needed, and who'd be happy if you did. It was a person whom you'd gladly donate a kidney to, if it came to it. Complete openness, complete trust, close contact and true attachment. In some sense this was even a passionate relationship – often much closer than the one you shared with your wife or your parents. And much more intimate, compared to your useful friends or oldest friends. "Women come and go," Marat had stressed at the time, "but a true friend will remain forever." A true friend cannot be replaced; he is one-of-a-kind. It's a very special relationship, and, just like true love, not everyone gets to meet their true friend.

Of course, Dimitri had agreed with Marat that they were true friends. They had even decided that, if there was ever a need, they'd donate their kidney to one another without question. But deep down Dimitri wasn't so sure. Not in relation to the kidney; he was happy to give that up, if it came to it. Marat had done a lot for him, he was grateful for all of it, and he could go on living with just the one kidney if push came to shove. The problem was that Dimitri felt as though Marat had already paid for his kidney. He was absolutely sure – he knew – that Marat didn't think about it on those terms. Still, it didn't change how Dimitri felt.

It's not that he had any other friends who he was nearly as close to as Marat. He just thought that their distillation of friendship should be expanded to include a sixth category – the rich friend. Dimitri couldn't stop thinking about how, in a friendship, just like in a marriage, it mattered whether one person was much wealthier than the other – even if it didn't exactly get in the way of the relationship and couldn't be summed up in words. It wasn't even a problem; there was nothing toxic about it. But still... it did make a difference.

For him, the friendship with Marat definitely hadn't been love at first sight. It was Marat who had shown up out of nowhere and decided to make Dimitri his friend – and he'd spent a lot of time and money to ensure it happened. Did Dimitri feel like he'd been bought? Well, not quite. Marat was an interesting, original, unique and charismatic person, and Dimitri genuinely enjoyed spending time with him. Dimitri wasn't doing it out of sheer gratitude, and most certainly not because of some financial incentive. However, it was Marat who had chosen *him*, searched him out, and made him his best friend. And it was Marat who always determined when they would meet. Marat was in charge of what they'd be doing, where they'd go, how they'd spend their time together. Naturally, Marat had more responsibilities than Dimitri – even though Dimitri knew that it was really because Marat thought his time was more important. Marat always expected Dimitri to oblige, because to him it was a given that Dimitri would always make time for him. In a way, Marat had the same expectations of Dimitri as of his employees – that they would always do whatever was being asked of them.

Marat was the one who had decided where Dimitri should work, where he should live, and what doctors he should be seeing. He dominated their relationship to such an extent that Dimitri wasn't sure how common that was among true friends.

On the other hand, perhaps there was nothing wrong with this. Maybe it was Dimitri's own fault for being so submissive. He always went along with things, didn't show much initiative, and planned his time according to Marat. Marat would probably respect any other plans Dimitri had, and might even be happy to go along with his ideas every now and then. Maybe. Most likely.

What's more, Marat was always going to have superiority over Dimitri – he'd achieved more and he was more successful. He didn't even have to make a show of it, it was self-evident. And this, naturally, created a certain imbalance in their friendship, even if none of them paid much attention to it. They couldn't be friends/competitors for the simple reason that Marat was already the victor in everything. Marat was far wealthier, he had climbed Everest, and he was incredibly well-educated and quick-witted. Dimitri, by comparison, was the former mathematical wunderkind who had played a bit of sport in his youth. That was it. The time when Dimitri had felt special in something and considered himself among the best had ended some time ago, prior to his twenty-fifth birthday.

Marat had come into Dimitri's life completely from the blue.

Dimitri had started making educational videos about maths: 'Explaining Fermat's Last Theorem', 'How to Apply Bayes' Theorem to Everyday Life', 'What is Game theory?', 'Poincaré Conjecture', 'Galois Theory', and so on. Marat had come across these videos and sought Dimitri out, almost immediately offering his money, cooperation, help and friendship. He had simply appeared and then remained in his life. Marat had decided that he needed a friend-mathematician whose thinking and education was different to his own; that it would be an interesting addition and enriching experience. Dimitri wasn't the only one whom Marat had sought out in this way – there was also a chemist, and a philosopher. Marat called it his High IQ Club. Eventually though, as the years went by, only the two of them remained.

Dimitri's opinion on whether he wanted to be part of such a club, or whether he was interested in having this friendship, didn't matter. But it would be wrong to say that Marat never gave anything back. Marat was, in fact, very generous – and not just in terms of money, luxurious presents or all-inclusive trips. It was a relationship underpinned by genuine interest, stimulating conversation and quality time spent together. It was, beyond a shadow of a doubt, a process that enriched them both. Yes, Marat had a senseless amount of money, but money was a weird kind of substance – and although it would be ignorant and arrogant to underestimate its importance in people's lives, Dimitri truly believed it would be more accurate to say that Marat had *even helped him financially*, rather than *just helped him financially*. And wasn't that the reflection of a true friendship: one in which you don't feel like sparing anything, and are happy to share something as important as money, even, without a second thought? There were plenty of so-called friends in this world who meticulously insisted all of their shared expenses were divided equally in half, unless – God forbid – they'd be tricked into paying a penny more. Such friends would never lend you any money, let alone help you out financially if they saw you going through a rough time. No, Dimitri concluded, helping a friend out with money was something that a more distant friend would never be capable of doing, and Dimitri truly appreciated it.

However, Dimitri also knew that Marat was using a tactic that was popular among all wealthy people – Marat knew that money could open any door, and secure almost any friendship or connection. Hardly anyone would say no to money – or the promise of it – which naturally accompanied a friendship with someone wealthy. That sort of friendship, even if it didn't produce any immediate benefit, was for someone like Dimitri a safety rope for unexpected situations that the future could bring. It was someone you could ask, if you really, really needed to – and that counted for something. Beggars rarely said no to moneybags.

Whichever way you looked at it, there was a certain asymmetry in their friendship from day one. Yet in spite of this – and mostly thanks to Marat's insistence, energy and interest – their friendship had over the years become very close. They spent a lot of time together, whether it was sports or relaxing, and it always felt like time well spent. For both of them. And wasn't that the most important thing in any friendship?

Meanwhile, Dimitri and Tsimber had returned to the Michelangelo replica.

"You know, it wasn't common in those days to depict Mary being young," Tsimber continued, a hint of fatherly affection in his voice. "But, look, she looks so young here. In fact, she looks a lot younger than her own son. And she's a real beauty, too. Christ sacrificed himself, God sacrificed his son, and Mary lost her son, but that's the law of life – you have to be ready to bear sacrifice. Not because some god needs it from you, but because, in some sense, there are only two paths available to all of us – the path of sacrifice or that of murder." *Pietà* had turned Tsimber into a philosopher.

"But she'll need some sort of a podium. She's not meant for being displayed on the floor like that, is she?"

"You're right, she shouldn't be standing on the floor." And now, having noticed that Dimitri wasn't interested in his musings, Tsimber changed the topic in a flash. "Most likely, she was displayed on top of some massive piece of furniture, perhaps a huge chest of drawers, a cabinet; or perhaps she was the biggest decor in some hall or large room; or placed at the end of some hallway. With the right lighting, she'd look very impressive."

"What did you mean when you said there are only two paths available – that of sacrifice or murder? Does someone always have to die?" It seemed now that Dimitri had, in fact, listened to the antiquarian's reflections.

"I wouldn't take it so literally, Mitya. Physical death isn't the only kind of death. You can feel dead while being physically alive, don't you agree? It's not easy being alive, and often, in order to stay alive, you have to sacrifice a lot of things, often things that are very important to you."

"I think that my friend will like it," Dimitri decided. "It's a classic. Michelangelo. An impressive, large object that looks very old and rare. Yes. I think this will do."

"Very good, very good," Tsimber murmured, satisfied, as he wiped the Virgin Mary's head with a handkerchief.

While he'd been out shopping, Dimitri's worries over Marat's plans for murder had loosened their grip, and yet he still wondered what would be the right action to take.

He couldn't just go down to the police station and tell them what Marat had revealed to him, could he? As well as being totally pointless, it would be a complete betrayal. So, should he be warning Twinka to avoid mushrooms in her diet? That seemed even more ridiculous. What's more, Dimitri couldn't work out what worried him the most about this situation – was it an egotistical fear of getting mixed up in some trouble? Or fear for Twinka's life? Or fear that he'd have to spend the rest of his life burying Marat's horrible secret, looking Ronia and their mutual friends in the eye and forever holding his peace?

He'd have to talk to Marat again, to further understand what was going through his friend's mind and to make sure he gave up on his ridiculous plan. Otherwise, God only knows what might happen – and there may be no way back.

Yes, he was going to buy Michelangelo's replica, Dimitri had decided. The present would astonish Marat, and that was the main thing.

CHAPTER 7

Oh, all this doubt! As time had drawn closer to their day of *getting acquainted* – which she herself had initiated – Twinka had felt even more tangled up in her feelings, totally lost in her thoughts and desires. At times it was like she was already experiencing all the shame, guilt and regret that would inevitably follow her perverse decision to implode her own marriage. It was wrong, and she – Twinka – was definitely not the type who'd do something so terrible and shameful. What had she been thinking! No. It was so wrong.

She was a good person. She always did the right thing, she never hurt anybody, she'd never violated the ten commandments. That was her essence; her identity. How had she even got that far? How had she started discussing something so reckless and stupid? Still, she didn't then pick up her phone to call it all off. No. Instead, Twinka had taken her phone and made a bikini wax appointment.

But no. It hadn't meant anything; it definitely hadn't mean that she had decided. And she had warned Cat that, following their day of *getting acquainted,* nothing would happen between them.

Still, she'd made an appointment to get her bikini line waxed.

What am I doing? She'd asked herself the same question over and over again, but couldn't seem to find an answer for it. It had felt like two opposing forces were fighting for power inside of her.

Twinka didn't like thinking how much her age had given rise to all these doubts. Thoughts about aging, no matter how unpleasant, were unavoidable. Thirty-eight was a lot. And how much longer would men be showing any interest in her? She had felt like a queen back in the day, able to grab the attention of and enchant all men. But now there was always some younger floozie about who enjoyed this special honour. It's not that being *the* most beautiful and attractive woman in the room mattered all that much to Twinka, but she wanted to be at least *one of them.* She was used to always being one of the sexiest women in the room.

In fact, she had only realised that it mattered to her the moment she noticed that the situation had changed. Okay, maybe it didn't exactly *matter to her* – but she enjoyed it. Those special, curious, undressing looks from men, which locked on her breasts, hips, ass and face. Looks that made men appear unattractive, banal, primitive, sometimes dangerous, but mostly simple and submissive – easy subjects for manipulation. When she could no longer catch these glances, she realised that she desired them.

Whether she wanted to or not, Twinka had confronted herself with the question: how much time would it be before she too would join that category of women who were no longer viewed with sexual desire? How much longer would she even have the opportunity to throw herself into a crazy adventure and board a ship that would, before long, have sailed for her? And had she experienced enough in her life to decline the offer?

Like all trips, like all real adventures, this one too involved the unknown. There was risk and danger. Naturally. But wouldn't she lose a lot more if she decided to run away from these potential risks and imaginary danger?

Why am I even on the pill, when we barely have sex?! Twinka had felt her anger towards Marat swell inside her.

At first he had spoiled Twinka, but now he was showing almost no interest in her. She felt as though he was avoiding being intimate with her. In the evenings Marat always gave clear signals that he was tired, that he had to get up early, and so on. And the days when Marat used to wake her up with his caresses and kisses, and they started their day with love-making, were long in the past.

On the rare occasions when they did have sex, it was nothing more than a distant glow of what it had felt like before. Yes, Marat knew how to make Twinka climax – he knew her better than anyone else, maybe even better than she knew herself. But her orgasms felt very different these days. Cold, quick, technical. And rare. If he himself had never shown Twinka that it could be different, perhaps she'd be less upset about it. But he had, and she longed to experience that enormous, reckless pleasure that could bring her to the brink of losing her conscience, which she had felt at the start of their relationship. Still, even though Marat's indifference deeply upset Twinka, was she going to use it as an excuse to sate her desires elsewhere?

A single accidental kiss during a wild party had made her lose all clarity over who she was. Should she succumb to being satisfied by a vibrator for the rest of her life? That didn't seem right. Twinka had tried to drown her desire in alcohol, tried to dull her longing and replace it with the enjoyment of wine, but that hadn't helped.

But even if she could muster an excuse, would it be enough? Could she live in sin for the rest of her life, knowing that what she'd done wasn't right? Would she be able to forgive herself? Oh, these damned doubts and contradictions!

Their day of *getting acquainted* had not ended up being cancelled.

Cat had booked a table for them in a little romantic restaurant right on the seafront. And he'd strategically planned everything. First, they had a glass of an excellent champagne. As they dined they finished half a bottle of red wine, then moved on to sherry with their dessert, and after that went for a walk along the beach. This time, alcohol was helping both of them. As soon as they got to the beach, and out of the public eye, Cat, who was standing behind Twinka, pulled her closer and locked her in an embrace. They stood like that for a short moment, looking out at the sea as their bodies grew tight and lewd. They both knew that this was consent. The sea smelled of seaweed and salt. Twinka had taken off her shoes and was holding them in her hands. She looked at her watch. It was exactly 19.19, and that too had felt like a sign.

Cat had started to kiss Twinka's neck. His arms were caressing her belly and her butt was pressed tight against his hips. And it wasn't just his arms – Twinka could feel the curiosity, interest and desire of his each finger. His touch felt very different from Marat's routine, familiar and perfunctory caresses. These were not the lover's arms that Marat used to hold her with during their early years of marriage: when sex between them had felt like the pinnacle of bliss – like the triumph of love and a merging of two souls. No, she felt nothing like that in Cat's arms, but they had still activated something in the pit of her stomach. It promised a purely physical – purely bodily, but powerful – pleasure. It didn't promise sex in the same form it had been with Marat, when they had loved each other passionately, nor the bland version it had eventually turned into. This was some third option; the kind of sex that Twinka had either never felt before or had long forgotten.

Cat had bitten Twinka's earlobe gently, and she had moaned in pleasure. Yes, this was consent. She desired these arms and these lips to search her, to investigate and get acquainted with her. The sea was playfully reaching for Twinka's naked toes. Every time it succeeded, Twinka cheered in childish excitement. She closed her eyes. The man and the sea caressed her, kissed her and cuddled her. Doubts, thoughts, shame, blame or regrets no longer plagued her. In that moment, she had only felt delight, calm and pleasure.

Cat had turned her towards him, and then they were kissing *for real.*

"Did you know that married people don't kiss?" Twinka had asked him afterwards, when they were on their way back.

Cat had laughed. "I guess you're right."

I haven't kissed anyone in ten years, thought Twinka. She was flushed and happy.

The day of *getting acquainted* had been a success.

CHAPTER 8

I should go and see Mum today, Marat decided.

It had been five weeks since his last visit, and Mum's unvoiced disappointment travelled the length of the city and reached him like radio waves. He had to go. Today. Marat talked himself into it. He should also get the air-con sorted before the heat of summer set in. When Dad had still been alive, Marat had bought his parents a luxurious house in a very desirable location next to the sea, built in the American modernist style. At the turn of the previous century, a Swedish ambassador had hired a local architect who had designed it, drawing inspiration from Frank Lloyd Wright. The ambassador used the house as his summer residence in-between the two world wars. Naturally, when Marat had bought the house, he saw it not only as a decent home for his parents but also as a good investment that would only grow in value, and which would be easy to sell on or rent out when it had served its purpose. Whether she had sensed Marat's pragmatic logic, or because of some other reason, Mum hadn't wanted to move into the new house for ages. Afterwards she'd complained that the house was too big for just the two of them, and how she didn't feel good living there.

Eventually, however, the spacious garden had coaxed Mum into overcoming her complaints. Mum had immediately started to change and improve the garden, spending all of her time there. If she wasn't working on the garden, she'd be lounging in a chair under the apple trees with a magazine in her lap. The garden was her only joy, her only entertainment and solace; she had fallen in love with it. Since Dad had passed away, Mum lived in the spacious, elegant house very modestly. Even though Marat was ready to bestow upon her anything she needed, and she always had a decent chunk of money in her bank account,

Mum tried to get by on her pension alone, taking as little as possible from the money Marat had given her. Marat couldn't understand why.

"You could have warned me that you were coming!" Mum complained, instead of greeting him. "I would have had some time to think about what I was going to make you, and gone out to buy some food."

"I'm not hungry, Mum. You don't need to worry about anything."

"Well, it's just good manners to give some notice." She made no attempt to hide her displeasure.

They walked into the living room and Marat watched as Mum opened a precious little mahogany box, took out four different bracelets and put them on, one by one. She placed three round her right wrist, and one round her left, doing so with such precision and determination that it were as if she were loading a weapon ready for a battle in which someone would inevitably die. Marat remembered some of the bracelets from his childhood.

Having finished with the bracelets, Mum tossed some beads on her neck. They were made of small, unpolished pieces of amber and joined together with a rusty wire, the colour of which perfectly matched the rough resin.

"So, how are you then?" she asked.

From her tone of voice Marat could usually infer just how guilty he should feel. However, today Mum maintained a neutral tone, as though she were doing so on purpose.

"I'm fine," Marat answered, trying to appear cheerful. "Look, I brought you some organic chickens. They're small but they've been bred outdoors, in nature, eating grains and earthworms, not some antibiotics."

"That was completely unnecessary. You shouldn't have spent money on my account. A basic chicken is good enough for me!" Mum showed no trace of excitement or gratitude, instead sighing heavily as she looked at the treats her son had brought, as though by doing so he had placed an enormous burden on her. She then tried to start a conversation.

"You better tell me what's new with you. How are you?"

"I'm fine, Mum, fine. Everything is okay. Best tell me how you're doing."

"Me? What about me? I live by myself. I never know anything, no one ever tells me anything, and no one comes to see me anymore."

"Hey, look, I've come to see you." Marat tried to be as gentle and loving as he possibly could.

Once more his mother sighed heavily and didn't say anything. Marat noticed that she had lost weight. She looked very thin and small, yet despite this a strict rigour of character was still evident in her frail and fragile body.

"I had a lot of work on. Really. You know how much I've got to manage."

"No. I don't know anything, because you never tell me anything." Mum was no longer hiding her mood.

"What do you mean? I tell you everything. What would you like to know? Ask me anything and I'll tell you."

"Well, I wouldn't even know what to ask you, because I don't know anything about your life. We're like strangers. You're bringing me chickens as though I've got nothing to eat! It's not chickens I need from you."

Marat was taken aback by how much bitterness, disappointment and perhaps even hate he could hear in Mum's voice.

"Oh, come on, Mum..." He really didn't know what to say. "I don't know what to tell you. I work a lot, I'm earning a lot of money..."

"As if money was the key to life..."

"I'm not saying that it's the key..."

"Do you spend any time with your daughter, or are you always just out and about, making money?"

"Of course I do." Marat felt hate announce itself inside of him. Why did she have to act like this? He was trying his best, wasn't he? He had bought her some lovely treats and come to visit her; he wanted only the best for his mother. The last thing he wanted was to have a fight.

"When did you last go out with her?" Mum said from the kitchen. She had decided that Marat should have something to eat after all.

"Mum, everything is fine. There's nothing you need to worry about."

"See what I mean? You never tell me anything! You just keep saying 'Go on, ask me anything', but when I do you don't care to answer. Do you call that a conversation? All you do is keep bringing me these blue chickens. There's barely any meat on the bone, what am I supposed to do with that? And they probably cost ten times more than a normal chicken."

"Listen, I was thinking that we should install some air conditioning in here," said Marat, trying to change the topic of their conversation, "otherwise it'll get too hot in the summer again. Shall I send someone over?"

"I don't need any air conditioning," Mum snapped back.

"What do you mean? Remember how hot it was last summer. It will be like that again soon."

"There's no way of telling what the weather is going to be like. It's hot today; it will rain tomorrow," Mum squealed back at him, annoyed.

Marat was quiet. Why was it that, of all the people on this planet, it was absolutely impossible to have a conversation with his own mother? He loved her, and he knew that she loved him, but she was simply unplayable like this. It was as if, no matter what he said, and no matter which words he populated his sentences with, it was all deemed by her to be wrong, upsetting, or – in the best-case scenario – plain stupid.

Mum had heated some soup in a small saucepan.

"Careful, it's hot," she said as she handed Marat the bowl.

I'm about to turn fifty. I can tell that it's hot, Marat thought to himself, but held his tongue. They sat in silence for a while. Mum's borscht was delicious as always. Marat loved the soups she made.

"Why aren't you having any sour cream?" Mum scolded him. "It tastes much better with sour cream."

"I don't want any sour cream, thank you."

"Oh, go on, try it, add a bit of sour cream! You'll see, it's so much better that way." Mum pushed the jar of sour cream closer to Marat.

Marat didn't add any sour cream to his soup, and yet again Mum sighed heavily.

I've offended her, he concluded. Now, more than ever, he wanted to get away from here. It hadn't even been half an hour since he'd arrived. *And she wonders why I don't come to see her more often?*

"So, what are we going to do about the air-con?" Marat forced himself to ask the question in a calm manner.

"I don't know. It's your house, do what you like. I haven't got any say here, have I?"

"Great. I'll send someone around next week," Marat replied formally.

There was a tall, old linden tree at the furthest corner of the garden. It was in full bloom and smelled wonderful. This was the perfect place, where one should feel happy; and Marat wanted, from the bottom of his heart, for Mum to be happy here. But she clearly wasn't. It was no excuse to act like this towards him, though. It wasn't his fault that she was unhappy;

he was doing everything he possibly could to change that. So why was she still acting like she was? Maybe she was depressed? Or maybe aging had brought on some change in her psyche? She needed a consultation. She should talk to a specialist; it must be horrible to live in such a glamorous house, with such a wonderful garden, and yet still feel so glum, intolerant and bitter for no apparent reason.

"Say hi to Twinka," Mum said, instead of a goodbye. "She calls me more often than you do. If it wasn't for her, I'd probably never see my granddaughter or know what goes on in her life."

"Okay. I will."

"Twinka is an incredible woman. So good and so kind... She's probably suffering being married to someone like you."

"Goodbye, Mum."

CHAPTER 9

Twinka had known exactly how it would happen.

Cat had rented out a barely furnished flat in a dull old apartment building for their secret rendezvous. It was located in that sad, boring part of the city that you'd not quite define as the suburbs, but wouldn't consider part of the city centre either. The building was a stone's throw from two of the city's busiest transport arteries, which was very convenient for their needs. Another important feature was the underground car park, only accessible to people who lived here, which gave them protection from unwanted witnesses. The flat was basic and characterless, and still smelt of its recent and, evidently, simple renovation. The walls, the wardrobes, the shelves, the fridge – even the rubbish bins – were all empty. It was immediately clear that no one actually lived here. There was a fairly large room with a sofa and a TV (which they'd never turned on), a basic kitchen with cheap kitchen units (which they'd never used) and a bedroom with a spacious bed, which was almost level with the floor. The flat was neither cosy nor homely, but Twinka could hardly say she'd noticed.

Even though she had been given her own key, Twinka had known that Cat would always be the one to arrive first. He would literally jump on her as soon as she set her foot in the flat. He'd press her against the door or one of the walls in the corridor and immediately, right there and then, start rumpling and undressing her; kissing her face, neck and forehead; biting her ears; shamelessly grabbing and squeezing her tits and ass. He'd growl and moan while he was doing it, like someone who was sampling the world's most exquisite recipes. His loud nasal *mmm*s would grow into energetic *emmmm*s and *ammmm*s, and finally – pleasure-filled *ahhh*s. He'd sound like a huge purring cat who wanted to eat her. These noises would make her smile, and it was because of them that she'd started calling him Cat.

Cat's attempts to undress her would be chaotic and messy, leaving her feeling uncomfortable yet wonderful at the same time. She'd laugh, imagining what she must have looked like – her, Twinka, in the corridor, with her coat still on, but with her trousers halfway down her legs. With her shoes still tied, but the bra under her jumper already open.

He wouldn't let her go. He wouldn't stop – not even for a moment. There was something insatiable, wild and boyishly charming about him. His purring and the constant kisses would completely disarm Twinka. She'd try to help him undress her, but she'd get all tangled up and fall on the floor. It would make Twinka laugh, while he became even more uncontrollable, insatiable and reckless. In-between his purrs, Cat would utter all sorts of funny and naughty compliments about Twinka's different body parts. It would make her wonder how she'd managed to forget when she'd been young, and had felt just as wanted and desired. What had happened to her life? How had she managed to forget what it was like? But she had. She'd forgotten it to such a degree that she'd stopped longing for those times. It was as though they had never existed. But they had.

These encounters were like a resurrection for Twinka – almost like an awakening from a deep slumber. It was the most incredible journey: filled with new impressions, tastes, smells and adventures, as though arranged by angels.

Sometimes they'd start making love right there, by the entrance door; other times they'd get to the living room or the kitchen, stumbling and screeching. Somehow, they never made it to the bedroom. Twinka enjoyed the fact that Cat could keep up the wild tempo. Cat was fast and quick and he didn't stop until they were both literally dripping with sweat, and fell on the floor or the living room sofa, completely exhausted. At this point, as opposed to Twinka, Cat had not finished yet, which made this pause feel very special. The tension was still there, and palpable. They had merely stopped to catch their breath, and were ready to continue at a moment's notice, though they decided to wait.

In that time they caressed and studied each other. They talked and kissed. Their hands were acting especially naughty, their bodies exposed, and then, at last, they continued. Twinka had never been with a man who was able to do it like this. He was different now – slow and gentle – and Twinka felt that he was close to climaxing, though he seemed to be prolonging the process. He would either cuddle up to her from behind, squeezing her tight; or have her facing him, his lips fixed against hers. He moved very slowly and calmly, so close and deep inside her. Sometimes, when she was on top, he would stroke her breasts or look straight in her eyes. So close and deep.

As much as the first part of their rendezvous would always feel like crazy fucking, the second part would be more like gentle love-making. As his sperm entered her, Twinka felt as though no other man on this Earth had ever made her feel like this. This was a completely new feeling for her: fuller and more wholesome than a simple orgasm. Her every cell – her whole mind and her psyche, every atom and molecule of her body – had experienced something freeing. Something that she had been deserving of for quite some time; something she had expected, and found especially nourishing. This thing that was happening between her and Cat birthed an addiction. It made everything else in her life seem so insignificant, and she felt like she'd completely lost her mind. It just felt too good to make Twinka think or worry about what she was risking, where it was going and how it would end.

The pleasure that Cat offered her was transient, evanescent and purely physical. But it was still a kind of happiness, one which Twinka had never experienced before and which, inadvertently, made her think about what else she may have lost or missed out on in her thirty-eight years on this planet. Such thoughts made her desire burn even stronger.

Later – after the funny, purring hurricane had passed; when the saturated pause was now behind them; and the slow, gentle resolution had taken place – they would once again rest. Twinka would curl up in Cat's lap, snuggling close to him. They would be talking, and then – an hour or maybe slightly later – they were making love again.

Then they got dressed and went their separate ways.

It happened just like that every time.

Twinka always stopped by a church before returning home. This was her church – the one she used to go to on Sundays with her dad when she was little; and the one she had stopped coming to as a teenager, but which had offered her solace years later when her first marriage had broken down. She knew everyone in this church: from the priest, to aunt Ginta – who would unlock the doors and lock up again, help keep the place clean, and look after everything when there was no one else there on weekday afternoons.

Twinka needed it to calm herself down and return to planet Earth. She hoped that the church's moist, cool and unhomely air would eradicate the pungent smell of love-making from her body; wash away the treacherously healthy blush on her cheeks, which even a shower didn't seem to be able to rinse off. She hoped that the lonely echo of her footsteps resounding from the church vaults, and Jesus's figure on a cross, would help to dispel the vivid memories of having just had a man inside of her. She couldn't go home right away; to do so would be wrong! It would be immoral to return home glowing and smelling of sex and another man. No, Twinka wasn't here to ask God for forgiveness. On the contrary – she was grateful to God for this opportunity, for this journey, for the chance to be reborn that He had granted her.

Almost a year ago – when all this had only started – Twinka had been so afraid that the feelings of guilt would ruin her life, that she wouldn't be able to look her husband or Ronia in the eye, that her conscience would eat her up alive... But nothing like that had happened. She simply felt happy. She couldn't even imagine that there might be one person who had spotted the changes in her appearance and behaviour immediately. He'd instantly noticed the *joei de vivre* in her eyes, along with an energy and lightness he hadn't seen in her for ages. He had straightaway noticed just how happy she was. Even the colour of her skin, her gait, and her movements seemed to have changed. Twinka seemed much younger and happier, and no visit to the church could ever hide it from him. From the man who knew Twinka better than anyone else. From Marat.

CHAPTER 10

Dimitri didn't have to wait long for a chance to talk to Marat. On Tuesdays and Fridays they would usually meet in Marat's private sports hall. Its walls were covered in pictures of Everest (and Marat's conquest of it), and in terms of its equipment, appearance and size, it would make any professional football or basketball club proud.

His house on Button Street wasn't located in a desirable part of the city. It was a suburb, which, at the start of the twentieth century, had housed a number of larger and smaller factories. As times changed, artists and creatives had started to flock to this area. Nowadays it boasted several independent theatres, a number of quaint art galleries and dainty little shops, as well as artist workshops, cafes, and the first hipster housing projects. However, just around the corner you could still find heroin addicts, hobos, abandoned buildings, poverty and ruin.

It was called Button Street because it had once been home to a button factory. Marat had bought a huge plot of land here, and had built an enormous house with his own private sports hall next to it.

Dimitri regarded anyone who went to the gym with a certain degree of arrogant scorn. He called them bodybuilders, and didn't consider them true athletes. What was the point in pumping one large muscle, then another one, when instead you could do some actual sport? The kind that developed a person overall, and where speed, flexibility, dexterity, endurance, explosive strength and technique were all required. A real sport – one that was demanding, and developed your character and personality as a result.

Dimitri had spent his childhood practicing Greco-Roman wrestling. Then, during university, after suffering a knee injury – which put an end to tournaments and the world of professional sport for him – he had turned to aikido. Dimitri worked at it for a long time, earning himself the black belt, and now he attended a Brazilian jiu-jitsu group, where he loved being superior to everyone else thanks to the experience he'd accumulated in his youth. However, Marat had managed to convince him to turn to strength training. Every ten years, after turning thirty-eight – Marat said at the time – men lose eight percent of their total muscle mass. And they had to start fighting this early, because suddenly realising it when you're sixty or seventy would be far too late. Or at least that's how Marat's theory went.

"For a man, aging is so closely linked to losing his muscle mass. Just look at elderly men – they're so tiny and withered, with arms and legs that look like sticks. But we'll fight it for as long as we can." Marat had been full of enthusiasm and determination.

And so they had started to practice Olympic weightlifting. Two, sometimes three times a week. And Dimitri was even enjoying it. The yelling that accompanied the lifting, and the noise of the steel barbells crashing on the floor, felt like mini testosterone explosions. He'd fallen in love with their training routine, even though he wasn't going to admit it to Marat. He was much stronger than Marat, too – significantly stronger – and a head taller to boot. There was something very satisfying in that. This was the only place, the only sphere of life, where Dimitri was considerably superior to his friend. Marat – even though he'd managed to climb Everest fifteen years previous – evidently wasn't very strong physically. While he was tough and tenacious, he couldn't do a thing with a hundred-kilogram barbell. Of course, you had to take the differences in their weight and body type into consideration. Past experience with training was clearly evident in Dimitri's posture. He was still an athlete – albeit an ex-athlete. Next to Dimitri Marat looked tiny, skinny and completely unprepared. It was evident that they were in two completely different leagues when it came to weightlifting.

Furthermore, the explosive strength and flexibility that weightlifting required were exactly the kind of qualities Dimitri had been familiar with since his days in fighting sports. Whereas Marat was only capable of some degree of explosiveness. In addition to this, the flexibility in Marat's shoulders and back was poor. He couldn't complete some of the most basic exercises, even without weights. For example, he more than struggled to squat with his heels down while holding a pole high above his head with straight arms. In fact, this was completely impossible for Marat, even if you were to give him a hollow stick instead of the metal pole.

Dimitri had always enjoyed feeling a sense of superiority. He'd taken up maths only because it came so easy to him and he could feel better than others without putting in much effort. Even now, he took every opportunity to demonstrate his abilities to resolve complex mathematical problems in his mind in a flash, and enjoyed the admiration and respect it produced in other people's eyes. For him, the chance to feel superior was a far better cure for melancholy than the best antidepressants. Consequently, Marat's sports hall had become the place where he received this healing therapy.

It has to be said, though, that training with Marat wasn't quite in line with Dimitri's understanding of how training should be. Marat often didn't show up, cancelling at the last minute. Obeying any rules, including those which he himself had set, to Marat meant limiting his own freedom. And he insisted that submission and discipline was the philosophy of slaves, which had to be extinguished at all costs.

On the occasions when he did show up, and despite him having hired a very experienced private coach, Marat would always be the one who determined what exercises they'd be working on that day. So the purpose of the coach was simply to assist them, change the weights, count their attempts and correct their technique. (Often it was just the two friends anyway, due to Marat changing the times of their training sessions so chaotically that their coach couldn't always get there on time.)

Today, it was once more just the pair of them.

"How's things at home?" Dimitri asked, once discussing politics and other news of the city was out of the way. They had moved from bench press on to deadlift, and now following that to clean and jerk.

"Meh," Marat replied, vague yet with a hint of annoyance, showing every sign that he didn't want to touch the subject.

"And how's the murder plan coming along?" Dimitri prevailed, posing the question as innocently as he possibly could.

"Please, let's not use the term 'murder'," Marat said, his mood all of a sudden ostensibly improved. "We're just talking about euthanasia, really. About freeing a patient who's condemned to horrible suffering."

"Correct me if I'm wrong," Dimitri objected, "but doesn't euthanasia usually refer to cases where a person wants to finish their life due to an incurable disease, or extreme suffering and pain that cannot be mitigated?"

"No, it's not just that. The direct translation of euthanasia actually means 'a good death'. What you're talking about are the legalities – the cases when it's permissible – while I'm talking about the essence of it."

"And what's the essence of it then?" Dimitri was curious.

"Okay. Let me tell you a story. About my classmate Kathryn. Now, I don't know what happened exactly, but thirty years ago, when Kathryn was still in her early twenties, her mother got very sick. She'd had a stroke or something similar, which left her bedbound and paralysed. She couldn't do anything for herself. Literally. Kathryn had to become her carer.

And so it continued for *thirty years*. Think about it. Just picture it. The daughter had absolutely no life of her own for *thirty years* – no private life, no professional life, no children, no husband, *nada*. Her entire life was looking after her paralysed mother. Now Kathryn is about to turn fifty, just like me... Is that right, in your wise opinion? Kathryn was a good, smart, wonderful girl. She really was. She could have done anything with her life. She had the chance to be happy, to start a family, to raise children – but she didn't do any of it. Instead, she had absolutely no life at all. She spent her best years – her *entire life* – working underpaid jobs, coordinating everything just so she could take care of her mother any spare moment she had. Is that right in your book?" Marat was heated and spoke with passion.

"And what are you suggesting? That she should have killed her own mother instead?"

"Of course," Marat said categorically.

"I don't know who would be capable of killing their own mother."

"I'm not saying that it's easy, but sometimes you have to do the difficult things in life," Marat said indifferently, shrugging his shoulders. "We've all become too meek, too cowardly and too compassionate. We need more of the Spartan character in our lives, more of the Spartan morality."

"And how would you like it if someone killed you in that situation?"

"I'm so sick of this argument – it's coming from the same *Oh, make sure you do unto others as you would have them do unto you*, blah, blah, blah. But it's wrong. Even if I didn't want it done to me, that doesn't prove anything. It doesn't matter what I want or like. I could wish for many things. For example, I might want to drink cognac every day, but I know that it's wrong. Besides, I can make mistakes too. The truth doesn't care what I think or whether I like something or not. The only thing that matters is whether the truth has been exposed by the strongest argument. And it doesn't matter whether someone likes it or not."

"Finally, I totally agree with you." Dimitri smiled. "So you're admitting that what you want could be wrong. You're even admitting that you're capable of making a mistake. Don't you think that killing your wife might be that? You want to kill her, even though the right thing to do would be to divorce her. You're just looking for the easiest path, in your opinion. What I'm saying is, you do want to drink cognac every day."

"This is exactly why I love you." Marat laughed as though acknowledging and appreciating the argument. Only his subsequent words showed no respect for Dimitri's actual question. "But let's not mix everything together. We're discussing whether I would want someone to kill me, if I was old, ill and helpless, and had become an enormous burden to my children. Well, in that case – of course! I definitely wouldn't want to get killed. Firstly, I'd attempt to kill myself, so that I wasn't an albatross around my daughter's neck. But if I couldn't do it myself I'd beg her to do it instead. And, since we're on the subject – I want you, as my best friend, to promise me now that you would kill me if I became paralysed and bedbound, with limited mental capacity. Promise that you'll kill me! Promise me!"

"I'm not promising that. That's like playing God, you can't..."

"Here we go again with your God... Your God is your imaginary friend. He's a bloody fairy-tale character! Cheburashka! The only difference being that this particular fairy tale was created not only for entertainment but as a mechanism to control our society."

"Stop it. First of all, Christianity is the basis for our culture. Secondly, if there is no God, then what else would stop people from doing whatever the fuck popped into their mind?"

"The only thing that can stop a person from doing anything is fear. Nothing else! That's why your God is threatening us with hell and eternal suffering. The Christian church actively supported slavery, racism, genocide, and the secondary status of women. The biggest wars throughout history were started by Christians. The Holocaust was the act of Christians, and to this day the Church is still covering up for paedophiles. And you're offering *that* as a moral compass?! Really? In that case, I think that Cheburashka would make a much better figure of moral authority."

Again, Dimitri regretted mentioning God. He knew better when talking to Marat. Nevertheless, he persisted with his line of questioning.

"But if your daughter decided that you're a burden to her, even though you weren't completely disabled and paralysed – would that too be allowed, in your world?"

"You know, Jack London has a lovely story called 'The Law of Life'. I recommend it. It's about the last days of an old Eskimo chief called Koskoosh. His tribe has to leave their ancestral land because there's not enough game and food to sustain them, but they can't take Koskoosh with them because he's very old. He's almost blind, and he's become a burden, and his son cannot feed his young family if he also has to look after his dad. But Koskoosh isn't worried about it. He knows there's such a thing as The Law of Life. See what I mean? Such is The Law of Life." Marat was ignited.

"What – so take him on a sleigh to the nearest forest and just leave him there?!"

"Yes. Unfortunately, if you've become a millstone and you're blocking the way for the young, then yes. Unfortunately."

"And when you're bored of your wife, then she goes on the sleigh too?"

"We're not talking about being bored," Marat hissed quietly. He could see where Dimitri was going with this. Dimitri was trying to talk him out of what was, in Dimitri's opinion, a foolish step and wrong decision. Dimitri cared about him. It was all completely understandable. Except Marat didn't want to be talked out of anything. He was already regretting having ever mentioned the topic.

"Yeah, I remember. We're talking about corks here, the fact that she likes to have a drink in the evenings, and that getting divorced would be far too messy."

"You know what else I hate?" Marat had decided to change the subject.

"What?"

"I hate spouse sex."

"What's wrong with it?" Dimitri didn't understand.

"Spouse sex is completely rational. There's nothing extra or special: anything that doesn't fit the purpose has been redacted over the years. It's like a short concrete road across a mountainous valley that has replaced the old, winding, exciting, picturesque path. There used to be peaks and troughs in the past, which made your heart beat like crazy. Dainty rope bridges that stretched across the abyss and took your breath away. There were places for rest with wonderful views, rare orchids and luscious smells; icy springs to have a drink from. And it was never, ever the same route. Every time felt like a new, unique adventure. It really did! But now, all of that has turned into a concrete road – ten minutes, and everyone has safely and happily made it to the other side. A boring, routine drive to get from point A to point B," Marat complained. "I wouldn't even call it sex. It's just satisfying your physical needs, really. I think it was Nabokov who called it 'sanitary sex'. I mean, the sort of sex that's necessary for good health – but it's not really sex at all. Do you know what I mean? It's not the kind of sex that brings the biggest pleasure in the whole world, that kind of sex that makes you lose your mind and forget everything; for which people are willing to risk everything, even their lives. Spouse sex, on the other hand, is some kind of fast-food substitute, like the McDonald's of sex, instead of that amazing, mysterious thing you used to enjoy in the past."

By now they'd finished up their training session and were heading towards the changing room.

"Listening to you," said Dimitri, "one might get the impression that any marriage is doomed from the start."

"I don't know. Maybe not all of them, but most of them for sure. It's just a fact."

CHAPTER 11

"You know what's the most important thing in a relationship between lovers?" Cat asked Twinka, gently stroking her bare back with the top of his palm.

"No," Twinka replied, disinterested, without opening her eyes or moving.

"The main thing is not to fall in love," Cat said with a heavy sigh. "Fall in love and it's game over. That will be the beginning of intolerable suffering, hours spent waiting, jealousy, pain, torment and depression. From there, everything would fall apart..."

With a sudden gesture, Twinka turned to face him. "Are you worried about me or you?" she asked, staring into his eyes defiantly, as though she herself didn't know the answer. For the first time, Cat noticed that Twinka's smile could be hostile and dangerous.

Cat wanted to warn her to pull herself together and not let any feelings fester. He wanted her to keep a cool head and remember that this was nothing more than sex and friendship – or therapy even. But nothing beyond that. They met up, spent some wonderful moments together, but it wasn't going to lead anywhere. It could not progress to, or end with, anything further.

Twinka understood these facts no less than Cat, and Twinka was very happy with these conditions. So there was absolutely no need to remind her of the state of play – and yet he did. Not very often, but he did. And it infuriated her.

Cat could feel Twinka's irritation. He realised he should not have said anything – it was very tactless of him. Cat was regretting making the comment, but he was still worried. He could feel that Twinka had become very attached to him – in a girly and passionate sort of way. He could feel it, and it frightened him. And he couldn't deny that he was also afraid of how much he had started to look forward to their dates – how everything else in his life seemed far less lustrous, intense or genuine as this.

"I'm reminding myself, gorgeous, only myself," Cat said, sending her a gentle smile full of warmth in an attempt to correct his mistake. "I don't deserve you." He let out a sad sigh.

Twinka didn't reply, and turned away from him again. Cat stroked her back softly with his fingertips: all the way down from her neck to her bum, then all over again, as far as his arm could reach – and then back up again, just as slowly. In some places he'd very softly scratch Twinka's skin with the tips of his nails.

"I love it when you do that," Twinka said, to prove that their argument was over.

They all love it, Cat thought to himself, though he said nothing.

CHAPTER 12

Visiting Mum had left Marat with a nasty feeling. He wanted to smooth things over between them, so he decided to go see her again the following week before the handymen got to work. He wanted to give Mum the opportunity as well. They had no reason to argue, let alone act disrespectfully towards one another. Marat felt weighed down by the way their relationship had warped. When did it start? What had happened? Why did almost every interaction with Mum turn into a putrid exchange of spiteful words, poisonous accusations and festering resentment? Marat didn't have the answer to any of these questions. He didn't even have a working theory as to why every conversation with Mum had become so fraught. During his childhood, and especially his teenage years, it was the relationship with his father that had felt tense and complicated – but it was never the case with Mum.

His father, a civil aviation pilot – a very disciplined and organised man – had always been extremely demanding and strict towards his son, whereas Mum always represented the haven of support and trust for Marat. He'd never had to question the unconditional love he'd felt from her. When did things change – and why? It was his mother's influence – her being a history teacher who devoured books – that made him fall in love with literature and study history. That should have made her feel proud of him, but all Marat received these days was judgement and constant, unfounded accusations. Why? Surely, there were worse sons than him out there?

This time he gave Mum a call in the morning, explaining that he'd be coming over later and thereby giving her some notice. He also took a small cake with him – he knew how much Mum loved having a piece of cake with her morning or afternoon coffee.

"Alone again? Without Ronia?" was Mum's verbalised assessment as soon as Marat set foot over the threshold.

"Mum, you know she's at school. And then she has after-school practice, plus homework. Every day is packed for her."

"School, practice... It wouldn't hurt her to skip it occasionally. When I'm dead, she'll be able to practice to her heart's content – God knows how much time I've got left..." Mum didn't even look at the cake, not even a n acknowledging glance. It remained on the kitchen table, still in its packaging.

"Mum, can you explain to me why we're always arguing?"

"The garden is in full bloom: petunias have been blossoming for a month, lavender and astilbes are just coming out. My roses are flourishing too, they love the heat. You could have brought your daughter with you," Mum said, her tone more sad than angry. This time, her bracelets and beads were already in place. Although they weren't the same ones she had worn last time, Marat still remembered them from his childhood.

"Mum, why can't we converse like normal people, just for five minutes?" Marat was very serious.

"Well, I'd gladly tell you, but I'm afraid you'll get all offended again," Mum replied, pouring some coffee into a pot.

"Please, let's talk it through. We're always acting like enemies," Marat insisted. He sincerely wanted to understand, and to resolve the tension.

"It's obvious. It's all very simple," Mum said, sitting down at the table with a heavy sigh. "I've become a burden to you. Obviously, old people are no use to anyone – they just take up precious space, spend all your money and demand attention. Believe me, that's not a very nice feeling to have."

"But it's not true, Mum! You're not a burden!" Marat was genuinely surprised that the reason for her attitude had turned out to be so basic and unfounded.

"See? You always start an argument, and then you ask me to explain why we're arguing."

"Mum, am I not looking after you? Am I not providing for you? Are you ever in need?"

"Oh, never mind..." Mum tossed her hand in defeat. "Yes, you do provide for me, thank you very much," she said with an even heavier sigh, clearly indicating that Marat hadn't understood anything. "By the way, when was the last time you went to your dad's grave?"

Marat didn't reply. The last time he'd been to his father's place of rest was more than six years earlier. At his funeral.

"Do you even know what it looks like now? It's probably overgrown."

"It's not; we're paying someone to look after it."

"Is that right? How convenient everything is these days. Simply marvellous. So, when I die, you'll just pay someone to look after my grave, too." Mum spoke with so much anger, her voice oozing with resentment and bitterness.

"Mum, do we *have* to talk about death?"

Only she is capable of pounding such intense feelings of guilt into me, in a matter of mere seconds, Marat thought to himself.

"You don't go to your father's grave, and your daughter doesn't even know where to look for it."

"Fine. I'll go visit Dad's grave. I promise."

"No, don't bother. You don't need to inconvenience yourself." Mum's hand gave another petulant gesture.

Marat fell silent. What was there to say? Yes, it was bad that he'd not been to his father's grave. Yes, Ronia didn't even know where it was. Yes, it was his fault for not establishing a tradition in his family of going to the cemetery a few times a year. For what it was worth, he couldn't remember having been taken to his great-grandparents' graves or visiting the cemetery an awful lot when he was a child. *Clearly, the interest in cemeteries increases exponentially the closer you get to your own grave*, Marat noted to himself, but he kept the observation to himself. He observed how Mum hadn't even offered him a piece of cake with the coffee. Clearly, today would see no resolution between them. Again.

"I'm a constant burden. The sooner I die the better, so you can pass it onto someone else, and you can finally live in peace," she continued.

"Mum, I keep telling you that you're not a burden to me," Marat said. However the fatigue, irritation and guilt caused by their conversation had transformed his facial expression into one that suggested the polar opposite.

"Of course..." said Mum, now openly mocking him.

"Mum, I think you may have depression. You should see a specialist. You know, you can actually cure it quite effectively these days." Marat had managed to pull himself together, and was making one more attempt to talk formally and constructively.

"You mean a shrink?" Mum looked at him quizzically, clearly taken aback.

"A psychiatrist. Or a therapist. I could recommend someone. In fact, I know a good specialist..."

"What a marvellous idea. You could shove me in a madhouse, pump me full of pills, turn me into a vegetable, and problem solved! No, darling, I won't let you succeed with your 'convenient' plan."

The revulsion she felt had given Mum a new burst of energy. Her eyes sparkled, ablaze with hate; her cheeks glowed with a healthy rose tint; and she had physically straightened herself. Her fragile body was suddenly filled with strength.

"Mum, why are you acting like this? Where have you got this idea from that I wish you harm? Have I ever done anything to you? So, why all these accusations? Where are they coming from? I just want the best for you. I can see that you're unhappy, and I want to help."

"Your generation has only two solutions to all problems – money; and if money doesn't do the trick, then it's obviously a mental health issue. Then you need a psychiatrist and pills. Money and pills – that's all you know." Mum had seemingly calmed herself a little.

"Okay, fine, I don't know what's best. Just tell me if there's any way I can help; if you need anything, just let me know."

"I don't need anything." She was sulking again.

"By the way, the workers will come over later this week to install the air-con," Marat said.

Mum didn't reply.

"Right, I guess I'll get going," Marat said, downing his cup of coffee and rising from his seat.

"Yes, darling, you best go. And hurry, you've got all that money that needs looking after."

CHAPTER 13

"Gosh, you scared me," Twinka said. She was sat on the terrace with two open bottles of white Burgundy wine on the table next to her, as well as two additional wine glasses – a large Bordeaux and a standard-sized Pinot Noir. Hearing Marat's sudden footsteps behind her had made her jump. "I didn't hear you come in."

"The trouble with having a large house is that you never know what's happening on the other side." Marat felt a vague and distant childlike glee for spooking Twinka. Yet he immediately chased the feeling away, chastising himself for having it.

"Sometimes it's best not to know, rather than being able to hear everything and wondering what all those suspicious noises coming from the garage could be." Twinka sank back in the chair. She seemed quite tipsy.

"Sometimes it's best not knowing – I agree with you there."

"Try this other one. It's a very young Pouilly-Fuissé – so elegant, like something we don't deserve."

"And why don't we deserve it?" Marat poured himself a little of the wine and remained standing.

"You know, I'd love to have someone sneak up on me from behind like you just did and force themselves on me like a brute," Twinka said, without looking at Marat.

"You mean you have rape fantasies?" For the first time that night, Marat looked at Twinka with genuine interest.

On a normal day, the tone in which Marat had phrased his question would have made Twinka avoid any further discussion. But this time she responded almost spitefully. "No, it's not like I want someone to *actually rape me.* But maybe I'd like you to take me by force sometimes."

"What do you mean – take you by force?"

"Oh, just forget it." Twinka took a large swig of the wine. Her spike of churlishness had passed. She was woozy, the evening was warm and pleasant, and she didn't want to focus on anything – which was what Marat was demanding of her. "Never mind," she said, and looked at her watch. It was 20.20. "Ha! How come every time I look at the time it's always displaying some ominous numbers?" She turned her stylish, oversized white fitness watch towards Marat.

"Just coincidence." Marat scrunched up his face. "Where's Ronia?" he asked.

"Dad took her to a concert."

"To a concert?"

"Yeah. Wagner, at the opera house. They'll be gone for a while."

"You know, the whole BDSM thing really isn't for me." Marat finished his wine.

"How can a man can get aroused by hurting a woman? By hitting her, pulling her hair and humiliating her. I just don't get it. I even tried watching some BDSM porno clips, for research purposes. Not only did it fail to arouse me – I thought it was sick. It's disgusting and I hate it."

"It's fresh, isn't it?" Twinka asked, leaning over to top up Marat's glass.

"Yeah, it still feels very new."

"If you want to try a grandpa, pour yourself some of this." Twinka pointed to the other bottle.

"Another Pouilly-Fuissé?" Marat asked. The label on the second bottle looked washed-out, and was eroded by mould in places.

"Yeah, this one's thirty years old. It's wine in your style – aged beautifully."

"You're not trying to tell me that you're into BDSM, are you?" Marat insisted, determined to get to the bottom of her comment.

"No, I guess not," Twinka said, her tone implying she was unwilling to continue with the conversation. What would be the point, since Marat had already made it clear that he thought it was sick. Was he expecting something else after that?

"But what did you mean when you said that you'd like to be taken by force?" Marat wasn't letting up.

"Nothing! Just calm down."

"No, I'm curious now, and I want to know." Marat was trying to sound sincere, sensitive and interested, as to encourage Twinka to continue. He had realised that his remark about how BDSM was sick had been too hasty, if he wanted to find out more.

"Actually, I'd like you to take me in any way at all," Twinka said. "I can barely remember the last time we had sex."

"Yeah," Marat replied, and poked his nose into the wine glass. "It's true," he said, but it wasn't clear whether he was talking about the wine or the sex. Suddenly all his interest in their conversation had dissipated. "I'm staying true to my theory – if you have the opportunity to choose, you should always go for a grandpa," he said after a while.

It's impossible to go wrong with a thirty-year-old wine. That was one of Marat's laws.

Twinka looked at her watch again. 20.27. She sighed, and poured herself more of the grandpa.

CHAPTER 14

Those who didn't know Twinka too closely were convinced that she always wore a kind and tender smile. Her parents used to call her their little angel. Even now, it was the first thing that came to mind whenever someone looked at her sweet, smiling face. Yet, once you got to know her a bit better, it became obvious that Twinka's eyes weren't always happy – and that what looked like a smile was just a constant expression, created by her facial features, that never left her face (not even when she was lost in contemplation, sad, or raging on the inside). If you did eventually notice this peculiarity, it was hard to tear your eyes away from Twinka's face – it was a secret, a paradox; a riddle that mesmerised, and which demanded you looked deeper and paid attention. For instance, if you saw Twinka now, standing by the mirror, you'd notice an expression of sadness, anger, and even a touch of despair that had overpowered her natural smile like a dark shadow.

"You know, it's sexy to have a belly," Cat had said to her. Or was it "It's really sexy to have a belly"? Or had he simply stated "A belly is sexy"?

Studying herself in the mirror, Twinka tried to recall his exact words. She was bothered by her instinct, which was that it wasn't sexy to have a belly, and this is why Cat had mentioned it.

Twinka examined her midriff from the front and both sides, sucking her belly in and then relaxing it again. She hadn't scrutinised herself like this in ages. *You know, it's sexy to have a belly*. While that may be true, her belly said to her 'first trimester of pregnancy' rather than 'sexy tum'. Until now Twinka had purposefully avoided this entire subject, though she always knew that the moment would come – the day when she'd have to admit to herself that her reflection didn't look good. Not one bit. Her tummy looked misshapen and foreign to her; she hated it, and it felt like the belly hated her back. Swollen and wobbly, it had begun living its own separate life, all in order to disgust her.

Twinka had carried a sandwich into the large, spacious bathroom that could have passed for a studio flat. She'd put a slice of cheese and tomato and a pinch of salt and pepper on toasted granary bread. Twinka rarely had breakfast, but today she had woken up feeling hungry. Now she felt as though the sandwich was smirking, surveying her with sarcastic glee. Twinka felt a sharp and sudden urge to have a glass of champagne, but she scolded herself for having it. She wasn't an alcoholic who started drinking from the crack of dawn.

But she was fat. Or almost fat. Her butt had grown bigger, too – and not in a sexy kind of way. It was simply bigger, void of any shape or form; it was heavier, with visible lines of cellulite circling the top of her hips. And the worst thing of all was that it felt like even her face had changed. It was puffy; her cheeks were swollen and her eyes had grown narrower; even her forehead didn't look like it used to.

Twinka had managed to avoid contemplating all these physical changes for some time now. For instance, when her high-heeled shoes became a burden – with her feet too painful and inflamed, and her no longer feeling like she could overcome great distances or obstacles in heels – she simply switched to low heel pumps without thinking much about it. When the exquisite lingerie she was used to wearing had started to cut into her flesh, she just switched over to cotton knickers. When her favourite dresses and skirts no longer fit her, she went and replaced them with new clothes. She justified it by thinking that it wasn't something to worry about, as she couldn't go on wearing the same clothes forever anyway. This entire time, she had managed to escape *that* word. She didn't consider herself fat. At least not until today. But now she had to do something.

Something radical and swift – except she didn't know what that might be exactly.

Of course, Twinka had considered experimenting with different diets, although she wasn't actually eating much as it was. She just couldn't work out where all this excess weight was coming from. Okay, maybe she did occasionally have a bit of cheese with her wine in the evenings, and perhaps a helping of prosciutto or the odd cracker with a sliver of pâté. Yes, she did indulge herself a little when she was having wine – but often that was the only thing she ate all day. She barely ever had breakfast, and lunch was rare for her. She ate far less than Marat, who never had issues with excess weight. It was so unfair. Marat could eat chunky steaks, fish, potatoes, anything he fancied, while Twinka seemed to pile on pounds just sniffing a slice of cheese. She didn't identify with advice that said to go for a run or take up a sport. She'd never done any kind of exercise or set foot in a gym, always managing to stay slender and fit regardless. No, that wasn't for her.

Should she be cutting back on wine? But what joy would then be left in her life? How would she go on, if the only hours that she actually enjoyed during her days were taken away? No, that didn't sound realistic. Rather, she wondered whether to stop taking her antidepressants, which she had started using a few years back. At the time, she felt like they had made her feel... if not exactly better – then at least less bad. That was probably the root cause of the weight gain. And now that she had Cat, she didn't need the pills anymore. Her weight would definitely improve – and, if she really had to, she could live without cheese. She could! So, everything would be okay. She had to cling on to that hope anyway – or else, what really did she have? She carried the sandwich back into the kitchen.

Nonetheless, Twinka felt like dressing up today. She wanted to look gorgeous, glamorous, sexy, and just *wow*. She wanted men to fancy her and women to envy her, just to feel a bit uplifted. No, she wasn't fat. She wasn't. And it was sexy to have a belly anyway, if Cat's words were to be taken at face value.

Because of him, Twinka had bought lots of new lingerie. And she had now laid out numerous sets on the bed for her to choose from. She wasn't going to meet up with Cat today – all she had on was her weekly visit to the psychotherapist. Today Twinka wanted to dress up for her pleasure alone. She loved the see-through, flesh-coloured Le Petit Trou set with barely visible embroidered love hearts. Those bra and panties looked so light and airy: the most delicate of petals caressing her hips, a gentle wind playing with shadows on her breasts. No, this set was too good – she'd save this one for Cat.

The second option was a rather conservative, yet high-quality Maison Lejaby set. No, this one wouldn't do either – it was from the "pre-Cat" period in her life. The tight bra, which created a beautiful form; the high panties that almost reached her belly button – it all belonged to the Twinka who had been a dutiful wife, not a passionate sinner. This may well have been Catherine Deneuve's favourite brand, as they explained in the store, but Twinka wanted to be much more sexy, provocative and bold today.

She placed a few more options on the bed, finally settling on a black Kiki de Montparnasse set, and her mood began to lift. She looked stunning in it, even despite her belly (her skirt hid it well). *Maybe I should have breast-enlargement surgery* was a thought that crossed Twinka's mind. *Larger breasts might make my figure look more... harmonious?* But she chased the thought away – no, Twinka liked her own breasts. She put on a claret-coloured top with a large neckline that left the straps of her bra exposed on the shoulders. It looked good, and Twinka was satisfied. A genuine smile had settled back on her face.

She proceeded to choosing a bag. This always felt like a complicated task. Her dark-red Birkin would go really well with this top, but it had been a present from her first husband. Besides, Marat considered Birkin bags tacky, so she almost never wore them anymore. In a completely different sense, the Anya Hindmarch bag suited her outfit too. Made of recycled plastic bottles, it bore the inscription "I'm not a plastic bag". Twinka held both pieces aloft, weighing up whether today she wanted to be a rich bitch or a rich bitch who was disguising herself as a middle-class intellectual. Eventually she settled on the perfect compromise and went with a black, medium-sized Dior bag, which she simply adored. She decided not to wear heels today – she had to lose a few kilos first (five to seven would be ideal), but that definitely wasn't beyond her. Besides, middle-class intellectuals who were gifted with good taste didn't wear heels.

CHAPTER 15

Michelangelo's *Pietà* turned out to be an even better present than Dimitri had anticipated. He delivered it to Marat on a Thursday morning – the date of his actual birthday – and by Friday evening, when Marat was having his birthday party, it was already on display, in pride of place. The sculpture was the first thing you noticed coming in through the main door. It was a perfect fit, as though it had been custom made for the space opposite the grand entrance, which had previously been occupied by a mirror and a low cabinet with drawers that stored keys and other knick-knacks on its broad surface.

In their place now stood *Pietà*. It was practically at the centre of the house, placed next to the entrance of the reception hall from where, if they turned left, the guests could enter the grand open-plan living room, or – if they turned right – they could access the upper floors by stairs, or go down to the swimming pool, sauna, garage and the utility rooms.

"Do you realise that you've given me a gravestone as a gift?" That was the first thing Marat had when he saw Dimitri. "The sentiment is clear – a man isn't supposed to live much more than forty or fifty years. Nature's intention was that by this point you would have produced enough heirs, and they would be able to live independently, so all your evolutionary duties would have been fulfilled, so it was time to go."

"Oh, it's not a gravestone. It's a meditation on the idea that there are only two paths available to a human being – either sacrifice or murder." Dimitri faithfully recited the antiquarian's words.

Marat laughed. "Whoever sold this to you must have forgotten to mention that Michelangelo designed the sculpture as a gravestone to a French cardinal who had requested it. His contract stated that it must be the most exquisite marble

89

sculpture in Rome. So, Michelangelo was simply fulfilling the terms of his contract."

Dimitri truly hadn't known. He felt a bit embarrassed. However, Marat looked excited and happy. *If he didn't like the sculpture, he wouldn't have placed it so centrally, so it's probably okay,* he reasoned privately.

Exhilarated, Marat rushed to tell every guest who arrived that Dimitri had given him a gravestone as a present. The joke continued for the rest of the evening, evolving and taking on different forms. Someone even managed to place a glass of wine in the Virgin Mary's left hand, which made the sculpture the object of everyone's admiration and the subject of numerous photos.

The present was a success, there was no doubt about that.

"By the way, do you know why sacrifice exists?" Marat said to Dimitri. "Countless primitive tribes committed sacrifices because they discovered that whenever they collectively killed someone who was innocent, the injustice and horror of the act stopped the war of all against all – for a time at least. So, in order for us to stop killing each other and protect ourselves from falling into an anarchy where anyone can just kill whoever they please, we have to, openly, publicly and collectively murder someone. The more innocent the sacrificial lamb is, the more insignificant their crimes, or the more similar they are to us, the better. Man is a very violent, extremely aggressive animal. A born killer: the most effective killing machine that nature has ever produced – and sacrifice is a way of us triumphing over this violence, at least for a moment. Take your beloved Christ – he was murdered for the same reason. It was a classic act of sacrifice. I wouldn't be surprised if someone believed that by producing this story – that we murdered the Son of God, that God had sacrificed His own Son – we'd have peace for longer. Naturally, the idea failed..."

"Wow, this wine is fantastic – what is it?" Dimitri was trying to change the subject. He didn't want to get into another debate about Christ.

But Marat wasn't listening. He gripped Dimitri's shoulders and led him towards the wine rack to top up his glass, all the while continuing:

"And so, you see, there are no 'two paths' of murder or sacrifice. Sacrifice is the same-old murder, but what's really interesting is that we still practice it today. Every now and then, we sacrifice someone; we publicly destroy someone who's innocent or almost innocent because we still need it. Do you understand? Even today, we crave it and we do it. You'd think that by now we would have developed some other mechanism to end the war of all against all! But no, we still do it. And we often rely on our law system to help us carry it out."

"I'm not sure if the Christian church would interpret crucifixion in the same way you do," Dimitri said, allowing for his glass to be topped up.

"Ha! Of course the church won't see it that way! The church is a mechanism of power and control, an opium for the people. It's important for them to indict everyone with the idea that your life must be a sacrifice, that having a shit life is normal. And people get caught up in that; they suffer and waste away their only life, hoping for some other, better, life beyond death."

"Attention everyone –" Twinka interrupted them – "I'm about to open a Petrus! When should one drink Petrus if not on their fiftieth birthday?! We have three bottles of an exquisite Petrus magnum. And one of them matches Marat's rule about good wine, its being more than thirty years old."

"Very true!" Marat interjected. "When else should one enjoy this symbol of philistines and the nouveau riche?" Marat didn't miss the opportunity to demonstrate his superiority over these two groups he clearly didn't think he belonged to.

"If Jesus turned water into wine, it would have been a Petrus!" Twinka laughed. "Jesus wouldn't have turned the water into some cheap drivel from the bottom shelf, would he?" She turned towards Dimitri, as though seeking support, but he stayed out of it. Every bottle of Petrus had been bought at an auction and delivered from France, with specialist transport maintaining the same temperature. And each had cost the same as an average family car.

Dimitri couldn't quite put it into words, but he felt that Jesus would have something to say about that.

"Fifty has always been a turning point." Marat raised his glass, having interrupted the chatter of the guests. "I remember my dad's fiftieth birthday, and the birthdays of his friends. It was like they all competed to create the most memorable party, inviting as many guests as possible. A fiftieth birthday is like a showcase of all your accomplishments: here's my house, my wife, my children, my friends; look at everything I've achieved in life. Clearly, the message is that once you turn fifty, everything goes downhill. That's it. The peak of your physical and intellectual capabilities belongs to the past. Your most productive years – filled with love, the effort of establishing a family, the birth of your children – it's all behind you, life has taken its course, and all that's left for you to do is to live your remaining years in as much comfort as possible. That was the feeling I got on my dad's fiftieth birthday. Of course, back then, certain social and biological norms existed, to ensure that things didn't deviate too much from their set course, and my dad didn't even dream of resisting them. He had accepted the rules. But you know what?" Marat paused. "I don't feel like doing that. Not at all. I don't intend to accept these 'rules'. I have decided to have another life – to start my life afresh. Thank you, Dimitri, for the gravestone – it's the perfect present for saying bye to my old life and for starting a new, different one. Most men stop developing and growing around thirty, thirty-five.

Around forty, most of them have let themselves go and become alkies. It's written all over their faces: 'That's it; my life is over'. And they know it. Some put on a bit of a fight – we call that a 'midlife crisis' – though there isn't much point in having these convulsions. Then those who haven't completely degraded themselves surrender to the current. In the best-case scenario, they rest on the laurels of their past achievements, trying to squeeze more out of them, some more successfully than others. But none of that's for me. I've had a wonderful life. I've been fortunate in so many ways, but I'm not interested in resting on the laurels of my fortune and drinking Petrus. I want everything, all over again. And I mean it. *Everything.* Except this time I have my past experience, I know myself, and I know the ways of the world. And, of course, I owe my gratitude to Twinka. You're one of my life's greatest achievements, my biggest thanks to you for everything." Marat kissed Twinka on the cheek.

"To another life." He raised his glass.

"To another life," one of the guests repeated.

"To another life," announced the rest in unison.

Dimitri and Marat's eyes met across the room. Dimitri's gaze held a question, and Marat's seemed to have the answer. It was affirmative. Dimitri no longer doubted what Marat had decided. They had known each other for a long time; they had spent a lot of time together, trusting each other with their biggest misgivings, problems, goals and desires. And now, without the need to utter a single word, they understood one another perfectly.

CHAPTER 16

Marat didn't believe in psychotherapy. He believed that a psychotherapist was a friend who got paid by the hour, and that people who had real friends or a family didn't need one. And Twinka would have been inclined to agree with him, if Marat hadn't stopped talking to her.

Because of that shift, the contrast between now and their first years of marriage was dramatic. At the outset, Marat had been interested in every detail of Twinka's life: her thoughts and feelings, how she'd spent each hour, and everyone she'd met. Marat wanted to find out why she thought this way or another, what she loved and didn't like, and why. Films, music, books, everything related to sex, her first marriage, her childhood, her parents – everything about her genuinely intrigued him. Marat could probe Twinka for hours, coming back with more questions later to clarify what she'd said. He was fascinated by what she was doing; he wanted to know her opinion on everything, from politics to running their household; and he always looked forward to hearing her thoughts. It was a genuine, deep interest in Twinka – one that she'd experienced for the first time in her life.

If he hadn't already read them, Marat made an effort to consume all of Twinka's favourite books, from Faulkner to Fernando Pessoa (after he found out the latter was Twinka's favourite writer and poet) – despite Pessoa's only being available in a foreign language. And he didn't do it to conquer her heart – there was no need. He genuinely wanted to understand who she was. And whenever he'd finished reading one of Twinka's favourite books, they'd discuss it for ages.

But now, all of their conversations revolved around Ronia or questions of a practical nature concerning their household. You couldn't really call them conversations – it was more like an exchange of the most basic and essential information. In the best-case scenario, they shared some gossip about their mutual friends and acquaintances.

Twinka envied Marat for having at least one genuine friend he could talk to – Dimitri. She, on the other hand, had only Marat, and their discussions had simply ceased, as though every possible topic had been exhausted. She still had Mum and Dad, of course, but that was different.

And so, unlike Marat, having a friend who got paid by the hour didn't seem like such a crazy idea to Twinka. Of course, it wasn't going to be the sort of friend you'd be able to call at any hour, or whose support you could rely on to help face whatever life threw at you. Still, it was close enough. As intimate as you could get, considering it was a paid service.

Lynda, one of Marat's employees whom Twinka had befriended (because she'd started suspecting that Lynda was more than just an employee), had mentioned 'this amazing genius therapist who literally works miracles'. And that's how Twinka had ended up at Anna's practice, which had become her most significant discovery of late.

They were almost the same age (Twinka was thirty-eight, Anna thirty-seven), though that was pretty much the only thing they had in common. Anna was a bit of a hippy, was covered in spectacular tattoos, and had a turbulent life story and two corgis. Having finally found her true calling, she'd graduated and established herself: seeing clients in her tiny one-bedroom flat on the first floor, a space packed with psychology and self-help books as well as plant pots of all shapes and sizes. The living room had a single window that looked out onto a small inner courtyard that Anna had turned into an improvised orangery. Whenever you opened the window, the flat was filled with lovely garden smells. It was very cosy.

During her first visit Anna had asked Twinka why she'd decided to seek therapy, and also what goal she had in mind for their sessions. It wasn't easy for Twinka to answer these questions.

Should she go ahead and confess about her issue with alcohol? She hadn't even admitted it to herself, let alone delivered a full confession to a stranger. She simply knew that Marat considered her drinking a problem.

Should she say that her problem was excess weight? Or her looks? Or the fact that she no longer had sex with her husband, though she was having it with someone else?

No. No matter how charmed she was by Anna, Twinka wasn't ready to reveal everything about herself to another human being whom she'd only known for a few minutes. But in the process of having to think about the best way to respond and describe all her problems without revealing too much, Twinka suddenly stumbled upon the words that she thought described her situation perfectly: she wasn't happy.

Yes. She was no longer happy. Her family, which had always been at the centre of her life – her foundation, the unit in which she had felt truly fulfilled – no longer felt like that, and she wanted to work out why. What had happened? Yeah, that was it: what had happened, when did it happen, and why? She wanted to get to the bottom of it.

CHAPTER 17

For a short while Marat had let his chauffeur drive him around in a limousine. Though he definitely didn't enjoy it. It made him too dependent, passive, and limited; it felt like it took away his control over the situation – and that didn't feel good. Marat enjoyed driving. Now, he only used the chauffeur when he'd been drinking, was planning to have a drink, or knew that it would be a nightmare to find parking wherever he was headed.

Marat loved cars. The opportunity to drive in a good, fast and expensive car; the chance to buy one and have it in his garage – that was his way of enjoying his fortune. Nothing gave him more pleasure than spending his money on cars. He didn't own a yacht and he didn't long for one; he didn't possess his own private jet; he didn't have a house in every metropolis; or a tour bus, filled with supermodels – none of that caught his fancy. To Marat, money meant freedom and independence. And having money meant that he didn't have to obey anyone or anything; he didn't need to waste his time on anyone or anything he didn't find interesting. It offered the opportunity to choose his own friends, and the people he wanted to spend time with – as well as cars. Cars meant a lot to him, and Marat was the proud owner of twelve. Four of them were parked in his garage, so that he could choose whichever matched his mood, the weather and/or how far or where he needed to go on a given day. More often than not, he picked a car according to his mood.

There was the 2009 Rolls-Royce Phantom Coupé that he loved looking at, and which he kept close despite hardly ever using anymore. Then there was the 2018 Rolls-Royce Wraith Black Badge, which he selected when he was tired, in a bad mood, had a long distance to travel, or was heading out with

Twinka or taking his daughter somewhere. It was Marat's idea of a family car.

There was also his brand-new Porsche 911 GT3. That one was for fast, mighty and glorious days, full of testosterone and the smell of sex, power and victory.

He also had a Porsche 911 Turbo S convertible for days that were similar, but with a more hedonistic touch. Days when he wanted to enjoy the beauty of life in a broader sense.

And finally, there was Marat's most recent purchase – the new Mercedes-AMG G 63.

Marat loved everything about this car. He loved that its design hadn't changed in the last forty years, that it was originally made for an order from an Iranian shah, that it had been used by forty-five different nations as an army vehicle, and that the Pope himself owned one. He loved that you had to apply pressure to slam the doors shut, and he loved the rough, metallic noise that accompanied the action. He adored almost every sound this car made, including the loud click when its central key awoke it, which sounded just like pulling the selector switch on a Kalashnikov.

He loved the low humming of the engine, which, although discreet, still made you feel a distinct sense of superiority. Marat felt an actual physical pleasure whenever he had the chance to push the gas pedal into the floor and subsequently heard the engine hiss like a whale. It felt as though the car had stood up on its hind legs, ready to destroy anything that would come into its path. The acceleration was amazing, and Marat revelled in it like a giddy little boy.

He even loved the way the moniker 'G-Wagon' rolled off the tongue; or the original German name *Geländewagen*; and even the cute-sounding Russian word *гелик* (*gelik*), which Dimitri sometimes used. Marat's G-Wagon was black, had tinted windows, and only a few chrome-plated details adorning its exterior. He loved his self-coined saying: 'The snow has to be white, the Christmas tree has to be green – and a G-Wagon has to be black'.

After the radical but visually almost unnoticeable updates of 2019, the G-Wagon had become easier to control, more comfortable and unbelievably fast. This enormous off-road vehicle could accelerate from nought to a hundred kilometres per hour in less than four seconds – a second faster than Marat's first Porsche 911, which he'd bought almost twenty years prior. Marat loved that this enormous, angular tank – which weighed almost three tonnes and had the aerodynamic shape of a small firewood shed – could beat the supercars of two decades ago when accelerating on a straight-line path. Of course, the feeling was completely different in a sports car. The sharpness of the steering wheel, the collision with the road, the break path, and the speed at which you could manoeuvre through the bends were all distinctly different. But even so, the rate at which technology had developed in a mere twenty years was incredible to grasp and left a deep impression on Marat. He knew, admired and enjoyed the possibilities of this vehicle and he merged with it like a master with his tool, as though the car were an extension of himself. At the same time, Marat loved the fact that the car looked discreet in traffic. And someone who didn't know better would struggle to distinguish the latest G-Wagon model from the old one. It was unusual for anyone to decipher that the car cost more than €200,000. In fact, it was this very concealment of his superiority that gave Marat the most pleasure. Whenever he wanted people to know it more overtly, he used the Rolls-Royce or GT3.

Cars gave Marat so much pleasure that he'd often plan his day in a way that he could drive somewhere. Today he had to go and collect some products from an eco-farm located outside the bounds of the city. He could have sent someone to get them, or paid for the delivery service, but he'd chosen to drive because it meant spending almost an hour on the road in each direction. For Marat, it was a kind of meditation – an opportunity to be alone with his thoughts, the road, and this wonderful car. He craved, and loved, the sanctuary this gave him, and often made important decisions during such drives.

Yes, he was going to do it. The idea he'd only toyed with at first had slowly crystallised and turned into a commitment. Suddenly everything seemed clear. He had decided.

"The simpler the plan, the less chance for something to go wrong," he reasoned aloud. "I'm going to fake a burglary. Whack her over the head with a bottle. And I'm going to do it tomorrow." Marat had no more doubts. "It has to look as if the burglars had lured Twinka into opening the door for them – and then she had either refused to give into their demands, or one of them had simply lost their temper and killed her. That sort of thing happens all the time. I'm going make a mess in my office today, to have it look as though the burglars had been searching for something. It's Thursday tomorrow, when I normally go for my long run. That's when it needs to happen."

Suddenly the plan was ready, to the smallest detail. Marat stopped the car. The free-range eggs would have to wait – he needed a moped.

On Thursdays he usually went for an eleven-kilometre run along the beach. Well, not exactly every Thursday, but relatively often. Usually he drove to a little pub called Neptune, located on the outskirts of the city next to the beach, and from there he would run for two kilometres along the dunes, then four more along the shore, and then another five on his way back (usually walking the last of these, to cool down). Then he ordered a green tea and a freshly squeezed orange juice at Neptune. He was usually gone a good three hours, including the drive there and back. So, the plan was simple. He'd drive to Neptune as usual tomorrow, leave his car and phone in the parking lot, then drive back home on a moped that he would have hidden in the dunes ahead of time. Then he'd "do the deed" and return to the beach on the same moped, leaving it somewhere where it would likely get stolen, then have some tea at Neptune as though he'd just returned from his usual run. It may not be the world's strongest alibi, he reasoned, but it was good enough. The main thing was to complete every step with utmost precision, without getting caught by the cameras installed outside his house. The farthest end of Button Street abutted the railway line, along which was a small footpath. And that footpath provided him with the ideal means of accessing Button Street while circumventing the surveillance. He had already examined all this thoroughly.

Then, obviously, the first suspect was always the husband. But if the police had no evidence linking him to the time and place of the crime, then it would remain at the level of suspicion. People would have seen him at Neptune around the time of the murder; his phone would have been there the entire time, along with his car. Of course, he would be absent for a little while, but it's not like you could tell the exact time of the murder inside a ten-minute window. Besides, how would he have got there and back in time without his car? The plan was solid. He didn't even have to worry about leaving his DNA or fingerprints in the house in general, because there would obviously be plenty of those around. He just had to make sure he didn't leave any when ransacking the office, or on the murder weapon itself.

Sat in his car at the roadside, Marat loaded a marketplace website on his phone. There were currently 1,849 mopeds for sale. He figured it was important to suss out which ones had been stolen. Having studied the site for a while, Marat bookmarked several ads. He went to make a call, but stopped himself just in time. No, it wasn't wise to use his phone. He had to get one of those pay-as-you-go SIMs.

Even though everything went relatively smoothly from there, the entire process took several hours. Marat bought a handset and a SIM card in a tunnel next to the railway station. He called a few sellers from the ads he'd marked, and only the third person he spoke to agreed that he'd pay €700 (rather than the €300 mentioned in the ad) if the seller would transport the moped beyond the city bounds, near Neptune. Since he'd been coming there for years to do his runs, he knew the area well. The tank had to be full, insisted Marat.

He was met by two teenagers. The sun was going down and twilight had started to set over the dunes. Emerging from the half-shade of the pine grove, Marat managed to spook them, even though the boys tried to hide their fear. Marat held the cash out in his hand – he'd withdrawn it earlier – so that it was on full display. His thinking was that the money would distract the teenagers from looking at him. Money always shifted people's attention away from everything else that was going on around them. The deal only took a few seconds. It was a shabby old Piaggio in silver. Marat cast a sceptical eye over the questionable moped.

"Let's hope it survives the journey," he muttered to himself.

The most important thing now was to hide the scooter so that it wouldn't be discovered by anyone until the following afternoon. He couldn't leave it in the cafe car park because that was kitted out with CCTV cameras. He would have to hide it somewhere along the dunes, which wasn't an easy task – Marat couldn't find anything to cover the moped with. Besides, the hiding place might have seemed like a good idea during twilight, but during the day it may turn out that the Piaggio had been left in an open space, visible to everyone, so he took his time choosing where to stash it. If the moped did get stolen overnight, then his entire plan would be put on hold, and he'd have to start the whole process again.

It had gone eleven when Marat finally returned home. Ronia was already in bed.

"I called you," Twinka said, but there was no judgement, suspicion or blame in her voice. "I wanted to know whether you'd be having dinner, or whether you'd managed to eat something on the way?"

"No, I've not eaten yet. I'd love to have some dinner."

"I left you something in the oven... Have you been working hard? Are you tired?"

"Yeah, quite a bit."

"I opened the white Rioja – would you like to try it? You'll love it; it becomes simply divine with age."

"Sure, why not," Marat said, looking at his wife, considering whether he'd like to sleep with her one last time. No, he didn't feel the slightest urge. "I need to finish up some work in the office," he said. "I need to find a document. And I may as well organise the papers while I'm at it."

"Yes, of course darling. I'll watch a film." Twinka was used to spending time on her own.

Having shut the door to his office and put on some leather gloves, Marat started making a mess, rifling through everything systematically. He tossed the contents of the drawers all over the floor, pulled books off their shelves, opened folders that contained important documents and scattered said pages around. Twinka rarely ever entered his office, so he didn't worry that she may have questions – and even if she did, what would it matter? Having done this for a bit, Marat felt worn out, and decided to go to bed. He went downstairs, gave his wife the usual kiss, still pondering whether to have sex with her one last time. But he felt too lazy for it. Marat was tired, so he just said bye and went to bed.

But despite the fatigue, he couldn't fall asleep right away. After a while, he heard Twinka put the alarm on and go to bed.

CHAPTER 18

"Tell me more about your first marriage," Anna suggested, lighting an incense stick, which she placed somewhere behind Twinka's back. Twinka was surprised that Anna never offered her any tea or coffee. She would have found it easier to talk and open up with a hot beverage in her hands, but she didn't dare ask. If she hadn't been so wealthy and elegantly dressed, she may have asked for one. But Twinka was conscious of the fact that people often considered those who were as wealthy as her to be spoiled and always expecting special treatment. She was afraid of coming across like a 'rich bitch'. Normally.

"I don't know. It seems pointless to talk about him," Twinka said, though she continued nevertheless. "He was older than me. Wealthy, respectable. Very serious. He owned several building supplies stores. I fancied him. The wedding was grand and spectacular: everything about it felt very respectable, important and expensive. I loved it."

"And when did things start going wrong?" Anna encouraged Twinka to go on.

I doubt whether someone who doesn't come from money could really understand someone who does, Twinka thought to herself, examining Anna carefully once more. There was nothing wrong with Anna, and she wasn't impoverished by any means – Twinka had spotted Anna's brand-new Porsche Macan. Still, someone belonging to the middle class would never be able to comprehend what it was like to be truly in the money. They didn't have a clue; not even the faintest idea of what life was like when you had so much. Twinka hated all their stupid clichés – that people like her didn't need anything; that they didn't have any problems; that everything came easy to them, and they didn't know anything about life's hardships. Anna probably thought along the same lines. Or perhaps she understood and appreciated the fact that Twinka presented her with a unique opportunity to get an intimate insight into the world of the uber-affluent.

"When did you first notice that something was wrong?" Anna repeated her question, having noticed how Twinka was lost in thought.

"I think I was like a trophy wife for him. How was I supposed to know that what we had wasn't love? I assumed it was."

"When did you realise that you were his trophy wife?" Anna was sat at a ninety-degree angle to Twinka, so that she wasn't situated directly opposite.

Twinka chose not to look at Anna – she was gazing outside the window directly in front of her eyes. "After we got divorced, I think." Twinka smiled sadly, slowly gathering her thoughts, as if she was afraid of wandering too quickly into territory that she'd abandoned so long ago. Even though it didn't seem particularly threatening, there was still a good chance she could step on something sharp.

Twinka continued after a pause. "A month or two after the wedding, it was like he just put me in storage, from which he'd collect me whenever there was some occasion or an event involving 'the wives'. He truly believed that, as long as I didn't lack anything in a social, financial or material sense, he'd done his duty. Looking back on it now, I realise how simple-minded, crass and boring he was. Don't get me wrong – he wasn't a bad person. No, no, he wasn't evil or anything. He was just incredibly basic. Do you know what I mean? He was boring. It was a huge disappointment."

"The classic joke comes to mind: 'Can a marriage of convenience ever be a success? Only if the calculations are done right'." Anna followed this quip with a look that urged Twinka to continue.

"What calculations? It wasn't like that. The reason I was so attracted to him was because he courted and wooed me like no one else had. He was miles ahead of everyone else purely because of his diligence. Besides, he seemed serious, strong and dependable. Everything felt fine. On the surface, he really resembled the perfect husband."

"So, there was no love or calculation involved. And what about the sex?"

"Oh," Twinka sighed. "I didn't even know what an orgasm was until I met Marat." Twinka was surprised at how easy she found talking to Anna. "I was so inexperienced. I had no idea that you could have several orgasms."

"Sounds like getting divorced was a wise decision?"

"Yeah. Fortunately, we didn't have any children. It's scary to imagine how life could have turned out if we did. I would have probably stayed."

"And why didn't you have them?"

"I don't even know, we just didn't. We discussed it and we agreed that we were in no hurry, though we didn't use contraception either. We felt like they'd just come into our lives when the timing was right. Yet they never did."

"Maybe somewhere in your subconscious mind you felt that you shouldn't have them?"

"Maybe."

"Did you feel relieved after you got divorced?"

The room smelled of incense, books and vegetation. Anna had a little diamond piercing in one of her nostrils. She looked more like the owner of a tattoo parlour than a psychotherapist, and that's probably what drew Twinka to her.

"I don't know. I mean, I definitely did, but not until later. It wasn't easy. He was very cross with me. He didn't understand what I was talking about when I said we had problems, but he promised to make everything right. He begged, objected and protested – he genuinely believed that everything was exactly as it should be. Of course, I felt very guilty, because he wasn't a bad person and he'd never done anything to harm me. I was hurting him without meaning to. I didn't enjoy it; not one bit. Luckily, my dad took care of everything in relation to him. I don't know how, but he's just good at stuff like that. In that sense, I can always rely on Dad – he'll always turn up and sort everything out just when I need it. But if we had kids, I would probably still be there, like a living corpse trapped in a coffin."

"I get what you're saying – marriage can be so cruel." Anna had a look of compassionate understanding on her face. "If you had to compare your first marriage to your second one – would they have anything in common?"

"They didn't... until now." Twinka let out a laugh. "Well, the main difference is that there was always a genuine, deep love connection between me and Marat, which made everything about it so different."

"Go on, tell me more." Anna was listening intently.

"Oh, Marat! Marat caused an absolute explosion in my life. He immediately occupied the entire space – he filled all my thoughts, my time and attention. Suddenly, there was only him. In the morning, during the day, in the evening – it was all him, everywhere."

Anna wasn't writing anything down. At least not while Twinka was present.

"It was very tough for me after the divorce. I felt intimidated. I had failed, and burned myself in the process. I felt like everyone else knew how to live life, except me. I even tried going on dates and meeting men, and there were a few who seemed nice and interesting. With some of them, it even led to something more, but I was wary of believing that I could make it work with those men, only to later realise that I'd made the same mistake. Everything felt hopeless."

"And that's when Marat showed up?"

"Yeah, that's when Marat showed up. Compared to the shopkeeper, Marat was in an entirely different league in every possible way. He was a historian who'd somehow set himself up as a financier, a banker and an investor. To this day I don't even know how to describe what he does. He doesn't want to have some label, or a stereotype attached to him, so he never tries to explain or help people understand what he does. In certain circles he's considered to be a genius; something to do with trading financial instruments. At least he used to in the past. He's also far more wealthy than the shopkeeper."

"He works a lot but he's never at home." Anna had intended to pose a question, but it sounded more like an observation.

"No! That's the biggest difference between him and the shopkeeper. Marat works very little. And what he calls work usually involves lunch with another banker or a lawyer. They meet in one of those select 'banker's restaurants', enjoy the best cuisine in town, consume a bottle of some distinguished wine, and that's work. To be honest, I don't think you could even apply the word 'work' to him. I used to tease him sometimes, asking whether he felt overworked today: had the oysters gone off, had the lamb been fully tenderised, did he feel a heaviness in his stomach after such a hard day at *work*."

"It sounds like he's set himself up rather well," Anna said with what sounded like approval, albeit her features betrayed a smirk.

"Yeah, he's set himself up well, there's no denying that." Twinka sighed.

"It's interesting, because even the wealthiest people don't always dare of doing, or aren't capable of doing, only what they like, especially those who are self-made." Anna had managed to wipe any expression off her face, so her comment sounded dry and formal.

"Do you know what *sprezzatura* is?" Twinka asked her, fetching a bottle of water with a heightened pH level from her bag.

"*Sprezzatura*? No, I've never heard of it." Anna looked interested.

"It's a principle that was developed by the Italian aristocrats in the sixteenth century, which was later adapted by all of Europe's aristocratic houses. They call it *effortless superiority* in the British elite schools. Essentially, it means that whatever you're doing, you need to do it perfectly – but you also need to make it seem like it didn't require any effort from you. Being superior to others is only half the victory – the highest thing you can ever strive for is to be better than everyone by a head, but in a way that looks like it didn't require any effort whatsoever. As though you did it without thinking."

"Intriguing..." Anna tilted her head towards Twinka, demonstrating active listening.

"There's a volume called *The Book of the Courtier*. I noticed it on Marat's bookshelf one day and asked him what it was. I'd never heard of it before, but after he spoke about this *sprezzatura* so passionately I realised it was a very important concept to him. It's his signature. At least he'd like it to be. Not only does he want to climb Everest – he wants to create the impression that it was all very easy and basic, sort of done in passing.

"Say, what do you, plebs, consider a big achievement? Reaching the summit of Mount Everest? Very well. I'll go ahead and do it.

"Yeah, Everest wasn't half-bad – I went there and did it. Now, what else do you consider to be important? Wealth and money? Fine. I made some money for myself, but just for everyday expenses. Education? Well, I've got three degrees.

"That's just who he is. He's taking a degree in theology, just so he can debate about God with more conviction, suddenly pulling a quote by Saint Augustine or Desert Fathers and weaving it into a conversation with a facial expression as if to say 'Oh darling, everyone knows that'."

"And where do you fit into all of this?" Anna cut in.

"That's a very good question."

"Have you been put in the storage room?"

"I'm with Ronia."

"In the nursery then?"

"We got married when I became pregnant. Then Ronia was born. Ronia – 'the robber's daughter' – Marat was convinced that this would be the perfect name for his own girl. The first nine or even ten years of our marriage were the happiest in my life. Those years were filled with absolute love, without anything overshadowing it. Everything was as good as it possibly could be. But then one day you realise that nothing's the same anymore... and I've no idea what happened."

"Okay, why don't we talk about that next Monday?" Anna said, in a tone that served as a reminder that their time was up.

"Yes, of course. All good things come to an end," Twinka replied sadly. She hadn't even noticed the time go by.

"We'll start from the same place we finished off today," Anna said.

"Yes, of course." Twinka had already got up. Her 'paid friend' had to get ready for her next client.

CHAPTER 19

As he attempted to fall asleep, Marat tried not to think about the murder plan, instead making an effort to focus his thoughts on something else entirely. He remembered how the evening had developed following the afternoon's wine tasting session. He and Dimitri had ordered a glass of cognac (not their first, either) on the restaurant's terrace and started talking about life. These sorts of conversations were what friends were for, and they were also what made life beautiful. Marat tried to recall the feeling, the smells, and the mood from that evening.

Few things brought as much pleasure to the soul as the first warm summer's evening of the year. The sky glowed late into the day, with a gentle sea breeze blowing. The city buzzed with energy and excitement, as if it had been eagerly awaiting the first opportunity to break free from its winter confinement and take to the streets. Despite the late hour, cafes were packed and windows thrown wide open. A student orchestra had gathered in the park across the street, playing *Moscow Nights*. Some people lounged on its benches, while others strolled around leisurely, soaking up the atmosphere...

Dimitri and Marat had chosen a secluded table on the restaurant's terrace. Marat wanted to smoke a cigar before they headed home. "Two cognacs, please," he ordered.

"Oh, not for me," Dimitri tried to object.

With a commanding gesture and look, Marat made it clear to the waiter that they would be having two.

The waiter turned to Marat, correctly interpreting who was in charge.

"What type of cognac would you like?"

"What do you have from Hors d'Âge?" Marat asked.

"We have A. E. DOR eleven and nine. We also have Gautier Tradition Rare – very reasonably priced – and, of course, Hennessy Paradis," the waiter replied with an air of pride.

"Have you got nothing from The Last Drop Distillers?" Irked by the waiter's haughtiness and the assumption that he might be interested in something as crude as the price, Marat posed the question solely to assert his dominance.

"No, sir, I'm afraid we don't have that one."

"Okay, fine. We'll go with Paradis then."

"Very well, sir," the waiter replied and hastened away.

"Classic," Marat muttered to himself, tracing the waiter's withdrawal with an exhausted look.

"It's too much for me on a Wednesday night. I've got work tomorrow," Dimitri complained.

"You're the one who said that your position is untouchable," Marat reminded him. "Just take the day off. Tell them I needed you."

It didn't even occur to Marat that pointing out their differing positions in the bank's hierarchy could come across as insensitive.

"You know, people worry too much about political freedoms, to the extent that they've become synonymous with the word 'freedom' itself. But that's only one aspect of freedom," Marat said, tossing one leg over the other. He used the restaurant's napkin to dust off his shoes, transferring a small trail of black shoe polish onto the fancy cloth before flinging it under the table. "Philosophers don't pay enough attention to things like having to go to work. Essentially, if you have a body, then you're no longer free by extension. If you need to eat, seek shelter, warmth or water, then you can't be truly free. The human body is the primary obstacle to experiencing freedom. The body is in charge of your routine. It decides when you'll defecate, when you'll be healthy or sick, what your sleep pattern is, when you should eat, how far you can run, how high you can climb, how much you can lift, and so on. The body even determines whether you'll be having sex today. It will just decide on a whim – 'It's not happening today' – and there's nothing you can do about it. Well, at least for us men." He paused dramatically before continuing.

"Next, if you have kids, then you have a whole list of duties and responsibilities. You're limited for about twenty years or so, even the most basic freedoms are no longer available to you. What's more, you have to actively think about money, shelter, food, medicine and everything else – because your children have bodies too, and there's no philosophy, ideology or religion that can satisfy their needs. And it's the same with your parents. You have a duty towards them – you can't just up and leave. Even if you did, that still wouldn't set you free. Because if you can't take care of your kids and parents, chances are you're not very good at taking care of yourself either. And there's more. Society's expectations and moral pressures, along with feelings of guilt and inadequacy, literally make you a slave to the opinions of others.

"And then there's fear. Fear makes you a slave to your own inner demons, and they affect every aspect of your life. The fear of pain and death; the fear of all kinds of diseases, poverty and hardships, and the fear of shame. There's worry, dread, anxiety – and every one of these steals a little piece of freedom away from you. Fear can even make you physically sick."

"And after all that, the government comes in with all its laws and taxes, telling you what you can or cannot do – what you can smoke and what drugs you can take. There's no freedom to be found anywhere, not even a whiff of it! But we'd love to have it, wouldn't we? That's why people take drugs. You take drugs and suddenly you're free. What an incredible feeling that is – to be free, at long last! There's no fear, no bondage, no opinions imposed on you, no agitation or shame – you've become like God. You're finally free. And that's why people get addicted – because it's tough being a slave. For our proud minds, it's insufferable."

Dimitri knew better than to say anything – Marat wasn't seeking his opinion.

Meanwhile, the waiter had brought them two glasses of cognac.

Marat dipped the tip of a cigar in his glass, put the cigar in his mouth and started lighting it. "Okay, let's ignore the problem of the body for a moment, even though it's not just the body's problem – it's a problem of money, economy, inequality: everything is connected there," Marat said when the cigar was finally lit. "Food, shelter, medicine – unfortunately, it all costs money. But if you didn't have a need for it – if someone was as wealthy as we are – then you'd still be left with all the other obstacles to freedom. So, what can we do about them?"

Marat smacked his cigar and Dimitri knew that he was about to answer his own question.

"Well, you could cut ties with everything that limits you. Family, society, the government, morality, the legal system – *everything*. But then we have another problem. When you cut ties, you're also cutting off any possibility of interacting with these aspects of your life. What kind of a life are you left with – do you become a monk? An ascetic? A recluse? You'd have to live like the wandering bandolero. That won't do, at least not for me," he concluded, before then continuing once more. "Lots of people would say it's actually the opposite – you can't set yourself free by giving up and running away from everything. They'd argue it's all about power. You don't just cut ties with everything that could limit you – you gain power over it. But I'd argue that, on many levels, this is just an illusion, too. Only gods have limitless power. Because power usually depends on your position at work, your situation, your wealth, or the act of suppressing others. And that can produce its own addictions and new types of bondage. Only gods can be free, omnipotent, and independent – for humans, that kind of power is out of reach. So, what option are you left with?"

Marat's tone and body language clearly indicated that something he considered extremely important was about to follow.

"There's only one type of power that remains, and which can give you a relative amount of freedom. Wisdom. Some say that knowledge is power, but I think that's nonsense, because you need to know how to apply that knowledge. And for that, you need wisdom. You need to carve your own individual path to freedom – that's your only option. *Your* personality: your unique signature that consists of your commitment in relation to every single obstacle that limits you. You have to cut ties with something, give up on something else, you have to subject someone to your power, or make peace with someone else. That's a huge undertaking." Marat raised his glass of cognac. "To wisdom."

They toasted, although Dimitri only took a little sip.

"Of everything you just said, the only thing I understood was that you need to be so wise and so rich that you can get away with killing your boring wife," Dimitri concluded with a smirk.

Marat ignored the remark. He dipped the tip of his cigar in the glass, licked it, took a few puffs, then plunged it back into the glass.

"Actually, I don't think wisdom is enough. One must also be brave," he continued. "If you want to be truly free, then you need to be ready to take a deciding step, to be capable of action and decision. Every other person must have had the desire to kill their wife or husband at some point, right? It's a fact. Do you think it's morality that's holding them back? No. It's just plain old fear."

"God forbid you ever find yourself surrounded by people who think like you and have the courage." Dimitri shook his head. "Just think about it. Any self-righteous idiot could suddenly decide what laws they want to follow, what's in society's best interests, and go on a killing spree, murdering anyone they don't like the look of. I'd like to be as far away as possible when that happens."

"I agree with you on that," Marat said, formally. "You should never let something like that happen."

"But you were the one promoting it just now!"

"No! Never. I'll explain it again – I'm only defending *my own individual* right to freedom. But you're so stuck in your clichés that you can't even comprehend what I'm saying. No, I don't want to act in accordance with the Categorical Imperative. And no, I'm not interested in the maxim of my will becoming universal law. Any 'golden rule' of morality – it's all just bullshit for the simpletons who don't use their own brain. Or are you trying to say that Islamic fundamentalists or Hitler's fascists, or Stalin's communists created decent material for general law-making norms because they were certain about their maxims of will? No, Father Kant totally missed the mark on that. Categorical imperatives are not a guarantee of anything good. 'Act only according to that maxim whereby you can, at the same time, will that it should become a universal law' basically means 'Do as you please, and if you don't know how to justify it, then just use God or an ideology to do as you please'," Marat said, before then ordering two more cognacs.

"What about 'Do unto others as you would have them do unto you?' Is this rule missing the mark for you, too?"

"No, it makes perfect sense – for the ordinary folk. But what if you're not an ordinary person? What if you come across tasks that an ordinary person would never experience in their entire lives? No one's counted how many people Emperor Constantine suppressed, how many more he ruined or how many he killed, just to instil Christianity and its morals as a universal law? Does anyone know how many heretics the church has massacred? Picture me being an emperor. Say I needed an effective social mechanism for controlling the mob. I pick Christianity, task it with unifying its own teachings and suppress everything else. How would your Golden Rule apply to this situation? What would the law sound like then? Whenever you become an emperor – make sure you pick Christianity? Is that it? The emperor cannot be guided by the principle of 'do unto others as you would have them do unto you' because he's in an entirely different category to them. It's true, isn't it? He decides who's a real god and which gods don't exist. He decides which gods should worshipped, and which ones should be forgotten. Right? He murders anyone who opposes him. He decides when it's war or peace, he decides over life and death, he determines the value of money, he creates laws, and for all those reasons he can't be compared to your average Joe."

"Hang on. I think I've read that theory somewhere," Dimitri interrupted with glee. "It's Dostoyevsky! Raskolnikov had his ordinary breed of people and the 'chosen ones'. Not only did they have special rights, but a moral duty to remove any obstacles in their path. Including murder, if necessary."

"Yes, of course. But don't you start comparing me to Raskolnikov! Look at me – do I remind you of the lame, lanky Christian and socialist Raskolnikov, on the brink of collapse?" Disgusted, Marat scrunched up his face. "Raskolnikov and I come from two completely different castes. Dostoyevsky's biggest weakness was wanting to entwine a moral message or a lesson in his novel. He ruined a perfectly decent story by doing that. I mean, he could have stopped Raskolnikov from killing that poor pregnant woman who'd become a witness. Everything would have been different then. Why did she have to show up? Only because he wanted to add his didactic to it. Raskolnikov could have just collected the evil hag's money and saved a thousand families from ruin. But no, Dostoyevsky wasn't interested in that. And why did Raskolnikov confess? He could have kept his mouth shut, but Dostoyevsky wanted to lecture us: to show that murder is bad, that it always comes to a bad end, and that, following a downfall, there might be a chance for resurrection. That's what he was trying to say, but the result was still the same – more preaching, using the same old quotes from the Bible. Lazarus, who'd started to rot and smell, could still be resurrected – that's what Dostoyevsky wanted to get across. But those are just fairy tales. Does anything of the sort happen in real life? Are there many murderers who don't touch the money they've stolen? How many of them confess due to a psychological pressure? And how can anyone believe that a corpse that's been rotting away for four days could be resurrected? It's all pure nonsense. Fairy stories for the ignorant mob."

"I disagree," said Dimitri, finishing up his drink. "What Dostoyevsky wanted to say is that a crime will always have unforeseen consequences. It has its own inner logic that always leads to something worse over time. And that's so true – it's literally always like that. You can't commit a serious crime and expect nothing to change. Everything changes, but you don't know in what way until you've done it. Dostoyevsky was a prophet – perhaps the only true prophet. The 1918 revolution happened exactly as he'd described it in *Crime and Punishment* and *The Devils*. First you kill the Tsar to free the people who'd been suppressed and humiliated. But then immediately after that, you must also kill the Tsar's wife and his children, along with all the other oppressors. And suddenly you've started killing the same people who were oppressed and humiliated, in whose name all the original murders started."

"Hmm, I'm not so sure... I think it's another cliché to say that Dostoyevsky was some kind of a prophet. Everything that happened in Russia had already been explained in Machiavelli's little book, except this was on a much bigger scale. Because it was Russia, not a single Italian kingdom the size of one Russian province." Marat crafted two delicate smoke rings that gracefully floated in the air. "But what I absolutely cannot stand is preaching, especially in art. If art contains a moral message, then it's no longer art. It's then become propaganda or a pedagogical tool – anything except art. And anyway, it's much simpler than that. I'm going to repeat myself here: the biggest portion of the population abide by the laws only because they're afraid of getting caught. All those who preach, they're just scared little cowardly shitheads. The minute they're out of the public view and no longer afraid, that's when the worst kind of behaviour comes out. From betrayal to awful things like raping little altar boys, I guarantee it." Marat had again become carried away.

Meanwhile, the orchestra in the park had started playing the score from *The Godfather*.

CHAPTER 20

"How's your sex life?" Anna asked.

"We don't have one."

"What, none at all?"

"No."

"When was the last time you had sex?"

"I don't remember." For some reason, Twinka was finding it much harder to be open with Anna this time round.

"Come on, surely you do," Anna chided her. "When was the last time – a month ago, six months, a year perhaps?"

"No, it was longer than that." Twinka looked out the window with a vacant stare.

"Over a year ago?" Anna asked.

"I'd say over two years ago," Twinka finally confessed.

"Oh." Anna's face reflected the gravity of the statement. "And how do you feel about it?"

"What do you think?" Twinka groaned. "It's driving me insane."

Anna didn't say anything – she waited until Twinka was ready to continue.

"Well, luckily I have Cat now."

"Cat?" Anna didn't understand.

"A man."

"Oh, right." Anna's expression transformed into a mischievous one. "You have a lover?"

"Yeah." Twinka was looking down at the floor like a shy little girl.

"Go on, tell me more." Anna adjusted her position in the chair, displaying an air of feminine curiosity.

"Err... Fine. I mean, everything's fine." Twinka didn't know where to start. "At first, I felt guilty. But then I realised that Marat is the one to blame. It's his fault that we don't make love. It's like he doesn't want it anymore. He must have a lover; maybe more than one. Yet for some reason I'm still the one who feels bad. It's just wrong."

"So, you think he has another woman?" Anna asked.

"I don't know. Things just don't feel right anymore. I get jealous of any woman he's in contact with, like some kind of paranoid idiot. Every time one comes on the scene, I figure he's probably sleeping with her. It's so humiliating." Twinka was on the verge of tears. And she would have liked to have had a good cry, but she had been long since numbed to the situation.

"Cat is helping me a lot. I mean, just the fact that he's there is helping. I'm less interested in what Marat is doing: he can sleep with anyone, for all I care. And Cat is just amazing." Now that she'd said all this, Twinka felt a sense of relief. She raised her eyes and looked at Anna quizzically.

"We should try and unpick the reasons behind this." Anna had dropped the act of a curious girlfriend and switched back to her professional demeanour. "If it's just a sexual adventure they crave, men don't typically stop sleeping with their wives. In fact, when a lover comes on the scene for them, it often in turn improves the sex in their marriage. But if the relationship has deteriorated for other reasons, a lover may be used as a means of filling the void, much like what Cat is doing for you. What I'm saying is –" Anna's tone had now become serious – "we must find the reason why you're no longer having sex. There can be a multitude of reasons."

"So, you're saying that the appearance of a lover can improve the married couple's sex life? Well, it's the first time I'm hearing about this."

"Yes, it does happen. For starters the lover helps to raise the husband's libido, and his testosterone levels go up. Not only does he *feel* younger, on a hormonal level he *has* become younger, and that can result in a more intense interest in his wife. Also, husbands often engage in a kind of 'masking strategy'. For example they'll show affection to their wives more often, as a means of preventing them from becoming suspicious. It also helps them deal with their feelings of guilt. That sort of thing does happen – but, like I said, we have to look deeper and work out why you're no longer having sex, and why he's sleeping around. That will determine everything."

"You know, I'm worried that he just doesn't find me interesting anymore. I mean, as a person or a woman. That's the root cause. And I wonder whether it's my fault."

"And what do you make of it?" Anna clearly wanted Twinka to elaborate on her theory.

"He said to me once: *You're more interesting than Nietzsche.* It was the most unusual and, consequently, best compliment I've ever received. And it meant even more coming from someone like him. He also said that he was less interested in having sex than he was getting to know me on a deeper level, and I don't think he was lying. Because for him, sex was just another way of getting to know me; only one aspect of the process of exploration. An important one, of course, but I don't think sex is all he cared about. He was interested in honesty, openness, surrender, emotion – all the elements that sex encompasses – and how these enabled us to get to know each other better. But now that he's figured me out, he's no longer interested. I think that's the root cause. He's simply bored with me."

Anna was nodding her head as though actively listening, urging Twinka to continue.

"Back in the day, sex with Marat was like one experiment on top of another. It gave him immense satisfaction to come up with things that were new to me. He wanted to do it in every kind of place possible; he wanted to experiment with toys; to make love to me while we were high on weed, cocaine, LSD, ecstasy... We used to do it for hours on end, under the influence of something or another. He always came up with something new and exciting. I think the most stimulating part for him was the prospect of discovering something that was entirely new to me. He absolutely loved taking part in something I was experiencing for the first time."

"To conquer, to acquire, to submit, to steal a woman's maidenhood – these are all typical aspects of male sexuality. When something happens for the first time, it's almost like he's taking your virginity again. So, that makes sense..."

"Probably. But I think Marat was also guided by something more philosophical – that anything real and genuine can only happen to us once. And that's why I think he found any new sexual experience with me so stimulating."

"Intriguing..."

"And pregnancy was another novel event for us. You know, I think Marat enjoyed it a lot more than I did. He was so excited. He showered me with attention. He loved watching my body change: how my belly swelled up and my breasts got bigger. He was fascinated by every little detail – my mood swings; my feelings, worries and fears – and I loved it. I felt so important to him, so special and safe. To be honest, it's only now that I realise just how amazing it was. I'd never been so happy in my whole life. If I had known back then that everything that was happening to us for the first time would never happen again – if I had realised just how special it was, if I had the ability to notice and appreciate every moment as it unfolded – I would have enjoyed it a lot more. I guess, over the course of ten years, all our novel experiences had come to an end; all aspects of my 'maidenhood', so to speak, had been taken from me; and his astonishing interest just dissipated."

"I'd venture to say that each new year – or each new day, at that – brings with it new experiences, all of which are happening to us for the very first time. Is it worth trying to make him perceive life in that way?" Anna suggested. "Relationships continue to evolve as well. Yes, spring is always followed by summer, and after that comes autumn, but everything is still happening for the first time. We get to a certain age for the first time, we reach a certain level of maturity – all this could be just as interesting, eh?"

"I don't know. Maybe. It just doesn't have the same energy; the element of surprise is gone. In any case his interest in me has waned, to say the least. And the worst thing is, I'm asking myself if it's all my fault? Could I have done more to keep his attention and interest in me?"

"And what do you say to yourself?"

"Nothing. I don't want to place any blame on him or myself."

"Is Cat your solution?"

"Yeah, sort of... And this time I'm definitely keen to fully take it in and appreciate it. Something totally new and genuine, full of life and beauty, is now happening to me again. Marat would understand..." Twinka laughed. "If I wasn't his wife."

CHAPTER 21

As he woke up on the morning of the murder, Marat noticed that he felt anxious.

Once Ronia had left for school, Twinka went back to bed.

As he enjoyed his morning coffee, Marat tried to tune into himself and understand what he was feeling. Was he having second thoughts? Maybe he shouldn't go through with his plan? It wasn't too late – he could still change his mind.

The sink was filled with dirty dishes, which really annoyed him. When he was a child, everyone would get up and clean their own plate as soon as they'd finished eating. It's not like it was hard. All you needed was hot water. You didn't even need any washing-up liquid, as long as you turned on the tap and ran the plate under it quickly once you were done. Was it really such a difficult task?

But no. Twinka would keep piling the dirty plates until they formed a mountain, and only then load them into the dishwasher. Or she'd wait for their housekeeper to do it. Worst of all, Ronia had, naturally, adapted her mother's habit. Even Marat no longer washed up after himself, because what was the point if he was the only one in the family doing it?

It was almost as if marriage was designed to make you discover your partner's worst flaws. You get the pleasure of hearing your partner fart and snore, seeing them get wasted and puke everywhere, being with them when they get high or sick, and experiencing their depression and mood swings. Marriage was a magnifying glass on your partner's weaknesses, imperfections, and those deformities in them that even they didn't know existed. And what outcome could this possibly lead to? You might still love them – but only as a relative, or an ally in combat, or a life partner. That in itself wasn't nothing. It was actually amazing, and it could be incredibly beautiful. It's just not what Marat wanted right now. He desired to live another life. He wanted to have a fresh start; one more spring. He wanted to have all the best things that life could offer, just once more. He was healthy, fit, and energetic enough to receive all those things. More than anything, he wasn't ready to just sit back and grow old, surrendering to the flow of life. He had never been one to follow the current, which is why he had achieved so much. And he wasn't prepared to stop.

No more doubting – Marat was determined. *It's only normal to feel a little anxious,* he reasoned to himself, *like you were about to take a big exam, nothing more.* Marat toasted two slices of bread, topped them with a spread of avocado, added a squeeze of lemon and finished with a sprinkle of salt. Meanwhile, his mind went over the plan once more. If there was a break-in, then something had to be missing. The best bet would be Twinka's jewellery; she had lots of expensive trinkets that criminals may want – watches, earrings, bracelets and necklaces. Easy to carry, easy to sell. It wouldn't be suspicious if they went missing. He'd have to bury them somewhere, out of sight. But it wasn't a high a price to pay, all things considered. He could tell the police that some cash got taken from his office, too. Not a bad catch for someone breaking in. Especially in terms of regular people's money.

Was there anything he'd forgotten?

Marat reminded himself that true wisdom came in being prepared for any outcome, so that nothing in life could catch you off guard. When Twinka was finally dead, he'd have to make the house look even more ransacked. He was sure to get a call from Ronia's school around four in the afternoon to tell him that Twinka hadn't shown up to collect their daughter. He would still be at Neptune at that time. He'd drive over to the school, collect Ronia, take her to her Taekwondo class, then head back home to work out (and then 'find out') what had happened to Twinka. Then he'd call the police, while ordering his driver to collect Ronia and take her to Mum's house from Taekwondo.

The unpredictability and novelty of everything that would follow – in terms of the follow-up investigation – felt borderline exciting to Marat, but he fought the urge to get ahead of himself and instead went through the sequence once more, this time from the very beginning.

Shortly after one p.m. he'd leave the house and drive to his usual running spot. Then he'd come back on a moped, sneak into the house through the back gate, do the deed, then leave the same way he'd come in, and drive back. He should have plenty of time. In fact, he could extend his stay at Neptune for a little longer, maybe have a meal? He'd done that on a few previous occasions, so it wouldn't look particularly suspicious. And while there he'd patiently await the call from the school.

As an extra precaution, Marat decided to change his clothes for the drive on the moped. Even if he was recorded on CCTV cameras somewhere else in the city, no one would know it was him. He found some jeans, sunglasses and an old, blue-green chequered windbreaker that he couldn't remember wearing for the last ten years. He stuffed everything into a backpack.

I'll wear this over my sports clothes, and I've got an old helmet I bought off those guys. No one will recognise me in a million years, he reasoned, pleased with himself.

Hold on – what about shoes? He had to change his footwear. He couldn't let anyone identify him, not even from the smallest detail. Marat found a pair of old, comfy trainers and his anxiety eased. He also picked out a pair of gloves – they'd be useful for his drive, as well as what would follow.

Now I'm ready, he told himself. It was only nine in the morning though. He had another four hours to kill. He didn't have anything else in his schedule today, and he felt restless.

The avocado on toast hadn't quite done the job, so he decided to boil a couple of eggs.

Years ago, still in his schooldays, someone had popped a question at a party: "Would you be capable of killing a man?"

Marat remembered his bewilderment as to how many of his schoolmates responded with genuine shocked (or convincing lies), insisting that they were incapable of doing anything of the sort. Marat hadn't understood it then, and found it even more perplexing now. What's the big deal? He'd find it a lot harder killing a dog or a kitten. Now, that would be both cruel and stupid. But a person? Even back then, Marat already knew that, if he really needed to, he could do it. Without batting an eyelid. And he was even more convinced of this today, as he sipped his coffee on the morning of the murder. Most people lived like zombies anyway. And some even behaved like especially evil, useless and toxic zombies: who caused so much pain and suffering to others, and whose stench permeated our world. Of course, Twinka wasn't one of them – she'd been so good and kind to him. But what was left for her – anything she could actually look forward to? She already felt unhappy, and would only continue to decay with time. It was funny that they'd never got round to discussing what funeral they'd like. They hadn't left any instructions for each other on what to do if one of them suddenly died.

Never mind, Marat reasoned, *I'll make sure everything is done in accordance with the highest standards.*

CHAPTER 22

Time went by very slowly. He didn't want to leave any earlier than he had to, but he also didn't want to see Twinka again. As he saw it, Marat had already said goodbye to her. Their life together had come to an end. Overall, it had been brilliant. Sixteen amazing years, and a wonderful daughter as a testament to them. That meant a lot, and now it would forever remain this way; only as a wonderful memory, in which he'd salvage only the good and beautiful parts. With a pure heart, he'd take utmost care of Twinka's memory. As soon as she was gone, loving her would become easy and enjoyable.

Once again, Marat went over all the details of his plan. He had considered every nuance, and everything felt right. He decided to pass the rest of the day at the bank, to avoid running into Twinka. And the fact that people would see him there was an added bonus. If the police suspected him, they could reconstruct his steps hour by hour, only to come the conclusion that he'd spent the whole day surrounded by people.

Marat had some more coffee at the bank – and, although it meant he had to have his fourth cup that morning, he was seen doing so by at least thirty people.

Finally, the time to leave had arrived. He had changed into his running gear while still at the office, and caught himself driving faster than usual, like he couldn't wait to kill his wife. And that was probably true. Like any tedious, messy chore, he wanted to get it over and done with as soon as possible.

Marat left his phone in the car and started running along his usual route – except today he was wearing a backpack. He was so excited when he saw that the moped hadn't been stolen: as if this were the only thing that could have gone wrong. Marat couldn't see anyone in the dunes, so he took the windbreaker and trousers out of the bag and put them on. He changed his shoes, stuffed everything else inside the backpack, and started heading towards home.

No, there's no chance that anyone would recognise me looking like this, he assured himself.

The journey took longer than he had anticipated. The moped's brakes were awful, and its front light wasn't working. Marat hadn't noticed this when he was buying the vehicle, and he hated it – the road police could pull him over him for that. In fact, it had been ages since Marat had driven anywhere on such a cheap and clunky old wreck. It gave him as much discomfort as the mismatched outfit he was wearing. The jacket looked stupid; it assaulted his aesthetic sensibility – no wonder he'd never worn it before. It was one of those 'mishaps' you could find in anyone's wardrobe. Even though he knew he was in disguise, and the whole point was to not look like himself, he still felt like a complete idiot; one without money or any sense of taste. He was deeply embarrassed. Having grown accustomed to the G-Wagon's comfortable discreteness, or the domineering, elegant superiority of the Porsche, he was suddenly on the same level as all the other everyday road users. All this ordinary cosplay didn't excite him at all. He couldn't wait to turn off into one of the little streets where no one could see him.

Marat parked the moped about a block away from his house and covered the remaining distance on foot. Their street was usually deserted during the day and, fortunately, he didn't bump into anyone. His journey had stirred inside him a small yet noticeable amount of displeasure and anger. However the ill-feeling wasn't aimed at anyone in particular, plus it had at least succeeded in pushing away the anxiety he'd felt in relation to this messy, albeit necessary, job.

Marat unlocked the basement door, entering the utility room next to the basement garage. He stopped and listened carefully. There was music coming from the house. Marat recognised the melody – it was Leonard Cohen's 'A Thousand Kisses Deep'.

Back when they made love, they had used to listen to Cohen quite a lot – Twinka adored having sex to his music. Marat smiled inwardly. It felt like a sign from destiny; as though this was exactly how it had to be.

As soon as he could, Marat ripped off the ugly jacket and trousers. It was absolutely impossible to picture himself accomplishing something as important as his wife's murder dressed like a complete buffoon. Although he'd need the clothes for his return journey, he tossed them angrily into a corner. Next, he removed his shoes. Marat wanted to sneak up on Twinka: a feat best accomplished in socks.

The moment had finally arrived, and Marat felt really anxious now. Though he wasn't going to spend any more time in contemplation. Again, he listened out for the sounds of the house. He couldn't hear anything except for 'Dance Me to the End of Love'. The utility room was packed with empty wine bottles, stacked haphazardly on the windowsill and crammed into boxes from manufacturers and online shops. Marat put the gloves back on, having taken them off momentarily while he removed his shoes. He picked up one of the empty bottles and quietly opened the door. His anxiety increased by a notch, but Marat pushed it back down – he didn't allow the feeling to enter his conscious mind. He'd learned that in the mountains. You'll always be afraid, but you can't allow fear to take hold of you – you must suppress it or shut it out before it's had a chance to paralyse you. You simply have to get on with whatever you've planned: taking it step by step; and focusing only on the task at hand, without letting your thoughts stray from it. That's how you conquer your fear.

There was a flight of stairs leading up from the basement to the ground-floor hallway housing Michelangelo's *Pietà*. Pausing halfway up them, Marat had several options. Twinka was usually in the kitchen around this time, which was itself connected to the spacious living room. Or she might be up on the first floor: either in the master bathroom, dressing room or bedroom. In fact, Marat realised he hadn't a clue what his wife got up to while he was out.

Although it wasn't too loud, the music prevented him from determining which room she was in. Marat hesitated for a moment, then he suddenly heard Twinka's footsteps. She was in the smaller guest room, which was situated closer to the main entrance to the house. It was designed for receiving people they didn't want to invite any further into the house.

Now nearing the top of the stairs, but still out of sight himself, Marat could hear Twinka heading from the guest room on her way to the kitchen. Peering out, he could see she was wearing that weird but expensive outfit that had always baffled Marat – one that registered somewhere between a nightshirt and a dress, yet never quite managed to be either. A rogue thought went through Marat's mind – Twinka looked desirable in it. But it was a tiny, fleeting, insignificant thought. It didn't mean anything, and it certainly didn't change anything. Marat felt no fear, no doubt, nor any worry. By now his actions had become mechanical. It felt like his body was simply carrying out the program it had been given, while he stood, indifferent, observing everything from the sidelines.

In the blink of an eye, he emerged from the stairs and into the area of the hallway just off the kitchen, and was standing directly behind Twinka. Somehow Twinka – just about to enter the kitchen – sensed him approach, and turned around. Their eyes met. Michelangelo's Virgin Mary, with the dead Jesus in her arms, was now directly behind Twinka.

With his arm already raised, Marat struck.

PART 2.
Confusion

CHAPTER 23

Before he even opened his eyes, Marat knew that something was wrong. He was in an unfamiliar place. Something didn't feel right, though he didn't know what it was.

He wasn't in his own bed. And this wasn't his bedroom. Marat couldn't feel the rest of his body, only his head – it was as if he was wearing a helmet made of lead. He could feel someone else's presence in the room. Marat tried to pull all his senses into focus, but he didn't yet open his eyes – as though he were trying to shield himself, afraid of them discovering that he was awake.

His brain was processing everything faster than he could formulate it. An inexplicable sensation, all of a sudden arising from within, informed him that this was a hospital.

Marat slowly opened his eyes. Yes, he was definitely in hospital – in a small room designed for two people, though the second bed was empty. He could move his arms and legs, but his body felt unnaturally heavy. He could see a tube attached to one of his arms, and that some sort of machine with a monitor was placed next to his bed. He realised that the top of his head was bandaged up, and that he could only open one of his eyes – with the other side of his face also covered in bandages. Marat tried to remember, and to work out why he was here and what had happened. But a void occupied his mind, and his strength was already leaving him: as though looking around and touching his own face was hard labour, so difficult and demanding that no energy remained for anything else.

The door opened and Marat shut his eyes instinctively. He felt someone next to the bed. They arranged his blanket, then did something else, and then he heard a voice. A voice he couldn't confuse with any other: it belonged to Twinka. The voice had jogged his memory, bringing everything back into focus. He remembered his plan, recalled the moped and the bluish-green windbreaker. He saw Twinka in the hallway and remembered the blow. Twinka should be dead. That was his plan, and he had gone through with it. But what was all this about? Perhaps he'd mixed things up and it wasn't Twinka? Marat didn't dare open his eyes. He felt her clutch his hand. She was right here, he could feel her breath. It was undoubtedly her – he recognised her smell and her touch.

Next, Marat heard the familiar jingling of the bracelets. So, his mother was here, too. She was putting or arranging something on the table by the other side of his bed. Marat had no energy left to process the chaotic thoughts that were running through his head in search of answers. It may have been the effect of the drugs, but whatever it was he had used up all of his strength, and he sunk back into unconsciousness.

The intense headache woke him. He had no energy to speak – he just groaned, in the hope someone would be nearby. But there was no one there. It hurt so much that he passed out again.

Marat had no idea how much time passed between the brief moments of consciousness. When he woke up the third time, there was a nurse in the room. The pain wasn't as extreme as before, but it was still unbearable.

"It hurts," Marat whispered.

The nurse seemed pleasantly surprised to hear his voice.

"You're up! Oh, that's good. Don't worry," the nurse said, adjusting something on his infusion pump. "You'll feel better in just a moment."

Again, Marat tried to process what had happened. He vaguely remembered his plan – or, rather, he remembered recalling his plan while he was lying here. Though nothing seemed certain anymore. He remembered Twinka being by his bedside – had it really been her? He wasn't sure about anything now. Had he maybe dreamed all of this? What part of it was a dream, and what part was real? And where the hell was he, and why was he here?

Marat tried to focus all his energy and, overcoming the pain, asked in a barely audible whisper: "What happened?"

"Your house got broken into. You and your wife were attacked," the nurse said. "Thank God the criminals had enough decency to call the ambulance on their way out. Otherwise, you may not be here," she added. "You were in a coma for two weeks."

Her voice sounded so lovely.

"It hurts," Marat whispered again. He had no strength left with which to process all this new information.

"Bear with me just a moment, and it will all go away," the nurse said, and her words came true. The morphine kicked in, the pain subsided, and Marat sunk back into a deep sleep.

CHAPTER 24

In his dream he was back in the park with Dimitri, only this time Twinka was there too. Dimitri was asking Twinka if she knew that it would be much more convenient for her if she was killed. They both laughed. Twinka even clutched her stomach, showing just how funny it was.

"It would be so convenient for me, if I was killed – I can't picture anything better," she said, writhing with laughter.

Then Raskolnikov appeared. Marat didn't recognise him straightaway. He looked poor and skinny, dressed in some dirty old rags. Raskolnikov went over to embrace and soothe Twinka. Suddenly she was no longer laughing, but crying. Marat was astonished that Twinka would let this strange, degenerate man, dressed in tatters, embrace her.

"I'm pleased that you came," Marat addressed Raskolnikov, "I've been meaning to ask you something – you never changed your theory, did you? The one about the 'chosen people' who are allowed to commit murder? You came to the conclusion that you're not one of them. You're too soft, weak and pathetic to be able to create any real change in this world. You couldn't even help a single person – not even after you killed the old hag and seized all her money. You're a catastrophic failure. You're nothing but a loser and a dirty old rag. Svidrigailov was the only one capable of doing something and helping someone."

"We all have our individual path. Each to their own," Raskolnikov replied with a sad smile. Marat's words didn't seem to anger him. "Each to their own," he repeated. "I found my path, but what about you – have you found yours?"

"Oh, don't start preaching the gospel to me!" Marat tossed his hands dismissively.

"Maybe I wasn't capable of doing good, even though I always tried – but what about you? Have you ever wanted to do anything out of charity? Yes, I killed the old woman. But not for my own pleasure. I took that sin upon me, but I didn't do it thinking that it was good for me. It's not out of selfishness that I chose to destroy my own soul. But you? You *wanted* to commit murder – and for what? What's your excuse?"

"Because a divorce is a huge mess, apparently," Twinka said. Suddenly everyone burst out in a loud and hearty laugh at Marat's expense.

"I wanted to kill you because you're not the same person I once loved," Marat said quietly. "You've changed. You've let the Twinka I used to love disappear. You're pretending to be the same person when you're actually someone else. You've cheated and deceived me."

"You're angry with her?" Raskolnikov asked him compassionately.

"Were you hoping I'd never change?" Twinka asked.

"I guess I was. Isn't that normal though? When you first get married, do you ever picture that this wonderful woman you're marrying will transform into an alcoholic in about ten years' time, then a devout Christian in fifteen, and God-knows-what in twenty? No, you get married thinking you'll spend the rest of your life with the person you're actually marrying."

"And what about you, Marat? Have you not changed in all these years?" Raskolnikov had morphed into a successful psychotherapist in an expensive and elegant office.

"Look, for someone like me, charity is easy. It requires no effort. For me, doing charity is easier than going to the barber's." Marat wasn't going to answer any of Raskolnikov's questions. He wasn't up for being analysed, and he wasn't about to let Raskolnikov take charge of the conversation. He would only engage if their conversation developed in the way he wanted. "In today's world, philanthropy is a multi-billion industry," he continued. "Charities are literally waiting in line to get my buy-in. I might save the Amazon jungle a little bit today, and tomorrow I'll buy a thousand meals to feed the starving children in Africa. And the day after tomorrow I might feel like kitting out a children's music school with violins. I could also ask my chauffeur to take all my old blankets over to a dog shelter in the evening – it's all just basic stuff. It's all so trivial that the soul doesn't take any part in it. What I've described here are all just different methods the ordinary, pathetic masses use to boost their self-esteem. This is how they pacify their fattened middle-class conscience. *Oh, he's a good person, he's given money to a good cause* – they can't help but brag on each other's behalves. It's all bullshit. Just the everyday life of ordinary simpletons. I mean, I could be kind to someone in traffic if I wanted to: giving way to some old lump of scrap metal; or I could hold the door open for a lady – none of that requires any effort. But to carve out my own individual path – even if that means something as drastic as murder – is something else entirely. I can be evil, if that's what's required to achieve a greater goal. And my soul is fully invested in that – it's a soul-searching exercise. Not that any of you would ever understand..."

"Right. So, from now on, evil will trade places with good." Raskolnikov smirked.

"And obviously," added Twinka, "wives are there to assist in your soul-searching – helping you to discover *just how much* of an asshole you can be." Evidently she was in the psychotherapist's office too – Marat just hadn't noticed it. "It's *so* courageous of you to sneak up on your wife and hit her on the head with a bottle! You're clearly a very special person!"

"You're making it sound like I've treated you badly. It's not fair. Surely, I've been a good husband to you?"

"You're a sociopathic... a psychopath! I don't even know what to call you anymore – a psychopathic, narcissistic, old piece of shit! Compared to you, Raskolnikov is a just an ordinary Bolshevik, but you – you're a real criminal." Dimitri had now replaced Twinka in the room.

"Oh, here we go again..." Marat said before starting his objection. "You're using the term 'criminal' all wrong!"

But Raskolnikov interrupted him.

"Let's kill him – that will be best for everyone," he said. "If good seems too 'ordinary' for this 'chosen man', then let's kill him – let's show him that we're not some ordinary simpletons."

"Yeah, he's just like Osama bin Laden – a self-assured criminal with a drive to kill," Dimitri chimed in.

"We have to kill him," Raskolnikov added. "Can you imagine how much taxpayers' money is going down the drain, paying for his medical expenses? What's the point of having him? What good is he to society? The minute he gets better, he'll start plotting another murder. Let's kill him! Let's kill him! He's even worse than that old hag I killed who made me famous!"

"And you call yourselves Christians." Marat was astonished. "Remember that it was your God who created evil, not me. Though it seems like he didn't create it for you to know good from evil. He did it so that you would know exactly what to do with people you don't like, and all in His name."

"Kill him! Kill him!" roared a stadium full of people. They were all standing, their faces twisted in anger. "Kill him! Kill him!"

Raskolnikov emerged from under his psychotherapist's table with a baseball bat in hand, and began striking Marat violently.

"You're as much of a murderer as I am," Marat groaned. "You 'charitable people' have learned and adapted every method from the people you call evil. God, it hurts so much! You murderers, you think you're better than me? Well, you're not!"

Everyone was laughing.

"You're evil! You're evil! We will crush you!" the crowd was chanting.

They were beating Marat for a long time.

When Marat had very little life left in him, Twinka shouted: "Okay, that's enough. Enough!" She got down on her knees and covered him with her body to protect him from the blows.

Marat woke up – the pain was excruciating.

CHAPTER 25

July's sunshine filled the room, too bright for Marat. Everything seemed crystal-clear in his memory now. He remembered his plan; how he got home, returning on his moped wearing that horrible blue-green jacket. He could recall getting into the house, what music was playing, and how he'd snuck up on Twinka from behind, and how he'd struck her. Every detail up until that point had come back to him. But what had happened afterwards?

"Your house got broken into; you and your wife were attacked." Is that really what the nurse had said to him? And what did it mean? *Why am I in hospital? What's happened to my head? And was it really Twinka who came in and held my hand – or was that just a dream?* A multitude of questions were scurrying around his head.

A doctor entered the room, accompanied by two nurses. He was a tall, good-looking man of around forty. "Good morning, I'm Dr. Weinberg. I carried out your surgery. How are you today?" The doctor's tone was formal, and he was rushing his words.

"My head hurts," Marat replied, though at that exact moment he could barely feel any pain.

"Follow my finger with your eyes, please."

Marat obediently followed the doctor's digit.

"Can you feel a cold sensation?" The doctor had touched Marat's foot under the blanket with something metallic.

"Yes." Marat could feel it.

"How many fingers are you seeing?" The doctor was showing two. "And how many now?" He was showing four. "Can you count from ten backwards for me, please? What year is it? Do you know who's the president of the United States?"

Marat knew the answers to all of his questions, which seemed to greatly please the doctor.

"You're going to be okay," the doctor said, "but you must rest. The trauma you suffered is very serious, and the healing process is incredibly important if you want to avoid any other issues from developing. The medication I've prescribed eases your pain and makes you sleep, which is the best thing for your brain right now. Now, if you don't get enough sleep during this period, you'll be prone to things like epilepsy, migraines, a chronic headache, and a string of other issues later down the line. So, you just need to sleep. No reading, no TV, no phone screens, you shouldn't listen to any music either – essentially, avoid doing anything that could put any strain on your brain. And shut that curtain –" the doctor was now addressing one of the nurses – "there should be no bright light in here."

"What happened?" Marat used the first available opportunity to ask the only question that was putting any strain on his brain.

"You and your wife were attacked in your house; luckily the criminals called the ambulance as they left, or you wouldn't have survived." The doctor had repeated what the nurse had said, almost verbatim.

Marat let out a heavy sigh. He still didn't understand anything, and his strength was already fading.

"What about Twinka?" he managed.

"Your wife didn't suffer much – we sent her home after four days to continue the healing process there. She had a concussion, but that's about it. It was a serious concussion, she lost consciousness, but it's not even close to your trauma. You have a very serious basilar skull fracture, in a very bad spot. We essentially had to reconstruct your skull on one side of your head. You survived only because you were brought to the hospital so quickly, and we were ready to operate on you as soon as you got here. But even so, the prognosis for survival was only about fifteen percent. The fact that you don't seem to have any neurological complications, and you've regained all your cognitive abilities, is nothing short of a miracle.

"Your wife, on the other hand, received a blow to the thickest part of the frontal bone, which is one of the strongest bones in the body in general. You could hammer bricks with that part of the skull, which was very fortunate for her." The doctor was chatty. "You, on the other hand, received a powerful strike to one of the worst possible areas – diagonally across the temple – and your eye has suffered as a result." The doctor was pointing at his own eye to illustrate this. "Usually, with a trauma like this, people don't tend to survive. So, you're very fortunate. Born under a lucky star."

"Yes, of course, very fortunate," Marat said almost inaudibly, shutting his eyes.

All his energy had been spent.

CHAPTER 26

This time Marat saw Cyclopes in his dream. These one-eyed giants from antiquity seemed to be his friends.

"You shouldn't take things so literally," said one of them. "I mean, you don't believe in fairy tales about resurrecting the dead, do you? The one about Jesus raising Lazarus four days after he died? Or his own resurrection? You don't believe in all that silly nonsense, do you? Then why do you believe in everything that Homer wrote?" The Cyclopes examined Marat with curious glances, their massive singular eyes fixated on him.

Marat didn't know what to make of this conversation, and the Cyclopes laughed heartily. It seemed to amuse them that Marat didn't know what to believe in.

"Well, at least you've no more doubts about Cyclopes, have you? You can see that we're real?" one of them asked, all of a sudden very serious. The probing, solemn gazes of the others penetrated Marat.

"No, I mean, of course... there's no doubt about *you*," Marat said. Though he didn't sound particularly convincing.

"Are you sure?" one of the older Cyclopes asked, his tone bordering on harsh. "Or maybe you want to touch me just to make sure?"

"No, no, I can absolutely tell that you're real. Very real."

"Of course we're real!" The Cyclopes looked happy again. "We definitely are."

Marat wasn't convinced though – some part of his logical mind whispered to him that Cyclopes couldn't possibly be real. *What Cyclopes? Are you mad?* his inner voice was saying.

"I'm afraid it's not enough." Having summoned all his courage, Marat addressed the Cyclopes. "You might feel real to me right now, but any reality that only I can perceive cannot be considered literal reality. Reality has to be interconnected with others. If I'm the only one who can see you when no one else can, it means that you don't exist."

"I don't agree with you." Twinka had appeared from the blue. She held a glass with a little wine in one hand, and a bottle in the other. "We each have our own unique reality, which is unlike anyone else's, and that's what makes us who we are. It's our identity – it consists of our memories, our fantasies, dreams, hopes, fears, and all sorts of small, painful, happy, tragic and other types of life experiences, which belong solely to us and determine who we are. And what could possibly be more real than what makes me who I am? Take our marriage, for example. You'd think it's a shared reality, but actually we both see it differently. Marriage is like two books that have been written by two separate authors. And when they read one another's work, one person's account will often not match the other's. Yes, some things will overlap – the names of the protagonists, some biographical facts, the setting – but everything else is inconsistent."

The Cyclopes were listening to Twinka with great interest.

"Yes, Twinka is right," they concluded.

"Marriage is like two books written by two separate people," one of them repeated.

"There's no such thing as a shared reality," Twinka continued, "we each have our own world, often a very lonely one. When I suffer, I'm completely alone. No one else could share this reality with me, even if they wanted to, and it's the most absolute and convincing reality that could ever exist for me. I am the most trustworthy version of reality for myself."

"Yeah... But it's not quite like that, is it?" Marat objected. He was enjoying this conversation with Twinka. He was happy that she was here and he was no longer alone with the Cyclopes.

Although they appeared to be his friends, everyone knows that Cyclopes would sometimes eat humans for breakfast.

"Our pain, our suffering, our love, our fear, and all of our hopes – our entire inner world – is unique to us, you're definitely right about that. But it's also shared, in the sense that we've all had these experiences and we recognise them. Others suffer, too; while they themselves experience love, fear, hope in addition to all sorts of trials in life, just the same way we do. From the dawn of time, we've been telling each other stories. And through these stories we've been able to turn our individual realities into shared ones. Other people recognise themselves in our stories; they recognise the commonalities, and therefore what's *real*."

"So, you're saying that you create realities by telling stories to each other?" The older Cyclops asked, intrigued.

"Something like that – we examine reality through storytelling; we search it and we test its boundaries."

"Well, there's no shortage of stories about Cyclopes," one of the Cyclopes said. The others enthusiastically agreed. "Which means we're real."

"Well... I wouldn't be so quick to draw that conclusion." Marat didn't want to upset his new friends, but the truth was more precious. "I mean, Cyclopes – that's on a completely different level to what Twinka was just talking about. Yes, we do all see things differently, we understand and experience them in different ways – but no one can physically see a Cyclops."

"What do you mean – no one can see us?" The Cyclopes were astonished. "You can see us, can't you?"

"The trouble is that no one has met you in a very long time, just like no one has seen people rise from the dead. On the other hand, people experience suffering, love, pain and a range of other emotions – and they go through trials – *all the time*."

"What do you mean – no one has met us? If you've been able to meet us just now, how can you dismiss the possibility that someone else has met us, too?"

"Oh," Marat gestured dismissively. "It's all just empty talk. Apparently the Virgin Mary reveals herself to people every now and then too, and Christ even talks to people – but it's all just bosh."

"Interesting," one of the Cyclopes said, the one with the most intelligent eye. "Just last night I was having an argument with a friend from Ephesus about whether the outer world exists or not. He said that it's all just an illusion – that we can't possibly know whether a garden exists beyond the window if no one is looking at it, and so on. It turned into a bit of a philosophical dispute... Anyway, eventually, towards the dawn, I finally managed to convince him that the outer world undoubtedly exists. It's real: you can touch it, change it, certain laws operate within it, which are the same for everyone. And you know what happened in that very moment? I woke up. That's when I came here and met all of you. But the argument that we had in my dream – believe you me – felt just as real as this conversation we're having right now. Except it turns out that I was asleep; but now I'm awake, just like you."

"But I'm not awake." With some part of his conscious mind Marat knew that he wasn't, although he was no longer sure about anything. These Cyclopes weren't as straightforward as they first appeared.

They're trying to say that their waking world is my dream, he thought to himself. *But if that's true, then what does that make my waking world? We were both asleep. He was arguing with a philosopher in his dream, and I was talking to Dimitri. I wanted to kill Twinka, and that's when we both woke up and met each other? Is that how it works?* Marat tried to focus his thoughts, but he couldn't shake the feeling that the Cyclopes were mocking him.

"I think one thing is clear: the dead don't dream. Am I right?" Marat asked. "And if the dead don't dream, then it surely means that dreams are just a phenomenon of our consciousness?"

"That's the thing. They're a phenomenon of our consciousness," the eldest Cyclops said to him, smiling. "You have to understand that sleep is death and death is sleep. It's our immortal consciousness – or mind, soul, or whatever you want to call it – which joins with the body and leaves that which it has joined, then joins it again and disconnects from it."

"Do you understand?" The Cyclopes were looking at Marat with hope.

"No, not really." Marat was honest.

"Have you noticed how small children refuse to go to sleep? They fight against it with whatever little strength they've got; they protest until the last possible moment just to stop themselves from falling asleep, even when they're exhausted and their eyelids are dropping. All their instincts are trying to stop their consciousness disconnecting from their bodies. They've not been taught yet that sleep – this 'little death' – is good for you, it's needed. Just like most adults never learn that death is just another way of their consciousness separating from their body. Do you get it now?" The Cyclopes were amazed that Marat didn't know such basic things.

"I do," Marat said, because he didn't want to upset his new friends. "I remember reading that the Greeks invented you because they couldn't find a way to explain how the Mycenaeans had built the famous walls along their citadel." He was attempting to change the subject. "Those walls were built with stone blocks that weighed about twenty tonnes, which couldn't be lifted by any technology known to the Greeks, so they figured that you'd built them. They named them The Cyclopean Walls."

"Oh, yes, the Cyclopean Walls – we've heard all about those..." The Cyclopes laughed. "No, unfortunately, we didn't build them. We don't work in construction; and Odysseus has never been to see us either, let alone got one of us drunk so that he could stab him in the eye. The Greeks loved telling those kinds of stories to each other to bolster their self-esteem."

"Hmm, I see..." Marat nodded. *If you say it didn't happen, then it probably didn't – how could anyone doubt the word of the Cyclopes?*

"This is what we've been trying to tell you. You shouldn't believe in all that bosh. We're blacksmiths, the craftsmen of gods' tools and weapons."

"And what about cannibalism?" Marat had finally mustered the courage to ask the dreaded question.

"Nonsense." The Cyclopes looked insulted. "Absolute balderdash, stupidity, lies. Fake news; – a political plot." They seemed genuinely appalled. "It was actually the Neanderthals who were man-eaters. They snacked on each other's babies too, by the way. They weren't vegetarians, that's for sure... Humans were terrified of them, which is why they filled their children's heads with fairy tales, to stop them from crawling into caves and walking around alone, so they didn't get caught and eaten by those enormous Neanderthals. And there were a lot of cases like that, too. It all comes from there. From those ancient days when humans and Neanderthals lived side by side. Which, by the way, was going on for quite a long time."

The Cyclopes were looking at Marat as though they were weighing him up. It was important for them that Marat understood and believed their words.

"When they say that Odysseus won a fight with a Cyclops, they were actually trying to say that humankind triumphed over the Neanderthals, who were far bigger and stronger than humans. But the Greeks had forgotten those ancient times, so they changed their stories in a way that seemed to make most sense to them at the time."

Suddenly, Dimitri had joined their company.

"Yeah, exactly," he affirmed. "That's all true. Humans didn't eat one another – they co-operated, learned how to forgive each other and discovered God, which is why they survived, unlike the Neanderthals. The Neanderthals were much stronger and tougher than humans, and their brains were bigger too. In theory, they should have become the crowning glory of creation, but it didn't work out that way. Humans survived, and the Neanderthals died out. The question is: why? Because the strength of humankind lies in God, in the ten commandments, in working together, in justice and morality, in the prohibition to kill and eat one another." Dimitri was speaking in a self-righteous *I told you so* tone. "The Neanderthals failed to unite. They killed each other and eventually went extinct, whereas humans did the opposite – they learned to work together, help each other out, and make friends. They discovered God and morality, and they survived."

"Yes, I agree," said Marat, "to the extent that when humans are in danger, they become reasonable, disciplined and united. A common, deadly, man-eating enemy really helps cement all that. As soon as there's any danger – a war, the threat of extinction – everyone starts acting sensibly. They suddenly realise that everyone has their own thing; they take up their dedicated spot; they obey authority figures and observe discipline. But as soon as danger is replaced by wealth, you get degradation, impunity, and decadence." His voice sounded tired as he was explaining all this. "Everything falls out of balance, no one wants to do their thing anymore – everyone wants to do something else. No one follows any kind of discipline, either; they don't respect those above them, they despise hierarchy. Everyone is suddenly so smart, and they do whatever they like. Just look around you – it's hasn't been a hundred years yet since the last world war. And everything was great at first – humanity was progressing like never before. But what's happening now? We're on the brink of collapse and everyone is too big for their boots. Stupidity and idiocy have taken over, no one is interested in acquiring wisdom, and power no longer has authority. Everyone thinks that their opinion is worth something." On some level, Marat was prepared to agree with Dimitri.

Twinka turned to Marat. "It's so clear to me now. You're just a Neanderthal." She laughed. "A genius with a super-brain who's still just a stupid man-eater, with no sense of morality or God."

"With his one remaining eye, he could even be one of us," the old Cyclops quipped. "He'd just need to grow a little taller."

The Cyclopes laughed.

The dream was fading, and Marat experienced the familiar onset of pain. He couldn't feel anything other than his head, as though it were separate to the rest of his body. The pain was burning and all-encompassing; inexplicable, insufferable, excruciating. He didn't want to wake up – he desperately wanted to carry on his conversation with the Cyclopes. With every last ounce of strength he had, he fought to stay in that place, to postpone his inevitable meeting with the pain, but no amount of willpower or strain could keep him there. Reality was charging at him like a high-speed train, and agony alone dominated that realm. His consciousness had decided to reconnect with his body once again, and nothing could stop its decision. The Cyclopes faded. Only pain remained. No more philosophical disputes, no intriguing questions. No ignorance, fear, or anything else – there was only pain. Not quite unbearable – just strong enough for him to remain conscious and bear it.

Marat screamed for help. But the only thing that came out was a puny moan that echoed in the empty room. No one heard it.

CHAPTER 27

"Hi, my name's Ralph Draco. I'm the chief inspector. I'm looking after your case. Do you think you may be able to answer a few questions?"

Police? With a tortured gaze, Marat watched the two men sat in his room.

"I can try," Marat said.

The two policemen were dressed like ordinary citizens. The older of the two – the one who'd just said his name – reminded him of a mouse or a rat. While the other one – a sporty-looking young man – hadn't even bothered introducing himself.

"Actually, I only have one question: what happened to you?" The chief inspector asked. His voice had an odd, stunted timbre – like the pitch was a little too high while the voice itself was too quiet: as though Draco didn't have enough breath or strength in him, or there was an issue with his larynx. Whatever the chief inspector would say, it came out like a slight wheeze.

Marat examined him carefully. His clothes seemed to have been bought over different years and from different shops. And although in different shades originally, all pieces of his clothing had over time somehow adopted a single dirty olive hue. Just as married couples came to resemble one another in their mannerisms and appearance, Draco's items of clothing had become a cohesive and harmonious blend, with comfort the underpinning, uniting characteristic. It was the sort of comfort you'd need if you were outdoorsy or lived on a farm. Draco's shoes looked like hiking boots. His trousers were made of some durable fabric, but at least they had a classic cut, without the several large pockets you'd expect from this type of apparel. It was obvious that Draco mostly valued the fact these trousers would do an equally good job whether in an office setting or beside a campfire. A sturdy, wide army belt completed the lower half of his outfit, though it didn't seem to suit the chief inspector. It was too manly and weighty for someone who looked so unsporty, and who had such a puny voice. However, it was easy to attach a holster to the belt, along with a string of other useful things, which is probably why he had purchased it.

Draco hadn't brought a weapon along though. Perhaps the chief inspector realised that the belt didn't suit him, and that was why it was covered by a polo shirt. Even though his clothes insinuated an active lifestyle or some level of athleticism, the chief inspector failed to leave a masculine impression.

There was something restless and jerky about him. His eyes seemed like they were always switched on and kept shifting around, along with his lips, which he squeezed and released constantly – as though he was maintaining an active and animated dialogue with himself. Overall, he would have left a petty impression: that is, if it wasn't for the determination, spite, cunning and confidence that flashed from his face.

"I don't remember anything." Marat hadn't hesitated to answer, because that was the truth. He too would have loved to find out what had happened to him.

"So, you don't remember anything? Nothing at all?" The chief inspector asked, incredulous.

The other policeman wrote something down in his notepad. He'd still not as much as uttered a single word.

"No. In fact, I was hoping that you'd be able to enlighten me."

"Right," Draco said, and his disappointment was palpable. His lips tightened again. "Your wife doesn't remember anything either."

Marat watched Draco's shifty, cunning gaze and his tightly squeezed lips. *He looks just like a rat!*

"She doesn't remember anything?" Marat repeated.

"Nope. Even though the trajectory of the blow suggests that she should have seen who attacked her." The chief inspector's tone oozed suspicion and discontent. "It would make sense that you don't remember anything. You were most likely struck from behind: it's hard to say exactly where, it all depends on whether the criminal was left-handed or not. You may have *just* seen him, whereas your wife *definitely* did. And her injury was hardly as severe as yours."

"I haven't even seen my wife since then," Marat said, making it clear that he couldn't help them further.

"Okay. Fine," the chief inspector replied. "Just one more question from me, if you have the energy for it. The criminals were looking for something in your office. What do you think it was? Did you keep anything particularly valuable there?"

"Cash," Marat responded, again without hesitation. He'd prepared his answer for this exact question, though he hadn't envisaged it happening under these circumstances.

"Cash?" The chief inspector repeated. "You kept cash in your office?"

Marat gave an affirmative nod.

"How much?"

"Some forty thousand or more."

"Hmmm... And why did you have so much cash at home?"

"Cash is a classic," Marat said in a tired voice.

"Come again?" Draco didn't understand.

Marat knew that he wouldn't have enough energy to explain it. "I just like it," he said.

"You like having cash around?"

"I do." Marat would have smiled if he could.

"Could there have been anything besides cash – maybe some paperwork, important files or documents? Was anyone interested in your business?"

"I don't know. I don't think so." Marat felt worn out. His head hurt, and it was probably showing.

"Okay. All right. That's enough for today," the chief inspector said, getting up. "Who could have known that you stored all that cash at home?"

"I don't know..." Marat's reply was almost inaudible.

"Okay, okay." Draco could see that Marat had no strength left in him. "Get well soon – that's the main thing right now." The police officers made their awkward goodbyes and rushed out of the room.

As Marat sank back into sleep, he remembered Twinka's eyes – the last look on her face. It must have only lasted a few tenths of a second, maybe a few hundredths – but it was enough. Marat recalled her astonishment and surprise, which had turned into disbelief, then fear. Real, primal fear of death – all in the infinitesimal amount of time as he delivered the blow. He would never forget that moment. And he knew Twinka would never forget it either.

CHAPTER 28

As opposed to his waking hours – marked by weakness, pain, and twilight – Marat's dreams resembled spectacular cinematic movies. They were clear, vivid and lively; sometimes repeating for several nights in a row, albeit in slightly different variations.

This time, he was somewhere in India. He was a guest in the Raja's enormous palace, located on an island in the middle of a lake or wide river.

For some reason – and much to Marat's disappointment – Raskolnikov had also been invited.

Not him again! I've got nothing in common with him. Marat was annoyed, but nonetheless subjected himself to the ruler's will.

The Raja received them on the roof terrace of his palace. A magnificent bird – a peacock or a pheasant, or something in-between – was pacing along the balustrade with a calm and noble gait. Marat felt strongly that this was a peaceful oasis of prosperity and happiness.

The Raja was an older man with a thick, greying beard and wise, serene eyes. He was wearing a luxuriant turban on his head and exquisite ancient overalls. They were covered in rich gold embroidery, although he wore them as though all that luxury was beside the point, like he'd thrown on the first thing he'd seen in his wardrobe.

A cold, refreshing drink was served.

"This palace is more than just a palace – it's also a symbol of society," the Raja explained. "You see, it has four floors. The top floor belongs to me – I live there with my wife and children. This is the floor of the Brahmans. Being a Brahman is a huge responsibility. On the one hand, you have the privilege of being here, at the very top. From where, as you can see, everything looks clear and tranquil." The Raja was gesturing at the surface of the water and the misty plain further ahead. "On the other hand, the Brahmans have to manage how people lead their lives. Without governance, a society couldn't exist."

"The third floor belongs to the Kshatriya. These people are very important, too. They're incredibly precise, disciplined, loyal and well-organised. The Kshatriya are warriors – they stand for order. It's the state's army and police. A country couldn't exist without Kshatriyas. These days, of course, they don't necessarily wear a uniform – Kshatriyas lead businesses, they're often the highest officials, and their skills are very much in demand."

"Beneath the Kshatriyas," the Raja continued, having invited his guests to follow him to the edge of the terrace, "are the Vaishya. Every floor of this palace is wider than the one above it, giving it the shape of a flat-top pyramid. Vaishyas symbolise the economy: without them, either, a country couldn't survive. They possess rare talents that others don't. They know how to create material goods. I wouldn't even know where to begin with that –" the Raja said, laughing – "if I had to lead a company, I'd probably go bankrupt within six months. Or if I had to manage a farm, I guarantee that nothing would grow on it. Everyone must do their own thing – that's the most important principle behind this building."

"And then, lower down, we have the Shudra. These people are also incredibly important. Shudras form the service personnel, and their responsibilities are many. They mop floors in hospitals, take out the rubbish, deliver orders, sew clothes, work in factories, clean after and care for people. A country also could not survive without the Shudras. If you didn't have Shudras, then someone else would have to do these jobs – the Vaishyas, Kshatriyas, Brahmans – and they then wouldn't be able to do their thing, and the country would collapse. Just imagine: if a surgeon had to take out the rubbish and clean the toilets, he wouldn't be able to perform procedures during that time. If a military commander had to herd sheep, he wouldn't be able to command an army during that time. And if a ruler had to wash his own clothes, then he wouldn't have time to read books and reflect on important decisions. But now, everything is in harmony. And so that's how Shudras are saving people in hospitals, strengthening the defences of the country, ensuring that everyone follows law and order, and enhancing wise governance in the country."

"Well, there's also the basement, but let's not talk about that..." The Raja walked away from the edge of the terrace. "And so that's how we live. This is the best formation of society known to man." There was pride in the Raja's voice.

"There's nothing good about it," Raskolnikov objected venomously, showing the Raja no respect. "Your caste system – it's simply a method of exploiting, discriminating and oppressing people. It's just a way for the elite to maintain their power and wealth. That's all it's ever been."

"Tell me, my dear," the Raja said kindly. He was pointing to coax Raskolnikov towards a comfortable couch under a white canopy, completely ignoring the latter's contemptuous and aggressive tone. "Tell me, do you think everyone is born with the same talents and abilities? Would you disagree with the claim that we're all different from the moment we're born? That some are born strong, others are weaker; some are well-built, others not so much; some are born with great gifts of the mind, others don't seem to possess them; some have incredible musical hearing, others are born without it; some have an excellent grasp of business, while others have no nose for it. Do you disagree with this?" The Raja had settled into the couch, and watched Raskolnikov with genuine interest. "After all, wasn't it you who had the theory that some people are special, while others are basic, trembling creatures by comparison?"

"Yes, people can be different. Yes, people are born differently. But what they *are* is not determined by whichever

160

caste their parents belonged to. Your Brahmans could have a child who isn't remarkable in anything. Maybe they turn out to be a complete scoundrel. Meanwhile, in a Shudra family, you may have a child who's more noble, spiritual and wiser than any of your Brahmans. Except, in your society, they'd have no opportunity to educate and develop themself. They'd have to spend their entire life taking out rubbish or serving drinks to the likes of you, even though with their abilities they could have ruled the country no worse than you – maybe even better."

"Yes, my friend, I'm familiar with all these modern theories." There was no resentment in the Raja's voice as he spoke. "Unfortunately, they all lack common sense. Think about it: if the karmic law has manifested in such a way that a Brahman's consciousness has transferred to a Shudra family, then it's not for nothing. It means that he's earned himself that exact experience and has to live through it; it means that he must learn something that only a Shudra's experience can offer. And it also means that in his previous life he had done something to merit this lesson. Perhaps he made some bad mistakes; perhaps he did a lot of things that go against the Brahman's code of conduct. It's not for us to decide which soul or which person is good or evil; who's noble and who's a simpleton. Who are we to determine such things? What do we know? What *can* we know about another person? Who are we to say: 'You look so noble and sophisticated, so wise and talented, you shouldn't be a Shudra – come and lead our country!' No, this way we'd be going against the karmic law and nothing good would come of it. I guarantee it – the law is such that Shudras cannot lead the country. So, even if it happened, it wouldn't be for the best. Whether you like it or not, such a law still exists."

"So, you're against democracy and everyone having a voice?" Raskolnikov remained antagonistic. "You'd love to see the caste system everywhere, wouldn't you?"

"My friend, the caste system already *is* everywhere. Regardless of whether you see it or not. A Brahman is a Brahman and a Shudra is still a Shudra – it's the same everywhere. It's like that here and it's like that where you live. It exists in democracy as much as it exists in monarchy. It's not possible to alter it, no matter how much you change your political systems. You can pretend not to see it, or pass a new law saying that we'll ignore the natural order of things, but nothing good will come of this. People will be born with different abilities. Just because you've implemented a decree that says from now on everyone will run equally fast, sing equally beautifully or understand maths equally well, it won't change anything. Certain people will continue to sing more beautifully than others, others will still run faster; some will have a knack for business, while others will gravitate towards maths – it's impossible to change that."

"You didn't answer my question: are you against democracy?"

"If I remember rightly, you had this man called Plato. And he said that only a madman would give sailors the chance to choose the ship's captain. You should never give that position to someone they like. You should give it to someone who has studied navigation, learned about seafaring and how to become a captain, passed his exams and accrued the requisite experience. Your Plato was a wise man, at least as far as he understood the most basic concepts," the Raja said. "It's the same with Shudras and running a country. If the Shudras started to rule and make decisions, it would be the same as sailors and boatswains thinking they don't need a captain anymore. Shudras are motivated by only one idea – how to deprive, divide, steal and squander. They have no idea how money is made, how a country is built, nor do they have any interest in learning such things. Shudras only want to spend whatever they have, enjoy life, and show off. To steal and to spend, and then call it noble justice – that's all they're capable of.

"And, as much as I love my dear Kshatriyas, unfortunately you can no more trust them with running a country. They make excellent executives, soldiers, officials and professionals; they know the value of order and discipline; but they have problems with vision and strategy. They're incapable of seeing the bigger picture – so they can't govern. And Vaishyas – those talented people, masters with a golden touch, the skilful businessmen – unfortunately they're no good at ruling either, because business should never be in charge of a country. I would even go as far as to say that, in some sense, business is anti-state, because it wants to turn the country into a corporation, to turn everything into a transaction and put everyone to work for profits. They genuinely don't understand that a country *is not* a business, and – pardon me, but if we didn't have the Brahmans, who would explain it to them?"

"So, only the Brahmans have the right to vote in your country?" Raskolnikov concluded.

"The only thing that matters is maintaining order." The Raja ignored the venom in Raskolnikov's tone. "It's important that a country isn't governed by Shudras, and that Brahmans steer clear of business or war; that Vaishyas continue to ensure people have bread on the table and goods, and that Kshatriyas don't have to plough the earth and tend to animals. As soon as this natural order is disturbed, everything falls apart – no one is in their rightful place anymore, no one is doing their thing; and, as a result, nothing works and there are hurdles at every step. This way, you'd spend your entire life tripping over things; going from one foolishness to the next, from one mishap or crisis to another – everyone would be angry and dissatisfied, and no one would be happy," the Raja said. "A country is like harmony, like music... like a symphony orchestra, wherein everyone plays their own instrument. Can you even imagine an orchestra in which the instruments were taken away and then redistributed among the musicians at random? What would you hear from them? A cacophony, horror, absolute torture – yet that's exactly what you're getting in modern democracies."

"I'm not interested in politics," Marat interrupted, "I'm a hedonist."

"My dear, I think you're a Vaishya." The Raja looked at Marat with a testing gaze. "You have a real knack for business."

"Personally, I wouldn't mind if Shudras were leading a country. I've got no objection at all," Marat continued. "You can always cut some deal with the Shudras. You can buy, frighten or trick a Shudra. I like the Brahmans too, but it's harder with Kshatriyas – they don't understand business, and I agree that they have no strategy or vision. Still, if I'm perfectly honest, I'm not interested in any of that. I'll survive no matter who's in charge."

"Yes, you're a Vaishya, my friend," the Raja deduced with a smile. "But you're wrong. You think that you can always cut a deal and bribe everyone, but you don't understand that there's no pleasure in living in a country that's overrun by poverty, lawlessness and corruption. There's no joy in living in a country where you have no decent schools or hospitals, and where the streets are dark and frightening. You won't be able to cut a deal with the Shudras then. No amount of money can make them govern a country skilfully, because they're simply not capable, just like I'm not capable of singing an aria in an opera." The Raja smiled.

"And you obviously think that I'm a Shudra," Raskolnikov interrupted, making it clear he felt offended. "Of course. It's all so simple to you."

"You're a Bolshevik," Marat cut in. "You killed that old hag, the usurer, so that you could take her money and help the poor, except you couldn't even accomplish that. Your

Bolshevik brothers did the same thing, but on the grander scale of all of Russia: they killed the rich, so they could divide the money amongst the poor – except, unfortunately, the money soon ran out. The problem is that if you want socialism to work, you have to keep on killing. The minute you stop is the end of socialism." Marat was making it clear how much he despised Raskolnikov.

"And you killed your wife because it was too messy to get a divorce. Now, there's an ideal to look up to," Raskolnikov said, his voice ripe with bitterness and hurt.

There were three Cyclopes in the distance, going about their daily business.

"Gentleman, let's stop arguing, shall we?" implored the Raja. "None of us can know our own karma. It's far too complicated. We can't predict it. If there was a simple manual for life, then we wouldn't have any problems. Unfortunately, it doesn't exist."

"Except maybe in the Bible," Raskolnikov disagreed.

"What nonsense," Marat said, disgusted. "You people have been preaching the Bible for two thousand years now. Plunder and murder – that's the only thing your manual has brought upon us. And anyway, no manual can be implemented without the Inquisition or the Gulag."

"But tell me, Raja –" Raskolnikov ignored Marat – "do you think that there are special people with the right to kill? Why can some, like Napoleon, murder thousands of people and still be considered a hero. While I – who killed one useless, evil, disgusting old hag – am considered a criminal?"

"Don't forget," Marat reminded Raskolnikov, "that you also killed the pregnant woman, so that she wouldn't tell on you. You killed her out of fear of punishment, which makes you a criminal."

"You're so thick, Marat! I didn't want to kill the pregnant woman. It was all Dostoyevsky's fault – I wasn't even planning on killing her. It was Dostoyevsky who decided that it was necessary for me to kill her. You forget that I'm just a figment of his imagination. The pregnant woman is Dostoyevsky's responsibility."

"You're right. I should be talking to Dostoyevsky. I don't understand why you're here in the first place," Marat growled.

"Gentlemen, please, let's not argue anymore." The Raja was somehow still smiling. "Really, let's stop, shall we? People have been killing each other and will continue to do so in the future, but death is just an illusion. I know that you've become so attached to your bodies that you no longer understand this, so I don't blame you for that. Come along, let me show you our wonderful garden by the river. A thousand flowers bloom there, and if you wish you can pick some of them – the garden won't suffer for it."

The next moment they were transported to the marvellous garden, which bordered a landscaped forest full of enormous, thousand-year-old trees. Gorgeous dogs and exotic birds lounged in their shade. All the animals seemed to be getting along, and somewhere in the depths of the forest you could make out a lion couple.

"Can you see that oak tree?" the Raja asked, pointing at a large, branchy and perfectly shaped oak. "Can you tell me how many acorns it has?"

Marat examined the tree. "It's impossible to say. Ten, twenty, maybe a hundred thousand?" he replied with a shrug.

"Yes. A lot of acorns," the Raja agreed. "And how many of these acorns will turn into an oak tree? One or two – maybe none. But that's nature's way. Each year this oak tree produces ten thousand acorns. Every one of them is programmed to become an oak; none want to end up as fertilizer for the soil.

Each acorn is trying hard, and one day some will turn into oak trees. But in the meantime, they're all just manure. You two are such acorns. You also tried, and I'm not saying that you won't succeed. It's never too late, not even the day before death."

One of the lions got up and gave a big lazy yawn before crawling even deeper into the forest.

CHAPTER 29

Marat was waking up. His consciousness had only just started to reunite with his broken body, but he could sense that Twinka was sat next to his bed. Marat had been afraid of facing this moment, ever since he had realised its inevitability.

Although he was terrified to look Twinka in the eye, he was also desperate to find out what had happened to him. Their encounter offered him some hope of understanding why he was here.

It has to be done, Marat decided, and he opened his eyes – or, rather, he opened the eye that wasn't covered in bandages.

"Oh hello," Twinka said. Her voice was warm and kind.

"Hi," Marat replied quietly. Twinka's friendly and compassionate tone had completely thrown him.

"How are you feeling?" she asked, sending him a charming, loving smile.

"I've been better," Marat answered, now even more perplexed.

"The doctors say you're going to be okay. You shouldn't rush your recovery though. You have to sleep it off, and you shouldn't be moving about too much."

"Yeah." Marat had heard all this already and wasn't interested. He pulled himself together and managed a question. "How are you?"

"Well... I hope you remember how you tried to kill me," Twinka said, followed by a laugh, as though they were talking about some funny thing that happened at a party, or an innocent drunken prank. "You know, it really surprised me. I was absolutely convinced that you felt nothing for me anymore."

Marat was listening carefully to what she said, but he was still none the wiser.

"Do you realise that you could have killed me?" Twinka asked, in a voice completely devoid of any anger or hatred.

Marat didn't understand. What was going on? What was she saying? Why was she acting so strange? The doctor said that his cognitive abilities hadn't suffered any damage – but what if they had? It was one thing to count from one to ten, or to do it backwards, but it was something else to grasp whatever was going on here.

"Anyway, the main thing now is that you get better. Everything will be okay," Twinka said, seeing Marat's confused and tortured face.

But what happened? Marat wanted to ask her. Then he realised that Twinka was talking to him as though he knew what had happened, so maybe it was better that he didn't ask her any direct questions. If Twinka realised that he didn't recall a single detail, she might hide something from him or twist the truth. *I have to find out what happened, without revealing that I don't remember anything,* Marat thought to himself. *But how do I do that?*

"They told me that you wouldn't be able to talk for too long, so I won't keep you. The most important thing right now is your recovery."

Despite his fatigue, Marat would have liked to continue this conversation. But "How's Ronia?" was the only thing that came to mind.

"She's good. She really wanted to come and see you, but I said it was too soon. I wanted to see everything for myself first. To work out whether it would be too traumatic for her to visit and see you like this. We'll come by in a couple of days though."

"Okay, good. You're doing the right thing." Marat squeezed Twinka's hand in gratitude.

Twinka bestowed one of her angelic smiles onto him and kissed him on the cheek.

CHAPTER 30

Mum came by the hospital every day, bringing Marat homemade chicken broth with quail eggs, as well as pasties. And she wouldn't leave until he'd finished the broth at the very least. She also kept watch to make sure he wasn't using his phone, reading anything or exhausting himself in any way. She did his laundry, so he would always have a fresh pair of underwear and socks, and rubbed his back with some liquid that smelled and felt a lot like pure spirit, before applying some cream on top. This was supposed to prevent Marat getting bedsores. She peeled and cut fruit for Marat and grumbled when he hadn't eaten it. Mum even cut his toenails and fingernails.

Marat wasn't sure if all of this was really necessary, but he didn't have enough energy to object or fight against it. He usually finished the broth and then pretended to fall asleep. Mum's presence wasn't as insufferable as it had been during their last few meetings, but Marat was mindful that she could turn at any moment. So he figured it was best not to engage in a conversation, but simply and quietly submit himself to her nursing and care. Fortunately, the doctors had imposed a rule that Marat shouldn't see visitors for more than an hour each day. Though Mum never stuck to the one-hour rule, there were times when Ronia came by to visit and Mum did have to leave, though she always did so reluctantly. However, she had to buy fruit and ingredients for the next day's broth, wash Marat's socks and underwear, talk to the doctors – and so there was plenty for her to be getting on with. Her behaviour gave renewed hope for forgiveness, truce and understanding, albeit through subtle indications. Their relationship was very fragile: they hadn't reached a mutual agreement, acceptance, or even any kind of understanding yet – and neither did they have full trust, or openness – but they had clearly made some progress towards it. It was still a far cry from the unconditional love between a mother and a son that Marat had experienced in his childhood. Mum's visits to the hospital hadn't reset their relationship to its preferable factory setting, but it seemed like they had taken a step in the right direction, which was a sure sign that not all was lost. Marat was very glad of this, and that was why he put up with all the fussing over his bedsores or the condition of his skin ("especially on your legs"). Perhaps they could use this experience as a foundation on which they could build something more substantial. He would like that. He really wanted to love his mother, and he wanted her to love him back. He was desperate for things to be less complicated.

CHAPTER 31

"Good afternoon, Fyodor Mikhailovich. Will you allow me to lend you some money? I've heard about your situation, and it's not right that a writer of your rank should be going around without a meal in him for three days straight." Marat had stopped Dostoyevsky close to the door of the Grand Hotel in Baden-Baden. "I can see the scorn with which these Germans look down on you. We must make things right."

Dostoyevsky was clearly taken aback, though he didn't reject the offer. "Who are you, young man?" he asked.

"My name is Marat. I am an acquaintance of Rodion Raskolnikov. Well, perhaps not quite an acquaintance..." Marat was mincing his words. "Let's just say we know each other. I'm nothing like him though," Marat disclaimed.

"Oh, I see, I see..." Dostoyevsky nodded. "It's good that you're nothing like him. Shall we go and find a nice spot somewhere? I know this little place around the corner. They have excellent sausages, truly, and the beer is very reasonably priced."

"Yes, of course," Marat agreed immediately. He remembered that Dostoyevsky had lost all his money at a casino a few days before, and had lived on nothing but tea since. "Let's go straight there. Let's get a decent meal – sausages with cabbage and potatoes sounds like an excellent idea."

Suddenly they were inside the restaurant. There was a huge bowl on the table filled with sausages, next to plates of stewed cabbage and steaming potatoes. There was also a bottle of vodka, sweating with droplets. They both had an enormous appetite, so they ate and sipped vodka, clinking their glasses in a non-verbal toast.

"And what is your theory, young man?" Dostoyevsky asked. "Is it the same as your friend Raskolnikov's?"

"Oh no. I'm, we're, completely different. I hate socialists – they only understand the meaning of stealing, squandering and living in depravity."

"Hmm, I see, I see..." Dostoyevsky said, though it seemed like he wasn't a very attentive listener.

"The only thing we share is that I wanted to test myself, too – to understand what I was made of, to awaken my soul, to take my essence into my own hands and shake it up. All that played an important role, although I'm not sure if that was my main motivation."

"So, for you, young man, it's a matter of course that you're allowed to commit murder, that you have such a right. Did I understand you correctly?" Dostoyevsky gesticulated wildly as he spoke, a sausage in his left hand and his fork in the other.

"Yeah, I guess so. It's a matter of course for me." Marat shrugged.

"And what about sin? Don't tell me that you didn't feel like killing a man was a sin? A vile sin?" Dostoyevsky asked, still gorging on the food.

"What sin?" Marat dismissed his words with a hand-wave of his own. "Sin is just a social construct. Yet another idea that we maintain and support because it had an evolutionary benefit for us as a species."

"A 'social construct', eh? That's an intriguing term..." Dostoyevsky studied his glass carefully.

"Fyodor Mikhailovich, you have no idea just how intriguing it is."

"So, it's a social construct, is it?" Dostoyevsky repeated.

"Of course. And if we studied what's behind it, all we'd find is evolutionary laws. Which means that my desire to get rid of my wife without causing a fuss, so I can go on spreading my genes, is only natural because it doesn't go against the core idea of evolution. You see, these days a family is no longer helping people spread their genes – it actually limits them. The concept of a family has changed from a useful evolutionary invention to one that's slowing evolution down – which is why the concept of a family is obviously dying out. You can see evidence of this everywhere: you can't miss it. People, of course, are still resisting it, holding onto the traditional idea of a family, even though it hasn't been functioning for a long time. And that's because we don't have a need or use for it anymore. You can have children and raise them outside of a traditional family. Every other marriage ends in divorce, and monogamy is more of an exception than the norm these days. But, once again, it's the Christians putting the brakes on everything – they don't understand that their traditional family concept is just one of the many forms that raising children and being together can take."

"So, you do have a theory after all." Dostoyevsky was smirking as he shook the fork (now with a sausage on it) in Marat's direction. "That's what I thought – that you have your own theory."

"Never mind." Marat once more tossed his hand dismissively. "I don't have a theory. I was just interested in philosophy and literature when I was young, so I can maintain a conversation if needed. As for my own life, I just meet challenges head-on, without dwelling on the method."

"And, naturally, you don't believe in God." Dostoyevsky clearly wasn't done, despite Marat's attempt to change the subject.

"Naturally, I don't," Marat confirmed. Judging by the course their conversation was taking, and their red cheeks, the vodka had started to work.

"But you wouldn't like it if, say, your daughter's husband had the same theory as you?"

"Why does no one understand me?!" Marat pounded his fist on the table, making the empty plate in front of him jump and the vodka glasses topple. "Is no one capable of ridding themselves of these Kantian dogmas?! Why does everyone believe that a private theory must always become the universal law? I don't want my daughter's husband to think like me. I don't want anyone to think like me. With all my heart, I want them to believe in God, to avoid sin and follow morality, to fear God's punishment, and so on. I'm Emperor Constantine: I want people to be Christians and fear hell; I want them to live peaceful, virtuous lives, observe the law, pray to God as often as they can and trust that He will help them. And I want them to look forward to their beautiful afterlife, without complaining about whatever happens to them in this one. That would suit me very well indeed – a world full of unthinking, obedient, modest Shudras, who bear their suffering without complaint and always look to the afterlife. Just perfect!"

"My young friend, I'm afraid you're absolutely right. You have nothing in common with Raskolnikov." Dostoyevsky, bent over his plate, was looking at Marat through his forehead. "You're much worse than Raskolnikov."

"Okay, so we're clear about me. But I'm not buying you dinner so that you can psychoanalyse me! I'm interested in your theory."

Dostoyevsky shot Marat a grave expression. He didn't say anything, just continued to eat.

"Everyone knows Raskolnikov's theory, as well as Luzhin's and Mikolka's," Marat persisted, "but what about you? What's your theory? That a murder, no matter how just, will always lead to more violence, and the innocent will always die? Is that your theory?"

"Yes, that too, that too," Dostoyevsky agreed, smacking his lips. He raised his glass for a toast, and downed it immediately following the clink.

"Okay, I'm not sure I agree with that. Obviously, it might be true, but it might not. I'm actually interested in another theory of yours. That rebirth isn't possible until a man has crossed a certain line, gone to the limit, taken a sin upon himself like Raskolnikov and Sonia did. And only then can he hope for rebirth. Did I interpret that correctly?"

"Well... Yesss—" Dostoyevsky let out a burp. It was obvious that he was only responding out of politeness now, and not because he wanted to share his theory with anyone. "Without crucifixion you couldn't have resurrection. Yes, it is so. Except sometimes you don't need others to crucify a man – he does it to himself." Dostoyevsky lifted his glass for a further toast, holding yet another sausage in the other hand. "Only then can man hope for rebirth. There's no guarantee, of course, but there is at least hope. But it doesn't apply to you, young man, at least not for the time being. You committed a sin for a selfish reason, which isn't quite the same as Raskolnikov's act and definitely not like Sonia's. They both took a sin and a punishment upon themselves, but you – pardon me for being so bold – are just a basic criminal." Dostoyevsky was looking straight into Marat's eyes with the sad gaze of an older man. Then another burp escaped his lips. "Let's drink," Dostoyevsky said.

"You're not using the term 'criminal' correctly. A criminal is someone who gets caught. Until you're caught, you're considered to be a respectable priest or a revolutionary, or even the nation's hero."

"You're a fallen man, that's what you are." Again, Dostoyevsky wasn't really listening to Marat.

"So, according to you, there's no hope for me then?"

"Why ever not?" Dostoyevsky objected. "We all have hope. You have hope for forgiveness, too."

"Ugh," Marat scrunched up his face in disgust, "another pathetic social construct, made up for the ordinary folk so they would stop killing each other. More social engineering. A basic paradigm for smoothing over conflict and escaping a string of endless violence. We can all forgive and move on, as though nothing ever happened. A very profitable concept, and one I *deeply* endorse."

"You're a cynic, my young friend. A cynic," Dostoyevsky concluded.

"I'm a realist. Forgive me for this, if you'd be so kind – and everything else..."

They clinked and emptied their glasses in silence.

CHAPTER 32

Marat's condition was slowly improving. His head didn't hurt as much or as often; he was able to eat more solid food; he could go to the toilet by himself – although he still wasn't permitted to read, and his screen time remained greatly limited. Consequently boredom had taken over from pain as the main problem. Marat was happy for every visitor he received, and was glad to see the doctor and the nurses whenever they called by. Yesterday Ronia and Twinka had come to see him, which was nice. And even now, as he watched the chief inspector and his markedly more athletic colleague enter the room, Marat felt a pang of excitement. This meant he might be able to elicit more details from them as to what had happened.

"The doctors tell me you're feeling better." Draco was polite, almost friendly.

"Yes, I'm much better."

"Have you remembered anything else?" the chief inspector asked, cutting to the chase.

"No, unfortunately I still don't remember anything. I'd quite like to find out what happened to me."

"Right. And do you remember what you were doing on the morning of that day?"

Marat sensed a steely, foreboding tone to this question. *This mousy man with his thin, receding hairline isn't as simple as he appears to be,* he thought to himself. He then took a moment to ponder the situation. Marat could remember everything about that morning perfectly clearly, but where was this question coming from?

"No, I don't," he replied, to be on the safe side.

"Oh, you don't?" Draco repeated, squeezing his lips.

"No. Everything feels so blurry; I don't want to get it wrong and by doing so accidentally tell a lie," Marat said. He was watching the chief inspector carefully. Draco looked so insignificant – as if he couldn't possibly have anything about him – but Marat was starting to sense that there was more to the chief inspector that appearances suggested.

"Now, here's the thing," Draco continued, as if thinking out loud. "We couldn't find your phone at the crime scene. Since there was no phone, we thought perhaps the criminals had taken it. So, we figured: if we find the phone, we'll find the criminals, right? Luckily, your phone was switched on and we did manage to find it. And do you know where we found it? It was still in your car, which was parked next to the cafe Neptune, some thirty-five kilometres from your house."

Marat felt a sudden sharp pain in his head, although the stabbing sensation passed almost as soon as it came. He had completely forgotten about his phone and the car.

"You know what's really interesting?" Draco looked at Marat. "The CCTV cameras show that you arrived there about an hour before the attack. But you don't remember that bit, do you?"

"I must have gone there for a run," Marat answered warily, resting his head back on the pillow. This conversation couldn't bring anything good, so he decided to start acting fatigued and unwell, which wasn't too difficult for someone lying in a hospital bed with a bandaged head.

"Yeah, you went for a run," Draco concluded, again as if he were talking to himself. "Running is good. Running is obvious. But, you see, that brings up a different question. How did you get home an hour later, if your car and your phone were still at Neptune? I'm pretty confused, to be honest," Draco said, though it was clear he was anything but confused.

"You drove to Neptune, you went for a run, but then an hour later you got hit over the head at your own house, about thirty-five kilometres away. You must have been running very fast indeed, to make it home in time. Faster than any runner in the world," Draco said, continuing his monologue.

"Well, I don't remember," Marat said.

"And without your phone. Do you always go running without your phone on you?"

Marat was silent, although it didn't feel like the chief inspector had expected an answer from him.

"So, I'm thinking – someone must have driven you home. I have no other explanation. It's weird, isn't it? And it's such a pity you don't remember who drove you home and why, because it's pretty safe to assume that this person is our guy."

"I don't remember anything," Marat replied weakly. Draco, sat next to his bed, smelt like an old school library; like dust and floor wax.

"Anyway, someone drove you home. Now, that would be one thing. But your phone..." Draco paused for dramatic effect. "Why did you leave your phone behind? Who goes around without a phone these days? It's very unusual." Draco pressed his lips and watched Marat, expecting some reaction from him.

Marat didn't say anything.

"You see, my work is so inextricably linked to criminals that sometimes I even catch myself thinking like one. I just can't think any other way anymore –" Draco made a helpless gesture – "and now I'm thinking: maybe you wanted everyone to think you were out for a run, when in fact you were planning on doing something else? Something secret and illegal in your own house, because the police could easily track your phone. You wanted us to assume that you were out running at that time, when, in fact, you were up to something at home. You wanted the police to think you weren't there, but then something went wrong – somebody hit you over the head, and your plan failed."

Marat still wasn't saying anything. He wasn't afraid as much as he was amazed and shocked at how quickly and easily the little rat-man had got at the truth.

"You know, there's just one thing I'm not sure about." The chief inspector continued to contemplate, pausing for a moment. "When we found you lying unconscious in your house, you were wearing gloves. It's summer, I'd say it's pretty warm outside, I'd even venture to say it's hot. Meanwhile, you've got leather gloves on your hands, in your own house? A jogging outfit and some leather gloves. Doesn't that strike you as unusual? Or do you always walk around the house wearing gloves? Does it get a bit too cold at night?" There was a touch of ridicule in the chief inspector's otherwise snarky tone.

Anger swelled inside of Marat. He wasn't used to being treated with such disrespect and arrogance by some inconsequential person.

"I don't understand – are you accusing me of something?" Marat pulled himself up until he was half-sitting on the bed and, as ferociously as he possibly could, turned to Draco. "What are you getting at?"

"Oh, no, no, no, don't worry," Draco responded, attempting to pacify Marat by feigning innocence. "How could we possibly accuse you? *You're* the main victim here," the chief inspector said, though his words dripped with irony. "You're the victim. You're lying in a hospital bed with a broken head. I'm not accusing you of anything. I just want to find out who wanted to kill you, who did such grievous bodily harm to you. You obviously didn't do it to yourself, I doubt your wife did either – the blow was far too powerful. Besides, someone called the ambulance while you were both unconscious. I need to find this person and bring them to justice. That's it. I'm not interested in anything else."

"Right." Marat lay back on the bed. He was genuinely starting to tire.

"Except..." Draco added, "I think you know who this other person was – the person your wife recognised as well. You're just not telling me for some reason. Maybe it's intuition, or experience, but I just can't help wondering..." Draco gestured with his hands, feigning helplessness this time.

Marat rose up on his elbows. He was thinking. Yes, the little rat-man was right. Twinka knew what happened, but she wasn't giving the police anything. Why? What *had* happened? Too many unanswered questions swirled and screamed like banshees inside Marat's head.

"I don't know who did it," he said.

"You don't know. You don't remember. No one remembers anything." Draco was back talking to himself. "So, you don't remember how you got back home then?" he asked again.

"I'm not quite following," replied Marat, "so, please, could you enlighten me – what sort of criminal activity was I doing in my own home, with an accomplice?"

Draco practically lit up. "That's a very good question. Excellent, in fact." It looked like he enjoyed being asked this. "I don't know," he said. "I don't know *yet*. Maybe you wanted to stage a burglary, for insurance purposes... I really don't know."

"That's utter nonsense." Marat rested his head back on the pillows, somewhat relieved.

"Well, anyway," Draco said, "we've actually managed to track down the other person who was with you at home."

"You did?" Marat was unable to hide his astonishment.

"Yeah, we think we know who else was in your house at the time of the assault."

"You should have told me right away!" Marat was truly intrigued.

"We checked all the CCTV cameras nearby. There's a little shop about a block away that has a camera that overlooks the junction that leads into your alley. Unfortunately there's no camera that captures the other end of the street, which is the route you used to return home. But this side does, and in that recording we saw a man who arrived at your house beforehand and left at the time of the crime. We asked around, and the neighbours said he hadn't come to see anyone else. So he must have gone to your house."

Draco fired up his laptop.

Marat was burning with curiosity.

"You can't quite make out his face unfortunately," Draco said. "But have a look anyway, maybe you'll recognise him." The chief inspector placed the device on Marat's lap.

The quality of the recording was rather poor – it had been filmed from quite a distance, from above – but Marat only needed a few seconds to know who the person in the video was.

It was impossible to mistake him for anyone else. He knew him, of course. He knew him well. Inexplicable weakness overcame Marat, and he thought he might lose consciousness.

The only other people who walked like that were beefy bodybuilders: setting their feet a little wider than everyone else, shifting their weight from one foot to the other – as though they had to be careful, lest the ground rock like a ship on a stormy sea. That's how all Greco-Roman wrestlers or Judo athletes tended to walk – always on the lookout for a sudden, incoming move. No, there was only one person in this world who walked like that. None other than Dimitri.

Marat's head was suddenly completely empty. He didn't have a single thought or emotion – it were as if his mind was refusing to process this new information. *Dimitri?* Marat didn't understand.

"Do you know him?" The chief inspector asked.

"No... I don't," Marat said, barely audibly, returning the laptop and reclining onto the pillows, completely exhausted.

"Right, just as I thought..." Draco mumbled to himself again. "Your wife doesn't know him either, nobody knows him, but the chief inspector has to work it out. Never you mind, the chief inspector will find out, don't you worry about that." The chief inspector had done away with any subtlety regarding his stance. "Just so you know, I always solve every case. The cards are now finally on the table."

"Can we finish please?"

That was enough news for one day.

"Yes, let's finish up." The chief inspector took his time switching the laptop off and placing it inside his black backpack. "You probably think this has nothing to do with me. But, unfortunately, that's not how these things work," he said, standing up. "A serious crime has been committed, and it has to be solved, and the guilty party must be brought to justice. That's the law, and the law is the law –" Draco grinned, seemingly at his own wordplay – "it's the only thing that can save us from chaos, right? You agree with that, don't you? The law is the only thing we have, the only thing that sets us apart from beasts."

Marat closed his eyes. He didn't answer. He was no longer interested in the chief inspector or the investigation. *Dimitri!* That name had devoured his entire consciousness.

Dimitri? What did this mean? That Dimitri was the one who'd struck him? *For some reason, he was in my house, he saw me, he knew what I was doing. He knew all about my plan, and he didn't let me go through with it. Is that how it was?*

CHAPTER 33

Despite the initial good signs and the doctors' optimism, Marat's healing process was not without its complications. Yes, his headaches had downgraded from constant pain to occasional flare-ups; and, overall, Marat felt fine – but the solemn faces of the doctors told him otherwise. The possibility of him regaining sight in his left eye was no longer on the cards. Equally, there were issues with the hearing in his left ear. The main question now was whether these would be the only long-term consequences.

By this point, Marat was used to living with partial sight loss, so he wasn't too worried. He was more preoccupied by the fact he still did not understand what had happened. Moreover, his anger over (and the humiliation inflicted by) Dimitri's betrayal was making him more embitterer by the day. Marat had lots of time to think, and so much to think about, that thinking had completely worn him out. Above all, one thing was clear: Dimitri, his best friend, had got in the way of his plan. What's more, he may have tried to kill him. Even if Dimitri hadn't succeeded, he'd caused a lot of damage. Dimitri's phone was switched off, and he hadn't come to see Marat, which only confirmed Marat's worst suspicions.

Marat was finally ready for his conversation with Twinka – that much he'd figured out. However, Twinka was now the one avoiding the conversation. She came to the hospital only accompanied by Ronia. She was incredibly sweet and kind to Marat, but she never stayed alone with him. Nonetheless, the opportunity finally presented itself. Marat had begged Twinka to bring him some fresh sandwiches and a cup of decent coffee for breakfast, and his constant complaints about the hospital food had made her agree to come by in the morning while Ronia was still at school.

"How's Dimitri?" he asked, sipping the coffee Twinka had brought him.

"Dimitri?" Twinka stalled. "Oh, I don't know. I've not heard from him," she said, matter-of-factly.

That wasn't entirely true. In the first few days after the attack, Dimitri had visited Twinka in hospital. However, they had agreed that while the police were actively investigating the case and asking questions, it was best if they didn't meet up, although they still texted each other occasionally.

"I think we should talk about what happened," Marat said.

"Or maybe it's best if we don't," Twinka said back, complete with one of her sadder smiles. "Let's just leave it as it is. What's done is done, we were both at fault, let's just leave everything where it belongs – in the past – and never mention it again," she urged him.

"No. I can't. I need to make sure that we're both on the same page with regards to what happened, that there's no guilt or blame between us." Marat caught Twinka's hand in his and tried to meet her eye. "That's the only way I'll be able to leave all this in the past."

Twinka freed her arm and stroked Marat's forehead gently. "But I'm in a rush. There's so much I need to do today."

"Twinka, what happened?"

"You know what happened."

"I want to know how *you're* interpreting what happened."

"What happened when?" Twinka's hand ceased its stroking. She was no longer smiling.

"You know when."

"To be honest, I'd really rather not remember that day." There was a touch of steel in her voice.

"Twinka, we have to talk it through," Marat pressed on. "We'll have to talk about it at some point anyway," he continued, even though Twinka had stopped responding. She stood by his bed with her eyes cast downward. "I promise I'll never ask you about it again if you tell me exactly what happened," Marat insisted.

Twinka knew that he'd keep on persisting. "All right, fine. What happened was..." she started reluctantly, formulating her words, "...you came home, I don't know how. Then you caught me and Dimitri. You got mad, hit me with a bottle, Dimitri got scared that you weren't in control of yourself and struck you with a bottle as well. He didn't mean to hurt you so badly, but he's so heavy-handed..." As Twinka spoke her head remained down, like a little girl who'd been caught doing something naughty.

Marat didn't say anything. He was thinking. The words "caught me and Dimitri" tore through his mind like a tornado, demanding all his strength and attention. Did they mean what he thought they meant? No, it couldn't possibly be true. Or could it? Is that why Twinka wasn't angry at him? She wasn't angry at him because she felt guilty? No, no, it couldn't be that. Marat felt completely exhausted. Dimitri and Twinka? His best friend and his wife? He felt physically sick, like someone had just punched him in the gut. *My best friend Dimitri? How could he? While we were eating, drinking and exercising together; while I trusted him like no one else – all that time he was sleeping with Twinka?! Dimitri?!? I bought him a house, I got him a job, I saved him from a criminal case, from prison. I paid for the best lawyers, I saved him from the grips of depression, I physically pulled him up to his feet! Everything he has is thanks to me: without me he'd be some homeless sponge, or he'd have committed suicide ages ago – and this is his thanks?! Dimitri!*

His head felt heavy, his thoughts were chaotic – how could this be?

The nausea worsened until he could no longer control it. Marat threw up all over himself and the edge of the bed. Twinka leapt away, barely escaping a stream of sick.

Dimitri, my best friend! And my own wife!

The vomiting didn't stop. Marat felt something bitter and chemical-like in his mouth. Even the sick didn't taste like it should.

Frightened, Twinka tried to clean up the bed, and handed Marat some water.

The nurse ran into the room. "What's happened?" she asked Twinka.

Tell her! Tell her what happened! Marat screamed in his mind.

A huge roll of blue paper towels appeared from nowhere, and the nurse hurried out of the room with the soiled duvet. Twinka looked terrified.

Marat couldn't even look at his wife – he wanted her to leave. Immediately.

"Marat, my darling, forgive me, please. I felt like you didn't care about me anymore, that you didn't find me interesting, that I was annoying, and a burden to you. It just... happened! I'm so sorry, my love."

It just happened, Marat repeated to himself internally. He had no more energy left. All he wanted was to be left alone.

Twinka didn't know what to do.

An awkward silence fell upon them. The nurse reappeared with fresh bedding.

Twinka sat down. Still acting like a little girl, she folded her hands on her lap. She didn't want to leave. No matter what, she mustn't leave. If she did, irreparable damage would be done, from which there would be no way back.

Marat was staring at the ceiling, breathing heavily. He let the nurse sort everything out and wipe his neck with a damp towel. He forced himself to thank her, and thereby convince her that it was okay for her to leave.

A long, heavy silence followed the nurse's departure, interrupted only by the sound of Marat taking sips of water.

Twinka wanted to say something to make the situation better, but she knew neither what nor how. She could hear Marat's heavy breathing in the tense quiet of the room. She lifted her eyes and looked at her husband for a moment.

Then suddenly...

Completely unexpectedly...

Totally inexplicably...

Against any rational assessment of the situation, and definitely without prior intention, Twinka let out a laugh – which surprised her as much as it did Marat.

Moments later and her laughter was now loud and hearty. Twinka's unexpected laughing fit was so out of place that it managed to stun Marat. *What's so funny?* he wanted to ask, but he remained silent. The last few minutes had brought with them simply too much to take in, and his heavy head couldn't cope.

As Twinka continued to laugh Marat fell back into bed, one of his eyes wrapped in bandages and covered with a large plaster. Half of his head was shaved and covered in further plasters, while on the opposite side his hair and stubble had grown back. Over the past few weeks he'd lost a lot of weight, and, to top it all off, he had just been sick all over himself. With his one remaining eye flashing with anger and hatred, Marat had suddenly appeared so comical to Twinka that she just couldn't stop laughing.

A helpless, defeated, pathetic old pirate, whose only eye burned with the eternal flame of hate.

Twinka knew how evil it was to be laughing at Marat, but she couldn't help herself. She felt like she was back at school: when her and her teenage friend had been overcome by a giggling fit during the most inappropriate of moments. The only difference now was that there was no one here to banish her from the classroom. Twinka did everything she possibly could to bring herself under control. But it only made things worse.

"Please, don't be angry with me, love," she said, still laughing. "We've all paid a heavy price for our mistakes." Twinka grabbed Marat's hand, looking at her husband so kindly and gently – just like she used to, an age ago, when they had first fallen in love.

Marat wasn't ready to make up. He wasn't ready to forgive and to stop feeling angry. But Twinka's laughter overpowered even his determined resolve. It was so contagious that, despite everything he'd felt just a few seconds ago, despite everything he could feel and think about – and against all odds – he smiled.

"I'm not sure," he said. "I feel like, once again, I'm the one paying for everyone and everything."

"Oh, come on, don't be so angry," Twinka said calmly, folding her hands on her lap.

"So, how long has it been going on?" Marat asked, trying to mask his emotions. He knew that if he wanted to find out more, he had to get his anger under control.

"Since that party last year." Twinka was honest.

Whether his energy was maxed out, or whether the truth and clarity had provided some modicum of relief or some small degree of closure, Marat suddenly felt nothing more than fatigue. All his anger, hate and pain, and the bitterness of the betrayal – all that had gone away, and he felt completely spent.

"Fine," Marat said, quietly and calmly, even though things still didn't seem clear to him. He had no idea how he felt or thought, or what he should do with all this new information.

"Oh, my poor pirate." Twinka smiled and kissed Marat on the forehead. "You need to rest."

PART 3.
The Right Thing to Do

CHAPTER 34

"Tell me about your parents," Anna urged. "What do they do?"

"Mum is a linguist, she used to work as an editor at a publishing house. Her entire life revolves around books. And Dad is a violinist."

"A violinist?" Anna sounded surprised.

"Yeah, he's the second violin in a relatively famous string quartet. He was very handsome in his youth, and I think that used to worry Mum. There was this cellist in the quartet and they were touring all the time – performing, staying in hotels... The cellist was married to the first violin, but then they got divorced, and there were rumours that the second violin had picked up the tune, so to speak. But I don't really know too much about it. Dad is very practical; someone who's got both feet firmly on the ground. If you didn't know better, you'd never take him for an artist. It's almost like he gets physical pleasure from fixing things, solving problems, and resolving questions. Whether it's mending the roof, the electrics, a piece of furniture, some equipment; or organising things so everyone has the right transport and tickets, and making reservations – whatever needs doing, he's in his element. I think organising and sorting things is actually his true calling, not music. I don't think his quartet would have acquired half of its success without his organisational talents and project-management skills. From buying instruments to overseeing their contracts, tours and CD recordings – he was always the problem-solver and main administrator. I've never got my head around how he managed to reconcile this pragmatic side of himself with his creative side, because he was a great violinist, too."

"That's so interesting. And do you think you've inherited his practical or creative side?"

"Hmm, more of the creative side, I think. I'm not very good at problem-solving. Dad is also a devout Christian – he believes in God. During my childhood, whenever he happened to be at home on Sundays, he'd take me to church. That's a very warm childhood memory for me – going to church with Dad. It felt very solemn, peaceful, and safe."

"Didn't Mum come with you?"

"Mum stayed at home, but she always prepared a big Sunday lunch for us, which we'd eat together at the big table."

"Does your mum not believe in God? Was that the reason she didn't go?"

"She says she does, but that she doesn't need the church to believe in Him. She doesn't like places with lots of people. That was probably the main reason. She's never been to the theatre or cinema, she hates crowded places. She didn't come to Dad's concerts. She'd go and listen to the dress rehearsal. Or, occasionally, when they performed in a smaller venue, she'd go along – but she never went to his bigger concerts."

"Sounds like agoraphobia. Do you know why your mum dislikes public places so much?"

"To be honest, no. We've always just respected the fact that she didn't like places with lots of people. She's very introverted and quiet, whereas Dad is anything but. He's extremely sociable. He genuinely likes people. To this day, he's still very active. When his quartet fell apart – like all bands eventually do – he put his violin down. So he doesn't play anymore, but he's an elder in the church. He helps them a lot: collecting donations, organising concerts and all sorts of events. He's definitely not a hermit."

"Sounds like they're polar opposites."

"Yeah, in some ways they definitely are, but it must have worked quite well. At least, Dad never seemed to have a problem with it."

"And what about Mum?"

"I'm not totally sure, we've never really talked about it, but I suspect Mum has felt lonely at times. Dad was never at home, though he always used to say: 'You're welcome to come along'. He invited her everywhere, but she just didn't want to go, although equally she was sad that she had to stay at home by herself. Well, not always, but I think at times that's how it was. But Dad was always good to her: he loved her and showered her with affection, which made up for it on some level. I don't really know; we don't talk about these sorts of things very openly in our family."

"I have a question for you on a completely different subject," Anna said, glancing quickly at her watch. "Tell me about your first childhood memory. What springs to mind?"

"Oh, I don't know."

"Have a think. What's the earliest childhood memory you have?"

"Hmm... the swing, perhaps?"

"Okay. What sort of swing?"

"Well, I'll tell you how I remember it, although sometimes I'm not sure if it really happened or whether I've imagined some of it. Anyway, we had this swing in our yard, and I loved being on it. I loved going high up and then feeling that funny sensation in my belly as I went back down again. I liked that it felt a bit scary, but really enjoyable too, and the fact that I was so brave and good on the swing. Yeah, I liked the swing a lot... And then this one time, I was swinging really high and somehow I came down. I fell down on the ground. It was totally unexpected, I don't know how it happened. I landed in a sandpit, so I didn't hurt myself too much, but I remember feeling the shock and surprise over what had just happened. Why did it happen to me? What was wrong with my darling swing?

"So, I stood up and looked back at it," Twinka continued. "All I wanted was to understand what happened, but right at that moment the swing came back towards me with full force. I'd gone up really high, and now my dear swing was coming back towards me at top speed. And it hit me. Right in the face," Twinka said. "Oh, how that hurt," she continued after a pause. "It knocked out some of my teeth, my lip was cut open, there was blood coming from my nose, my dress was all covered in blood. I remember putting my hand to my face, and my hand being completely covered in blood. I thought it was so cruel. I couldn't understand how that swing could be so evil. It had ejected me – wasn't that enough? Why did it have to deliver such a painful blow? I could have forgiven it, if it had just tossed me aside. I really had gotten carried away, and wasn't watching myself. But the blow, and the blood – I didn't deserve that at all. It was very unfair. I never went on that swing again. Not because I was afraid, no – I was just hurt and angry. Not at all the swings ever, but at that one."

"That's a very good story." Anna smiled. "It's funny that you remember this particular event because, on some level, Marat has done what the evil swing did to you."

"How could these two things be connected?" Twinka didn't understand.

"We often ask about the earliest memories in psychotherapy, because they could point towards a trauma. As in – it's not for nothing that you remember that specific event. You remember it because it was a traumatic experience, and sometimes these very early experiences shape the rest of our lives. Sometimes they repeat, like we're stepping on the same rake, again and again."

"So, you're saying that I was affected by the swing hitting me in the face?" Twinka didn't understand.

"Yeah. In a sense, you learned the hard way that sometimes life can hit you in the face. I don't know – maybe that's worth exploring deeper?"

Twinka didn't reply. She was trying to follow Anna's train of thought.

"And it's not only life that hits us in the face – usually the things that give us the most joy will also hurt us the most, and especially when we try and understand them. As soon as you ask too many questions, you get punched in the face by life," Anna carried on.

"Hmmm, I'm not sure..." Twinka's forehead had morphed into a crosshatch of astonishment and doubt. "To be honest I think it's far-fetched. It sounds a bit woo-woo to me."

"I mean, I don't know either, we're just talking really, but I'm wondering whether Marat is like the swing in some sense? Maybe it's a pattern that keeps repeating?"

Twinka's dazed look was full of disbelief.

"Well, okay, I'm not saying anything for certain." Anna had registered Twinka's scepticism, and she didn't want it to get in the way of their conversation. "How did it end with the swing – did you manage to forgive it?"

"No, I don't think so." Twinka smiled as she reminisced. "I think Dad dismantled it, or something like that."

"So, Daddy is the one who always solves everything. He dismantled the swing, he helped to dismantle your first marriage. Except he always comes on the scene a little too late. Is that fair to say?"

"What do you mean – too late?" On top of being confused, Twinka sounded annoyed. "Do you think he should have dismantled the swing before it happened? Or to have never allowed me to go on it, or to get married? Do you think that would have been the right thing to do?"

"No, of course not. I was just speculating."

Suddenly, Twinka felt like Anna didn't understand anything. She sulked inwardly.

Maybe Marat was right – psychotherapy is just some pseudoscience, like homeopathy.

CHAPTER 35

Marat couldn't stop thinking about Dimitri. It felt as if hate was burning him alive: stealing all his energy, consuming all his thoughts and killing any pleasure or interest in anything else. The doctors had allowed Marat to use his phone, with two conditions: that he'd limit his screen time to a few minutes at a go, and use it for no more than hour a day. In addition, upon the first sign of fatigue, he was to stop using it immediately.

Marat wasn't interested in world events or financial markets, or work. Pornography was the only thing that could distract him – he masturbated two, three, sometimes four times a day – whenever he managed to get himself aroused. Every time he finished he deeply hated himself, aware of just how pathetic he'd become: alone in this room with a broken head and a missing eye. No other pirate had sunk so low. He complained to the nurses about his headache even when he didn't feel any pain, just so he could get more pills that made him sleep, which for a brief moment took him out of this pathetic and humiliating existence. He knew that hate was self-destructive: it was never a good counsellor and it was obstructing his recovery, preventing him from getting out of this fucking hospital. Although he was cognisant of all this, Marat just couldn't stop marinating in the hate.

For a year, his best friend – whom he'd trusted more than anyone else in the world—

For an entire year, his so-called best friend had been sleeping with his wife like it was no big deal. Out of all the women on this planet, why did he have to pick Twinka?

Who does he think I am? After everything I've done for him, he doesn't feel the slightest bit of gratitude. He didn't even respect me enough to steer clear of my wife. How could I be so blind and stupid? How did I not see that I was just a cash dispenser for him; a supplier of goods, a problem-solve; someone he could call any time of day, who would jump in and solve all his problems. How convenient.

The most brutal and ruthless methods of revenge paced around Marat's mind.

A lion, tearing Dimitri apart.

Or Dimitri being buried alive: his knocking, cries for help and attempts to escape the coffin growing ever distant as the covering of soil thickened.

In other scenarios Marat saw Dimitri drown without him lending a hand. Or Dimitri, by himself, locked inside a burning building.

But none of these fantasies brought Marat any satisfaction. Each time he came back to reality, Marat realised that *he* was the one going through absolute agony. He was the one in hospital, and he was the one who'd been deceived and betrayed. He was blind in one eye and deaf in one ear. Marat's actions were being investigated by the police, and it was his wife who'd been sleeping with his best friend. They may even be doing it right now!

He had to get out of there, and back on his feet again. *That* needed to be his sole focus. *I'm going to leave and sort everything out*, Marat resolved. *I can't just lie here, doing nothing.*

Marat had ordered a custom eye patch from a company that renovated antique car seats. He wanted it to be made of the finest luxury leather, like the one that James Joyce had worn when he lost sight in his right eye. When the tailor arrived he tried it on. The eye patch was a true masterpiece, made of soft black leather. The part that covered the eye was shaped like the letter 'U'. The upper strap extended across his forehead, while the lower strap ran along his left ear. The two straps connected at the nape of his neck by means of a clip. The length was adjustable.

Joyce's bandage probably wasn't quite as fancy as this one, Marat thought to himself as he put in an order for two. *I'll show them who's a 'poor pirate'. Dimitri made a huge mistake by not finishing me off. A classic mistake,* Marat thought, returning to slumber once more and with it his fantasies of revenge.

On this occasion, Dimitri was buried neck deep in sand. In front of him, but just out of reach, was a glass of water and a bowl of fruit. Marat was sat on a chair nearby. They talked about life, about friendship between men, about whether murder ever could be justified, and whether the act could give you any pleasure. Dimitri was dying and Marat watched it happen...

As soon as he woke, Marat announced that he was discharging himself. He'd observe bedrest for a week and attend all his examinations, but he would be moving back home. He couldn't stand being here a minute longer.

Since he didn't want to return to the house on Button Street, he moved into his townhouse instead. The townhouse was one of the first properties he'd bought. It was not as spacious as the other one, and it didn't have a garden, a gym or a pool, but it would do. He didn't want to be living under the same roof as Twinka. He wasn't prepared to forgive her yet. He needed some space.

Since it was her fault, he left it to Twinka to come up with a way of explaining this all to Ronia.

CHAPTER 36

T: I told him everything.
D: And what did he say?
T: What do you think...

Dimitri didn't reply, which somewhat surprised Twinka. It was typically her who either didn't reply or who cut their conversations short, leaving Dimitri's messages hanging on *seen.*

She didn't dwell on it, mind. It mattered not a jot to her, plus she didn't have the headspace to deal with Dimitri's problems too.

Anyway, she didn't care, and she was late for her appointment with Anna.

Despite the doubts that Marat had sown in her mind, and the occasional feeling that Anna didn't understand her, Anna's tiny flat with all the books and the improvised greenhouse outside the window had become the only place where Twinka felt truly safe and comfortable. It was her sanctuary. She couldn't imagine how she would survive this period without Anna.

"I don't know how I feel, to be honest. It just feels like a huge mess."

"Did he really intend to kill you? Like, actually murder you?" Anna made no attempt to disguise her astonishment.

"Yeah. I found it hard to believe as well, but it is what it is."

"And what was your first reaction when you realised what had happened?"

"God, it was awful. I'm ashamed to even admit it."

"Go on."

"Okay... Well, when Dimitri came over that day, he couldn't help himself. He literally jumped on me, and we were making out in the small guest room – we have this little room by the front door where you receive people you don't want to invite any further into the house. We were kissing very... passionately. And then, as soon as I saw Marat, I realised he'd caught us. He was livid. At that point, I didn't know that he'd planned this all along. I don't know why, but I enjoyed seeing him so angry."

"You enjoyed it?"

"Well, I felt guilty, but also sort of happy, maybe even relieved. In fact, perhaps at the back of my mind, I had always wanted him to catch us. I don't know why – maybe you're better at explaining this – but yeah, I was almost delighted."

"And it was only afterwards that Dimitri told you that Marat hadn't actually caught you –instead that he'd planned to kill you all along? And he would have done it, if Dimitri hadn't appeared, just at the right moment?"

"Yeah, but I found out much later, in hospital, when Dimitri came to visit me for the first time."

"And how did you feel when you first heard the news?"

"I don't know..."

"Try to remember. You gave such a good description of feeling happy and relieved. Maybe it's because you initially thought that Marat wasn't indifferent. There was still love there, and you could finally see some emotion – even if it was negative, it was powerful. And then it turned out that wasn't true. It wasn't a spontaneous attack, caused by jealousy, right? He wanted to kill you in cold blood."

"Oh, everything feels so muddled –" Twinka paused, taking a sip of water from the little bottle she carried around with her – "I just can't be angry with him. I don't feel any hate or rage towards him. I probably should, but I don't."

"Is it because you feel guilty, despite everything?"

"No, I don't think that's it. I have no regrets. I'm not upset that Marat caught us."

"Are you living together?"

"No, we decided to live separately. I'm staying at our house on Button Street, and he's moved into his townhouse. Every day I walk past that statue of *Pietà* where it all happened, and I don't have any bad feelings. The only thing that worries me is: how do I explain all this to Ronia and how do I ensure that she never finds out what actually happened? That's the only negative aspect that comes to mind. Funny, isn't it? Stockholm syndrome, maybe?" Twinka's eyes quizzed Anna.

"It's very complex," said Anna, then shaking her head. "No, I don't think we're dealing with Stockholm syndrome here. I think that you do feel guilty about your affair, but now, after everything that's happened, Marat can't really be angry with you, because what he did was even worse. So, that makes you quits. In fact, you may even have the upper hand. Perhaps that's why you feel quite pleased. You've managed to successfully escape a potentially dangerous situation; a huge issue, which, by all rights, should not have ended well for you. And Marat has no right to blame you for anything. You're the one holding all the trump cards. You can choose to stay with Marat or to leave him – who would question your decision now? So, I think, what you're feeling is relief. You wanted to go on an exciting journey, feel intense emotions and experience an adventure. And that's exactly what you got, and the only price you had to pay was a bump on the head. It's not a massive price, all things considered, which is why you feel relatively delighted with everything."

"You might be right," Twinka said, although her tone signalled that she didn't quite agree with Anna's assessment. "Now, I know this may sound weird – we've never talked about it before..." Twinka didn't know how to begin.

"Talked about what?" Anna gently prodded.

"You know, Marat loves arguing with believers. He's like an aggressive atheist. It's like a sport to him – all it takes is for someone to mention that they believe in God, and Marat starts asking all sorts of provocative questions, talking about imaginary friends, and showing off his knowledge of the Bible."

"Oh yeah?" Anna looked at Twinka with an intrigued expression.

"And, of course, when he realised that I believed in God, he started teasing and provoking me. Not quite as viciously as others, and he didn't do it in an insulting way as such – but still. And you know what was the only answer I could give him?"

Anna was fully engaged in the conversation: her body still, and her attention fixed on Twinka.

"The only thing I could say was that I don't believe in coincidences. Do you know what I mean? I believe in God because I don't believe in chance. And when something bizarre happens... It takes me a very long time to process. I mean, how could anyone believe that things happen at random?" Twinka was looking at Anna intensely, expecting some answer or an affirmation from her.

"Okay. Go on..." Anna was bent forward, a thoughtful and focused look on her face.

"I mean – how? It's such an extraordinary string of events. Did all this happen purely by chance – the fact that Marat had revealed his plans to Dimitri, and Dimitri came to see me, on the right day, at the right hour, to prevent the worst-case scenario from playing out? And we're all alive and well. It's like we've been given another chance. Did all this happen totally at random?"

Anna was clearly confused, though she tried to hide it. "So, you believe that –" she was searching for the right words – "God has some sort of plan in relation to all of you?"

"I think that God protected us. I think that He has given us another chance. It all seems pretty obvious to me, because things could have taken a very different turn."

For the first time, Anna saw firm conviction flash in Twinka's eyes.

"Things could have turned out differently. Marat could have succeeded in killing me and taken this awful sin upon himself. Ronia could have effectively become an orphan, because Marat would never make a good father to her – not with such a heavy sin in his heart. And he would definitely get himself a younger wife, or he could have got himself arrested. Imagine the suffering that Ronia would have to endure. If everything had worked out exactly as he'd planned, Marat would have killed me and himself in the process, while deeply scarring Ronia. I really don't believe he would have wanted that. It's the work of the devil."

"So, you think it was the devil who tempted Marat to kill you?" Anna ventured to clarify.

"I know that this may sound strange to you, but yes, it's something like that." Twinka was relieved – she felt better for sharing her thoughts. "Marat may be an atheist and a hedonist, but he's not a bad person. I know him."

"And that's why you can forgive him so easily, because he's actually a victim – the victim of Satan's temptation?" Anna's questioning gaze bore into Twinka.

"Well, when you put it like that, it sounds stupid, but you did ask me how I really felt about it." Twinka sulked, intuiting that Anna found it hard to accept what she'd just heard.

"No, it's not stupid," Anna denied with enthusiasm, "not at all. It just hadn't occurred to me, that's all."

"I don't know if you've ever had the feeling that God hasn't abandoned you, that He is present in your life, that He's a real force who can influence what happens in our lives?" Twinka wanted to explain it further.

"I understand," Anna said, so as not to seem out of sync with her client, but Twinka could sense that it was disingenuous.

She doesn't understand anything, Twinka thought to herself.

CHAPTER 37

The arrival of the police and his subsequent arrest didn't come as a surprise to Dimitri. Twinka had already told him what sort of questions the police were asking, and that they had video footage of him turning onto Button Street around the time of the attack. Dimitri knew that the police had his voice on record too, from the call he'd placed to the emergency services. He had hoped that none of this would be enough from which to identify him, but deep down he knew the police would find him eventually.

And even though Dimitri had taken all this into account, he still wasn't prepared for it. Not one bit. He hadn't found a lawyer and, most importantly, he hadn't considered what he would say when the police asked him why he was there. He still didn't know what was the right path to choose – should he tell the whole truth? A partial truth? Or something else entirely?

In short, should he save Marat by carrying the can himself? Or should he tell the police *everything*, and let them arrest Marat for attempted murder?

Merely considering all these questions was incredibly taxing. It was so distressing and tiring that he had continually postponed the thinking and decision-making part of the process. Moreover, all his thoughts about what had happened were intertwined with equally pressing and unanswered questions about him and Twinka, or him and Marat.

Until now, Twinka divorcing Marat and being with Dimitri hadn't been a remote possibility. And because it was impossible, Dimitri hadn't allowed himself to consider it. Neither of them had. But everything was different now. A new door, previously off-limits, was suddenly accessible to Dimitri. It hadn't opened yet, but it was there, and Dimitri couldn't ignore it. All of a sudden, Twinka had become much more than a lover or the elegant and beautiful wife of his wealthy friend, the conquest of whom stirred his senses and puffed up his ego. Twinka had become a woman in her own right. Someone he could potentially spend the rest of his life with. And he knew she was the one. Fate had brought them together, and she was the best thing that had ever happened to Dimitri.

Suddenly, everything that had seemed clear, stable and solid had been made fluid. Now anything was possible, which was exciting and terrifying at the same time. Seemingly overnight, his life had taken several unexpected turns, all of which were complex and challenging. He knew that the decisions he made now would determine the rest of his life, and that he wouldn't be able to go back and alter them. Plus, they didn't affect Dimitri's life alone. He was terrified of this massive responsibility, embodied by the decisions that lay ahead of him.

Still, he felt surprisingly calm when he saw the police car approach. And he held onto this sense of inner peace all the way to the station, and afterwards as he waited inside for the chief inspector to arrive.

Yes, he knew that if he'd prepared to face this moment properly – if he had considered all the possibilities, thought it all through and made his decision – he would have had every opportunity to avoid being put behind bars following his arrest. He could have walked away from the police station that very same day, if only he'd prepared to confess how his actions had prevented a murder. That his actions had, in fact, saved a life. He knew exactly what Marat's intentions were and he got in the way, at the last moment, using force permissible for self-defence. He'd saved Twinka from certain death. It was all very simple. He had nothing to hide. He'd done nothing wrong, and he wasn't a criminal. On the contrary, he'd done the right thing.

Still, the realisation of how significance the moment was, how important his decision would be for everyone involved, made him hesitate. No. He wasn't ready. He needed more time.

Which is why Dimitri refused to testify and submitted to his arrest. He would remain behind bars for three nights until the judge decided what security measures to apply next. In fact, Dimitri was pleased he'd been arrested. These three nights spent in solitude were just what he needed. There would be nowhere for him to escape to, and so he'd be forced to weigh everything up and reach a decision.

A rather large policewoman with dry, blotchy skin escorted Dimitri to his detention cell. She didn't look him in the eye. She didn't glance at his face either, as though she just wanted to get it done and over with, with as little interaction or contact between them as possible. Dimitri was put in handcuffs, with his hands bound in front of him. He found it bizarre that you had to take an elevator to get to the prison, as it was located on the upper floor. They barely squeezed into the elevator – that's how big the female officer was, and Dimitri sensed that she felt awkward about it. He could smell her overly sweet perfume. He wondered whether her uniform had been made-to-size for her, and whether she'd had to contribute toward the cost. He caught himself thinking about everything and nothing: all except the one thing he really should be thinking about.

The large lady led him into a windowless room. There, a male officer told him to strip off before carefully searching Dimitri's clothes. Dimitri noticed that the man's shoes looked dirty. The female officer, still smelling of the sickly sweet perfume, remained by the door, pressed against the wall and side-on to Dimitri. She didn't look at him, although he knew that she could see him. It wasn't like he cared – he just wondered whether they all stood like that, next to that door, watching other naked men and women being examined.

Horrified, Dimitri realised that his boxer shorts weren't as fresh as he thought. Two disgusting brown trails ran along on the inside. He was overcome by an overwhelming feeling of shame. He was so embarrassed. He wanted to explain to the police officer – and especially to the fat lady, who wasn't even looking his way – that he wasn't some dirty old pig, and he wasn't a criminal either. He was here of his own free will, and he was not a bad person. On the contrary – he was the good guy. He was the one who'd saved Twinka's life.

But Dimitri knew how weird it would sound to say anything now. (And whatever he said would sound like whatever real criminals would say when they were here.)

He looked over at the fat lady, as though asking her whether she knew that he wasn't the baddie, that his shoes were usually always clean, as were his boxer shorts, and that he wasn't who he appeared to be. But she continued to ignore him.

And then, all of a sudden, Dimitri broke down. He knew that, objectively speaking, he was exactly what he looked like. Even if this ugly, dirty shell – these two skid marks in his boxers; these dirty, disgusting shoes – did not belong to his true self, nevertheless it was, based on the evidence of reality, a part of him. At least for now. He didn't believe that he was currently the way he *actually* was. But these really were his dirty shoes. And it was his own shit, from his own dirty arse, that had made the skid marks. That was the truth, plain and simple.

And maybe it was even worse. Perhaps this *was* his true self whom they were stripping and searching. Maybe his shell was the self-righteous, honest Christian man who lectured Marat about how a crime would always have its consequences, how it would always set into motion a string of events that couldn't be foreseen – but who failed to understand that *any* sin had consequences. And it didn't have to be something as extreme as murder – the tiniest sin had far-reaching, destructive ramifications. A small lie gives rise to another, and an insignificant betrayal leads to a far greater one. And here he was, because *he* had broken one of the ten commandments. He had coveted and slept with his best friend's wife. An act the Bible explicitly prohibited, but which he'd gone and done regardless. He had known exactly what he was doing, and it hadn't stopped him from leading Twinka into temptation, from talking her into it and getting her addicted to it. It hadn't seemed so bad at the time because no one had been suffering, but that's how it always appeared at first. A sin was a sin, and it would always have consequences, and that's why he was here.

Suddenly, Dimitri realised that it was out of kindness that the woman hadn't been looking at him. She didn't want to face this kind of crass and common ugliness that she encountered so often. She witnessed it every day, all the time, and she just couldn't bear it anymore.

Then, just like that, the horrible moment had passed. Dimitri put his dirty underwear and shoes back on, and the fat lady escorted him to his cell.

The dirt, and the sour, disgusting smells of his cell in the short-stay unit caught him by surprise. It was like he could smell everyone who'd come before him. The only clean item he could see was the thin blanket he'd been given. There was no bedsheet though, and no pillows nor towels. The huge officer gave him a small toothbrush, a tube of toothpaste and several pieces of toilet paper, which she tore from a toilet roll as he looked on. That's when their eyes met for the first time. He wanted to ask why she couldn't just hand him the entire roll. And it seemed like she wanted to say: 'Do you want to ask me why I'm not giving you the roll, just like everyone else does?!'

No. Dimitri didn't want to ask her anything. None of that mattered anyway – there were bigger things that demanded his attention.

There were two beds in the tiny cell, each pushed against a different wall, with mattresses covered in some material that resembled tarpaulin (they looked as if someone had gone over them with a wet rag). A round, bright lamp hung from the ceiling. Dimitri continued to be shocked by the sheer stench and uncleanliness – he had thought that contemporary prisons were a grade above this. However, his first impulse of disgust soon dissipated, and he tried to frame it in his mind as a monk's quarters. His arrival here was a stimulus, an encouragement, a catalyst, to help him to make his important decision. This was exactly where needed to be right now, and he would humbly accept, endure and pass this test.

It was hot in the cell, and the bed was a little too narrow and a little too short for Dimitri. He took off his shirt and shoes. After a moment's hesitation he removed his trousers too, leaving him in nothing but his boxer shorts. He twisted the blanket into an improvised pillow. There was a ventilation shaft on the ceiling, right above the bed, which emitted a paltry yet irritating stream of cold air.

So... To give his friend up to the police, to say that Marat had planned a murder... Was that the right thing to do? His initial reaction was no – it didn't feel right. *You don't rat on your friends. You just don't!* Marat had been taught his lesson, he was obviously going to lose his eye, and no one would benefit from his spending years in prison for attempted murder. Those years wouldn't make him reconsider his actions any more than he already had; he wouldn't be released 'a changed man' – indeed, knowing Marat, it would probably have the opposite effect. Dimitri had also to consider the trauma that Ronia would endure if her father was jailed for trying to kill her mother. Who could live with that knowledge? No, that wasn't the right thing to do.

On the other hand, the law demanded that he, Dimitri, tell the truth. If he didn't, he'd become a lawbreaker himself. So was that what he should do? But, laws and morals aside, there was a deeper, ethical dimension that stated that you never double-cross your friends. Dimitri felt this with more conviction than ever before. What would remain of the definition of friendship if the notion "don't betray your friends" was taken out? This aspect was self-evident, and people knew this instinctively, just like any of nature's laws. And yet society's law demanded that Dimitri deceive his friend and testify against him, which would see Marat sent away for years. What path should he take then?

The spartan interior of his cell made Dimitri study the additional touches made by prior occupants – which, surprisingly, were in no short supply. For example, someone had tried to cover the bright lamp on the ceiling by sticking newspaper around it (you could still make out its print on the murky glass). Previous inhabitants had also scraped various slogans onto the walls.

lie and thou shalt be forgiven, one of them proclaimed.

don't leave the room, some jester had written.

god is, another declared.

Of course, Dimitri had to admit to himself that the definition of a friendship also forbid one's sleeping with the other's spouse. God's commandments specifically prohibited coveting a friend's wife, let alone having sex with them. Dimitri had broken this commandment.

However, this act hadn't seemed to cause him much internal turmoil. *Twinka is my friend, too*, he reasoned. *And Twinka was much happier with me – she loved our dates, she needed them. It was Marat's fault for not giving her enough attention.*

It definitely hadn't been the right thing to do, but maybe it wasn't as bad as all that. If Marat hadn't found out, no one would have been any worse off – in fact, they had all gained something, hadn't they? Even Marat. Didn't he benefit from his neglected wife feeling happy and content? It wasn't like Marat had any less of Twinka whenever she was with Dimitri. No, he hadn't really taken anything from him.

The situation was definitely not ideal, but it was okay. At least, it didn't seem to tear Dimitri's conscience apart.

Nevertheless, the decision Dimitri was about to make held enormous gravity. It was one thing to sleep with your best friend's wife, but something else entirely to put them behind bars while you carried on making love to said wife, or even embarked on a new life with them. That was probably how things would progress if Dimitri chose to go down that route.

Dimitri wanted to weigh all the pros and cons in his head, but it was absolutely stifling in the cell: it must have been at least thirty degrees. The weather outside was unusually hot for October, too.

He attempted to focus and think.

The biggest pro, in terms of if chose to tell the truth, was that the police would set him free and his reputation wouldn't suffer from all of this. In fact he'd be hailed as a hero, having saved someone's life. Marat, on the other hand, would be nothing more than a failed murderer. Marat would go to prison and his reputation would be ruined.

However, if he chose to protect Marat, then the police would probably twist the story: making him, Dimitri, the villain. He'd already been put on trial once – for assaulting his ex-wife's partner – and now it would look like he had attempted to kill his lover's husband. In the absolute best-case scenario, he'd be set free owing to a lack of evidence. But he could also be sentenced and sent to prison – because everything pointed to Dimitri sleeping with his best friend's wife and wanting to kill Marat so that he could be with Twinka. He could spend many years behind bars.

What would people think of him then? They wouldn't know that, by taking this vow of silence and admission of guilt upon himself, he would have saved his friend from ruin. Indeed, everyone would believe the exact opposite: that Dimitri was sleeping with his best friend's wife and therefore wanted to kill him. That's what everyone would believe. They'd despise and slander Dimitri; his name would be mud. The court of public opinion would judge him without hesitation, and, in that context, hand him a life sentence. Considering Marat's enormous wealth, Marat wouldn't care about his reputation or what others thought of him. It wouldn't really affect Marat's life. But for an ordinary person like Dimitri, it would be incredibly tough to live with the mark of Cain.

Who would hire me? I wouldn't be able to get a job, not even as a maths teacher. And would Marat even appreciate my sacrifice? He's probably added me to his list of enemies, and has already plotting my murder. Is Marat even capable of forgiveness? And is he able to think about anything rationally at the moment?

Dimitri deciphered someone's barely legible writing on the wall:

god knows all your thoughts.

I wonder what tool they used to carve that? he thought to himself. The wall seemed to be inviting him to leave his own statement; some legacy of his own amid the never-ending stream of prisoners passing through this cell. Dimitri felt united with all of them – the ones who had come before him, and the ones who were yet to arrive – whether they were guilty or innocent, and whether they stayed here for long. He wanted to write something, though he didn't know what, and he couldn't find anything sharp that he could use to do it.

Then an idea came to him. In some sense, if you looked at the problem from a different perspective, he owed Marat. So, perhaps it was only fair that Dimitri took the blame upon himself. He was in debt to Marat for his affair with Twinka, and that was how he could repay him for the betrayal. And then, afterwards, maybe they could... well, not be friends exactly, but at least let it lie. Was that the right thing to do?

From yet another perspective, though, wouldn't it be better for Twinka if Marat was put in jail? She'd be able to unshackle herself, to get a divorce, and to start afresh with Ronia – free from a violent husband. Now that would be right, wouldn't it? Surely, that would be best for her?

Dimitri re-examined the cell. There was a small metal table fastened to the wall, with a chair next to it that was screwed into the floor, while on the opposite side was a separate area with a toilet. There was a window, but the only means of accessing it was by stepping on the table. Dimitri tried, but it was very uncomfortable. As he moved to straighten his back his head banged against the ceiling, so he bent back over and instead took to his knees on the table, just so he could look outside. And because the table was relatively small, he had to press his knees together tight and then crane his neck, just so he could look outside. It was incredibly uncomfortable, so Dimitri ditched the exercise.

He wondered how he could get his hands on an implement he could use to inscribe a message on the wall. Others had managed it, so there had to be a way. The best idea Dimitri could come up with was using the flap on the zip of his trousers. Since he could fasten his zip without it, he broke it off, acquiring him in the process a half-decent scraping tool.

This small victory gave him immense satisfaction. If only he could solve his moral dilemma just as easily. Oh, what should he do... ?

CHAPTER 38

That chief inspector is rather good, Marat thought. *I really didn't expect this. If everything had gone according to my plan, I wonder if he would have caught me then? He'd probably come close, but I don't think he'd be able to crack it. He doesn't know anything about the moped, just as I suspected, and he hasn't managed to capture my return on the CCTV cameras. I would have probably succeeded... It's just my luck to get such an intelligent chief inspector! As much as I dislike him, Draco reminds me of an upper-caste intellectual. There's probably only one percent of them in our entire society. And how many of those work for the police?! They shouldn't even have people like him, at least not working as inspectors. And one of them just happens to be investigating my case.*

Marat had always been fascinated by a high IQ – it was as if he could smell one a mile off. It was like he and the chief inspector were somehow related, even though Draco was his polar opposite. Because one law remained constant: that, no matter the circumstances, it was always pleasant to encounter an upper-caste intellectual. A superior mind had the power to attract, fascinate, enthuse and inspire you. And even if the owner of such a mind happened to be your enemy, that mind still demanded respect and admiration.

Marat came up with an excuse to visit Draco. He wanted to find out whether the chief inspector had uncovered anything new, as well as to get a better idea of what he was thinking. The police still had Marat's car and phone, which they'd picked up at the car park by Neptune when they thought that the potential suspect had stolen them. Marat realised that he could request for his belongings to be returned to him. Well, he could try, at least.

When he phoned Draco the chief inspector greeted him very politely – he was almost friendly. Draco enquired about Marat's health and seemed pleased to hear that Marat was feeling much better.

"Yes, of course, you can pick up your things. Just fill out a request form, drop it off tomorrow around eleven, and I'll take care of the rest." There was no suspicion, blame or judgement in the chief inspector's voice.

That cunning bastard, Marat thought, following their conversation, which had only made him want to see Draco more.

The next day, Marat entered Draco's office. To his surprise, though, there was a girl present in the room, sat on a small couch. She looked about eleven – with long, frizzy, ginger hair – and she was drawing something on a notepad. The last thing Marat had expected was to see children at the police station, and he didn't quite know how to react.

"Annabella; this is Annabella," Draco explained, having picked up on Marat's bafflement. He turned to the girl: "Annabella, say hi."

Annabella reluctantly turned away from her sketch. Her eyes were drawn to Marat's eye patch, though she didn't say anything.

"Hi, Annabella," Marat stretched out his hand out for a greeting. "My name is Marat. And I'm not a pirate," he tried to joke.

"Hi," Annabella said quietly, stretching her hand out in return, her eyes now facing the floor. They shook hands.

"You have to look them in the eye! Whenever you're greeting someone, you have to look the person in the eye," Draco told the girl, though by now she had already withdrawn her hand and retreated to her notebook.

"Annabella is on a school holiday; she's waiting for me to take her shopping. We need to get some new trainers and a tracksuit, plus a few other bits."

"Oh, right." Marat was truly surprised. For some reason, the idea that the chief inspector might have kids hadn't occurred to him. "I don't want to keep you. I can come back another time..." Marat's sentiment was genuine – he really was ready to leave.

"Oh, no, don't worry! Annabella is used to it, she's here quite often. Dad has to work, and nothing can be done about it. Annabella knows that. Right, my sweet?"

She didn't reply, and just carried on drawing.

Marat felt uncomfortable. He regarded Annabella again, and in doing so noticed how beautiful and very unlike her father she looked. Marat then acquiesced to Draco's energetic gestures inviting him to take a seat.

He sat down on a chair by a desk, so that Draco was opposite and Annabella was now behind him.

"You know, I'm so pleased that you stopped by; really pleased," Draco said.

Pleased? That was an interesting choice of word, Marat thought to himself.

"How's your health?" Draco asked politely.

"I've been better," Marat replied, pointing to the bandage.

"You know, it kind of suits you," the chief inspector said with a smile.

Was there a dash of irony and ridicule in what the chief inspector had said? Or was Marat reading too much into it?

"Yeah, you had a serious trauma; very serious. The doctors said it's a miracle you even survived," the chief inspector continued compassionately, as though he'd picked up on Marat's suspicions.

"Yeah, that's what they say."

"The prosecution think that it could be interpreted either as an attempted murder or grievous bodily harm."

Marat shrugged. The office smelled of sweat and cheap lunch.

"It's really good that you came by though – see, I have another question for you, almost a private one. 'Off the record', so to speak." The chief inspector sat down opposite Marat in the other visitors' chair. "So, I did some digging. I looked up a few things about you on the internet – don't worry, just standard procedure really, nothing out of the ordinary. And I found this lecture you gave a few years back. Do you recall it? You were invited by the MBA students, and your lecture was called 'The IQ and the real caste system'. Do you remember?"

"Yeah, I think I remember something. It's all a bit foggy though, it was a quite a while ago."

"It was a very interesting lecture. Absolutely fascinating. I liked this bit in particular," the chief inspector turned the computer screen towards Marat. It was a video of Marat stood at a lectern in front of a packed lecture hall. He was wearing an elegant suit, its jacket sporting a pocket square. "Any individual with an IQ above 140 is different from others – is like someone who's seven feet tall, compared to a person of an average height," he spoke with passion. "Except the difference isn't as obvious or visible. In the case of intellect, a person with an IQ above 140 still exists in a world full of idiots, just like a seven-foot-tall basketball player lives like a giant in a world populated by tiny people.

"The unequal distribution of IQ – one of the main inequalities that exist among people, and one that has the biggest socio-political impact – is a taboo subject in our society. For example, such differences would be self-evident in sport: no amateur tennis player would be surprised or upset if he couldn't score points against the world's fifth-hundredth-ranked player, let alone one of the Grand Slam champions. Everyone would understand how, ever since childhood, a professional tennis player has been trained for one, single goal – to become a better tennis player. They put all their energy into perfecting their talent, and over the course of tens of thousands of hours they have accumulated such experience, ability and skill as to make them untouchable to a simple tennis enthusiast – even if the latter were talented; even if they had been training three times a week, an hour each time, for the best part of a decade. Obviously there's an insurmountable abyss between an amateur and a professional tennis player, whose talent has been shaped by their parents, coaches and tennis consultants ever since they were little, as well as string of other specialists: like physiotherapists, medics, psychologists and nutritionists.

In the same way, no amateur boxing enthusiast would ever dare challenge a professional fighter. And anyone who loves long-distance running understands that they wouldn't stand a chance against an Olympic marathon runner.

And so, in sport, the gulf between a professional and a plain amateur is crystal-clear. But it's not the same when it comes to intellect. The differences are just as vast, but your average idiot can't spot them. They don't see any difference between themselves and people who possess a high IQ, even though it's the same as not being able to tell the difference between themselves and their sporting idols.

The bitter truth is that there exists such a thing as the intellectual caste system. And the majority of our socio-economic and political problems stem from putting leadership and decision-making in politics, the media, government and the justice system in the hands of people who aren't physically or biologically suited to the task. Regardless of how much time, work and effort they've invested into improving their skills. They're not equipped to solve our moral dilemmas, nor any intellectual or leadership issues they come across, which is why they ruin everything.

If we want to evolve beyond the Dark Ages – if we want to move towards a better, more developed world – we need to respect wisdom. We need to give wisdom its rightful place: create a cult of wisdom, mould a society that considers it to be the highest virtue of all. We need to create a 'sophiocraty' – this is what needs to be at the heart of a new world order. We need to respect our biological differences in terms of hereditary intellect, and establish a system whereby everyone occupies the place best suited to them."

Draco had stopped the playback.

Marat was looking at the chief inspector with a quizzical expression. "What about it?" He didn't understand. "Don't you agree?"

"Well, I'm actually interested in something else, from a purely professional standpoint..." The chief inspector was fidgeting in his chair, as though he was genuinely intrigued. "You must have heard of Daniel Kahneman, the Nobel Prize laureate?"

Marat gave an affirmative nod.

"Right. And for many decades now, this Kahneman has been asking people to answer one simple question: if a baseball bat and a ball cost one dollar and ten cents, and we know that the bat costs one dollar more than the ball, how much does the ball cost? What would you say?" Draco cast a flattering smile Marat's way, then waved his hand nonchalantly. "I mean, I've no doubt you'd have the right answer. But, you see, it turns out that most people say the ball costs ten cents and the bat cost a dollar. Of course, it will come as no surprise to you that the answer is—"

"Five cents," Marat said, interrupting the chief inspector in order to show off.

"Exactly. That's exactly right! The ball costs five cents and the bat costs one dollar more – which makes it a dollar and five cents," Draco confirmed.

Marat didn't say anything. He was still in the dark as to where this conversation was heading.

"But then there's something that confounds me," Draco continued, "which is the fact that the level of education or intellectual development doesn't seem to be a factor in producing the average number of correct responses to this question. More than fifty percent of Harvard's and MIT's students – people who'd passed the world's toughest and most thorough selection processes; people who were on top of their IQ game for their age category; people whose intellectual excellence was beyond any shadow of a doubt – one in two of these overachieving types gave the wrong answer to the simple question about the ball and the bat! Do you know what I mean? In your upper-caste system, every other person wouldn't be able to give the right answer to a basic question! I often come across criminals who think they're geniuses, that they're the product of some higher caste, but then I catch them like I would some amateur teenager."

Marat remained in thoughtful silence.

Meanwhile, Annabella had moved over to a small cabinet that was crammed with teapots, cups, opened tea-bag boxes and a big packet of ground coffee. She had pulled out a small jar containing honey and was in search of a spoon. Marat noticed that Draco always had his attention on Annabella, and that her movements made it harder for him to focus on their conversation. It was bizarre that such a vile, despicable man could have fathered such a beautiful daughter. *It's like they're not even related,* Marat thought to himself.

"So, we must build a new world order then?" Draco asked after a pause, squeezing his lips tight. "Which will be led by the intellectuals? Your so-called 'upper caste'? Is that right?"

Marat looked at Draco like a student who had, once again, received a bad mark. "Look, personally, I'm not interested in political power. I don't care about creating a theory or fighting for everyone to follow one particular school of thought or think like me," Marat explained in a tired voice. "I'm not interested in any of that. I don't care about politics, I don't expect the government to provide me with anything, I take care of everything myself. I don't expect the government to solve any of my problems, I always rely on myself. I'm astonished when I look at those who are fighting to keep or change something officially: like those who want to maintain the current definition of a family, or anyone who wants to force the government to legalise or prohibit what you can smoke and snort. I couldn't care less about any of that. I'll have whatever family I want to have, and I'll smoke whatever I want to smoke. I'm going to believe in whatever I want to believe – those are all just external factors for me. Which, by the way, tend to be quite complicated and unfavourable in most areas of life, so only an idiot would make their life dependent on them. I'll play with whatever cards I've been dealt. It's like rain, or snow, or frost. I don't like the rain, but I adapt to it, and I get through the rainy days. In the same way, I don't like seeing idiocy in politics. But somehow I adapt to it and survive. And if it got so bad that I just couldn't take it anymore, I'd move somewhere that had a more favourable climate, literally or metaphorically. People with an individual strategy – those are the ones who get into politics: it's their way of playing their cards; their tool for gaining recognition, power, connections, fame and other resources. Naturally, it's always the mediocrities who are trying to get ahead in politics – they don't know the first thing about politics, but that doesn't stop them from trying to weasel their way in. Politics make mediocrities feel that, for once in their lives, they're more significant than they really are. They can't get this anywhere else – otherwise they'd be sat in an office. But here, you see, the Shudras get to vote for them – and, all of a sudden, the television and press are all interested in their stupid opinions." Marat was climbing through the gears. "And what you're showing me here is just a lecture, a demonstration; a flexing of muscles, so to speak – it's not my political ideology. I just like to show off; I like being admired; I like it when people listen to me, when they applaud; and I enjoy flirting with the students. I love all that, not the politics."

"Right. Showing off, flirting with the students... How fascinating..." Draco sounded disappointed. "Then you're not interested in building a new world order, ruled by the clever ones? A 'sophiocraty', as you called it?"

"It's impossible." Marat gave his characteristic dismissive hand-wave, though he remained tense. "There simply isn't a system that could sustain it. A democracy? No, because your average Joe can't comprehend the most basic concepts, let alone what's best for him long-term. Idiots aren't capable of finding their place – they always want to do someone else's thing. And they're usually bad at their own thing as it is, let alone something that isn't theirs. But they're too stupid to acknowledge that! You see, there's no way out: because democracy doesn't work, but without democracy you'd be left with a dictatorship. And in that system, of course, anyone can pretend to be clever and usurp power, even if they're not. There'd be no third party that could independently determine who should be where in the societal hierarchy. It wouldn't be possible, because they'd immediately seize or corrupt the third party. In short, it's all just talk, and there's no salvation for us. Of course, I don't believe that you should only be able to tell which caste you belong to by who your parents were. It doesn't work that way – that only leads to more injustice and suffering. I believe that a Brahman can be born into any background; like the Dalai Lama's coming from a peasant family. However, we've never had a system that ensures the true Brahmans take their rightful place. If we did, then we'd all be living in a better world. But it's impossible."

"Ah, but don't forget that every other of your so-called 'Brahmans' wouldn't be able to tell how much the ball cost. And the rest would think they're allowed to do anything. That's when they end up at my door. And just like that –" Draco snapped his fingers – "their freedom is gone."

"Well," Marat started, "in my case..."

He stopped himself just in time.

What had he almost confessed? The chief inspector had subtly angered and provoked him, and he had almost said, with injured pride, that Draco hadn't managed to catch him yet.

Oh God, that should never have almost happened. I need to be more careful, he thought to himself. Watching the lecture, and seeing the child in the office, had completely tamed his usual vigilance.

Draco, of course, noticed everything. "In your case – what?" he asked.

"Well, in my case, I've never had the audacity to imagine that I'm allowed to do anything I want." Marat felt himself jump through the corrective hoop. "To quote the Bible – everything is permissible, but not everything is beneficial." He'd adopted a provocative tone, trying to distract the chief inspector's attention from the mistake he'd just made.

"Or do you, by any chance, believe that you're so intelligent that you haven't been caught as of yet?" said Draco, calling a spade a spade.

Annabella was back on the sofa, with the jar of honey in her hands.

"If you've been gathering evidence about me," Marat had regained his self-control, "then you should already know that I always play by the rules – a run-in with the law just isn't something I need in my life. Such things are expensive, and cause a huge mess. So I always pay my taxes, and I don't exploit any loopholes to save money – I can afford it, so I don't need the stress of coming into conflict with the powers that be. Those are inadequate risks. Imagine if you were trading with financial instruments. If you managed the position sizes correctly, you'd still make a profit even if you made a make a mistake on forty-nine percent of all occasions. In fact, you can be right even less than fifty percent of the time and still turn a profit. If you make a mistake only one-in-three times, and manage the position sizes without getting too emotional, then you're truly exceptional. But if you wanted to, say, kill someone, then all you'd need to do is make one tiny mistake and it's game over for you – the consequences would be catastrophic." Marat spoke with arrogance and scorn, as though completely sure of himself. "Clearly, someone with my experience in risk management would never take such a step. Only a buffoon would play a game where a single mistake, one single position, would lead straight to their ruin." Marat sounded so convincing that he almost believed his own words.

In fact, it suddenly dawned on him, having heard himself make the argument out loud, that the idea of murdering his wife was a huge mistake. Really, how could someone like him – someone with so much experience in risk management – come up with something like that? However, this wasn't the time or place for metacognitive contemplation, so he parked that thought.

"Oh, by the way, did I tell you – we obtained a sample of the suspect's voice," said Draco, changing the subject. "He'd phoned the ambulance from Twinka's phone. Did you know the switchboard records all incoming calls?"

Marat shrugged.

"Would you like to listen to it?"

Marat already knew who the voice sample belonged to, so he wasn't particularly interested. However, he realised that it would raise further suspicions if he refused. "How interesting," he said. "Sure, let's hear it."

"You know, I have to say that in my experience this is the first time that a criminal attacks the victim and then, literally minutes later, phones the ambulance. Don't you think that's odd?" The chief inspector's eyes scrutinised Marat.

"I don't know. I've got no experience in this area," said Marat, swerving the question.

"Okay, well, let's hear it." The chief inspector pressed a button on the keyboard and Dimitri's voice resounded from the small computer speakers. It sounded surprisingly calm to Marat. He tried to picture the scene. Both he and Twinka lying there unconscious, while Dimitri coolly dictated the address.

"Isn't it strange though?" the chief inspector repeated, before responding to his own question. "Most unusual. Who does that?"

"Yeah..." Marat said quietly.

"So, do you know this person?" The chief inspector asked in a strict voice. All of his friendliness had dissipated.

"No. I don't," Marat answered just as firmly.

"You don't?" repeated the chief inspector. "You don't know him at all?"

"No."

"Well, let's hear it again, maybe it'll jog your memory," Draco said, and replayed the recording.

"I said I don't know him," Marat stated, without relistening to the clip. He had come here of his own free will; his curiosity had led him here, nothing more. But, as it turned out, Draco had set a trap for him. Several traps, in fact.

"Very interesting," Draco carried on muttering. "Very interesting indeed. Tell me, since you're very intelligent – I mean everyone says so, and your IQ is 160, so you definitely belong to the upper caste. You must have some theory about who attacked you?"

One hundred and sixty-five, actually, Marat corrected the chief inspector in his thoughts. He was starting to wonder whether coming here had been a bad idea. On the other hand, if he hadn't, Draco would have probably called him to the station for questioning anyway.

"I'm expecting good results from you," Marat replied. "You're a professional, you're very experienced – and it's *your* job to find out what happened."

"I know, I know. Of course. And I will, don't you worry about that. In fact, I think I may have worked it out already." Draco's voice was void of any judgement or reprehension.

"You have?" Marat couldn't hide his astonishment.

"Oh, yes, I'm more or less clear on what happened. I just have this little weakness, you see..." Draco flexed his fingers to demonstrate how insignificant and small his weakness was.

Annabella had placed the honey jar and the spoon next to her on the sofa. She was drawing something again. The jar had tipped over, though thankfully it was closed and so no honey had leaked out.

"...I love it when a criminal confesses."

"And why would they?" Marat didn't understand.

"What do you mean?" Draco didn't understand either – or pretended not to. "An offender has to realise that what they did was wrong – that's the best-case scenario. They realise that it wasn't right, and they won't be able to live with such a heavy burden. They need to crave their punishment, as a way of getting redemption. That should always be the end goal of my work, and of the work of our entire legal system."

"I see." Marat stood up, a smirk on his face. "Well, do what you must."

"Goodbye." Annabella had spoken for the first time, loud and clear.

"Goodbye, young lady." Marat stretched out his hand and they shook. Annabella was looking straight into his eyes now, and Marat sensed she'd been carefully listening to every detail of their conversation.

It suddenly occurred to him that Ronia was in school today. So, it wasn't a school holiday. Had Draco brought his own child here on purpose, just to distract him, to make their meeting seem less formal and more sociable, hoping that he'd open up and drop his guard? Was this girl even his daughter?

CHAPTER 39

Annabella was indeed Draco's daughter. And she really did have a day off school, due to some teacher training. However, Marat's suspicions weren't completely unfounded. Draco could have spoken to Marat in the interrogation room, rather than his office, but he chose to talk to him with Annabella present. Since Marat's own daughter was of a similar age, Annabella's presence should have fostered trust between them: making Marat feel like Draco wasn't his enemy or opponent – simply a single father who had no one to leave his child with – and to give the appearance that prosecuting Marat wasn't the single, most important thing in his life. Draco had even considered telling Marat about Annabella's late mother – his wife had died of cancer when Annabella was only two years and four months old – to imply that it wasn't all that easy being a lone parent to a young girl. But he'd changed his mind at the last minute and decided not to play that particular card, thus saving it for later use. Either way, Draco's goal was to make Marat feel relaxed, so that he could lull him into a false sense of security and disarm him. Only then could he hope that their conversation would go the way he wanted it to. Marat wasn't the sort of person who was easily pressured or intimidated. Such tactics would only mobilise Marat to increase his focus and muster all his strength to repel the attack. No. Draco's extensive experience had taught him that the best way to deal with smart, self-assured individuals like Marat – individuals who'd achieved so much – was through the use of flattery and a tactful manipulation of their guard. Draco knew that his usual tactics – of intimidation, wearing suspects down, and bluffing – would not be effective against Marat. And although Draco hadn't learned anything radically new, he was still pleased with the way their conversation had turned out.

Marat had been fairly open and candid, and they had chatted on seemingly unrelated tangents long enough to help Draco get a good idea of him as a person – and to understand Marat's way of thinking, character and reactions through close observation of his body language. He felt he had a good sense of Marat's personality, which would aid him further in his investigation. Luckily for him, Marat was *extremely* confident. Draco didn't class him as a narcissist, as Marat did seem to possess some ability to feel empathy (such as when he said he was willing to drop by at a better-suited hour, so as not to interrupt the quality time between a father and his daughter). The main tell of a narcissist was their complete lack of or inability to feel any empathy.

No, Marat wasn't a narcissist – he was just extraordinarily full of himself. He genuinely believed that he belonged to some upper caste. This belief was deeply ingrained in Marat – he was convinced karma or nature had bestowed upon him some sort of supremacy. He didn't think it was something he'd gained through hard work, or by developing himself, but rather something he'd genetically inherited. He believed he was born to be superior, just like a seven-foot basketball player was born to grow taller than everyone else. It was nature that had made him tower above the others – that's how Marat thought of himself. What's more, he had clearly demonstrated that he also possessed all the typical deficiencies of character that self-assured people like him usually did. They relied too much on their supremacy, they were careless, and they underestimated their opponent. This made Draco almost ecstatic. Marat hadn't considered everything – he'd arrived ill-prepared, heedless, and absolutely convinced that he'd be able to tackle any situation that was thrown at him; forever staying one step ahead, as though Fortune were always smiling on him.

Oh, no, my friend, Draco thought to himself with a smile, as he patiently waited for Annabella to pack her things so that they could go to the shops. *I'll crack you like a nut. I love working with people like you. Those are my favourite cases. It doesn't matter what IQ you've got, because your arrogance will turn you into a fool.*

"Show me your drawing, sweetheart," Draco said, picking up Annabella's notebook. The first page he opened showed a large pirate ship with a one-eyed captain at its helm.

CHAPTER 40

Walter Keiko was one of the country's most seasoned and established criminal case lawyers. A grey-haired man in his seventies, he was still actively working. His physical movements may have been slower than they once were, but he retained his impeccable natural judgement, which was enhanced by the solid layer of experience that he'd acquired over the years. His two sons were just as perfect – both had become lawyers, continuing the family tradition. However Marat only trusted Keiko senior, whom he'd known and worked with for years.

After Dimitri's arrest, it was finally time to call Keiko.

There was no point in Marat holding anything back, so he didn't. However, he did find it somewhat uncomfortable to open up and tell the old, wizened man absolutely everything: from his conversation in the park with Dimitri, to his recent visit to Draco's office.

"You know what's the first thing that comes to mind?" the old man said with benevolent irony after he'd finished listening to Marat's story. "If there was some beginner's manual for murderers, the very first sentence would read: 'If you're planning on killing someone, don't tell anyone'."

Marat smiled. He appreciated the sarcasm. "Then I probably shouldn't tell you how badly I want to run Dimitri over with my car... at least three times... then another three, just to make sure he's dead."

"No, you probably shouldn't. Because if I started suspecting that you were serious, I'd have to report it to the police."

"Right. Then get me a copy of *Murder for Dummies*. Sounds like I need it."

"At my age, I didn't think anything could surprise me anymore, after all the criminal cases I've seen. But you have succeeded. Frankly speaking, I'm flabbergasted – you're such an intelligent man. So, what's all this about? It will soon be half a century since I started defending all sorts of murderers, despots, burglars, wife-beaters and brutes. Do you know what they all have in common? Violence is their only available resource. It's their last resort."

There was a small ceramic dish on the conference table in Keiko's office, filled with tiny squares of Swiss chocolate. Marat reached in and picked one up, relieved it of its shiny wrapper, and ate it.

"For those who are weak, violence is their only strength," Keiko elaborated. "When you've got nothing else – no money, no sense, no real power, no authority, and no wisdom – when you have absolutely nothing, then all you're left with is violence. It's your only chance to feel powerful, even if it's just for a moment. Which is why people like you rarely resort to violence."

Keiko watched as Marat made the chocolate wrapper into a ball and rolled it back towards the ceramic dish. The tiny, messy, crumpled sphere contrasted sharply with the elegant restraint and order of the room. Marat looked at Keiko, trying to assert whether the lawyer had spotted it too. That is, the fact that the leftover wrapper besmirched the previously pristine room. *He hasn't accounted for that*, Marat thought to himself, somewhat disappointed.

"In most cases, whatever the powerless are trying to achieve by using violence and force, those who possess intelligence, wealth and power can usually achieve through other means. In the worst-case scenario, they outsource violence as a service. But you – what kind of a devil possessed you to act like this?!"

"I don't know. It seemed like a good idea at the time. Maybe because people don't tend to do things like that, or maybe because divorce seemed like an even worse option."

Marat was rapid and businesslike, as though they'd been dwelling on an insignificant point for far too long.

"Tut, tut," said the respectable lawyer, shaking his head.

"Okay, picture the world we live in." Marat decided to explain after all. "We've all convinced ourselves – or, rather, the Christian church: those maniacs of social control who have been brainwashing us for centuries... they've convinced us – that the formula 'till death do us part' is good and natural when it obviously isn't. The traditional form of marriage has long been dead. It's no longer relevant, and it doesn't exist in nature anyway. Every other marriage ends in divorce, and that's not to say that couples who decide to stay married live happily ever after. These days, some people take the oath 'till death do us part' twice, maybe three times in their lives, without considering that it's just as silly to believe in it as it is to believe in some imaginary friend who listens to your prayers and fulfils all your wishes."

"I like your radical thinking –" Keiko smiled warmly – "I'm less pleased with your radical actions."

"It's interesting that I've obviously always considered myself to be very intelligent." Marat took another chocolate from the dish. "Twice in my life I've been asked to complete the full IQ test, clearly for a reason. I got 165 the first time round, and 140 the second. I'm close to having three degrees, and I've made a substantial profit on the financial markets. And yet sometimes, when I look back on some of my decisions, I'm ashamed of how stupid they've been, despite their not seeming that way at the time. You can't even trust your own IQ, even if it's 165! It still won't protect you from stupidity. How can that be? And why?"

"You tell me..." The veteran lawyer let Marat vent.

"It's scary, right? If I can't trust my own mind, my own sense of judgement – which is well above the average – then what can I trust? What should I lean on?"

"That's a rather serious question," said Keiko, nodding approvingly. "Here's all I can tell you. Your case, in terms of the criminal process, is actually quite straightforward. If you testify that Dimitri was the one who attacked you, then – in his defence – he will say that he knew about your decision to murder your wife, that he was sure you'd started to fulfil your intention, and all he did was use physical force to prevent the murder. Not only is this permissible by law – in some sense, it was also his duty. Of course, we'll deny and question everything he says, but nonetheless our position will be fairly weak – everything will point towards him being right. And if – God forbid – your wife corroborates his testimony, then Dimitri will be released, whereas you'll be arrested for plotting and attempting a murder. With my help you won't have to remain in prison for too long – but still, I'd wager five to seven years. Not to mention the damage to your reputation, your business, and so on."

Marat sighed. The chocolate didn't taste good. It was too generic-tasting, and lacked a character to it.

"No, here's option two. If you and your wife stick with your current testimonies – that you don't remember anything and you don't know who was in the house with you at the time, or who attacked you – there will be no direct evidence against Dimitri. He may have been there, but only after the attack, when he found you both unconscious and did the right thing by calling the ambulance. Why didn't he wait for the ambulance to arrive? Well, he got confused and scared that he'd get the blame, and the fact that he didn't offer any further aid can't really be held against him. In this scenario, he'll walk free, and everyone will continue to lead their lives as before. That would be the best outcome – from what I can see, anyway."

Marat crumpled the chocolate wrapper haphazardly and pushed it towards the first one. *It doesn't look so bad anymore,* he thought.

"Everything really depends on Dimitri. This isn't the typical dilemma for a prisoner, because every scenario would work in his favour; whereas we're only interested in the second scenario, in which he cooperates. Otherwise, the situation could get quite tough."

"Oh, Dimitri will cooperate. He's not going to start a war with me," Marat said.

"What makes you so certain? He may want to see you put behind bars, so that he can take your place next to Twinka. He saved your wife's life, they were lovers before the incident, and this could bring them even closer." The lawyer's eyes bore into Marat.

"Because Dimitri believes that cooperation is always the best option for society. Apparently that's related to game theory, which he was telling me about the other day," Marat said, though his voice didn't sound very confident.

"Hmm, I don't know." Any trace of a smile had faded from the lawyer's face. He was shaking his head. "What I do know is that people don't tend to forgive those they've betrayed or let down. Dimitri betrayed you – he deceived your friendship, and so he'll never be able to forgive you for it."

"How do you mean? I don't get it." For the first time during their conversation, Marat's interest had been piqued.

"If you've acted disgracefully towards someone – if you've hurt them, deceived them, abused their trust, cheated, humiliated, or caused suffering to them – that will make you feel pretty bad about yourself. Whether you do it consciously or not, it makes you question who you are. Are you a good person? Are you worthy of being human? These feelings will continue to gnaw at you deep inside. They are so uncomfortable, to the extent that you start thinking: *Well, how do I get rid of them?*

"Naturally, you don't want to blame yourself, so you start blaming the victim.

"It's not me who betrayed him – he was a scumbag and deserved it.

"It wasn't me who raped her – she provoked the animal inside me. I didn't actually want it. I'm not really like that.

"Some people hate their victims so much that they end up killing them. That's the only way to get rid of the blame that lives inside the victim, which you can't help but want to do as a criminal. They have to murder the victim for whatever atrocity they themselves committed, or at least pile all the blame on them. The victim provoked the action, so, technically, they deserved whatever happened to them. There's no other way: because admitting to yourself that you're a bad person – a complete moral reprobate, so despicable and pathetic – is near impossible."

"So, you're saying that Dimitri will never forgive me for his sleeping with my wife?"

"For sleeping with *his best friend's* wife, yes," the lawyer corrected him. "He'd find it extremely difficult to forgive you for it." Keiko smiled ruefully. "To justify his actions, he'd need to convince himself that you deserved it. And a judgment that rules you as the guilty party would serve as a confirmation of this, making him feel a great deal better about himself."

"But then he'd be betraying me twice. And, according to your theory, that would only make him hate me more?"

"Yeah, he'd hate himself. And you by proxy. But he won't realise that until much later."

"So, you think he's going to tell the truth?"

"I think it's a real possibility. And he'll probably embellish the truth." The lawyer's gaze was expecting affirmation from Marat.

Marat picked up another chocolate, but hesitated to unwrap it. "Okay. But, in any case, it would be his word against mine, and I'm more successful than he is. A rich man's word always carries more weight," Marat said, anxiously tapping the still-encased chocolate against the table.

"Of course – except in court," Keiko objected firmly. "Anywhere else you're absolutely right, but not in the courtroom. In fact, it's probably the opposite." Keiko watched the square in Marat's fingers.

"But I'm the victim here! He's the one who was sleeping with my wife, and he almost murdered *me*!"

"True." Keiko gave a heavy, theatrical sigh. "If you hadn't left your car by Neptune, then we could have worked this out somehow. But now, if Dimitri testifies that you were planning on murdering your wife, and your car was parked by Neptune – which indirectly corroborates his story – then things don't look so sunny for us." Keiko sighed again.

Marat tossed the chocolate back into the decorative dish, causing another square to skitter out of the container, landing on the table next to the crumpled papers.

What a mess, Marat thought to himself, annoyed.

CHAPTER 41

Help me, God! Don't leave me now. Show me the right way,
give me a sign, spark an idea within me! How should I act?
Give me wisdom, God, grant me the clarity of mind so that I
know what's right, and give me courage to act on it! Down on
his knees, with his back to the door, Dimitri was praying.

How do I avoid making a huge mistake? How should I act,
so that you don't judge me and I don't judge myself? What's
good and what's right? Marat is my friend – my best friend...
Oh, God, what should I do? Dimitri's entreaties were sincere,
passionate, desperate.

How can I be sure that I'm doing the honourable thing?
Arrogance is his biggest vice, and he became entangled in his
own philosophies, losing sight of good and evil, like all atheists
do. Forgive him for his sins, oh Lord, and save his soul! And
please give me clarity, God, so that I know what to do. Marat
has done so much for me. He's helped me a lot, and I don't wish
any harm to come to him. I'm grateful for everything he's done
for me. But will I be acting in good conscience if I don't testify
against him? And would he, without receiving his just
punishment, continue living in his delusions? If he doesn't get
his comeuppance, won't that only make his actions bolder in
future? And if I do testify against him and tell the whole truth,
will the time in prison cure him of said delusions? Would that
be the right outcome? I'm his friend and I've already betrayed
him by seducing Twinka. Oh, Lord, why have you put this heavy
decision on me? Why are you making me take on this
responsibility? I don't know what's right!

"You shall not bear false witness against your neighbour,"
that's what the eighth commandment says. But is it always
proper to give a true testimony, even if it goes against your
friend? Is the deeper meaning of this commandment to always

say good things about those who are close to you? And never, under any circumstances, talk behind their back? To always be there for your loved ones and to guard them from gossip? But does this principle apply as far as me going to prison only because I want to protect my friend from punishment? If we had committed a crime together, that might change things, but we didn't. Oh, God, give me a sign! What's the decent thing to do? What outcome would be best? Oh, Lord, grant me clarity of mind, wisdom, and strength to do what's right, in accordance with your will!

Dimitri's prayer was interrupted by the clanking of keys in the lock. He'd already become acquainted with the prison's fixed routines, which is why this noise at such a late hour surprised him. He was back in bed before the door rattled open. There was only one thought flashing through his mind: had God really heard his prayer, and delivered the sign he'd been asking for?

"Good evening." The chief inspector peered through the door with a smirk on his face. The door shut behind him. "I was just on my way home, but I thought I'd drop by and see how you're settling in," Draco said, as though his office was here, in the prison.

Dimitri sat up but didn't reply, trying to work out what was going on. He had asked God to send him a sign; he had asked Him to aid his understanding, to know what path he should take – and suddenly, out of the blue, the chief inspector was here. Was that just a coincidence? How should he interpret this?

Draco sat down on the bed opposite Dimitri's. Despite the hot weather, the chief inspector was wearing a suit – albeit with the tie missing – while Dimitri had nothing but his underwear on. This underlined the huge difference in status between them.

"So, then," Draco was looking directly at Dimitri. "How do you feel? Have you started settling in? Are you used to it yet?"

Dimitri didn't feel like he should respond. His provocative gaze bore into the chief inspector, though he was embarrassed by his nakedness and his grimy, sweaty underwear. When Dimitri was arrested, it hadn't even occurred to him to bring a fresh pair.

"Did you know that the punishment for committing grievous bodily harm could be up to six years? Although it's very likely that the court will classify it as an attempted murder case, in which case the sentence will be tougher." Uttered in Draco's tiny voice, the threat sounded particularly revolting. "Surely, you already know that your lover's husband has spent two weeks in a coma, then lost sight in one of his eyes and hearing in one of his ears after a prolonged process of recovery? So, you see, the consequences of your crime are very serious indeed. I think you punched your lover only for the sake of appearances – I reckon she's just playing along, it's quite easy to fake that kind of a trauma."

Dimitri was struggling not to react. "Why have you come?" he asked, aggrieved.

"Because I know you're innocent," Draco said.

"Well, if you already know that –" Dimitri sounded surprised – "then what am I doing here?"

"Oh, no, don't blame me," Draco said innocently. "You did this to yourself. If you had told me everything right from the start, exactly as it happened, there would be no need to arrest you. But you didn't, did you? So, what was I supposed to do? Those are the rules of the game, I'm afraid."

"And what sort of a game is this then?" Dimitri was livid. "You know that I'm innocent but you're still going to accuse me and let me go on trial?"

"With all due respect, it's totally up to you," Draco gestured helplessly with his arms. "If you tell me everything, exactly as it happened, we'll part on friendly terms and I'll nail the guilty party – the one who mysteriously appeared in his own house wearing gloves, having secured himself an alibi ahead of time."

"You didn't answer my question." Dimitri wasn't letting up. "If you don't get any solid evidence against the guilty party, then you'll just go ahead and accuse me. You'd pursue an innocent man because I refuse to cooperate. How long did you say – seven years? You'd put me in prison for seven years, knowing full well that I'm innocent. Does that sound right to you?"

"Right and wrong – it's all very complex. As they say, life keeps us in check, so we don't get too big for our britches. Okay? So, even though I agree with you in principle – it wouldn't feel right if you, as an innocent man, had to spend the next seven years behind bars – I still won't be able to prevent this injustice from happening, unless you help me out. Basically, my hands are tied." Draco shrugged his shoulders, his arms once more issuing a gesture of helplessness.

"This is blackmail," Dimitri objected, "pure blackmail!"

"Oh, God forbid, who said anything about blackmail?" Draco parroted Marat's dismissive hand-wave – he seemed to be enjoying the conversation. "I'm just trying to explain how the system works."

"Well, don't blame *life* for throwing problems our way," said Dimitri, "it's *people*, like me and like you, who are responsible when things go wrong. *We* are the ones who take the wrong actions, making it look like there's something wrong with life." Dimitri had changed the tone of their conversation – he hoped that Draco would listen to him and realise his mistake.

"Well, why don't you do something about it then?" Draco raised his voice suddenly. He was almost shouting – as much as his tiny voice permitted him. "Do the right thing already, for fuck's sake! Give your testimony, tell the whole truth, help the investigation, so that we can find out what actually happened!

Help the system things right! Do it! Just do the honourable thing! Am I really asking too much?! But you're not listening to me, are you? So, what do you expect?" Draco took a deep breath and continued, this time more calmly:

"So, you want other people to do the right thing? Meanwhile you can do whatever you want; whatever's easiest and most convenient. Now, does that sound right to you?"

Dimiri lay idback down and stayed silent.

"Okay, fine. I'm leaving already. I can see I'm not a welcome guest." Draco had simmered down. "But if you carry on like this, then you'll soon realise what a delight any unexpected guest can be, when you're in prison. Mark my words – not even a year will go by before you're happy to see whoever visits you, even if it's me. But why should I come and see you? And who else is going to come? Do you think Twinka will come? Or Marat? Yeah, well, you can hope all you like, it's no skin off my nose," Draco said, knocking on the door and waiting to be released. "Goodnight, Dimitri."

Dimitri turned to face the wall, determined to finish what he'd started.

Twinka, Dimitri had scraped next to where someone had inscribed tallies marking the days – every four vertical bars crossed through by a diagonal line.

It was unbearably hot in the cell and constant sweating had made Dimitri's skin clammy. He felt dirty, lonely, and utterly pathetic. He finally realised why the newspaper scraps had been stuck to the lamp in the ceiling. The lights never went out in this prison.

PART 4.
Bad Cards

CHAPTER 42

"So, you've decided to testify then?" Chief inspector Draco looked extremely smug – his mood appeared almost festive.

"Yeah," Dimitri replied, looking extremely serious and focused.

"Great. Let's get right to it then, shall we? Start from the top. And, if anything is unclear, I'll jot it down and ask you to clarify, once you're finished."

"Earlier in spring this year," Dimitri started, "over the course of several conversations, Marat revealed his plan to kill his wife Twinka. Our first conversation took place on the Wednesday just before Easter. At that point, he'd already considered several ways he could commit the murder, like lethal poisons and toxic mushrooms. At first, I didn't think anything of it. But over time my suspicions grew stronger, especially after his fiftieth birthday, when Marat talked a lot about his desire to start a new life.

"That's when I decided to warn Twinka. I called her and said that we urgently needed to meet and talk. Twinka agreed to this, and we happened to meet on the same day on which Marat decided to realise his plan and murder his wife. We'd arranged the meeting for during the daytime, as Marat was usually out then. I arrived at their house and we started talking in the small guest room – the one that's closest to the main entrance. I hadn't quite managed to explain my reasons for coming over to Twinka yet. She got up and went into the kitchen to get something. That's when I suddenly noticed Marat, standing behind her. He was wearing gloves, holding an empty bottle in his hand, and it looked like he was about to strike her on the head with it. There was distance of about four, maybe five metres between us. Knowing Marat's plan and that he was about to kill Twinka, I – I genuinely don't know how, but somehow – in one leap managed to grab an empty bottle from the coffee table next to us, land by Marat's side and hit him over the head with that. I landed the blow at literally the same time Marat's landed his – or maybe a hundredth of a second before, because his blow had lost its power and it looked like he was just gently placing the bottle on Twinka's forehead. Then Twinka fainted – not so much from the impact as from the shock, I think – although I suppose even a falling bottle can cause quite a lot of damage. Anyway, the fact is, they were both unconscious.

"I got confused, I didn't know what to do. I decided to call the ambulance from Twinka's mobile and then, having ensured that help was on its way, I left. There was nothing more I could have done to help them."

Dimitri had clearly considered what he was going to say, and his testimony sounded like a well-rehearsed speech.

"It wasn't my intention to harm anyone. I acted out of pure instinct, in the only way I thought possible, to prevent Twinka's murder. I didn't have time to consider my options or what I should do – I used whatever was at hand to prevent a murder from being committed," Dimitri added to his speech.

"Hmm... I see, I see," Draco muttered under his nose. "So, it was around Easter that Marat revealed his plan to kill his wife to you. Why did you wait several months before you warned Twinka?"

"Well, at first, I didn't take it seriously. I didn't believe that anyone was in any real danger. People come up with all sorts of fantasies all the time."

"But then, later on, you began to suspect that there was, in fact, some real danger involved?"

"Yes."

"So, why didn't you go to the police at that point?"

"Well," Dimitri was confounded. "I wanted to discuss it with Twinka first, as I still wasn't one hundred percent sure. She knew Marat better than anyone – I mean, she was his wife, so I figured I'd decide what steps to take after I had a chance to talk with her."

"I see..." Draco was chewing a pen, away with his thoughts for a moment. "Tell me more about your relationship with Marat."

"We're very good acquaintances. He wanted to support my YouTube channel; that's how we met."

"Ac-quain-tan-ces," Draco repeated slowly, writing the word down. "And how would you describe your relationship with Twinka?"

Dimitri started to fidget. He'd known that this question was coming; he was expecting it; he knew that he wouldn't be able to hide the truth from the chief inspector. But still, he would have rather avoided the subject altogether.

"We had a... an intimate relationship," Dimitri forced himself to answer, in as neutral a tone as he could muster.

"In-ti-mate," Draco repeated, as he committed the word to paper. "And how long have you been having this 'intimate relationship' with Twinka?"

"About a year."

"One year..." Draco continued to scribble. "And, tell me, how intense was this 'intimate relationship'? How often did you see each other?"

"Twice a week usually."

"And is it possible that Marat could have found out about your relationship?"

"I doubt it. I don't think anything would have made him suspicious, since we were always very careful. Even if he'd followed her, all he would have seen was Twinka entering an underground car park of a block of flats every now and then.

And I always made sure to arrive early or leave late: usually doing so on foot, and using one of the other exits. So, no, I don't think he knew."

"Right." Draco carefully wrote it all down. "And do you have any idea why Marat wanted to kill his wife? What was his reasoning?"

Dimitri's relief was palpable – the tough part was over. He could talk about Marat till the cows came home.

"Marat believed... believes," Dimitri corrected himself, "that divorce is very complicated. It's traumatic for the children, it's extremely painful for the wife, and it's the source of constant guilt for the husband. Everyone who goes through divorce has to live with these uncomfortable feelings for the rest of their lives. He also believes that there's nothing left for a woman who's past forty, except for loneliness, menopause, depression and alcoholism. Well, at least that's what he thought... *thinks*... about Twinka. He believes that a woman turning forty is the same as a man turning eighty. And, according to him, he'd be saving Twinka from all the suffering that comes with a divorce, and the miserable life that she'd inevitably endure. He believed that it would be best for their daughter, too – that he'd be saving her from getting traumatised by her parents' divorce; while also saving himself from perpetual guilt, thinking that he was the cause of everything. According to his logic, everyone would be gaining something from Twinka's death, as though it were a good thing overall. He thought of it like euthanasia."

"And murdering his wife didn't seem to stir any feelings of guilt for him?" Draco asked, sarcastically.

"No. He believed that death would be more convenient for her."

"Her own death would be more convenient for her..." Draco looked incredibly smug as he jotted this down. "Were those his actual words?"

"Yes, they were. And it really pissed him off when she left the corks on the corkscrews."

"Oh? Left the corks?"

"Yeah – he said how much he hated when she opened a bottle of wine, removed the cork and left it on the corkscrew."

"Right. I see. She wouldn't remove the corks..." Draco scribed. "Well, it all seems pretty straightforward to me –" he handed Dimitri his testimony for signature – "I won't keep you any longer, you're free to go," he said. "Go home, take a nice, long bath and get some rest. If I think of anything else, I'll be in touch."

CHAPTER 43

"It sounds like you and Marat have fundamentally different ideas about life: did that not cause any problems between you until now?" Anna had clearly considered what Twinka had told her during their last session, and wanted to unpack the subject further.

"No, not really, to be honest." The window facing the courtyard was open again, and Anna's office was filled with the lovely aromas of damp soil and tomato plants, as well as other garden scents that Twinka couldn't quite place. Twinka filled her lungs with the fresh air then exhaled with a heavy sigh, sinking deeper into the soft armchair. She felt so free and safe here.

"An aggressive atheist and a true believer isn't your typical couple..."

"I don't know." Twinka shrugged. "I think it's because, deep down, any atheist is seeking God. They've chosen a different path, but the end goal is the same. Does that make sense?"

Anna seemed intrigued by the discussion, though she disagreed. "From an outsider's perspective," she objected, "it may seem that Marat doesn't only not believe in God and shows no inclination to find a path towards him, but that he feels like God himself, or aspires to be god-like. He has a god complex. He believes that if he wasn't constrained by society, his family and societal norms, he could fully actualise himself and become like God. He'd have carte blanche to do whatever he wanted. And we already know that he thinks he has the right to decide who lives and who dies."

"That's true, but if someone is as preoccupied with God as Marat is – I mean, he studies and talks about the subject constantly – then, as you say, shouldn't we look for the root cause?" Twinka didn't want to argue, but she did want to explain her perspective.

"And what do you think is the root cause?"

"I don't think Marat is a true atheist, like those who believe that human DNA just happened by chance. As in – a hurricane is raging through a prehistoric jungle, and the next thing you know, Shakespeare's complete leatherbound works are lined up on top of an oak table. What are the chances of that happening? I don't think anyone could believe in such happenstance, not even Marat. The thing he mostly objects to is the Bible."

"As in he doesn't believe in Jesus?"

"Yeah, pretty much. As long as you don't get into arguments with him about what's in the Bible and you don't insist that everything in there should be taken literally, our views aren't all that different."

"So, you found a shared position you could both agree on – is that what you mean?"

"Well, not quite... I think over time the issue became more significant. At first, it felt like an intriguing intellectual frontier for both of us. I found his perspective genuinely fascinating, and took on board everything he said. And vice versa. It was always an engaging conversation. But that changed as time went on."

"And what do you think changed?"

"Probably the same thing I mentioned before: he lost interest in me. At times I've even felt like he gets annoyed by my perspective."

Anna didn't respond, tacitly encouraging Twinka to continue.

"For me, it's like this – I can genuinely feel God's presence all around me. I can feel Him physically, and I can see His existence in my life. But for Marat, God is like an intellectual quest: a cultural and anthropological phenomena; anything but reality. He'd never understand what it's like to feel God as ever-present and real. Sometimes I've wondered whether he's felt jealous or angry that God is so present in my life but not in his," Twinka said, with confidence and passion. "So, we didn't find a shared viewpoint. It was actually the opposite – we realised our perspectives were far more polarised than Marat had thought. For example, I'm not interested in studying the Bible. I don't care about the details, the different interpretations. I don't know which version is right, or what the historical inaccuracies might be, or why the Old Testament is full of stories that seem to go against Christian morals. But that doesn't change anything for me. God is still real. God is just as real as the two of us sitting here. But I don't know how I could ever convince someone who doesn't feel the same way. And I've never bothered to try."

"Okay, tell me more. So, the feeling that God is as real as you and me, and that He's present in your life – have you always had that feeling, or did it develop at a certain point in time?"

"I think it probably happened slowly, gradually. In fact, it was largely thanks to Marat because he made me think about it a lot more. And there was this one time... Marat and I had just got together; it was at the very start of our relationship – maybe two or three months in. We'd driven to this cabin in the woods for a holiday. It was incredibly romantic: we spent most of the time in bed, of course. It was in the afternoon; we must have fallen asleep. I woke up and Marat was lying next to me. The curtain had been left ajar and this bright, slanting afternoon sun was flowing into the room through the slit. I felt so happy, fulfilled, and at peace... And then, suddenly, I saw God sat on the windowsill, dangling his legs and smiling."

"What do you mean? God was just sat there?!" Anna had been incapable of hiding her astonishment. "Like an old man with a beard?"

"No, more like a child."

"Like a child?"

"Yeah, like a child, only bigger. Like angels in paintings: only a bit bigger, and without those silly wings."

"And how do you know it was God?"

"Because it was Him, and it wasn't the only time it's happened. Usually I can only feel Him, I can't always see Him. And I've no doubt that He was there when Marat attacked me. Of course, I've never told Marat: he'd just say I dreamt it, or I was hallucinating – like when you're in that weird mental state between sleep and wake. But this was different. He really was there. I'd even go as far as to say that we made contact; I think He allowed me to see Him. But it doesn't matter, because even if that hadn't happened, I can still feel His presence in my life."

"That reminds me of stories about guardian angels." Anna was thinking out loud.

"But they're all just words," said Twinka, "and it's hard to describe God in words. Any description will be incomplete and incorrect. Which is why people like Marat, who have a very rational mind, can't understand it. All they see are inconsistencies in the description, so they conclude that the thing being described must also be incomplete. But those are two separate things."

"The map is not the territory," Anna said, without thinking.

"What did you say?" Twinka didn't understand.

"I mean there's a lot of truth in what you said, and I can see why Marat fell in love with you – you were definitely an intellectual challenge for him, an equal in conversation, yet one with a completely different perspective and outlook on life. He probably found it very exciting to be with you."

"He did," Twinka confirmed sadly.

CHAPTER 44

"A love triangle... what a cliché – the most boring cliché of all," Marat said, pacing back and forth by the large table in the conference room. "Your wife and your best friend. A stab in the back. I guess no one ever expects it – no one thinks it could happen to them." It looked like Marat was talking to himself, making no attempt to hide the venom that was growing every day.

It was important that they meet. They were all adults, and smart ones at that, and so they should be able to sit down at the same table and, looking one another in the eye, talk through what had happened. And, more importantly, what would happen going forward. Only by doing so could they hope to turn the past into something they may just about be able to live with.

Marat had suggested the meeting. And, with some hesitation, Dimitri and Twinka had eventually both agreed to come. Dimitri's being released from custody and Marat's discharging himself from hospital had made it possible.

They arranged to meet on neutral territory, and chose to convene at the bank, where they were now sat by the large table in the swanky conference room. The mood was tense – everyone felt uncomfortable. Marat was standing while Dimitri and Twinka sat opposite one another, avoiding locking eyes while in Marat's crosshairs.

"Well, what more can be said? What can be done here?" Marat had calmed down,now and made a gesture to minute how he'd understood that there was no point in getting angry. "We can't have a third wheel, can we? One of us has to leave. Right, Dimitri?" Marat asked.

Dimitri finally lifted his gaze and spoke up. "You know what your problem is? In prison, I was thinking a lot about what Tsimber said when I bought you that sculpture. You chose murder, even though the only honest and ethical path available to you was sacrifice."

"Oh, yeah? How very interesting. And, obviously, you did the right thing and chose a sacrifice – you sacrificed our friendship."

"I'm not saying that I did the right thing. But just because we've made mistakes in the past doesn't mean that we can't make different choices going forward, and become better people. Think about it – what if it's the people who have made the biggest mistakes who have the most potential to become truly exemplary?"

"How wonderful!" Marat said, jeering. "I mean, why don't we just all become better people, forgive each other and just carry on, on good terms?"

"Marat, you need to realise that you can only draw water from two streams: you can either take something that's missing from others, or take it from yourself. To steal or to sacrifice – those are the two choices available to us. Say, if you didn't have enough money, then you could either steal it from someone else, or sacrifice your own time, effort and energy to get it. Those are two different outlooks on life. It's like a law – if you want to obtain something precious in life, you need to sacrifice something you already have that's precious to you. People who don't have any resources, or those who aren't capable of sacrificing anything – those are the people who choose to steal and murder."

"Oh, spare me your Christian nonsense, please! Sacrifice is the most revolting of all murders. Sacrifice involves killing the scapegoat. It's a collective act to murder an innocent soul, to stun the crowd into abstaining from killing, at least for a while. It's the most primitive social engineering. So, stop with the sermon and answer my question: we can't have a third wheel, can we?"

"Yeah, I completely agree." Dimitri was looking directly into Marat's eyes now. "You're absolutely right – one of us is a third wheel. And it's obvious that you're the one who should leave, and let me and Twinka be together."

"Ha! Is that what you think?" Marat asked, in mock astonishment.

"Yeah. You're the one who wanted to murder Twinka. Because, apparently, she'd be better off dead. You're the one who thinks there's nothing good ahead of her. You no longer wanted her around, so it's pretty obvious to me that if anyone should leave, it's you. You're the one who wanted to get rid of her. Twinka will stay with me."

Marat didn't say anything. He put his hands on the table, leaned in towards Twinka, and scrutinised her with his gaze.

Twinka continued to look at the floor, and didn't say a word. Her hands fidgeted anxiously under the table, her fingers fiddling with the clasp of the handbag on her lap.

"Well, then..." It sounded like Marat had made a decision. "Personally, I think we've been acting out this melodrama for too long, and I think it probably is my time to leave. That seems like the right thing to do. It's never too late to start a new life; not even the day before death, right?"

Finally, Twinka lifted her gaze and looked at Marat, as though asking him whether he really meant it. For a while they just stared at one another.

"There's just one small problem," said Marat, breaking the silence. His tone was menacing. "The problem is that you both betrayed me. You betrayed my trust, my friendship, and my love. You: the two people closest to me. I've never let anyone closer. I always treated you as well as I possibly could, and both of you—"

"But Marat—" interrupted Twinka.

Marat didn't let her finish. He pulled out a sizable revolver – it was heavy, cool, and fit perfectly in his grip. He pointed the gun at Twinka.

"...you're the one who left me, Marat," was all that Twinka managed to say before he sent several bullets in her direction. Twinka fell, wounded.

Dimitri went for Marat. Chairs were toppled, and you could hear Twinka's moans, but this time Marat was ready. He was faster than Dimitri, sending the bullet right into his friend's chest. "Committing adultery is the only sin that's mentioned twice in the ten commandments! Twice, you pathetic Christians! It's forbidden to covet your friend's wife, let alone sleep with her! Where's your piety now – where's your love of Christ, your morality?" he shouted, sending another bullet towards Dimitri, this time aimed at his forehead. It felt good. "The Old Testament commands stoning people like you – it's *moral* to stone people like you, it's written in God's own law, it's a natural law – the oldest of all laws! To kill your cuckhold wife and your best friend who's slept with her. Not only is that permitted in the Bible – it's actually my duty, lest the world sink into total chaos and everyone starts doing whatever the hell they want! This is what all natural laws are built on – it's the foundation! You both deserve to die!" Marat walked up to Twinka and their eyes met. Twinka, gravely injured, knew what was coming and had reconciled herself to it – there was no more fear in her eyes. Marat sent a bullet straight through her forehead, then walked up to the unconscious Dimitri, into whose chest he dispatched another. It felt so good...

That's when Marat woke up. The wonderful feeling was quickly replaced by the solemn realisation that real life was far more complicated.

Yes, they both deserved to die – especially Dimitri – he had no doubt about that. In fact, would Marat even be able to live with himself, if he didn't kill Dimitri? So, the real question wasn't about forgiveness. There was absolutely no way of forgiving a betrayal on this scale. Even if he wanted to, it was literally impossible. The question was: will he be able to carry on living without avenging this perfidy, this hurt and humiliation, with blood? Would anyone on this earth be capable of letting it go? If so, how did they do it? He didn't feel the same level of hatred towards Twinka. If she'd slept with someone other than Dimitri, he may have even been able to forgive her. After all, Twinka was right – he had neglected her.

But there was no excuse for Dimitri.

Marat put some coffee beans in the grinder, switched it on and watched – or rather, listened – as the blade milled them.

How could anyone live with this trauma: your best friend – the person you've trusted more than anyone else, whom you've helped in every possible way – and your wife; carrying on behind your back, like you're some kind of idiot...

How do I live with this? There really are only two paths – sacrifice or murder, Marat thought to himself. *How will I live, knowing that he's close by? I'll wonder how he's doing; I'll stalk him; I'll wait for something bad to happen to him; I'll take every opportunity to sabotage him; and it will go on like that for years, probably for the rest of my days. My entire life will be poisoned by this hatred. Evil and insistent, it will never quieten, unable to act out its desire for revenge. No one can live like that. But if I tried to accept it, to live with it and forgive – that would mean breaking, castrating, torturing, and sacrificing myself. And all in the name of what? Why? To stop myself from murdering someone?* Marat's head was hurting. *Killing someone is always an option – it always has been. The Old Testament instructs people to kill both guilty parties in this scenario, which is obviously the right thing to do. It's the only proper outcome, all options considered.*

Yes, maybe killing Twinka wasn't the smartest idea, especially doing it myself. But now, to stop myself from killing Dimitri – that would, once again, be the wrong action, wouldn't it? If I can't kill Dimitri, then I have to kill myself. And it would be far better to sacrifice myself than live with this outcome.

Marat poured some hot water over eight teaspoons of freshly ground coffee in a sizeable mug.

Is it even possible to forgive? What's the right action here? Should I call Dimitri and say: "Listen, it was stupid of you, but I forgive you. I hope you live happily ever after, and may everything work out in your favour." What, just like that?

His head was hurting unbearably now. Marat found his tablets and returned to the dark bedroom. Darkness was his only friend – it helped ease the pain. Taking small sips, he slowly washed the tablets down with the coffee.

CHAPTER 45

It was Friday. Shortly after one p.m. a police car parked up outside Marat's townhouse, while another arrived at his Button Street residence. Chief inspector Draco approached the townhouse, followed by the plain-clothed subordinate who had been at the hospital yet had never said his name, as well as four uniformed police officers.

Marat understood everything immediately. Dimitri had told the truth. *Damn it. Fuck! May he burn in hell, the bastard! First, he sleeps with my wife, then he almost kills me, and then he gives me up to the police. What a wonderful friend! A 'true friend'!*

Marat was suddenly overcome by weakness. He had still harboured hope that Dimitri wouldn't cross this final boundary. "Fuck, fuck, fuck. I've been a complete idiot, expecting him not to. How could I make such a huge mistake?" A multitude of uncomfortable questions exploded in Marat's mind, as though there'd been a shoot-out in his head.

"Hi, hello," Draco, unable to conceal his pleasure, was literally rubbing his hands with glee. More than ever before, he reminded Marat of a little, gnawing rat. He turned towards Marat. "It's you we've come to collect this time," he said, "definitely you. You see, we just can't wait any longer."

"What do you mean, you can't wait any longer?" Marat repeated.

"Oh, you know – I told you the other day; I enjoy when a criminal confesses, but sometimes the evidence is so overwhelming that the prosecution wouldn't see any cause for delay. So, you see, you have to come with us now."

"If I must, I will." Marat wasn't going to demean himself in front of these pathetic little people. He didn't feel any self-pity, fear, or regret – the only thing he could feel was an overwhelming, all-encompassing, burning hatred towards Dimitri.

The chief inspector allowed Marat to call Keiko before he seized his phone.

Consumed by thoughts of Dimitri, Marat didn't even notice that the police car he wasn't travelling back to the station in – the one that was carrying Draco, his inspector and two of the uniformed officers – wasn't itself heading to the police station, but in a completely different direction.

Meanwhile, in the house on Button Street, Twinka was preparing to drive to Ronia's school. Lessons finished at three-thirty p.m., and Twinka liked to arrive just after three, so that she would be closer to the school gate in the row of other parents' cars. She had been planning to stop at the butcher's shop on her way over, and so when Draco arrived with his three companions – two of whom were dressed in police uniform – she was just about to leave the house. Twinka had no idea that Draco had engineered all this so that he could surprise her at this exact moment.

"Hi," Draco greeted her. This time, his tone was neither friendly nor polite. He didn't even wait for an invitation to come in – he just entered, as though Twinka's only task was to hold the door open.

"I have a few questions for you," he told her.

She looked at her watch, stunned by the behaviour of the police officers. "I'm actually just on my way to collect my daughter from school, so I haven't got much time."

"That's okay, don't worry," Draco said. "Like I said, I only have a few questions for you. All you need to do is tell me the truth, and you'll make it to school in time. And even if you don't, that's fine, because I already notified social services to go and collect Ronia. I don't know if you know, but we have this protocol in our country whereby a child is placed in a crisis centre while their parents are being detained or arrested – so you've got absolutely nothing to worry about."

A horrified Twinka's eyes grew large as saucers. "What?!" This may have been the first time in her life in which any trace of a smile and/or warmth completely disappeared from her face. "What did you say?? What did you just say?!?"

"I suggest that you listen very carefully to what I have to say." Draco's tone was icy but calm. "Come, let's sit down."

Draco's colleague touched Twinka's elbow, as though wanting to chaperone her, but she snatched her arm back and perched on the living room sofa next to the chief inspector.

"Don't worry, everything is actually quite simple. I literally only have a few questions. And it's very important that you tell me the truth, not your usual phoney tales about memory loss. Dimitri has already revealed everything anyway – we know all about your relationship. We know that it's been going on for the past year, and we know what happened on that day. We know absolutely everything –" Draco was emphasizing his every word – "but, for the sake of proper process, I need your testimony as well. If you continue to lie and mislead the investigation, then I'll be forced to take appropriate action, which, unfortunately, means that you'll likely miss the school run. And so will your husband – in fact he won't be able to do the school run for a while, as he's just been arrested. Now, you wouldn't want to delay the investigation by giving a false testimony, would you?"

Twinka didn't answer – she was trying to comprehend everything that was happening. The fact that a figure in public office was openly threatening to kidnap her child and place her in some crisis centre seemed completely preposterous and mind-boggling to her. But what if it was true? *Oh, God...* Twinka felt like she couldn't breathe. What should she do now? If Marat was here, he wouldn't let anything happen to her, of course. *Keiko!* She would ring Keiko! Twinka started scrambling around for her phone.

Draco watched on with a healthy dose of arrogance and curiosity.

Twinka didn't know that Keiko was unavailable – he was already with Marat in the interview room, and hadn't been allowed to take his phone in with him. All she heard was the perpetual ringing on the line.

"Right, let's get straight to it then, shall we?" said Draco with an air of self-satisfaction, having loitered with an arrogant smirk as he waited for Twinka to put down the phone. "I thought you said you were in a hurry."

"Well, if you already know everything, then what could you possibly want from me?" Twinka didn't understand. She felt desperate.

"Only your honest, genuine testimony, nothing more. So, let's not waste any more time." Draco placed a recorder on the table. "Tell me what happened on the day of the attack. Start from the moment of Dimitri's arrival."

Twinka was finding it hard to focus.

What the hell is going on? How can they just do this?!

"Did you understand my question?" Draco's tone was threatening.

"Yes... Dimitri called me and said that he wanted to meet up – as soon as possible. And so I said he should come over," Twinka answered, almost absentmindedly.

"Okay, and what happened next?" Draco urged Twinka to continue, while his athletically built subordinate recorded Twinka's answers on the interrogation form. He had already filled out Twinka's name, surname and other details ahead of time.

"Next," Twinka tried to pull herself together.

Did they say that Dimitri had told them everything?!

Draco looked at his watch demonstratively. "Perhaps you'll find it easier to answer these questions at the police station."

"No, wait. Dimitri and I... we were lovers," Twinka said, overcoming herself.

The plainclothes inspector diligently transcribed her answer.

"Yeah, we knew that already – we're more interested in finding out exactly what happened after Dimitri arrived," continued Draco insistently.

Twinka had hoped her confession would end this horrid attack, but it hadn't.

"We started to kiss," she said. She hated this chief inspector, this whole situation. She felt humiliated. She wanted to cry, run, disappear.

"Please go on," Draco said in a cold tone.

"I went to the kitchen and suddenly Marat was behind me – he wanted to hit me."

"And then?"

"Dimitri saw it and attacked Marat. That's it." Tears were forming in Twinka's eyes, but she pulled herself together.

"How long were you kissing Dimitri before you went into the kitchen?"

"Oh, I don't know..." Twinka thought she would suffocate from the humiliation. A large swig of cognac would come in handy right now.

"Was it just kissing?" Draco continued his cold, hard line of interrogation. "Or something more?"

"Something more," Twinka replied. She wanted this to stop.

"Were you having sex with Dimitri at the time of Marat's arrival?"

"No, we were just kissing." Twinka couldn't believe the audacity of this rat-like man.

"So, you had your clothes on – were any parts of your body naked?"

"We were just kissing, but Dimitri can be very passionate, so he was kissing my lips, face, neck – that's all." Twinka couldn't understand why all these details were required – why were they trying to humiliate her like this?

"Tell me, did Dimitri tell you about Marat's plan to kill you?"

"No – he told me about it afterwards, much later."

"What exactly did he tell you?"

"He said that Marat had told him a while before Easter that he wanted to kill me; that getting a divorce would be a huge mess and that there was nothing positive ahead of me anyway; that he couldn't bear how I always leave corks on corkscrews; and that he'd have a better relationship with Ronia, if I wasn't in the picture."

"See, that wasn't all that difficult, was it?" Draco was now marginally more polite. "That's it, that's all from me today. We'll definitely have some follow-up questions, but they're not urgent, and I don't want to keep you any longer. Just a few signatures here and we're done. See, you'll get where you need to be on time."

No one in Twinka's life had ever treated her with such inferiority or contempt, or used their position of power to talk down to her to such an extent. Nowhere close to it. She had never felt so humiliated by anyone in her life – not to mention that no one had ever threatened her or blackmailed her like this. She had never felt so helpless and powerless either. Twinka felt like she'd been violated, ridiculed, and disgraced. She signed her witness statement.

Having shut the door behind the police officers, Twinka stood pressed against the door for some time. Then she sunk to her knees. She noticed that the officers had dirtied the floor by keeping their shoes on.

"God, please, give me strength! Please, I need strength, hallowed be thy name, thy Kingdom come, thy will be done, as on Earth as it is in Heaven, and forgive me my trespasses as I forgive those who trespass against me. God, give me strength, oh Lord, please, give me strength!"

After a moment, and having calmed down a little, Twinka rose and went into the kitchen. Usually she abstained from drinking before Ronia came home from school, but today she really needed some cognac to pull herself together.

CHAPTER 46

Marat didn't know it, but they'd put him in the same short-term detention cell in which Dimitri had spent the previous few nights. The cell reminded Marat of a concrete coffin. The walls were a depressing shade of grey-blue, and it reeked of dirt, urine, chlorine, as well as something disgusting that he couldn't quite place.

He tried to remember all the good things he'd done for Dimitri. How he'd helped him. And it was a long list. How anyone could act like that bastard had was beyond him. And why had the police taken Marat's watch? Why couldn't you have a watch in prison? *How many hours have gone by?* he thought constantly. *How long have I been here?*

"What time is it?" Marat shouted, kicking the door. "What time is it?"

"Shut up," someone answered in a tired, firm voice.

Right. He had to calm down, or else he'd lose his sanity. There was no point in getting frantic – Marat understood that too. He got up on the table to look outside the window, but in doing so bashed his head against the ceiling. Then he had to bend over uncomfortably, so as not to fall off the small table and still be able to look outside. There was a flyover in the distance. Judging by the intensity of the traffic, Marat tried to work out what time of day it might be. It was still light outside, but it was summer, and it remained light for a long time in those months, so he couldn't tell anything from that. The traffic jams seemed to have ceased, so it could be seven or eight in the evening, maybe nine... No, it was best to think about something else. He got down from the table.

Perhaps I should meditate? It's a shame I didn't learn meditation when I still had the chance, he thought. He remembered reading somewhere or hearing from someone that it was important to follow your breath when meditating. He sat down on the bed with his back against the wall. He couldn't put his legs in the lotus position, though he could easily sit with his knees bent and legs crossing one another. He closed his eyes and tried to inhale slowly, focusing all his attention on his breathing.

No, there was no point. He felt ridiculous. How could he meditate when there were all these noises coming from the corridor beyond his cell? Doors were being opened and closed with a metallic clanking; people were walking about; you could hear fragments of conversation. Marat couldn't ignore it, he couldn't relax and not let it inside him, although even the short moment of conscious breathing had seemed to help a little. Marat felt calmer. He should sleep, he thought – but how? There was no pillow, and the light was still on. Marat undressed, then used the blanket he'd been given as a bedsheet, laying it down underneath him (he didn't want to sleep naked on this disgusting mattress). He put his trousers under his head as an improvised pillow, but the bright light was disturbing him, so he wrapped his shirt around his head. This helped block out the light a little. Marat curled into a ball, folded the edge of the blanket over his feet, and somehow managed to fall asleep.

Marat dreamt that he was in a park. The linden trees were giving off a wonderful aroma, grey concrete paths snaked around him, and a little further along there was a pond. Marat observed himself, as if from a distance. He was wearing a stylish Savile Row suit jacket with just a vest underneath.

Marat heard two elderly women arguing immediately after passing him.

"He's German."

"No, he must be English!"

Raskolnikov was sat on another bench, and he and Marat exchanged venomous looks. Raja was in the park, too – he'd taken a small elephant with a golden embroidered blanket on its back out for a walk. He and Marat greeted one another from a distance, before Marat then spotted Dimitri: walking along the path, swaying a little, setting his feet a little wider than everyone else. That's how Greco-Roman wrestlers tended to walk. You could tell it was him from a mile off. But Dimitri turned into a side road, so their paths didn't cross.

"Oh, why – why did you do it?! Everything was so good! We were best friends! Why did you have to do it?!" Marat shouted after him – yet no sound came out, and so he concluded they must have just been his thoughts.

Marat woke up. Only now did he notice the clumsy, fresh scraping on the wall just above his eye level. For a moment, he couldn't believe what he was seeing – he was staring at it, almost in disbelief; even tracing it with his fingers to check it was really there.

Twinka, I love you, the writing said.

CHAPTER 47

"In two days' time you'll be transported from this pre-trial detention cell to a larger prison unit where they house anyone who's detained for a longer period of time," Keiko said. The lawyer was wearing an expensive suit with an accompanying neckerchief. Marat had a tracksuit on.

The lawyer's visits were the only moments Marat looked forward to – the only times that felt like something remotely resembling normality and whom he'd been in his life prior to then. The old sage Keiko was the only person who cared for Marat; and Keiko did so in a composed, professional manner, with no trace of pity nor judgement.

"My people met with the prison's management team – we have our contacts there – and we agreed to arrange a good non-smokers' cell for you. You'll have two cellmates: they're nice, intelligent people. One of them has been sentenced for money laundering; the other for rape, though I think he's not actually the culprit – the case looks suspicious, I think they're going to review it. Anyhow, they're non-violent and they don't have any mental health problems. Those are two of the biggest no-nos in terms of cellmates. Just one of these elements can make your life a living hell, with the worst-case being when you have someone who's violent *and* suffering from psychosis or schizophrenia. But we'll do everything we can to protect you. Your cellmates are well educated, and I think you'll have a lot in common with them."

"I want to be alone. Can't you do something, so I'm by myself?" Marat didn't believe he'd find anything in common with these two people.

"I can, but I really don't recommend it," the lawyer said confidently, with a hint of somebody in-the-know. "Time will go much faster when you're with others, and there will be a better chance of you maintaining your mental health: not sinking into depression and so on. Bad cellmates can turn your life into a living nightmare, but if you happen to come across good folk it can really help."

"I can't imagine how I'm going to survive five years. I'm terrified that this will be too much for me."

"Firstly, it won't be five years," Keiko said, trying to cheer him up. "In the very worst scenario I'll get you out after three, maybe two and a half. Don't worry, you'll adapt to it. The main thing is to keep yourself busy with something. Set yourself a goal, turn the defect into an effect – learn a foreign language, read some Proust. You had a plan to write your book. Get to it. Two and a half years will fly by."

"Yeah: an instruction manual on how to gain success in life, written by a prisoner." Marat smiled sadly. "Freedom has always been the most important thing in my life, the only thing I've ever wanted more than anything. Not money. Money is just a tool that can set you free: to spend your time as you wish, to avoid doing what you don't want to do, to be with people you want to be with, and to avoid being with those you don't like – that's the only reason for having money in the first place. And now? A walk at seven a.m. – for an hour, in some kind of cage – because that time is most convenient for the guards. Added to that, every degenerate prison guard can shit on you, punch you, do whatever they like to you. I really don't know how I'm going to survive this."

"I'll tell you a story that one of my clients, whose case was in some ways quite similar to yours, once told me. I don't know if it will help, but the story went something like this...

"Once upon a time, there were two monks. Buddhists, I believe. They knew that life was nothing but suffering: full of desires, attachment, temptation, illnesses, aging, the people around you, the government, politics, money – and all of this

274

creating only more suffering. One of them decided to isolate himself from it all. Every day, while he meditated, he built a wall to surround him as he meditated. Brick by brick, he constructed a barrier that would keep out all distractions – everything he found annoying, anything that might steal his attention – so that nothing would interrupt his practice of calming the thoughts that were jumping around his head like monkeys. He didn't want anything to get in the way of him achieving clarity. Everything that was in any way distracting would just bounce off the wall and remain outside.

"The second monk had chosen a completely different approach. He had decided to rise above. Every day during meditation he, in his thoughts, rose above all temptation, all negative impulses, conflicts, fear, envy, power, money, politics, relationships – he rose above it all.

"And then one day, when their work was done, the first monk discovered that he'd built a wall around himself. He was in prison; he couldn't see the city or the people, or the sea, or the mountains. There was no sound; light barely got through, and that which did was dim: so as not to disturb or worry him, and to let remain completely still.

"Meanwhile, the second monk had learned to rise high above all the houses and the treetops. A majestically beautiful bird had landed on his shoulder; he was looking in the distance, at the mountains and the sea; but underneath him monkeys played and the city life was vibrant – people were celebrating, falling in love, arguing and suffering. Life was running its usual course, people lived their lives; but none of that could touch the monk anymore. The events all around simply reflected off of him – just like an owl's cry bounces off the water in a lake. Just like the moon and the stars reflect in a still pool of water without being able to worry or affect it. Both monks had managed to distance themselves, and each in their own way – but only one of them was free.

"So, the moral of the story is: freedom isn't found solely in the way we control and manage the world around us. Freedom lies in our independence from the world, from people and circumstances – and you can only achieve that sort of independence by elevating yourself high above all the noise. Freedom isn't some external phenomenon. Freedom is the making of your inner world. People try to distance themselves; they run from that which worries and annoys them, or which drives them crazy; they try to shut things out of their lives – but it's impossible. You can only achieve true freedom by being able to watch it all from above, with peace."

"That's a good story, I'll think about it." Marat's attitude towards Keiko by now bordered something like obedient humility. Marat treated Keiko like a father or a teacher. Keiko could feel this, and he seemed to be flattered by it.

"I used to believe that money is freedom," Marat said with an air of sadness, seemingly unaware that he was giving voice to his thoughts. "You have money and therefore you're free. Do whatever you like. And the more money you have, the more freedom you have. And I was sort of free, but only within a certain sphere. Freer than lots of others, but not properly; I wasn't satisfied with it. And now I'm in prison. What a great outcome."

"Well, the main thing is to keep your chin up." Once more Keiko tried to rouse him. "You're young, you're only fifty. I promise you that, worst comes to worst, I'll get you out before your fifty-fourth birthday. You've got half of your life still ahead of you. Besides – and I'll allow myself to say this – it's the best part. Look at me: I'm seventy-six and I'm still working. I'm running an office, and the thought of retiring hasn't even crossed my mind. You'll have plenty more time. Nothing has ended until it is really over. What I mean by that is: while you're still alive, you can live for another fifty years – which is why, as I said, you should use this challenge to your advantage.

276

Study, read, write, come out of here stronger and wiser. And don't worry about the circumstances. Luckily, money and connections can get you a lot around here. I think we'll be able to resolve most things in the external world. All you need to focus on is dealing with your internal world."

"Please, could you use that money to arrange a small detail in the 'external world' – could you get me a knife and fork, so that I don't have to eat with a spoon?"

"I may not be able to do that right away," Keiko said, followed by a laugh, "but I think I'll be able to get you a plastic knife and fork in time."

CHAPTER 48

"I want to talk about something."

This time Twinka didn't wait for Anna to suggest a subject for her to focus on, or for Anna to start with a question – she used her own initiative. She'd been mentally preparing herself for this moment for a long time, and she felt ready.

"I want to talk about alcohol," she ventured bravely. "I think I need to do something about it."

"Okay, sure, tell me more about it," encouraged Anna.

"I think I have a problem."

"Why do you think you have a problem?"

"I'm not the type of alcoholic who drinks so much that they can't leave the house, or who gets those horrible hangovers whereby they're shaking inside and it's impossible to stop drinking. No, that's not what it's like for me. I wake up every day, make breakfast, get Ronia sorted for school, do drop-off, and often do the pickup later on too. In the evening, we always prepare everything we'll need for the next day: we choose what we'll both be wearing, we pack our bags. I make her dinner. Et cetera.

"And so it's not like alcohol gets in the way of our lives. But, at the same time, every afternoon – around two, three, maybe four o'clock – I feel a strong urge to drink. Actually, it's been creeping earlier and earlier. Sometimes even as soon as I wake I get the impulse to drink. But I manage to suppress it until lunchtime. And when I have my first glass or two of wine, I don't feel drunk or tipsy – that's when I start to feel normal and do all the chores on my list. Certainly no one ever notices. Then I have some more, and so on until the evening. When I go to bed around midnight, I see that I've finished two bottles of wine – or three or four on some days. I don't even feel like I'm drunk, because it's been so gradual throughout the day, but I realise that it's still a lot."

"And that's how it is every day?"

"Well, yeah. Though on Fridays or Saturdays, if we have a party or go to some event, then it's even more."

"More than three bottles of wine." Though her demeanour remained serious, Anna didn't hide her surprise.

"Well, it's not like I'm counting every glass, but it's around that."

"I see. And what or when made you suspect that it might be a problem?"

"Several things..." Twinka sighed heavily. "Well, I guess my looks are the biggest problem. Look at my face – that's not what I used to look like. It's puffy, it looks horrible; I'm walking around wearing sunglasses; I no longer go to those restaurants or cafes I used to like, because I may run into someone I know. I don't want them to see me like this. My weight is increasing all the time as well."

"Right," Anna nodded her head earnestly and with compassion. "What else?"

"Well, that's the main thing. And... if I was being completely honest, I think that if the traffic police were to stop me – even if it was during the first part of the day, when I haven't had anything to drink yet – the reading would still show I'd been drinking. I can literally feel it. And I feel physically awful. As I say, I don't have a hangover as such, but when I wake up I'm already tired. I don't feel fresh and rested in the morning – I feel as if I've been working hard – and it only worsens as the day goes on. I also get restless and anxious, with this only interrupted by one short moment of feeling good – that being when I have my first or second glass of wine. Yeah, that's when I feel good. Extremely good, I'd say."

"Have you tried to quit, or to limit your alcohol intake?"

"Of course. Every morning I wake up thinking, *I won't have a drink today*. Someone said to me that if you can last two weeks without a drink, then you're not an alcoholic. And I've tried."

"And how did it go?"

"I don't know whether it counts, but last year I went to this retreat in Bali. There was yoga, meditation, zero alcohol, a healthy diet. And I managed to last two weeks without any problems. But it's not the same at home. I can't do it at home."

"You must realise that there is a reason behind your drinking. People don't drink for no reason, right? What do you think the reason might be?"

"Ha, take your pick!" Twinka barked a short laugh. "I'll take a wild guess – maybe the fact that my husband tried to kill me, for starters?"

"As far as I understand, it began long before."

"Well, yeah, some time before. Actually, if I'm honest then I think it started back in our good days. Marat was really into his wines and champagnes; we used to drive around France a lot, going to different vineyards and exploring the world's best wine cellars – that was our life back then. We were happy and in love; we travelled to the world's best restaurants just to have lunch. We stayed in the most luxurious hotels, where we drank the most exquisite wines and champagnes. That was all wonderful – it was more than wonderful. Before then, I'd practically never drink alcohol. Prior to my meeting Marat, I never used to have more than two glasses of wine in an evening. It all started with Marat. Then he did his mountain training, so he managed to stop at one point, but I carried on. I don't know if that was because of the problems we had. I really don't... Maybe I was simply living my life, going with the flow, enjoying it. Either way I didn't think there was any risk involved. All our friends used to like a drink too, and it was fine; no one seemed to have any problems because of it."

"I understand," said Anna, nodding her head in confirmation. "And then, when the problems between you started, alcohol felt like a natural remedy, just within reach?"

"Maybe. But it's only now that I understand I drink too much and that it affects how I look and feel. I stopped eating properly a long time ago, yet, somehow, I'm still gaining excess weight. I have bags under my eyes; my skin and my hair looks horrible. I can physically feel that my body is struggling with it. I should really ditch the habit and stop, but I just can't physically do it."

"Oh, it's not as bad as you say with your skin, hair and weight," Anna tried to console Twinka.

"I wake up thinking: *No, I shouldn't drink. That's it. I'm not going to have a drink today.* But come lunchtime and I've already started toying with the idea that I should have a glass of something. That I'm allowed to, because I need to get through this horrible period of my life. And as soon as I come out the other side, I'll stop drinking. But right at this very moment that would demand too much from me. It's already tough right now: I can't take on additional challenges. Do you see what I mean?"

"I do."

Anna let Twinka talk.

"Marat is in prison. Everyone is looking at me like I'm some animal on display in a zoo; they're asking me all sorts of questions. Ronia's asking me questions, too – I don't know how to respond. And then Dimitri still wants something from me as well. It's hard enough to deal with all of this – I can't then fight my addiction on top. It's just impossible right now."

"But a different part of you realises that you should quit."

"Yes, another part of me says I should quit. I can't even look at my own reflection anymore, I can't stand the way I look

– it's not me; I want to throw something at the mirror and smash it! It can't go on like this, and yet it does. I know that as soon as I leave here and go home, I'm going to open a bottle of wine right away."

"I understand," Anna said calmly, when Twinka had finished speaking. "Drinking is a very natural defence mechanism. It's a way of temporarily drowning out all the problems, questions and emotions that are swirling around in your head. Alcohol seemingly gives you a chance to pause, to stop thinking for a moment; it offers a moment of disconnection, a moment of comfort – which is very important to you right now. Nothing else can offer you this feeling of comfort. It's understandable, and yet, as you yourself realise, the price you're paying for these moments of comfort and disconnection is too high. And the truth is that disconnecting doesn't actually help to solve any of your problems. Alcohol helps us to avoid thinking during times when we really should be thinking. *That's* the problem. Alcohol helps us to relax when in reality we should be pulling ourselves together. The problem is that, eventually, not only does alcohol fail to help us solve our problems – it actually creates new, additional problems on top of our existing ones. Things like bad health, challenges in relationships, breaking the law even. Alcohol deepens depression and prolongs its treatment. It aggravates other health problems too. Alcohol really is a poison."

"I understand all this, and it's easy to say it," said Twinka, interrupting Anna's lecture, "but I don't have the energy to be strong. You're saying that alcohol helps to avoid thinking during times when you should be thinking, but I don't have the energy to face any of these thoughts. And if I did face them, I'd simply lose my mind. I need this respite: these moments of disconnect, unconsciousness; this sleep that isn't refreshing, and leads me to wake up tired, but which at least allows me to continue functioning."

"I know, it's definitely not easy," Anna agreed. "If it were, then alcoholism wouldn't be one of the most difficult problems on the planet. I think people will end global warming sooner than they'll end alcoholism. But it is possible to quit! That's the only thing you should know at this stage. What I need from you right now is just this one tiny step: I need you to believe that it's possible to stop drinking; and, if you choose to do so, you'll be able to stop. You're not the first person who's been in this situation, and you won't be the last. People have managed to overcome it – maybe not all, but many of them – and you can be one such individual. It's possible to quit. It's even possible to maintain a social life and see your friends without drinking; as unbelievable as it may sound to you right now, it's all possible. You can do it because you're not weaker or worse-affected than others who have done it – that's what I want you to realise. I'll arrange an appointment for you with a narcologist, and we'll create a plan together. Luckily, at the age of forty, it's definitely not too late to start a new life."

"Yeah, I know – it's never too late; not even the day before death."

"Exactly," Anna agreed, smiling. "We should always remember that."

CHAPTER 49

No matter how hard Marat tried to stay strong and to not give up or give in to depression, his first few months in the large, proper prison were much tougher than he had imagined. Everything was far worse. First, the persistent thoughts about the five-year sentence. Five years felt like an eternity. Five years sat on his chest, crushing him. Five years...

Although Marat was counting the days, five years was still five years. There was no way around that. Four years and ten months would still seem like an eternity, and even if Marat believed in Keiko, who said he'd be released much sooner, it didn't change anything. Two years and six months would still seem like an eternity, except with a treacherous hope attached to it, alongside the risk that it may be far longer. Marat realised that it definitely wasn't a good idea to be counting the days, so he stopped. They were all just abstract numbers, and each felt like an eternal, unbelievably long stretch of time. He tried not to think about time at all. To take each day as it came, to focus only on the day ahead. As much as he could, he tried to blunt himself – to stop feeling anything, to stop thinking about anything – but it just wasn't possible. His thoughts circled back around, they haunted and tortured him, and every one of them was excruciating.

Marat suffered in the prison on countless levels. The cell, which was too hot in the summer, now felt too cold. But even the worst physical discomfort was nothing compared to his greatest challenge of all – namely, spending twenty-four hours in the company of people he hadn't chosen for himself. Under normal circumstances, he wouldn't be anywhere near them, he wouldn't exchange a single word with them, he wouldn't send a single glance in their direction. Keiko had put a lot of effort into ensuring Marat shared a cell with these two 'nice, intelligent people', but Marat immediately hated them (although he tried not to show it).

The rapist turned out to be a weak, pathetic character – some government official whose colleague had accused him of raping her after some Friday night drinks. She had told the story in vivid detail and cried passionately, and she even had a few bruises on her body, and his sperm was definitely inside her. No matter how he'd denied it, and explained that everything took place with the full consent of both parties, no one listened to him. The prosecution had found tiny particles from his colleague's skin underneath his nails, and scratch marks on her that seemingly explained this. He'd sworn that he was innocent, that he could never do something like that to a woman. Marat was so disinterested in the man's case that he switched off every time the fat, pathetic idiot started up on the subject.

The money launderer turned out to be an arrogant ex-lawyer who'd organised a small illegal trade of cigarettes with fake excise duty stamps, and as a result now considered himself a distinguished criminal. He took *huge* pride in it. This had been his second time being put on trial: the first, he'd managed to beat the charge; but now he had been sentenced to six years in prison, two of which he'd already served. As well as a member of the criminal elite, he thought of himself as a seasoned prison veteran.

The man talked about himself incessantly.

"Cigarettes bring in as much profit as drugs, but the sentences are much softer, and you're not being followed by police units with drones, dogs, scanners and informants. Cigarette business is for those who are smart."

Despite his deluded sense of status, the money launderer treated Marat with respect. Like all the pathetic little people, he instinctively felt a need to suck up to everyone who was wealthier than him, while acting especially mean towards those who were worse off than him – people like the rapist. To his mind, money was the only measure of success and the only mark of a person's character. If Marat were a free man, he wouldn't waste a second in the presence of this pathetic, jumped-up little creep, but now he had to cohabit with him and listen to his crumbs of 'prison wisdom', which were mostly acquired from films.

There was absolutely nothing for Marat to talk to either of this cellmates about. The money launderer was only interested in bragging about the Bentleys, Porsches and Range Rovers he'd owned; and which influential people (according to his standards) he'd been friends with, had gone on a bender with, and so on. He also loved looking back over his pictures from the good old days, and – while doing so, of course – imparting all his memories on Marat via a detailed commentary.

The rapist, who was obese and had diabetes, spent most of his time bemoaning his ill health and misfortune. Whether it had occurred naturally or by design, he occupied the lowest rank in the invisible three-man hierarchy of their prison cell.

Neither of Marat's cellmates read any books, though the money launderer did offer Marat, who didn't play any card games like the others did, a game of chess. However, after hopelessly losing a few games, the put-in-his-place launderer lost interest in playing. Furthermore, they couldn't even agree what to watch on TV. The money launderer was only interested in films about criminals, prison and the mafia. The rapist, who wasn't into movies, loved anything politics related. He was equally invested in domestic and foreign affairs – particularly the conflict between Israel and Palestine; the US presidential elections; and the actions of Turkey, NATO, Russia and China – and didn't want to miss a moment's coverage of the news. When watching it, he always added his own commentary (statements such as "China will always do whatever is most convenient for them", and "You can't intimidate the Russians with sanctions, they're used to suffering"). As a result, and to appease both of Marat's cellmates, the TV was left on almost all of the time – alternating between news coverage and mafia movies.

Marat would have loved to just sit in silence and read or think, but, stuck in this small space with these two scumbags, he couldn't even hear himself think. (And even if he had been able to, all he'd have heard was his seething hatred for these two characters, prison life, his situation.) He longer for the evening, and lights-out time, to arrive; although even the night didn't bring much relief. The fat rapist snored, or else groaned and moaned in his sleep, while the money launderer cursed him for doing either. For his part the money launderer fidgeted restlessly, farted frequently, and often masturbated too.

"If you don't do it, your equipment won't work when you get out of here," he had once justified to Marat.

Being confined in the company of these animals was far worse than simply being in prison, and Marat demanded Keiko do everything in his power to secure him his own private cell. His entire life, Marat's only drive and motivation for making more money had been so that he'd be immune from predicaments such as this. Yet now he found himself trapped in prison: a hell that contained all the things he hated with the most passion. He had absolutely no freedom here, and he even had to share his captivity with two idiots whom he couldn't escape; whom he couldn't avoid seeing, hearing, smelling and generally sensing. Marat suffered from their very presence, from the mundanity of it all, from a complete lack of private space, and, above all else, from the fact that he was forced to show respect to and get along with these bottom-feeders.

"Being in prison is exactly like being on the outside. It's essentially the same life. A prison is nothing more than a condensed model of our society," the money launderer explained. It was one of his go-to (and frequently rehashed) nuggets of 'prison wisdom'. "You don't think you were really free on the outside, do you? The exercise area was obviously larger, the food was a bit better – but that's pretty much it," concluded the self-satisfied idiot, obviously expecting Marat's approval (whereas all Marat wanted was to hit him in the face). All that prevented Marat from losing his self-control the knowledge that by doing so he would worsen the atmosphere in their cell. He simply could not risk making it even more unbearable. Besides, if he was being completely honest, he didn't know whether he'd win the fight.

Marat could stand it no longer. "I'm losing my sanity in here," he said to Keiko with absolute solemnity. "I will literally go insane. I don't think I can survive this."

CHAPTER 50

They agreed to meet at their usual spot – the flat. Until recently, Twinka had ventured there with excited anticipation, glowing and happy. They'd experienced so many moments of ecstasy in that flat, and had derived so much joy and pleasure from one another. But things had changed.

Twinka was worried. She had no idea what it would be like, or how she would feel. Would the familiarity of the flat rekindle some of those feelings – or were they gone forever? She didn't know whether she even wanted some of that secret, forbidden happiness to return, or whether she'd rather just forget it entirely.

The door was already open and, as usual, Dimitri was waiting for her. As soon as Twinka crossed the threshold he was beside her, locking her in an embrace. Twinka offered no resistance and they stood there, motionless, for a few minutes.

"Everything will be okay," Dimitri said.

Twinka didn't know how to respond. She untangled herself from his prolonged hold, slowly removed her coat and her boots, and walked towards the living room. She sat down on the sofa and pulled her legs in beneath her. It looked like she was smiling a very sad smile, but Dimitri knew her better than that. She wasn't smiling at all.

Dimitri threw himself down on his knees in front of Twinka, and put his head on her lap. Twinka ruffled his hair gently.

"How do you feel?" he asked.

"Ronia is constantly reading articles about Marat that she's found on the internet. I don't know whether she's looking them up herself or whether her friends are sending them to her."

"Fuck!"

"The only thing I can tell her is that none of this is true. And then she asks me: 'Well, what is the truth then?'"

"And what do you say to that?"

"That it's all just one big, tragic misunderstanding; that Daddy loves us both very much; that he's angry at Mummy, but he didn't actually mean to cause any harm."

"But you know that's not true, right?" Dimitri got up off the floor and sat down on the sofa next to her.

"Well, I think it is."

"In what sense?!" Dimitri didn't understand.

"I think it *is* just a misunderstanding, and that he does love us both."

"Twinka!" Dimitri made no attempt to hide his horror and astonishment. "If I hadn't decided to warn you and hadn't happened to be in the right place myself, at the right time, then he would have killed you. Don't you get it?! He would have murdered you, and we would not be sat here, talking, today. Don't you understand?!" Dimitri had a hold of Twinka's hand and was squeezing it firmly while looking directly into her eyes. "You'd be dead!"

Twinka averted her gaze. "I think you're right." She sighed. "But I think that I'm also right."

"How do you mean?!" Dimitri was baffled. There was a touch of irritation in his voice. "You do realise that if there are two mutually exclusive statements, then one of them must be false?"

"I don't know."

"It's a simple fact."

"None of this is very simple." There was prickliness in Twinka's voice too. She got up and went into the kitchen. "Have we got anything to drink?"

"I'm afraid not."

He could have taken care of it ahead of time, Twinka thought to herself, but she didn't say anything.

"You're not going to blame me for what happened, are you?" Dimitri asked.

"I don't know. It's hard for me to comprehend it all."

"I saved your life, you know," Dimitri said. "And now I feel like I've done something wrong."

Suddenly Twinka felt that this conversation, this encounter between them, was helping her find the inner clarity that had been missing all this time. Yes, it was good that she'd come. It was good that they were talking.

"I often wonder why you didn't just push him," she said. "In fact, it would have been enough to just raise your voice at him. But you nearly killed him. The doctors say it's a miracle that he even survived. Tell me, in all honesty – did you intend to kill him?"

"Oh, come on!" Dimitri was unpleasantly surprised. "You remember how it all happened. It was all so fast, so unexpected, that I had no time to consider my actions."

Having made sure of what she already knew – that there was nothing in the fridge – Twinka roamed the empty cupboards anxiously, then went back into the living room, with Dimitri following her.

"And why," snapped Twinka, "did you have to tell the police everything?!"

"Hopefully you don't think that I'm the one who should be in prison?" Dimitri continued to look genuinely shocked.

"They would have let you go anyway, but you made sure that Marat was put behind bars. Was that the right action to take?"

"Twinka, darling, if I had known that this is what you wanted, I would have stayed in prison myself. But there's no logic to what you're saying. Why wouldn't you want the person who attacked you, who planned your murder meticulously, to get away with it and carry on living with you, as though nothing ever happened?"

"And did you ever ask *me* what *I* wanted? Did you ask me to share *my* thoughts?" There was reproach in Twinka's voice.

"But, Twinka, my love, I was in prison."

"By the way, Marat is running a multi-million business while he's in prison, with his lawyer's help. He's also sending presents to Ronia, and writing her letters – but you couldn't even be bothered to write one tiny letter to me." Twinka was venting her anger. It had been stewing inside her all this time; although, until a few minutes prior, she hadn't even know it was there.

"I didn't have a lawyer," Dimitri said, as though in surrender. Twinka's anger seemed to have punctured him.

"And why didn't you have a lawyer, Dimitri? Why?"

"I don't know," Dimitri answered quietly, without lifting his eyes. He genuinely didn't have a clue.

Twinka sighed heavily – her anger had subsided as suddenly as it had erupted. She was never one to court conflict, and she hadn't come here to shame or reprimand Dimitri. What was the point of doing that now, anyway?

"Sometimes I feel that maybe I would have been better off, if I'd been murdered," Twinka said, having regained her calm.

"Don't say such nonsense. If you had died, Ronia would be put in an orphanage, because Marat would still be in prison."

"I was wondering why I have been given this fate." Twinka spoke as if she did not require an answer. "Did I do something wrong," she continued, "or make a mistake – maybe I'm the one to blame for everything? Maybe I shouldn't have fallen in love with him, I shouldn't have married him, I should have been a better wife... And, obviously, I shouldn't have let you kiss me. And I definitely shouldn't have slept with you."

292

"Bullshit! It's not your fault. You wouldn't blame a rape victim, just because they dressed up nice. He's a murderer, and there's no way you could have known it. You couldn't have foreseen it." Dimitri tried to embrace Twinka, but this time she didn't let him.

"Twinka, I love you. Did you know that?"

Twinka's eyes widened – she really hadn't expected this. "I know that the most important thing in a relationship between lovers is not to fall in love," she replied coldly.

"That's true, but I've fallen in love with you."

"Well, then you've made *the most important* mistake." Twinka's icy tone indicated that it would be better if he didn't explore the topic further. "You know what I've realised after all this time?" she continued. "The fact that I love Marat. Yes, genuinely, I love Marat. I thought that it was all over between us, that it was all in the past, but it's not true."

"I don't get it. He wanted to kill you! Seriously. And he would have succeeded. He had planned it all, down to the smallest detail. He'd left his car, made it look like he'd gone for a run, and returned home in secret with one thing on his mind: to kill you. And he'd then return back via the way he'd came, as though nothing had ever happened. It wasn't like a spontaneous burst of anger – he'd taken the time to carefully plan every step."

"I know."

"Then how can you possibly love him?"

Twinka's expression was one of resolved exasperation. "I know it's stupid and there's no logic to it, but I'm afraid that this is exactly what it's like in life – there isn't always much logic involved."

"I really don't get it. I've always been amazed by those women who choose to stay with an abusive husband, just because they simply can't leave."

"You sound just like my dad."

"Well, your dad has a point. Plus, he loves you and he's a clever man, so maybe it's worth listening to him."

Twinka shrugged her shoulders indifferently.

"Think about those women who live with violent partners for years – because *you're* becoming one of them." Dimitri felt that it was worth expanding on his argument, since Twinka's dad had said something similar. "They're probably telling themselves similar things – that it's all so absurd; that love isn't rational, and it can't be helped – even though we all know that the right thing to do when you have a husband who beats you, is to leave."

"But Marat doesn't beat me!" Twinka laughed. "And I'm pretty sure he won't attempt to kill me a second time. You should be worried about that more than me."

"You really think it's the right thing to do?" Dimitri was staring into Twinka's eyes, searching them desperately.

"Ha, here we go again. What's the right thing to do? That's a great question, except the answer never comes that easy. And you keep forgetting that I have a daughter. I have to take her into account."

"But what about us?"

"What about us?"

"I love you."

"Dimitri, my darling, can't you feel how much things have changed? Nothing is, nor ever will be, like it was up until that horrible day," Twinka said.

With each passing moment she felt – with greater and greater surety – that she really didn't feel anything for Dimitri now. She was completely indifferent towards him... maybe even a little disgusted.

"But things were so good between us. It had never felt better."

"They were, Dimitri. But looking back on it now, the world we used to have seems so distant and strange that I can barely remember it anymore. I sort of remember what we got up to here, but I can't comprehend how it all worked – and you've changed completely, too."

"No!" Dimitri was shellshocked – he felt that he was losing Twinka. "I'm the same person!" He tried to embrace her again, but she evaded him.

"That world, in which we were lovers, doesn't exist anymore, okay? The order which made it possible, no longer exists, and I need to organise all this chaos somehow."

"But Twinka..."

"No."

And she left.

The winter this year didn't feel proper – there was no frost, not much snow; only darkness, cold, damp, greyness, wind and helplessness.

Twinka didn't stop by the church.

CHAPTER 51

"How do you feel?" Keiko asked compassionately.

Marat looked terrible. He hadn't shaved, and his only eye looked sunken and glazed. His skin had taken on an unhealthy shade of pale grey.

"I'm fucked," Marat replied.

Keiko was taken aback. Marat had never used that sort of language before.

"I can't sleep," started Marat, having realised that Keiko wanted to hear some sort of explanation. "The rapist – dickhead, fucking pig – is always snoring, moaning and wheezing. And that other animal is either farting and wanking. It's impossible to sleep! I'm basically lying there with my eyes wide open, just hating them. I hate them more than anything."

"Right." Keiko tried to get accustomed to Marat's new manner of talking.

"I might fall into a bit of a slumber for a few minutes every night, but I haven't felt fully rested since I got here. My head feels like an empty bucket. I didn't feel this shit even when I was on top of Mount Everest."

"Right. We'll arrange a different cell for you," said Keiko, trying to console Marat.

"My life has shrunk. It's like a tiny nut, made entirely of hatred. I can't see or sense anything other than those two disgusting pigs, and how much I hate them."

Sensing his opportunity, Keiko interrupted Marat:

"And we have another problem."

"What?"

The lawyer retrieved a few celebrity magazines from his briefcase. Two had Marat on the cover.

"millionaire-turned-wife-murderer behind bars" one of the headlines proclaimed.

"only a miracle saved this woman from her murdering husband's plan" announced another, accompanying a big picture of Twinka. She was in a car by their house on Button Street.

Marat glanced at the magazines but didn't read them. Neither did he say anything.

"It looks like Dimitri's testimony has leaked. They've printed all of it. About the corks and the corkscrews, too." Keiko looked worried.

"Isn't that against the law?" Marat asked, though looking too tired to be infuriated by this.

"It is, but it can still happen nonetheless."

"Let's sue everyone, starting with Draco."

"It could be someone else."

Keiko's reply hadn't sound determined.

"What do you mean? How else could Dimitri's testimony have leaked?"

"Well, the testimony was given to the police. Then it arrived at the prosecutor's office, and then it was sent to the court, who decided that an arrest would be the most appropriate safety measure. On top of that, it could have even been someone from the prison administration who took a copy of your case file while you went outside for a walk. What I mean to say is that several people could have had access to your case, at various stages. And, of course, we can't rule out Dimitri himself."

"You think it was Dimitri?"

"Well, if I'm being totally honest, I think it was the prosecution. The news seemed to have been announced first by those old friends of your..." Keiko smiled knowingly. "And, as you know, their entire branch of investigative journalism is based solely on leaks."

"You mean that news portal? The one we sued a while ago?"

"The very same."

"Motherfuckers! Those fat, sex obsessed, scandal hungry bastards. They've got no lives of their own, so all they can do is sit around and think of ways to ruin everyone else's. Let's sue them again," Marat said in a venomous tone.

"I'm afraid we're likely to lose again." Kciko was now trying to ignore the way Marat was expressing himself. "We should take care of our own version."

"Or maybe it was Dimitri?" Marat mused. "He wants to be seen like the good guy in all this."

"Well, you know him better than me. We shouldn't dismiss that option entirely. But he's not even mentioned in these stories. They're saying that your wife managed to survive and recover as though by miracle."

"I can't think about this right now. I felt better being six thousand metres above ground than listening to the bodily functions of these two Shudras all night. I can't get hold of any pills either. I'm begging you – please, do whatever you have to do to get me another cell. It's fucking torture!"

"I'm trying. But we are in a prison, and it's very overcrowded. They're saying they already did a favour for us."

"You know what's the worst thing? The fact that, whenever I do manage to fall asleep, I have dreams. Normal dreams, in which I'm free. Then, suddenly, the disgusting wheezing from that fucking rapist wakes me up again. For about half a second I don't know where I am, and then suddenly it hits me: I'm in prison, with these two assholes. It's like I'm being arrested, over and over again. Every time I wake up I get a new, earth-shattering shock to the system, as I'm forced to emotionally relive it all, and be reminded of how the absolute worst-case scenario has played out."

"I know that words won't help much right now," Keiko said, his voice calm and empathetic, "but you'll get used to it. Trust me. People can adapt to anything – and pretty quickly, too. We're an uniquely adaptable species. Whoever can't do it, essentially dies."

"Looks like I'll be in the latter category then..."

Keiko smiled knowingly. "You won't. I know you." His voice held paternal warmth.

Keiko's attitude and words really did seem to console Marat a little.

CHAPTER 52

Immediately following his arrest, Mum had tried to visit Marat. But with Keiko's help Marat had managed to postpone their meeting. That is, until it was no longer possible to stall her...

Upon seeing Mum, Marat's heart sank. She looked terrible; far worse than when Marat had last seen her. She seemed to have shrunk, and looked both shrivelled and incredibly fragile. Her powder couldn't conceal the unhealthy spots on her skin, while her movements were slow and unsteady. She had tied something that resembled a fashionable sweatband around her right wrist, which was supposed to stop her bangles from sliding off. There was only a small watch and a single bracelet around her left.

"They won't let me see you," Mum said, wasting no time on small talk. "They don't want me to visit you."

"I know."

"So, how are you then?" Mum asked, her voice ostensibly perking up. Marat detected the sarcasm immediately.

"I'm well," he replied quietly, followed by a sigh.

"'Well'?" Mum repeated, as though this was exactly the sort of answer she'd expected. "You're doing well?"

Marat didn't know what to say.

"Never been better, eh? Ronia's probably doing really well, too. Her dad is in prison and all her classmates, and all her friends, know why. Brilliant. Have you seen what the press are writing about you? The internet is full of these stories."

"Mum, why did you come?" Marat did not have the strength to listen to her arguments.

"Why did I come? That's a good question actually." Mum dropped the mask of irony and sarcasm, and spoke frankly.

"Maybe to see my son in prison one last time before my death comes, so I can die in peace and loneliness."

"Mum, I'm really sorry that things worked out this way."

"Oh, you're sorry, are you? Sorry that you didn't quite manage to kill the mother of your child? Or sorry that you got caught?" she said, giving him both barrels. "Oh God, the things I have to live through at the end of my life..."

Marat said nothing.

"Do you even realise that I can't leave the house because I'm so ashamed?"

"I understand," Marat said quietly, hoping Mum would calm down.

"How could you do this to me? Have you been taking drugs? How could you even come up with something as stupid as this?"

"I don't know," Marat said. It was his turn to cast his eyes downward, and he let her scold him like she used to in his childhood.

"Did you consider my feelings, even for a second? Do you have any idea what it's like for a mother to live through something like this?" There were tears in her eyes.

"Mum, everything will be okay," Marat said. He was close to tears as well. "Remember what Dad used to say – it doesn't matter how many times a boxer is knocked down: the only thing that matters is how many times he gets up. We'll both get through this, it will be okay."

"It's never going to be okay – that's the thing! All that's left for me is to die, ashamed and alone – that's what you've accomplished. You've robbed me of any hope. And people can live without lots of things, except for hope. You can survive any difficulties and get through anything if you still have hope, but what hope is left for me? Tell me – what can I possibly hope for anymore?" Mum was dabbing at her eyes with a tissue. She was embarrassed by her tears. She'd vented all her anger, and now she was starting to realise that this would achieve nothing. She wanted to calm down. And so she tried to change the tone of their conversation.

"Is your lawyer any good?"

"Yeah, he's good," Marat replied, still facing the floor.

"I mean, how good could he be, if he couldn't even arrange for me to see you?"

"Trust me, he's good. I've known him for a long time."

"He told me that you could get five years. Five years! I won't be around that long."

"It's not –" Marat sighed – "going to be that long."

"You could have waited before I died, so I wouldn't have to live through this."

"Mum, how are things with you? Do you have everything you need?"

"Yes, thank you, I'm doing fantastic, they installed the air conditioning. Thanks to them, when I'm dead, no one will be able to discover my body for months. It will be nice and cool, and well-preserved." Her malicious, ironic tone had returned.

Marat realised that it was her way of trying to hide her sorrow and despair. Suddenly, he felt absolute clarity in his conscience.

I'm going to murder him! I'm going to kill that bastard and strangle him! Mum and I have to live through all of this, and it's all because of Dimitri. I'll never forgive him for it. I'm going to kill him!

While being escorted back from the visitation room, Marat let the anger consume him. In the stuffy prison cell, he was met with the quizzing looks of the money launderer and the rapist.

And I'm going to kill these two worthless beasts as well, he thought to himself.

CHAPTER 53

"You've never really talked about Dimitri. Tell me what he's like?" Anna suggested.

"Dimitri..." Twinka thought on this happily. She was in a cheerful mood today. "...Dimitri is gentle, which I liked. He's quite big and strong, but also tender – I think he's very sensitive and vulnerable, even though he tries to hide it. He'd like to be like Marat, but at the same time he's convinced he's better than Marat."

"In what way?" Anna asked.

"Well, he always scoffs at how Marat has climbed Everest, how Marat thinks he can do anything, how he has everything. I think he believes that Marat is too shallow, he shows off too much, he's too full of himself."

"But in what sense does he want to be like him?"

"Well, you know: Marat is the sort of person nobody likes, but who everyone wants to be like."

"Is it envy then?"

"Yeah, probably, but there's something more to it as well. Dimitri always wanted me to tell him that he was better than Marat in bed. He wanted me to feel like he could please me more than any other man. For example, he'd always ask me: 'Did you enjoy that?' And I'd reply: 'Yeah, it was amazing.' Then he goes: 'Was it better than when you're with him?' And I'd say: 'It was different.' Then he goes again: 'But was it better?' I mean, he said it sort of jokingly, but it felt like being favourably compared mattered to him. You know, Marat never asked me whether he was the best lover I'd ever had." Twinka laughed. "He's probably convinced that he is."

"Or he doesn't care," Anna interjected.

"Or that," Twinka agreed. "Yeah, it's probably that. Marat never compares himself to anyone else. Well, maybe except for some historical personalities; whereas Dimitri compares himself all the time, especially to Marat. They're so different in that sense."

"I suppose you could call it self-sufficiency. Marat is self-sufficient: he doesn't need to prove anything to anyone, including himself. Whereas Dimitri probably needs to prove to himself all the time that he's not a loser. He needs to prove to himself that he's able, capable, talented, that he's in no sense lesser than Marat. He may be lacking some external symbols of status – he's not as wealthy, his house isn't as big, his car isn't as good, and his wife isn't as beautiful – which makes him seek out other signs of proof that he is an Alpha male, no worse than Marat."

"I'm not sure. But it sounds like it could be that. It's so weird though because there's actually nothing wrong with Dimitri. Of course, he's not as well off as Marat; but he makes a good living, he's got this reputation of being a maths genius, plus everyone respects him – so he's definitely not a loser."

"Maybe subconsciously he believes that, as a maths genius, he deserves much more. Maybe he thinks that he should be in Marat's place, rather than just one of his employees?"

"Oh, what are men like..." Twinka laughed. "And they still have the audacity to make fun of women for their ways."

Anna acknowledged this moment of female solidarity with an affirmative smile.

"What else can you tell me about him?" she asked.

"Well, to be honest, he was better."

"In what sense?" Anna didn't realise her meaning.

"I mean at sex. He was undoubtedly better, he was unbelievably good. So good that I thought – *How can I have lived to the grand age of forty, never knowing that it could ever feel like this?*"

304

CHAPTER 54

Keiko's tale about the two monks turned out to be the most useful advice he'd ever given to Marat. More and more often, Marat recalled the story and tried to picture himself as the monk who rose high above the houses and treetops, leaving the everyday rabble beneath him. And he was starting to realise the moral of the story, because there were moments when he managed to achieve something similar, elevating himself above what was going on in his cell. He rose above that which was happening in the physical space wherein his body was located.

Marat remembered Keiko's words: that a monk's mind is like the steady surface of a lake, off which the owl's cry echoes – or something like that. And he had attached himself to this image. He imagined that his mind was like the absolutely calm, mirror-like surface of a deep lake: onto which everything that happened was reflected, without causing a single ripple on the surface. A war or a massive fire could be raging around the lake, or people could be screaming at one another in its vicinity, but it still wouldn't cause the top layer of the water to stir, let alone penetrate its depths. And even if something like that did happen – even if someone were to throw a stone at the lake – that would be just a fleeting moment; a brief, one-off splash. And even then, if you kept your eye on the stone, you'd see it sinking slowly and calmly towards the bottom. Nothing could disturb the stillness of the lake, and nothing could hurt it.

Envisaging the lake in his mind really did help Marat a lot. He thought about it at night, with his eyes closed, as he tried to fall asleep. And now he had also started thinking about it during the day. At first, he only meditated on it with his eyes closed, but now he could focus his attention on the lake with his eyes open, too. He could switch off the rapist and the launderer's insufferably stupid conversations; their arguments about politics; the latter's arrogant 'lessons in life'; as well as his snarky remarks and the rapist's annoyance at them – none of it could reach Marat anymore. Thanks to the lake, Marat had managed to adapt to the rapist's snoring and moaning and the launderer's flatulence and masturbation. He could still sense, see and hear all of it – it was impossible not to – but it didn't cause a reaction inside him, as though it all remained external. Marat had become the lake. Whatever those little people were doing on its shores no longer affected him in any way. He felt rescued by this feeling. It gave him hope that he'd survive this, and Marat clung to this like a drowning man to a floating rafter. You couldn't quite get on it and relax; you couldn't even cling to it properly – but it was still a refuge, just like the image of the lake was. It couldn't save Marat completely, and not all of the time, but it was at least something to hold onto. And, most importantly, it helped him fall asleep at night, which counted for a lot. It was just enough for him to harbour a hope that he would get through this. If only he had tried something like this sooner.

He found it very hard to remember how it had been when he was annoyed by the corkscrews or the corks that hadn't been removed, or by Twinka's stacking the dirty plates in the sink. How insignificant all of that seemed to him now. The amount of annoying, insufferable and disgusting things that were going on around here made everything that had happened in his life until then seem like the Garden of Eden. Except, of course, back then, with his famous IQ, he wasn't capable of seeing it. Now, it seemed so self-evident. How could he have been such a fool? He, of all people? And if it wasn't possible for him to trust his own judgement, how could he possibly go on living? How could he be sure that he'd be able to stop himself from making another huge mistake: one that seemed like a good idea in the heat of the moment?

Marat imagined a religious person saying that God had made sure Marat went through this experience in order for him to find purpose and meaning, so that he'd understand what an arrogant idiot he'd been and would realise his big mistake. It would serve as a positive and reassuring narrative. He could even say his heartfelt thanks to God for teaching him this invaluable lesson and granting him this newfound wisdom. But Marat didn't believe in God, and so there was no consolation in that.

This week, Marat was going to be transferred to a smaller, two-person cell. And what made this news even better was the fact that, at least to begin with, he'd have it to himself. Keiko had finally succeeded in arranging this. The transfer alone was excellent news – because, no matter how well he was doing with the lake, Marat still wanted nothing more than to get rid of the potentially innocent yet incredibly pathetic rapist and the deluded joke of a money launderer. He hoped that he'd never have to exchange another word with these Shudras as long as he lived.

Nine weeks had passed since he'd first entered prison, and they had seemed incredibly long. During those weeks, he'd experienced, survived and overcome at least as much as he had done in the previous thirty years. No Everest, no travels, no books, exhibitions nor paintings, nor women – except for Twinka – had ever managed to penetrate his soul on such a deep level; had moulded and tortured him so. Nothing in his life had ever inspired as much soul-searching as these last few weeks spent in prison.

Somewhere in the depths of the lake – like a little, yellow fish – a new clarity had appeared. It signalled that there would come a time when he'd be proud of this experience. He'd regale stories of prison life to his friends and acquaintances alongside those of Everest. And, faking modesty, he'd pretend not to notice the looks of respect and admiration that people would give him. The only thing he had to do was figure out a way to get out of here. The adventure hadn't been all that bad in the end – it had been a very interesting experience – but still, he'd had enough.

In order to ensure he was set free, he had to start preparing for his trial.

CHAPTER 55

Heading over to Anna's, Twinka took a bottle of mineral water with her. The writing 'pH 10' was clearly visible on the bottle. It was the only water she ever drank.

Some time ago, a friend she'd met at a wine tasting had told her that a famous doctor had said to her: 'If you drink a glass of water with a high pH level in-between glasses of wine, then the wine won't cause any damage to your health'. Even though Twinka forgot to have the water in-between the glasses of wine, at least she drank it during the first part of the day.

"It looks like I'm going to have some problems with Dimitri, too," Twinka said, carefully studying Anna's face for her response. She wondered whether Anna was just as excited for their weekly sessions as she was: so she could hear the latest news first-hand. Did Anna have many clients whose life had turned into such a mess? Maybe having a lover wasn't that special – even if he was your husband's best friend – but having a husband *in prison* for attempting his *own wife's murder...* That probably didn't happen all too often. Her story was worthy of a novel.

Really, Anna should be offering me a discount for giving her a front-row seat to this show, Twinka thought to herself.

"Problems with Dimitri?" Anna really did look intrigued.

"Yeah, I'm struggling with Dimitri. It sounds like he's fallen in love with me all of a sudden," Twinka said. "He wants me to be with him, and it's so... I don't even know how to describe it. He was the one who always stressed that the most important thing in a relationship between lovers is not to fall in love. And I was always the one who was afraid that I'd end up falling for him."

"And did you fall in love with him?"

"Yeah, I think I did a bit. Maybe. Or maybe not. I really don't know."

"Go on..."

"I can't really tell you much more because I don't feel it anymore. I'm done. I don't feel anything towards him. I no longer even find his company pleasant. He's sending me messages and I don't even want to open them."

"Did you ever discuss a plan whereby you'd divorce Marat and live together?" Anna asked.

"No! No way. They were best friends, so it had to remain a secret. That's why he obsessed so much over the details. He had meticulously chosen that flat, and he always arrived on foot – he never took his car, so that both our cars would never be seen in the same parking lot at the same time, even though the parking was reserved for and only accessible to those living in the building. He would always arrive long before me and leave after I left. He'd use a different entrance door every time, and so on. No, the plan was always to do it in secret. And, to tell you the truth, we enjoyed it – the taste of the forbidden fruit."

"Did you particularly enjoy it because Dimitri was Marat's best friend?"

"I don't know. I doubt it. I can't explain it because, of course, looking back, it seems really silly that it had to be Dimitri of all people."

"But it's not like you could choose between different lovers," Anna interjected, rushing to Twinka's aid, "it wasn't between Dimitri and someone else."

"Yeah... it just sort of... happened."

"And what are you planning to do now?"

"I already said to him that it's not going to work. I don't even feel particularly sorry for him. I mean, it's his fault, really."

"What is?"

310

"Everything."

"Because he told the police?"

"Well, that too. But he's the one who seduced me."

"Oh, I see. That's interesting. Tell me more."

"I didn't want to have an affair. I didn't want to sleep with him – he talked me into it. He manipulated me; he used psychological tactics on me, exploiting all my weak spots, until I finally gave in. But I never actually wanted it."

"But you enjoyed it, didn't you?"

"Well, yeah, I did – but what does it matter? It's like giving drugs to a teenager and saying: 'But you enjoyed it, so that's alright'."

"Or could it be that you're trying to transfer all the responsibility for what happened over to Dimitri? I mean, you're both adults, you had fully consensual sex, and not for a day or two – it went on for a year."

"But if he hadn't led me into temptation, none of this would have happened. Yes, I was weak when it came to him. I need to admit that to myself, of course. But if he hadn't started to twist my arm, then none of this would have happened. Right? I would have never ever made the decision to cheat on my husband. I swear. I never even had the desire. I agreed to this relationship just like Lolita agreed to be in a relationship with Humbert. And we don't believe that she actually agreed to it."

"I don't know," Anna said, unconvinced among other things. "Lolita was twelve, wasn't she? You're not twelve years old."

"Yeah, but I think we should investigate further this idea of consent." Twinka, for her part, seemed to have given this a lot of thought, and seemed very confident in terms of her position.

"It's very interesting that you brought up Lolita –" Anna spoke slowly, as though she was still exploring what she was going to say – "do you think it means that you see yourself as a little girl who's been thrown into adult life much too early, without feeling ready for it? A little girl who's used by men; and it feels so wrong, because she's still just a child. Children should be protected, nurtured, looked after – not abused. Is that what you expect from the men in your life: that they'd nurture, love and protect you, but they end up abusing you instead?"

"Yeah. Maybe. But don't we all want to feel like little girls with someone looking after us? Someone who nurtures and protects us, and we just love him in return? Isn't that what we all want, deep down?"

"You mean, they'll act like loving fathers, and we'll love them for it like we loved our own fathers?" Anna tried to clarify Twinka's train of thought.

Twinka wasn't listening. "We want them to be good to us and never let us down," she continued. "If we're being completely honest, isn't that what we all desire?"

"I don't know. Do you think that's what we all desire?"

Twinka didn't answer. Sometimes Anna's annoying habit of repeating what she had just said infuriated her, along with Anna's reluctance to give her actual opinion. Twinka knew that this was probably central to Anna's professional code. But even so, why couldn't they just have a normal, human conversation every now and then?

"You know what, it's complicated," Anna said, as though having read Twinka's mind. "We're all different. For starters, not everyone has had a loving father. For some it's the opposite – their parents may have been overbearing and put too many limitations on them, so now they crave independence more than anything else. Others may desire an equal – a partner who's also their best friend and teammate. Some might value the fact that he'd be good father material for their children, while others don't want to depend on any man. They may have big ambitions: a successful career, or to build their own business and generate their own income. If they have a man in their lives, then he's not a priority – the main thing is that he doesn't get in the way of their success, which makes his role very marginal. So, I think there's all sorts of cases."

"Well, yeah, I suppose," Twinka agreed, though she was annoyed. "Anyway, it doesn't change the fact that Dimitri used me. I have never had that feeling with Marat, but Dimitri manipulated me. That's how I see it."

"But you didn't feel like that before, did you? When did you first realise this?" Anna seemed relieved that the focus of their conversation had returned to Twinka's feelings.

"I realised it after our last conversation here," Twinka said, feeling a strong desire to have a swig of an old, strong, juicy Bordeaux. Pauillac 2000 vintage would be perfect right now. She took a sip of her heightened-pH water, hoping it would wash away her thirst for alcohol, at least momentarily. "It was when you said that Dimitri thinks that he deserves more in life. That he should be in Marat's place. Do you know what I mean? Because I think you were right. I think that, for Dimitri, it was more than just sex with any odd woman. It was important that I was Marat's wife. You hit the nail on the head there. He tried to prove to himself that he was no worse than – and maybe even better than – Marat. That he could get the same things as Marat. Maybe he could take something from Marat, so that he could feel like he was in his place and better than him. And I was an idiot for not seeing it sooner. I thought that he wanted *me*, but he didn't desire me at all – he desired Marat's place," Twinka said, making a point of looking at her watch. She wanted to end today's session. They'd been talking for long enough. She wanted to go home, be on her own, open a bottle of wine and unplug from everything. There had to be another box of Château Mouton Rothschild with Pauillac 2000 vintage. It had a logo of a golden lamb.

That will do the job, Twinka thought, laughing inwardly. That's what she would drink today.

CHAPTER 56

"How's your new cell? I hope you're not too bored being on your own?" the old sage Keiko asked, probably expecting praise or gratitude in return. Marat knew that it hadn't been easy for Keiko to arrange his being alone.

"It's perfect. I've never been bored when I'm by myself. Thank you so much, I really appreciate it. I really do," Marat said from the bottom of his heart.

"We do what we can." Keiko smiled a self-satisfied, falsely modest smile.

"Listen, I've had time to consider everything," Marat said. "Solitude can really help you gather your thoughts. I'm getting bored of being in prison, so I've come up with a plan."

"Oh?" Keiko was very willing to listen.

"I'll tell you exactly how it all really happened."

"Right." Keiko tore a fresh sheet from one of his large notepads, ready to write it all down.

"So..." Marat looked very focused and serious. "Twinka and I, my wife... Our sex life had hit a bit of a dry patch, so to speak. You know, it happens in a marriage. We've been married for a long time, we've tried everything, there's nothing new left, and so the sparks are no longer flying."

"Right..." Keiko gave an affirmative nod.

"I mean, sixteen years – it's not like the first three or even six years in that sense, right?"

"Yeah, you could say that," Keiko cautiously agreed.

"And so, Twinka had told me that she had this rape fantasy. Obviously, she didn't want to get actually raped, but it was along those lines. She'd be alone at home and then some stranger would sneak up on her from behind and take her by force, brutally and ruthlessly. Those were her exact words. So, there I was. At first, I found it absolutely unacceptable. It sounded unhealthy to me. But I'm the sort of person who likes to try new things, so I decided that I'd give her that kind of experience, and there'd be much for us to discuss afterwards. So, it came about from her own initiative. She suggested it. She did, not me." Marat was looking at Keiko, as though making sure that the lawyer had understood everything.

"Yes." Keiko nodded his head, then waited.

"So that's why I came home. That's why I left my phone in the car: so that she couldn't get hold of me. I wanted to really get into character, you know. That's why I put the gloves on – so that she couldn't recognise me by my hands when I attacked her from behind. I was wearing a mask, too, but I ripped it off as soon as I saw what was going on – Dimitri must have taken it. I thought Twinka might call the police, and I was willing to prolong this game a little longer, perhaps not even revealing that it was me right away. I didn't really understand her – I don't think she did either – when she told me of this particular fantasy of hers. Nonetheless, I let my imagination go, thinking that, perhaps, this stranger could appear in the future, and we'd know it was me. Or, in another scenario, perhaps she wouldn't know it was me. Both options were open. We would finally be onto something interesting. That was my thinking anyway. Does it make sense so far?"

"Yes, it's very interesting." Keiko was looking over his notes.

"Good. So, that's what happened there, from my side anyway. Of course, I would never dream of killing my life partner. Never! I love her. All those stories, saying that I'd plotted to murder her: those were invented by her lover, who actually wanted to kill *me*. By the way, not only did he plan to kill me – he was obviously looking for the promissory note in my office. He owes me quite a lot of money. He clearly wanted to get rid of me and with it his debt, which is why he'd ransacked my office. It was Dimitri who did it. He came up with all those stories about me revealing my plan to kill my own wife to him. It's ridiculous, isn't it? If I wanted to kill my wife, would I be discussing it with anyone, months ahead of time? Who do you think I am? My IQ is 165. I would never come up with something so stupid."

Keiko continued to write Marat's story down in silence.

"And, just so there are no misunderstandings," Marat's voice sounded categorical and much louder than usual, "I never had any intention of killing my dear wife. I have never discussed anything like that with anyone, let alone plotted it. Dimitri's testimony against me is a complete lie, from the first letter to the last, and it's obvious what motive he had for slandering me."

"I understand." Keiko had now finished writing, and placed his pen down. He laid back in his chair, crossed his hands over his chest and continued looking over his notes.

"But you did hit your wife with a bottle?" he finally asked.

"Well, maybe I did. I was in a state of emotional lability. When I arrived, I saw my wife orally satisfy my best friend. I'm sorry, but I lost my temper, my mind went blank. I lost my self control. I wanted to stop it, so I may well have hit her, though I don't remember any of it. In fact, that's the one moment I don't recall clearly. The last thing I remember is seeing my wife on her knees, with my best friend's cock in her mouth."

"Understood." Again, Keiko was writing all of this down.

"I'm not going to waste any more of my time in prison." Marat also laid back in his chair, crossing his arms over his chest.

"And how would you explain why we hadn't come clean with this version straightaway?" Keiko asked, looking at Marat very seriously.

Marat realised that Keiko was actually asking him what he should make of the fact that Marat had told him the entire truth during their first meeting.

"Let's start by agreeing that this is not just some version of what happened," Marat said very firmly, locking directly onto Keiko's eyes.

"Yes, I understand." Keiko had never seen Marat look so aggressive.

"You do realise that I suffered a very heavy trauma to the head, that I'd just woken up from a coma – my chance of survival was less than twenty percent. And because of all the things that happened – my best friend and my wife's betrayal – I couldn't think straight. I didn't know what actually happened and what was a lie. Everything was muddled in my head back then. Luckily, my recovery was successful and now I can remember everything clearly. As it actually happened."

"Yes, I understand. Well, that could work, I agree," Keiko said after a pause.

"Excellent!" Marat crossed one leg over the other, satisfied. He hadn't expected anything other than consent.

"Yes, and I also want to press charges against Dimitri for attacking me. He's the one who wanted to kill me. He was motivated by the debt he owed me, and he wanted to get rid of me, so that he could take my place. You've seen him, haven't you? He's tall and he's bulky, he's a trained wrestler. He's much stronger than me: if he'd wanted to stop me, he'd have no problem in doing so. But he wanted to kill me. He was acting with a single goal in mind – to murder me. That's why he was lurking around our house, looking for an opportunity to attack. And finally he found it. He should be the one who's put on trial. I want him to be in my place, behind bars."

"Right, I see." Keiko made yet more notes. "Well, we might have a case for crossing the boundaries of self-defence."

"He wanted to kill me!" Marat raised his voice again, ignoring any objections. "And to marry my wife, who would inherit all my money. He's the murderer."

"How about this," Keiko said formally. "We'll prepare an extended version of your testimony, based on what you've just told me. I'll have a chat with Twinka: the key is that she confirms in writing what you've said." Keiko's questioning gaze bore into Marat.

"She'll confirm everything because, obviously, it's true – we did have that conversation," Marat said with confidence. "If she says that we didn't, then we'll ask for a lie detector test. She won't be able to deny that this conversation did happen, and she shared her desire with me."

"Great, excellent." Keiko started gathering his papers. "I'll bring you your testimony, so you can make any changes, coordinate facts and sign it. Then we'll submit it and get you out of here. That should be our first priority. We'll see what else needs doing afterwards."

"Do it," Marat ordered sternly.

CHAPTER 57

"Ask yourself a question," Anna suggested.

"Me?" Twinka didn't understand.

"Yeah, today you're going to ask yourself a question," Anna restated. Her voice sounded much like a reception teacher who'd just proposed a new game to the children.

"I don't know what to ask." Twinka was flummoxed.

"There must be a question you're looking to answer, which even I don't know anything about."

"Hmm... I really don't know," Twinka said, although it looked like she had processed the rules of the game. She was clearly thinking.

"Have a think. There's no rush," Anna tried to encourage her.

"Well, okay, I do have one question – was it all just a coincidence?"

"Right. Good. And what do you think?" Anna seemed to be enjoying her reception teacher act.

"I wonder whether, the way our lives turn out – is it all in our own hands or is it fate? Is it all just part of God's plan and His will for us? How much depends on me, and how much of what I call my life is actually beyond my control, and always has been?"

"I understand." Anna was finally serious. "That's a really good question. And do you have any ideas?"

"Well, if I had the answer, I probably wouldn't be asking." Twinka was no longer sure whether she liked this game.

"You told me before that you believe in God because you don't believe in coincidences. That you see all of this – Dimitri being in the right place at the right time to save you, and the fact that such coincidences are almost impossible – as the act of

God's will. I think that's how you put it," Anna said, very gently now, trying to encourage her.

"Yeah, that's what I said. I said I believe in God because I don't believe in coincidences. And it's true that I feel God and His presence around me. But at the same time, He still lets me make mistakes. He allows me to sin and make wrong decisions. I don't know why. Since my childhood I've believed that our Father is in Heaven; but shouldn't a loving father protect us from taking the wrong steps? Shouldn't he lead us away from that, somehow? I don't know. I guess I don't really believe that God in Heaven is just a metaphor – I've always thought that He genuinely is like a father to us. But then again, a father takes care of his children: he doesn't just bark out orders at them – do this and don't do this – then leaving them to get on with their lives, all alone. I don't know. A father doesn't usually do that. I suppose it could be that I didn't feel Him in that moment when I made all those wrong decisions. If I had done, I may have acted differently. I don't know why it's designed this way."

"So," replied Anna, "I guess your question is – how much of your life is created by your own mistakes or the decisions you make, and how much is... How should I put it..." She was searching for the right words. "How much is an act of God? To what extent does He get involved?"

"Yeah, I guess that's my question."

"An old joke comes to mind: 'We must believe in luck. For how else can we explain the success of people we don't like?'" Anna, afraid of getting stuck in theological debate, had tried to make their conversation a bit more playful.

Twinka made a sour smile.

"If you were to ask me," Anna continued, "then from a purely psychological point of view, we see it differently. In the model that you're proposing – if I understood you correctly, of course – there is the individual and then there's God. Man and his actions, and God and His plans and actions – and everything that happens in life is the result of an interchange between these two forces: man and God. It's a deep, mystical, enigmatic, and very intimate bond. And, the way I see it, there are lots of unknowns in this relationship. We don't fully understand ourselves, so naturally, we cannot understand God either – but this bond exists nonetheless, and man is always nurturing, perfecting and strengthening this relationship their entire life.

"On the other hand, the model we use in psychology is quite different. Instead of the 'man–God' dynamic, we see multiple factors at play. In psychology, a human being is not something uniform or complete. We have our emotions, the conscious and subconscious mind, our values, traumas, the way we were raised, different cultural and environmental factors, plus our societal and physical factors too. And all of them play a part in affecting us – they determine what we think, how we feel, what decisions we make.

"Then there's other people, too: with their individual emotions, traumas, values, thoughts. And they all affect us in several different ways, whether we realise it or not. We also have a personality type that's not the same as it is for others, and which makes us have a range of reactions to different situations. Then, of course, we also have our differences in education and intellect. There are a range of factors, within us and all around us, that determine how our life turns out. How does that sound to you? Does it make any sense?" Anna tried to show that she wasn't interested in forcing her views on Twinka; that all she wanted was to have a conversation about it.

"Actually," mused Twinka in response, "it's crazy to think that we can never really know the people we've spent years living with – people who are very familiar to us and feel relatively good to have around. Even if we know them well, we can't be sure whether they'll just decide to hit us over the head with a bottle one day."

"Yeah, that's true. Although it's probably much easier to understand the people around us than God," Anna said with a laugh.

"If we could understand God, we'd probably call it science," agreed Twinka. "We had this discussion once, me and Marat. I mentioned that even Einstein believed that God doesn't play dice, and Marat got all fired up. Apparently, Einstein had never believed in the sort of God I believe in, he had never thought the way I think, that it had been taken completely out of context, and so on. But he also said that Stephen Hawking had reacted to this by saying that not only does God play dice, but he sometimes throws them where they cannot be seen and found. And I thought that was well said. Even the most intelligent physicists are not able to uncover how the dice have been scattered."

"And how did that make you feel?"

Twinka hated it when Anna asked these sorts of questions. Though she also understood that this was exactly why she was paying her. "I don't know." She sighed once more. "I'd like there to be a Father in Heaven who doesn't let me make a mistake and sin; someone who holds me back. But He lets me do anything I want! So, it's like I can't rely on myself and I can't rely on Him either."

"Is it really that bad? Maybe you just had your guard down for a brief moment and weren't focused on avoiding sin?"

"Yes, I gave into temptation. But it doesn't really help. I had time to doubt, hesitate, to think it all over. It wasn't a spontaneous act, and it didn't happen purely by accident either. I made a conscious decision and I carried on, and it didn't even seem like such a bad idea at the time. Quite the opposite, in fact – I derived so much pleasure and happiness from it that I was literally glowing. Why didn't Father in Heaven give me a sign? Why didn't He hold me back? And what if the same thing is happening again now, with something else? What if I'm doing something that seems right, but sooner or later will turn out to be very wrong? Or if I'm not doing something that I should be because I don't feel like it, but then later on it will turn out that I should have done it, and I'll deeply regret it? I always pray to God to give me wisdom – and do you think He listens? I really don't know. I pray that He gives me the knowledge of good and evil, that would be plenty. It might sound simple, but I'm no longer sure of anything. Everything is so muddled."

CHAPTER 58

"I had a chat with Twinka," Keiko said, followed by a satisfied cough. "It's definitely good news for us." He was searching for the appropriate form. "Twinka is ready to officially confirm that you had a conversation about... How should I put it –" Keiko hesitated – "fantasies of a BDSM nature. And that the one you brought up really did take place."

"Of course it did," Marat spat in an arrogant, common-sense-confirming tone, as though he'd never even considered the thought that Twinka may not remember their conversation or choose not to confirm that it happened.

"Twinka's testimony is very significant, it will help us a lot. I'd even wager to say that it's a turning point."

"Very good." Although Marat gave Keiko this praise, it was evident from his voice and body language that he considered this to be a small formality that had already been discussed and should not be dwelled upon.

"The only thing is, she said that they weren't having oral sex – though she did admit to kissing Dimitri – so I removed that detail. Other than that, the testimony is ready."

"She had been sleeping with him for an entire year; she had put it in her mouth multiple times. What difference does it make whether it happened at that exact moment or not?"

"Best to stick with what she's already testified." Keiko didn't seem comfortable with the topic of oral sex. "Let's stick with what's in Dimitri's testimony, which was confirmed by your wife – there's no need to question their testimonies on this matter. In fact, it's good for us that she didn't deny they were kissing. It gives us space to further develop our version."

"Okay, fine, I don't care," Marat agreed grumpily. "I just think that oral sex would create a more emotionally charged image."

"The more facts we can prove or use to corroborate our story, the better. Kissing is as good as proven, and that's what's most important right now. Let's not fix something that isn't broken."

"Okay fine, whatever." This time, Marat seemed to have come to terms with the fact that his idea had been rejected.

"The prosecution will definitely have questions to clarify how you got from the Neptune car park back home."

"I can tell them all about my moped – I don't know how they never found it." Marat's passion had been reignited almost instantly.

"That's great – you'll need to explain that, so it's obvious that we have nothing to hide. It's also important that no one helped you during that moment."

"Yeah, we've got absolutely nothing to hide. We'll give them the truth, the whole truth, and nothing but the truth." Marat radiated confidence and conviction.

"As soon as we submit all this, I'll ask them to drop the charges and close the case: because there is no evidence that points towards your intention to kill your wife, and the only eye-witness they have is a pretty shady character. Twinka has no complaints against you; she's suffered no lasting damage health-wise, so there'd be a good basis for us to close this case. But I won't lie to you – I get the feeling that the prosecution will want to see this go to court," Keiko said with markedly less optimism.

"How can they go to court with a case of attempted murder, if they have absolutely no evidence for it?"

"I agree with you, it's just one person's word against another's, and Twinka's statement indirectly confirms our version. However..." Keiko issued a heavy sigh of his own. "Even with court and prosecution, there's always a subjective human factor at play. It's ever-present. It's crucial what the people involved in the case actually think and believe. Who deserves their sympathy? And who do they have an aversion for? It shouldn't be that way, but it's always a factor."

"What are you trying to say?" Marat made no show of hiding his discontent.

"That I've felt a certain... How should I put it," Keiko hesitated. "Not exactly enmity towards you, but definitely a certain kind of hostility. And that makes me worried."

"The enmity of the masses? A disdain for the rich?"

"Maybe that, or perhaps it's something else – but there's definitely something in the air."

"Just get me out of here. I'm the victim in this story, I'm the one who suffered irreversible damage to his health." Marat pointed at his eye patch.

"We'll get you out of here, don't worry. I just feel like they're trying to slow things down. The prosecution already knows that there isn't a lot of evidence. Their case is weak, so they want you to stay in prison for as long as possible. If someone's already in prison, this alone can create a strong conviction in people's subconscious minds that they're a criminal. Because only criminals are sent to prison, right? If you're in prison for your wife's attempted murder then, most likely, you are the attempted murderer of your wife. Do you follow me?"

"So, the most important evidence they've got is the fact that they've already arrested me?"

"Something like that. Not by jurisdiction, of course, but psychologically. Judges are only human, too."

"Unbelievable. What happened to law and order? I thought that law was the best thing we had!"

"Well..." A vague smirk appeared on Keiko's face. "Sometimes the prosecution and the court are convinced, deep down in their hearts, that the person *is* actually guilty and so

326

deserves to be in prison, even when the evidence isn't all too convincing."

"But they're breaking the law!?" Marat looked genuinely astonished. "Servants of the law – breaking the law themselves?!"

"Yes, that's true, of course. But you know, law is one thing and justice is something else. And these two things are always bound closely together. Once you know this, it becomes clear why the servants of the law decide to act according to what they consider to be justice, rather than doing it 'by the book'."

"But that's what a lynch mob is – they can't do that! What would happen if everyone started to act in a way they believed to be just or right?!"

"I completely agree with you; according to the law, it shouldn't be like that. I'm just trying to explain the difficulties that may be ahead of us." These words made him sound helpless. "I've already heard talk that they're planning to carry out a psychiatric examination. As soon as we mention the term 'emotional lability', we won't be able to avoid that. And they'll probably come up with more. Plus, they'll want to delay things." Keiko had now resumed his formal, professional tone.

"The law is on our side. They have no evidence and never will – just get me out of here!" Marat, on the other hand, had resumed his employer's tone: one that brooked no opposition.

Their conversation was over.

CHAPTER 59

They met in the room that was intended for so-called 'conjugal visits' from one's spouse. Those who were entitled to them, had a spouse, and wanted to do so, could meet here twice a year. Just the two of them, for up to forty-eight hours. Keiko hadn't succeeded in getting Marat out of prison before his court date, but he had managed to arrange a ninety-minute window of uninterrupted alone time for Marat and Twinka. You couldn't normally get these sessions while on remand , and so it just went to show how much money could buy around here.

Arriving at the prison, getting searched, and enduring a careful examination of all her possessions and pockets took quite a bit of time, and definitely wasn't one of the most pleasant experiences that Twinka had ever had, though she endured it without complaint. She was then taken to the meeting room and told to wait until Marat was escorted in.

Twinka sat on the only chair opposite the bed, fidgeting with the clasp of her bag.

"Hi." Marat smiled at Twinka as soon as he appeared in the door, but the smile looked uncertain. Marat wanted to turn everything into a joke, to forget it all and start afresh; but he had no idea what was on Twinka's mind, and how she felt about what had happened.

They didn't know how best to start the conversation.

"How's Ronia?" Marat asked.

Twinka sighed. "It's not easy. She doesn't understand anything, so she's asking me a lot of questions and reading stuff on the internet. Of course, I'm always saying that it's not true – that Daddy didn't actually want to kill Mummy – but it's all very complicated."

"I didn't want to kill you," Marat replied. "You believe me, don't you?"

"Are you saying that I should try and explain it to Ronia by saying that it was just a bizarre sexual game between us that didn't go quite as intended?"

"Well, she's a little too young for that... But in general, I think that's exactly how you could try and explain it to her."

"Because of your intellect, no one believes that you could be so stupid as to come up with this idea to kill me." Twinka laughed. "Whereas they would definitely believe it if you said I had some crazy sexual fantasies."

"I don't know what came over me. Believe it or not, I really don't understand how I could have arrived at something as stupid as that."

"Unfortunately, half of this country knows how you arrived at that: because they've all read about how annoyed you were about the corkscrews; about how it would be better for a forty-year-old alcoholic woman to get murdered rather than drag out her pathetic existence, which would only become more miserable with each passing year. By the way, how did Dimitri know about the corkscrews?"

"Clearly, I must have told him about them." There was a hint of annoyance and fatigue in Marat's voice. If Twinka had come here to nitpick and dish out blame, then it would be better if she left.

"Were you really that annoyed about the corks? You could have just said." There was no anger in Twinka's voice. To his surprise, Marat thought he heard a faint echo of the mutual flirty teasing they used to engage in.

"Dimitri..." Marat wasn't in the mood for flirting. "Why did it have to be Dimitri, of all people? Could you not have chosen someone else? Someone who wasn't my best friend?"

Twinka seemed to have focused all her attention on her bag. She opened and closed it, as though she were checking whether the clasp was still working.

"I suppose I could say the same thing as you. In that how, looking back, I don't understand how I could have arrived at that decision. But if we're being completely honest, then it's not true. I know how it happened. Of course, it wasn't the right thing to do, but I don't regret it. He gave me something beautiful and important, which I needed at that moment."

"And you're surprised that I wanted to kill you."

"No, I'm not." Twinka smiled.

"Do you want a divorce?" Marat asked.

"Do you?"

This room was one of the most pathetic and saddest places that Marat had ever set eyes on (and lately, he'd been inside many sad and pathetic rooms). It was even more miserable than his cell, because someone had tried to give this room an air of normality, of cosiness and happiness. Except, of course, they hadn't succeeded. The ceiling was bleached white and the walls were painted a light orange up to eye level, then above that the yellow of butter. A bland yellow curtain covered the barred window, intended to match the rest of the room. There was a small vase on the table, and in it were three plastic flowers that looked like calla lilies. Cleanliness was the only positive quality that could be ascribed to this place, yet there was a price even for that little pleasure – the barely noticeable though still unpleasant smell of disinfectant.

"There's not much you can wish for in this situation." Marat gave a helpless gesture with his hands.

"I've been thinking a lot about it, of course." Now it was Twinka who became serious. "You know, it may sound weird, and I can't explain it with any logic, but I think that – thanks to us both having fallen so low and gone so far – there might be hope for us yet."

"How do you mean, there's hope?" Marat was surprised.

"I mean, divorce would probably be the easiest option for us – but the right path isn't always the easiest," Twinka said and reached towards Marat, stroking the side of his face where his bandage was. "We have a duty towards Ronia," she continued – it was evidently something she'd been thinking about a lot – "we need to show Ronia that everything is okay between us. It's the only hope we have to shield her from the drama of all this. She has to be able to see that it was all just a misunderstanding. We need to show her that we're both just human – we made a mistake like everyone does, we've paid a steep price for it, and we've both learned something."

"And what have we learned?" Marat looked just as serious.

"I don't know, but I think we should do more good. And we should instil that in our daughter: I want to encourage her to be a good person."

"And what will that give her? Nothing. If you're a good person, you'll just end up being used by everyone – the good guys and the bad."

"Marat, aren't you getting sick of this?" Twinka said. Her tone was both surprised and annoyed at the same time. "Don't you think your philosophy of super-egotism has completely failed? Can't you see that's why you're in prison, having brought all this misfortune upon us? Don't you think that – however paradoxical it may sound – the more egotistical a person is, the unhappier they become? Can't you see that in order to feel happy, you need to forget about yourself?"

"I'd like to point out that I'm here only because of Dimitri," Marat wasn't going to cede ground, "and that bastard, Draco, of course. And anyway, have I ever treated Dimitri badly? No, quite the opposite – no one else had ever done as much for Dimitri as I did. And what did I get in return? He was sleeping with my wife, and then he sold me out, so that the police could put me behind bars. If I hadn't been a good person, sought him out and helped him, he would have never done all this to me. How can you not see that?"

"It's not that simple. You're the one who started this chain of events, not Dimitri. You put him in a situation that could have no positive outcome. But he did what he could and saved my life."

"And I've always treated you kindly, too."

"Yeah, of course." Twinka laughed. "Except when you almost killed me!"

"Because you were sleeping with my best friend!"

"Look, let's be honest – is that really why?"

Marat pretended not to hear the question. "I do agree with you though," he said, "we have a duty towards Ronia, and I'll do everything in my power to fulfil it. I just don't want to fill her head with soppy clichés. I don't want her to become part of the herd."

"She doesn't stand a chance with a father like you." Twinka laughed again. "Maybe with all your talents you could come up with a philosophy that would make the world a better place, without making you weak. To do good and to be strong, and to take a stand against evil – that's what we could teach her."

Marat sat on the bed, his back against the wall. He was silent, and away with his thoughts.

"Where is all this fear of being used coming from anyway?" Twinka continued. "Is a strong person supposed to have so much fear? So what if you get used? Because you will. Of course you will! You won't get appreciated; people will forget to thank you. But so what? Let the weaklings and paupers have their way, who cares? Because there will be someone who appreciates it and someone who will say thank you – and you need to be good for your own sake, not theirs."

"My sake? So, it is egotism after all. You're saying: drop your ego and accept mine instead because it's somehow better." Marat made a dismissive gesture with his hand.

"Okay, fine, call it egotism if it helps you accept the strategy I'm proposing. Either way, you'll still gain from it, maybe far more than you did when you weren't concerned with doing good. And people will love you."

"To be honest, I don't think it's as straightforward as choosing a different strategy." Marat was very serious now. "In order to be good, you need, first and foremost, a desire to do good. But I just don't see any reason for wishing people well, at least not most of them. They're all stupid, evil and two-faced. Besides, it's not like any of them would wish good things for *me*. So then why on earth – and, honestly, give me one good reason – should I be good to *them*? They're destroying this country, our century, our environment; the air we all breathe, the water we drink! And you can't negotiate anything with them, because they're just incapable of understanding the most basic things. They fuck up absolutely everything – the politics, the economics, the planet – everything! So, why would I commend them? Will that somehow make them smarter or less evil? I highly doubt it. It's never happened before, and it won't happen now. Or ever. I have more compassion for pigs who have just been let out of their pen, because at least they won't be harming anyone. No, it's just not happening. Well, it's not like I necessarily *want* bad things to happen to them – I just don't see any reason to wish them well. And the few people I have been favourable towards and done good things for – they've paid me back with hurt and betrayal. And you're saying that I should be doing more for people? No. I'd rather stick to my strategy of service–payment–goodbye."

"Marat, this will end badly."

"It's already ended badly," was Marat's autocratic response.

"Nothing's ended. All this will pass, you'll get out of prison, and then it will all depend on you. As you like to say: it's never too late to start a new life – not even the day before death."

"Why does speaking the truth always get you into trouble?" said Marat, seemingly ignoring Twinka. "Why is our world set up that way? If you dare to share your actual thoughts, if you don't think *exactly* like the rest of the group, then you're guaranteed to have problems in life. It shouldn't be like that, should it?"

"Well, if you're so bothered about it, why don't you invest your energy, skills and money into something that would make the world a better place? Why don't you muck in, and start improving it in some way?"

"If only I believed it was possible – but it's not. Saying 'improve the world' is just like saying 'improve the winter, so it's summer again'. It doesn't work – we can only do it through winter, a catastrophe, fire, death, war, the plague... There's no other way. We must first fuck everything up to the utmost degree, before we can start improving things."

"And have you fucked everything up to the point that you can start improving things?" Twinka laughed.

"I guess I have." Marat himself smiled.

"Are we also going to be following the process of service–payment–goodbye?"

"We have Ronia, so I guess we'll need a slightly more complicated process." Marat was looking into Twinka's eyes with a serious gaze. "Essentially, we're in a contractual relationship with Ronia. By letting Ronia into this world, we have already signed a contract with her and we have a duty to fulfil it until she comes of age."

"Yeah, and I assume this contract has a clause that says her parents will do everything they possibly can to not end up in prison?"

"Yeah, that clause exists," Marat agreed sadly. "Well, then, let's take care of her," he added, following a moment's silence, "and let's try and raise her to be as intelligent as possible, smarter than both of us. Then, hopefully, she'll be able to face the world herself."

"I'm happy with that plan!" Twinka laughed again, but this time it sounded kinder and sweeter. "Come here." She got up from her chair and went over to Marat. She gently caressed her husband's head and touched his forehead softly with her lips.

Marat could only utter a sigh, which conveyed everything – his regret, a plea for forgiveness, as well as the unexpected pleasure of relaxation. Their lips touched. Marat was trembling all over. "Oh, Twinka," was all he managed to say. Twinka kissed his lips, his cheeks, his nose and forehead; she bit his lip and started to unbutton his trousers. On her initiative, Marat fully submitted to her.

The next moment, Twinka was on her knees. She knew that Marat enjoyed this the most. Twinka wasn't rushing – at first, she took it in her hand, as though caressing and admiring it. She was looking into Marat's eyes – she was getting herself ready, tucking rebellious strands of hair behind her ears as Marat waited patiently. Then, slowly, she put it in her mouth. With her free hand she was working around Marat's balls. She was doing it slowly, stopping every now and then, and gazing into his eyes almost the entire time. He couldn't stand the teasing any longer – he wanted it to happen now, so she increased the tempo. Twinka felt how turned on he was, and she wanted to feel it inside her.

The prison bed was incredibly squeaky – you could definitely hear it all the way from the corridor – but it only made them laugh.

"Let's break this bed," Marat said, with Twinka on top of him. "Let's destroy it!"

And she didn't hold back – the prison guards would have certainly heard her moaning, as well as that of the bed.

They had never felt so open and free, aroused and in love. They fell deeper into one another – in the way you can only do with someone you have already loved for a long time.

CHAPTER 60

Marat didn't get to enjoy the solitude of his new surroundings for long. The prison was overcrowded, and even Keiko couldn't ensure the two-bed cell remained private.

The name of Marat's new cellmate was Theodor. When Theodor first arrived, Marat stared at him in astonishment, like he was some sort of alien. Theodor looked like a small and scrawny boy of no more than twenty years, yet his entire forehead was covered with a massive tattoo. This was the first time Marat had seen anyone with a tattoo on their forehead. NO FEAR it read, in large writing, and it was practically bisected by a scar that looked almost vertical. There were other scars across his face, too. They were from a fight in a bar. As Marat later learned, someone had smashed a glass against Theodor's face. (Two, in fact, because Theodor had remained standing after the first.)

Theodor also had other, smaller tattoos elsewhere on his face and body. Under his right eye was a miniature lightning symbol that looked like a tear, while a skull adorned one of his temples. There was also a cross under his left ear along his jawbone, and a cobweb further down on his neck. A Batman symbol stretched across his shoulder blades, and his fingers housed strange symbols that Marat didn't recognise. However, none of these were any match for the inscription that dominated Theodor's forehead.

Theodor was twenty-six, and he was a murderer.

Marat had never seen anyone like him – he couldn't avert his gaze from the boy's face, nor could he find the right words to summon for a greeting. Theodor, on the other hand, didn't raise his eyes to meet Marat's. He walked by silently and made himself comfortable on the vacant bed.

Having somewhat come to his senses, Marat felt that Theodor would appreciate it if Marat didn't say anything or ask him any questions. As a sign of goodwill, Marat pushed some pâté and a packet of crisps, both of which lay on the otherwise empty table, towards the boy. Having then picked up a book, Marat reclined onto his bed in silence. Aside from the tattoos, the boy didn't look particularly dangerous. In fact, he looked wretched.

The silence ensued, though it was devoid of tension. Theodor seemed grateful for the questions that Marat didn't ask, for the opinions he didn't share, and for his silent support, which he could feel, even though had not yet lifted his eyes to meet Marat's. Not once, not even with a nod, had he thanked Marat for the snacks and the delicacies, the tea, the razor, or the brand-new toothbrush that Marat gave him to replace the small, clumsy prison-issue one. Theodor didn't have anything – no things, no money to buy something at the prison shop; nor did he have anyone on the outside who could help him. His only possession was a tattered motorcycle magazine: the issue in question dedicated to determining the year's best models across a range of categories.

Somewhere between the fifth and the ninth day of silence, it became clear to both of them that they would become best friends.

Roughly around the same time, Keiko – with whom Marat met every day, in order to prepare for the trial and coordinate his testimony – introduced Marat to Theodor's criminal case and showed him the boy's court materials. Keiko had marked the most interesting pages with yellow sticky notes. During one of their meetings, Keiko patiently waited while Marat finished reading the file. Theodor's story went like this...

Aged fifteen, Theodor had run away from home, rescuing himself from a violent stepfather. Since then, he'd lived in a gloomy district of dockworkers, prostitutes, smugglers, and other dregs of society. Having had very little formal education, Theodor had somehow managed to train himself to become a mechanic. He worked in a little workshop, where he fixed scooters, motorbikes and bicycles. The prosecution, however, suspected that he was actually dismantling, altering and selling stolen vehicles. It had never been proven though, and he hadn't received any charges on this count.

With his extremely slight build, and now existing amid the harsh reality and nebulous pecking order of street life, Theodor found himself in a constant state of stress and insecurity. The type wherein you are kind of respected, but not quite. And so you spend every day holding on (even if it's by your fingernails) to the thin ledge that separates those who command respect from everyone else. Every hour of every day, you have to carefully consider how you should behave and what you should do to maintain your status, so as not to find yourself suddenly on the wrong side of the line. Fortunately Theodor had a stable job and a steady income, which counted for a lot. The reason he was able to hold onto his job was because he barely ever used drugs and he didn't overindulge in alcohol, although the latter also made it harder for him to fit in.

His tiny frame and accompanying lack of physical strength were a problem in a society where violence was part of everyday life. Violence was a means of communication, and a method for solving even the smallest of conflicts. Theodor carried a screwdriver on him, and from his early days his eyes burned with a clear and desperate determination to kill or be killed in order to maintain his respect at any given moment. This look and resolve protected him, but only as far as not tipping him over the edge. From here, all it took was for one unfortunate event – like some joke uttered at a bar, which saw everyone in stitches – to lower him to the bottom step of this already miserable existence. It hadn't happened yet, although Theodor always felt as if the tide could turn at any moment.

His first tattoos helped, as though they imbued him with some sort of mystical protection. (as did the screwdriver in his pocket). The feeling was especially pronounced when he added the skull on his left temple. Others valued and respected him for it. It saw Theodor rise a little in the hierarchy of the docks. Almost everyone had tattoos around here – but not on their head or face, which is what made Theodor's skull special, and he enjoyed the attention and respect it earned him. And, for the first time in his life, Theodor felt quite relaxed at their local bar. This, in a dark basement, was fittingly called, The Basement. It was where the local who's who would gather. He felt like someone who belonged, like he was part of the pack. Life felt good. And so, Theodor decided to strengthen his position, and take another – more significant and serious – step to, hopefully, rise a little higher still. He decided to cover his entire forehead with a tattoo.

Without much hesitation, he settled on NO FEAR.

At first, the letters NO appeared: resulting in the admiration he had been expecting from those around him, as well as respect, acknowledgement and a number of questions. If only he'd been smarter – and stuck with just the mysterious and tantalising NO – then his life would have taken a different course. But the thought of doing so never even entered Theodor's mind. He was convinced that this was the right course of action, and that every extra section that followed would bring him even greater success.

A few months later, the tattoo NO FEAR was finished. At first, everything played out as he expected. When he first walked into The Basement, Theodor met by expressions that screamed praise and admiration. That was, until one of the local gangsters – a sad little pimp or a drug dealer – came up to him and asked, "So, you're not afraid of nothing, is it?"

"Nothing," Theodor responded with pride.

"Not afraid of me either then?"

"No." Theodor had managed to hold his opponent's gaze and his voice didn't tremble.

Then, for the first time in his life, he felt what it was like when someone smashed a half-empty beer glass in your face. The beer and the blood gushed all over his clothes.

"Fuck you," Theodor said, without thinking; and received a second glass, losing consciousness. As he fell, the screwdriver in his pocket pricked his groin.

This event in itself wasn't enough to tarnish Theodor's reputation. Though it would have been if he never returned to The Basement.

So he went back, and, as soon as he walked in, he was approached by another local criminal authority. Clearly, the tale of "Theodor who wasn't afraid of anything" was a popular one in The Basement.

"So, you're not afraid then?" the guy asked him with a smirk, while the whole bar cheered him on, eager to see the show.

"No," Theodor answered calmly.

Theodor was ready. It was about to be the most important moment of his life. He knew it was coming, and was fully focused.

This time his assailant wielded a bottle of beer; the attack neither particularly fast nor dangerous, as the man was not expecting Theodor to put up any resistance. But Theodor dodged the blow and pushed the screwdriver right into the man's fat stomach. Again and again. He couldn't remember the rest.

Theodor woke up in hospital – one of his hands was handcuffed to the bed frame. Someone had smashed a bottle over his head before he got arrested.

The prosecution claimed that Theodor, having set out to The Basement with a screwdriver in his pocket, was going there with the intention to murder, even though he didn't know who he was going to murder, and so no extenuating circumstances could be applied. This entire situation was caused by Theodor himself: as, one after another, he made all the wrong decisions, and was fully aware of their consequences.

The judge was rather considerate towards Theodor and leaned towards self-defence, which Theodor's pro-bono defence counsel had maintained. There was no doubt, insisted, the lawyer, that Theodor would have been murdered – if not on that particular occasion, then some other time – and he really was fighting for his life. The final verdict testified to the fact that the judge was especially furious over the prosecution's suggestions that Theodor should have foreseen that he'd get beaten up for having such a tattoo on his forehead, and therefore Theodor should not have got it in the first place and/or should not have been going to bars. The judge issued a clear signal that no tattoo could justify the act of violence directed at Theodor. The words NO FEAR didn't offend anyone; they weren't rude; they didn't hurt anyone's feelings; they weren't considered provocative. Theodor hadn't intended to offend, insult or provoke anyone by getting the tattoo, or to put his own well-being or life on the line.

As a result, the judge sentenced Theodor to three years in prison for breaching the limits of self-defence. It was far less than Marat might get for only attempting to murder his wife.

CHAPTER 61

Mum died in her garden, a week before the trial began, next to her beloved petunia pots. The neighbours noticed that she'd had a fall and wasn't moving. By the time the ambulance arrived, there was nothing more to be done.

For Marat, light, expected sorrow mixed with immense relief. It was good, at the end of the day. It was for the best, he was sure of that. Her life had become a huge burden for herself, and for him of course. Yes, this was a good outcome. Besides, Mum had died beautifully – in her own garden, without any needless suffering.

Deep down, Marat could feel something akin to grief or sorrow, but he wasn't going to dwell on it. *This is good news. I have to move forward,* he told himself.

Mum's suffering, and the sense of guilt that accompanied it, had suffocated Marat this entire time he was in prison. He wasn't worried about his own reputation, or the months he'd lost by being in prison, or even how this would affect Ronia. All of that was uncomfortable, of course, but he saw it as work – problems he needed to resolve – whereas his mother's suffering was something else entirely. The damage for her was unsolvable, irreparable, irreversible. The knowledge of this was always there: poisoning his days and torturing him at night. The feelings of guilt and shame burned his stomach, made his back ache, and weighed heavily on his chest. But now, it was all over – Mum was no longer suffering. And that was good. Very good.

Twinka made all the funeral arrangements, and the judge allowed Marat to attend the service, though he didn't permit him to attend the wake. Marat had to be back at prison within four hours – any delay would be considered as an attempt at escape. Mum had left detailed instructions for everything concerning her funeral: who should be invited; what music should be played; which photographs should be on display; what flowers should be laid down by the coffin; what shoes, clothes and beads she should be dressed in, including which bracelets should be put on each wrist. Everything had been planned to the smallest detail, and so it wasn't particularly difficult to organise.

The ceremony took place in a small farewell hall at the crematorium. The décor, although ascetic, was not too gloomy. In accordance with tradition, the coffin was placed on a small pedestal in the middle of the hall. The funeral guests could stand next to it for a while, place their flowers, even sit on the chairs positioned a few metres back. It was like they were immersed in a piece of performance art designed to make them contemplate how much time was left before it would be their own funeral. Marat didn't recognise most of the silver-haired ladies and their husbands who had come – Mum's fellow students, colleagues and peers – most of whom were reduced to tears by seeing another affirmation of death's inevitability.

Having patiently waited for an opportune moment, Marat politely asked everyone to leave, so that he could say his farewell to Mum in private.

"No, you stay," he said to Twinka, locking the door of the hall from the inside.

They walked up to the coffin. Marat embraced Twinka and she cuddled up to him, thinking that he was looking for consolation and compassion. But when Marat slid his hands down to Twinka's bottom and grabbed it, it was clear he had something else on his mind.

"Marat!" she shouted, both surprised and shocked.

Marat squeezed again, bringing her closer towards him. Twinka couldn't free herself, but she bent her head back as much as she could, so that Marat couldn't start kissing her. Marat flattened his face against her chest. Twinka tried to push him away, but he held her in a firm grip. She lost her balance. To avoid tripping, she instinctively leaned on the coffin, moving it out of place as a result. She let out a quiet shriek, which only made Marat laugh.

"Marat, stop it," she begged, "you're insane!" She was worried her screams could be heard from the outside, and would attract attention.

But Marat didn't stop.

Twinka was wearing a black formal dress – it was tight, slightly longer than knee-length and utterly unsuited to a quickie. Marat tried to lift it, but he didn't succeed. He managed to unzip the dress at the back half-way, though that didn't help much either.

"Marat, I can't!"

"Yes, you can," Marat said, and continued to undress her.

"Marat," resisted Twinka, once again forced to hold onto the coffin. "No, Marat, you can't do this!" There was fear in her eyes.

"She's all for it, believe me," Marat said, and didn't stop.

Twinka realised that Marat wouldn't give up. She was afraid they'd tip the coffin over and Mum's body would fall out onto the floor.

"Okay. Wait." Angrily, she stopped Marat. "Let me do it myself then."

Marat stepped back and watched Twinka roll her dress down to the floor. She was wearing black laced underwear, from her favourite Le Petit Trou collection. Marat exhaled a heavy breath of excitement and rushed to slide off his trousers. He was ready for action. Twinka stepped out of her dress, with her back turned against the coffin. Marat pulled her towards him and tried to twist her around, so that her back would be towards him.

"No, no, no!" Twinka shouted, and freed herself from Marat's grip. She wouldn't do it while staring at Marat's mother's dead body!

Twinka walked towards the back wall of the hall, which was furthest away from the entrance door. Marat obediently followed. To his delight, he discovered that Twinka was wet, which made him want to make her orgasm, so she couldn't say that she didn't like it afterwards. He tried, but he was too aroused – he'd been forced to resist for far too long, so everything was over within a minute, and he came inside her.

Twinka didn't know how to interpret this. *Does he think I'm still on the pill? Or is he finally open to the idea of having another baby? I'll have to discuss this with Anna.* These thoughts raced through her mind while Marat, moaning with pleasure, made his final thrusts. Whatever it was, the fact that he came inside her surprised Twinka and, on some level, even made her happy. Did he trust her again? Could they have a future? Did this mean that he still loved her? That they could, perhaps, have another baby?

"You're completely insane," Twinka said, getting dressed.

"And you look good," Marat replied, radiating satisfaction.

They straightened the coffin, making sure it was still where it was intended to be.

"I should go, it's time," Marat said. "Make sure everything is just as she wanted it to be."

"Yeah, okay." Twinka couldn't hide her smile – she was excited about what had just happened here.

CHAPTER 62

Marat's trial went on for two weeks. It was during this time that Twinka started to drink in the mornings. She didn't even notice how, but instead of wanting her morning coffee she now went straight for the champers. She chose ones that had almost no fizz – Jacques Selosse became her regular.

In her entire life, Twinka had never gone through anything as tough, horrific, humiliating and excruciating as this trial. *Sometimes I feel like I'd have been better off being killed,* she often caught herself thinking.

Even though it was a private hearing, the fact that Marat was on trial for attempting to murder his own wife was a well-known fact. No one dared to ask Twinka what had happened and how she was feeling, but she knew that these questions were in absolutely everyone's mind. It was utterly unbearable. Twinka had only been called in once to give her testimony (instructed by her lawyers, she had exercised her right to abstain from testifying against family members), though even that in itself had been harrowing enough.

The cameras; the waiting outside the courtroom door, surrounded by journalists, until she was called in; Marat's broken, miserable, silent stature as he sat on the defendant's bench, a police officer by his side... It all left her stunned and scarred.

Twinka felt so horrible that at times she couldn't even think. She could only watch herself, as though from a distance; feeling alienated, and never quite grasping what was really going on. How could their – by almost every metric – wonderful life: in the beautiful house, with their amazing daughter, their friends, their parties and dancing, the excellent wines and food... How could all of that have suddenly morphed into this living nightmare set in a courthouse? Everything that was happening felt so unreal to her: like it was a bad dream; something utterly surreal. She could only participate as a passive observer. And drink champagne. The champagne was reserved for the first part of the day, and wine was for the evenings. Or, sometimes, cognac.

The worst thing by far was the effect all this was having on Ronia. Twinka was worried about her. She couldn't take the internet away from her daughter, and no matter how hard Twinka tried to prevent it, Ronia had already learned everything. Now Twinka had to find answers to Ronia's questions – but how? How could you possibly answer: "Is it true that Daddy tried to kill you, Mummy?"

"No," Twinka would always say, "it's not true – it's all just one big misunderstanding." She didn't know how to explain the misunderstanding: all she could do was hug Ronia as they cried together. Then she would say: "We have to keep going", and ask her daughter to go and do her homework or read a book while she went to pour herself some wine.

If I could just feel hatred or anger towards him, that might make things easier, Twinka thought.

But she didn't feel anything like it. In fact, if she hadn't been able to recall the hefty blow with a bottle of Paulliac 2000 vintage then she probably wouldn't even believe Dimitri's stories. Marat and murder?! It sounded so inconceivable – too brutal, too dirty, too vulgar, for someone like him. But it was impossible not to believe it. She had managed to look Marat in the eye, and found there was no hatred there, nor anger. Those weren't the eyes of a madman, or someone consumed by rage. The only thing that was clearly visible in them was determination – cold, dispassionate commitment.

Yet despite this, Twinka couldn't feel anything other than pity for him. She realised that it was illogical and wrong – an inexplicable paradox – to pity a murderer, a brute. To pity him over how pathetic he looked, sat there on the defendant's bench with his one remaining eye. But that's exactly how she felt. She felt sorry for Marat.

She didn't want this. She didn't want Marat to suffer. If Draco hadn't set her into a tailspin with his threats about putting Ronia in a crisis centre, then Twinka would have never given such a testimony. But how could anyone prepare for something like that? How can you possibly assess all the circumstances and choose the right path at a moment like that? It was impossible. No wonder the police resorted to such tactics.

Dimitri called her one evening. Her feelings towards him had completely changed.

"How is it possible?" Twinka asked him. "You are probably two of the most intelligent people in this entire city – two grown-ups, both with excellent educations, both so erudite and experienced. Can you explain how you managed to get into this mess together? How did you do it? How could you get yourself into this situation?!"

"There's no 'us'," Dimitri said, resentful. "It wasn't 'us' – it was Marat. I don't think I've done anything wrong in this situation. I tried to talk him out of it, to change his mind, and I saved your life. How could you possibly compare me to him?"

Twinka said nothing in response.

Nonetheless, Dimitri inferred a tangible doubt from her silence, and the invisible wall that was now between them grew taller.

CHAPTER 63

Keiko's team did everything they possibly could to make Dimitri come across like an outlaw.

Everything Marat knew about Dimitri was put to use. And, of course, as Dimitri's best friend, he knew a great deal.

Keiko asked Dimitri's ex-wife and her boyfriend who'd been beaten up to testify in court, and they jumped at the opportunity to portray Dimitri as an unstable, rude and aggressive type: someone who was more than capable of resorting to blind, unprovoked violence.

Afterwards, Marat's lawyers described Dimitri and Twinka's relationship without sparing any details, aiming to show that Dimitri had good motive to kill Marat and lie about him in court. Keiko spent ages analysing the fact that Dimitri, giving his testimony to the police, had described Marat simply as 'an acquaintance', even though they had been best friends and Marat was the person closest to Dimitri: as evidenced by the intensity of their correspondence and phone calls, their time spent together, as well as everything that Marat had done to help Dimitri. By doing this Keiko wanted to show that one couldn't trust a single word that Dimitri said, and that he was a treacherous snake undeserving of an ounce of compassion or sympathy. Keiko's long, eloquent soliloquy outlined how one couldn't rely on this kind of witness testimony as the sole basis for sentencing Marat.

Meanwhile, Marat – even though he was in prison – had made sure that Dimitri was laid off from his job at the bank. The fact Dimitri was unemployed was immediately utilised and used against him. Marat's goal wasn't only to discredit Dimitri as a witness in court – Marat craved revenge. He was determined to cause Dimitri as many problems as possible; to destroy him in as many different ways he could think of. And, for the time being at least, he seemed to be succeeding.

The "friendly loan" Dimitri had received for his house wasn't so friendly anymore. Losing his job and being late on one payment was reason enough to repossess his house. Other banks and pension funds were no longer queuing up for Dimitri's services.

With his reputation in ruins, Dimitri's depression resurfaced. He was psychologically, morally and financially ruined, whereas Marat was experiencing the exact opposite. Even though Marat was in prison, he looked healthier and more energised with every passing day; more capable of regaining control.

Meanwhile, Dimitri had moved into the flat he had used to rent for hooking up with Twinka, though this didn't turn out to be a good idea. Everything – even the bare walls of the flat – reminded him of their many blissful, passionate, ecstatic hours spent together. It was a painful reminder of better times; days in which he still had everything: friendship, love, sex, success, and money; those in which he was a well-respected, even admired, individual, and the future seemed ripe with the promise of further success and happiness. Everything around here reminded him of the wonderful existence that had since vanished.

What did I do wrong? Dimitri asked himself, over and over. *When did I make a mistake?*

At times, Dimitri felt as though every decision he'd made had been a mistake; that everything he had done had been wrong. He was wrong to have kissed his best friend's wife at the party that night. It was even worse that he'd talked her into sleeping with him. And it was despicable to have then carried on doing so. How could he not see the damage all these decisions would cause as he made them – or, at least, the risks involved? How could he, as a maths savant, fail to realise just how dangerous it was?

On other days he felt like none of it had been his fault. It wasn't because of their affair that Marat had decided to kill Twinka – at least, it hadn't been the main reason. And Dimitri had definitely done the right thing by preventing it. Maybe the fact that Twinka had become so close to him was, in some sense, the reason why he had been so worried about her, and how he had found himself at the right place at the right time. It was God's will that Dimitri be there and save an innocent, beautiful, precious life, which was about to be taken by a sociopathic bastard. He had been Twinka's guardian angel, and he shouldn't feel guilty about that. And was it wrong to share the entire truth in court? Probably not. Why should he go to prison and let that narcissistic egomaniac win again? So that Marat could say he'd climbed another Everest? So that Marat could write more books, and sprout his arrogant bullshit ("*How you can achieve any goal in life, as long as you're intelligent enough*")?

No, his saving Twinka was not even a matter of virtue – it would simply have been stupid for him to act in any other way.

However, even this thought failed to make Dimitri's outlook any brighter. Whether it was a result of the mistakes he'd made or an amalgamation of other factors, he had reached the lowest point of his entire life, from which he could see no way forward.

The court ruled Marat not guilty owing to a lack of evidence.

PART 5.
The Day Before Death

CHAPTER 64

Twinka greeted Marat at the prison gate. Even though she wasn't a big fan of it, she had driven to collect him in his favourite car. She knew her husband would enjoy sitting back behind the G-Wagon's wheel.

They shared a formal kiss – in that way married couples kiss when they greet one another at the airport – and Twinka helped Marat put his things in the car. He had two bags filled with clothes, books and everyday items. Marat was still holding one of the books in his hands.

He had aged visibly: his hair had started to turn grey, he had quite a few wrinkles on his face, and his skin was dim and pale. He looked gaunt and older than his years. In less than twelve months, he'd aged by at least a decade.

"Well, that was an adventure," Marat said, shutting the car door with strength and determination, and enjoying the familiar, masculine sound. "The experience was definitely more impressive than being on Mount Kailash. Except maybe it went on for a bit too long – I almost got used to it by the end," he reflected, adjusting the driver's seat. He tossed the book he was holding onto the car's dashboard. "Just picture what an unusual creature man is: he can adapt to anything. At first all I could feel was total shock and paralysis – I thought that I wouldn't be able to make it, that I'd lose my mind or die – but then you get into your routine, certain rituals; you have your worries, little jobs, breakfast, lunch, dinner; then it's time for making tea, books, letters, TV, meditation – life carries on. I mean, there were certain inconveniences, of course, certain restrictions and challenges – but who doesn't have them?"

Marat talked intensely, as though he had just been picked up from the airport having spent a long flight deep in thought.

"What's that book?" Twinka asked, sounding a bit cautious and reserved. It was like she was waiting and watching, still unsure as to how she should act and feel.

"Oh, I had to wait until they sorted all the paperwork this morning. I read a bit of Faulkner to pass the time. *The Sound and the Fury* – a work of a genius, of course."

"Yeah, it is," Twinka agreed, but Marat wasn't listening. Neither did he seem to notice her lack of enthusiasm about him being released.

"You know what I'm going to do? I've decided to make the world a better place after all."

"Are you going to go into politics?"

"Oh, no! I'm going to become a philosopher. I want to be a – whatchamacallit – *maestro di color che sanno*. A teacher of the wise."

"Oh, I see..." An ironic smile flashed across Twinka's face.

"Yeah. I used to think that our main problem was having too many idiots, but now I feel that the problem must be defined differently. It's not that there's too many idiots in the world – it's that we're all stupid. I'm an idiot, too. If only there was a way to change it... Do you know what I mean? We need to work out why the smart, intelligent, educated people with high IQs are susceptible to idiocy. It's a real problem. How can it be that people like us – people like me – can't see the awful nonsense of the decisions we've arrived at? How can it be? And why is it? That probably causes more problems than the actions of the idiots. It shouldn't be happening. We have to find a way to ensure that intelligent people get the test with the baseball bat right. And it should be possible, because they're intelligent, right?" Marat's only eye sparkled with determination and glee. "If we lived in a world where – at the very least – intelligent people didn't behave like idiots, then we'd be able to reconcile ourselves to the fact that idiots are, and forever will be, idiots. But, for now, it is what it is."

"And what should we do to ensure that the smart ones don't act like idiots? Any ideas?"

"Not at the moment, though one thing seems clear: perhaps you need another person – or several unrelated people – with high IQs, who also have access to all the information, and with whom you can have an open discussion. We're built in a way that we can perfectly spot other people's mistakes and weaknesses, while we fail to see our own. So maybe what we need is advisers."

"But you had Dimitri, didn't you?" Twinka said with a cool smirk. "You couldn't get an IQ higher than that, or more openness. I mean, you didn't hide anything from him, but it still didn't work."

"Ah, but you see – he wasn't an authority to me. And that's the problem. He's a Shudra; a playmate. The same way he was for you."

"They called me from your office," Twinka said, after a longer pause than normal. "Some of your colleagues want to congratulate you; to see you, even if it's just five minutes. They asked me what time you'll be home."

"Not today. I don't want to see anyone today. How's Ronia?"

"She's at school."

"I have to say I'm a bit anxious about seeing her."

"Everything will be okay. As long as you don't try to kill me again," stated Twinka, very seriously. "Please, don't."

"I won't. No murder, no sacrifice. I promise. It was a very stupid idea. Well, except for Dimitri, of course. Dimitri no longer has a place under the sun," Marat added, with equal seriousness, following a pause of his own.

"Oh, I'm joking." He laughed, having noticed Twinka's facial expression change. "It was a joke."

CHAPTER 65

An older man – some fisherman – discovered Dimitri's body. It was floating in the canal somewhere between the shipyard and the docks. Two kettlebells, weighing sixteen kilos each, were tied around Dimitri's legs, which caused the body to surface vertically, so that only the head and a portion of his light-blue shirt were visible above the surface. In the dark water, it looked almost white.

The early morning was overcast, windy and unpleasant. The air smelled of late autumn. The weather forecast promised rain, and everything so far was pointing towards it being accurate. It was shortly after six a.m. The prosecutor on duty had arrived early, but the experts were late. The night shift would finish at eight a.m. To attend to the body before this time meant that the shift would be made far longer, and nobody wanted that. It was much more convenient to just hand the body over to colleagues who would be starting work at eight.

The policemen found a waterproof bag in a pocket of Dimitri's that was designed for either athletes who did water sports or tourists. Inside the bag was a little note, housed in a transparent document case.

"I DROWNED MYSELF IN THE FRAGRANCE OF HONEYSUCKLE," read the all-capitalised writing.

Also in Dimitri's pockets were a few coins and pens, a set of keys and a credit card, the latter allowing them to immediately identify the body.

The policemen who had been first to arrive at the crime scene believed that everything pointed towards suicide. However, the prosecutor remembered that – until recently – Dimitri had been a key witness in a high-profile criminal lawsuit, and so he decided to wake Draco.

Considering Draco's prior involvement, he too was assigned to investigate the circumstances of the death. Draco arrived at seven-forty a.m. at the place where Dimitri's body lay on the shore, the kettlebells secured to its legs. The night-shift staff had arrived too, and grumpily carried out their checks, desperate to finish the work quickly.

"Your opinion?" Draco asked the expert dressed in specialist overalls, who was squatting next to the body. The wind was picking up and blowing the first drops of rain towards them. Though it wasn't properly raining yet, it was clear that it would be soon.

"Looks like suicide," replied the man, sounding indifferent. "At least one of his legs seems to have been broken from the impact with water, though I won't be able to tell you much more at this stage."

"Where could he have jumped from?" Draco asked.

"I don't know, that's something for you to investigate." The expert yawned. "Behind the shipyard, there's a railway bridge, stretching over the canal. They use it to transport materials, but it's not too high – maybe some four metres above water. People who commit suicide usually pick higher places, but maybe that's why he needed the weights – to be extra sure." Somewhat reluctantly, the expert had shared his opinion.

"How long has he been in the water for?"

"With the hot weather being over, the water is quite cool here in the deep. It would have been at least ten days, maybe even a couple of weeks – I won't be able to give you an exact date at this stage," he once again disclaimed.

"No signs of a struggle?"

"Well, there are some scratch marks and bruises, but they could have been caused by the current dragging him along the bottom of the canal. It looks like he tied the kettlebells to his legs himself – with some serious knots, and duct tape as well:

probably to make sure he wouldn't be able to escape – then lifted the weights in his hands before jumping. You can be pretty sure you won't get very far with thirty-two kilos tied around your legs, even if you wanted to. Like I said, it's most likely suicide."

"*It looks like* suicide," Draco corrected.

"All he had to do was work out how deep the canal was." The expert had paid no notice to Draco's remark.

"He was a mathematician, he knew how to do that," Draco said, more to himself than anything else.

The expert shrugged his shoulders. "I'll let you know when I know more."

"Looking forward to it," Draco said, before zoning in on the body. He had something else on his mind. Dimitri had an enemy – someone who was vicious, immoral and ruthless – and this enemy had been released from prison, where he had first landed due to Dimitri's testimony, a few months prior.

And now Dimitri was dead. Was it just a coincidence? No, probably not. These events were probably linked; in fact, Draco was in no doubt that they were. But how?

Draco was willing to admit to himself that he didn't want it to be suicide. And this was not because, if it were suicide, he'd have to deal with another uncomfortable question: that of how ethical his own investigational tactics had been in relation to Dimitri. Wasn't Draco the one who provoked Dimitri to take the first step on the path that eventually led to this?

No, Draco was not afraid to face uncomfortable questions.

Draco didn't want it to be suicide because it would be *exciting* to once again investigate a case in which Marat was the prime suspect. There was something about him that drew Draco in.

As for the uncomfortable question – on his way here Draco had already managed to ask and respond to it himself. Of course, he – Draco – wasn't and couldn't be considered guilty. Not in the least bit. He was only doing his job; and, as usual, he did it very well, brilliantly even. The suspect was found and handed over to the prosecution, so he had done the right thing: following to-the-letter what the spirit of the law instructed.

The fact that the court let Marat walk free was another story – that was the court's problem and nothing to do with Draco. The police and the court system were set up solely for the purpose of preventing anyone who decided to dispose of their wife only because they were no longer interested in her, from actually doing so. Because actions like these would always be followed by unavoidable punishment. That was the whole point of the system. That had always been the point of any primordial forms of delegated governance; that was its deeper meaning, all the way since ancient times. And Draco had carried out his work, so that the mechanism of governance would function just as it was intended: the guilty party was caught. He couldn't be held responsible for the fact that Marat had managed to wriggle free at trial.

What could Draco possibly blame himself for? The fact that he pushed Dimitri a bit? Or that he tricked Twinka, so that he could get her testimony before Marat's lawyers got to her? But both of their testimonies were true! Draco had only given a little encouragement, to both of them, to do the right thing – was there anything wrong in that? Sometimes people needed a little motivation, a bit of a push in the right direction. And Dimitri? Most likely, as Twinka's lover, he would have testified against Marat anyway. No, Draco didn't blame himself for anything. Besides, it hadn't yet been established whether this really was suicide. And even if it were, it was unclear what had driven Dimitri to it.

"I need about twenty police officers – we must search both shores and find the place he could have jumped from. We need to look for a roll of duct tape, a knife or some scissors, maybe a bag," Draco commanded, "and, quite possibly, some sort of vehicle for transportation. He couldn't have walked all the way here carrying those kettlebells. We're looking for a suicide or a crime scene."

CHAPTER 66

It had started to rain, which felt like an omen for a greater kind of storm. Draco walked towards his car, ready to drive to Button Street.

By the time the chief inspector arrived at the familiar building, it was pouring down. The gate, which had been easy to open before if you reached for the bolt on the inside, now had an intercom and electronic keypad installed.

"What do you want?" Twinka's voice resounded through the speaker. The sound was a little distorted, but Draco could still make out the unmistakably vicious tone.

"I have a few questions," Draco said, bristling up under his umbrella, which wasn't built to withstand such strong winds.

"Send me a summons, call me into the police station, I'll come with my lawyer, goodbye!" Twinka said firmly, before cutting the intercom.

Draco pressed the bell again.

"Dimitri is dead," he said.

After a pause that seemed to last a long time, Draco repeated: "Dimitri is dead."

The gate clicked open.

Twinka was waiting by the door.

As soon as Draco's foot crossed the threshold, Twinka let him know he was to go no further. They were in the small living room that received such visitors: the one in which she'd been kissing Dimitri on that fateful day, before Marat had arrived to kill her. Twinka stood opposite the chief inspector, blocking the doorway. She was wearing light blue jeans that emphasised her shapely legs, as well as a white shirt. Her hair was tied up, and there was a hateful, venomous smirk on her face.

She really was a beautiful woman. Draco had never really clocked it before, but Twinka was stunning. He shook the raindrops from his umbrella. The chief inspector realised how drenched and pathetic he must have looked, and it wasn't a pleasant thought.

"What's happened?" Twinka asked, in a tone that clearly signalled that she wasn't about to let him manipulate her a second time.

"Earlier this morning, we discovered Dimitri's body. I don't think he died of natural causes," Draco said with as much humility as he could muster.

Twinka's fighting spirit depleted. "Okay, sit down," she said. Confusion – or perhaps some obscure, nebulous sorrow, a deep sense of loneliness – took over her. *Dimitri – dead? How can that be?*

Draco sat on the chair and waited. His body language signalled humility and gratitude, though he wanted the news to sink in fast and subsequently pacify Twinka's resistance and rebelliousness.

"Is your husband home?" he asked, joined by a squeezing of his lips.

"No. He's away in the mountains, he's climbing. What happened exactly?" Twinka asked, trying to avoid looking at the man whose appearance alone made her want to vomit.

"We don't know, we don't know... for now." Draco didn't even mention suicide as the most likely version. "When did you last hear from Dimitri?"

Twinka had to think. They hadn't seen one another since their meeting in the flat, although Dimitri had continued to text her. Reluctantly and somewhat lazily, Twinka had eventually replied. Dimitri had wanted to see Twinka. He explained that he'd done the right thing, that he'd acted in a way he believed was best for her. Every day he confessed his love to her, while

Twinka's responses remained cold. When Dimitri stopped texting, Twinka felt a sense of relief.

The thought that she should reveal the details of their last correspondence to this sleazy, soggy rat disgusted her. No, she wasn't going to tell him anything. No matter what had happened to Dimitri, she would never cooperate with this person; she would only speak in Keiko's presence.

"I don't remember," Twinka said decidedly. "I have nothing else to tell you. Please go." She regretted not leaving Draco outside in the rain.

And it was then that the news Draco had brought began to sink in.

Had Dimitri killed himself? Had he realised that they had no future together? Had he sacrificed himself ("We can't have a third wheel, can we...")? Had Dimitri decided to check out, just like that?

Oh, God! Twinka desperately wanted to look at her phone, to see what Dimitri's last message to her had said, but she didn't want to do it in the chief inspector's presence.

"Please, just leave," she said in a pleading voice.

Draco didn't move. With his lips still squeezed tight, he took a deep, nasal breath before releasing it with a hiss. "Why can't you just let me do my job?! Someone has died, and I need to investigate the circumstances of how it happened. I will need to ask you all these questions anyway, so why are you making things more difficult for yourself?"

"Because you're a crook – a mean, dishonest person. Please, just leave!" snapped Twinka, tears in her eyes.

She really is a stunning woman.

Draco caught himself having a very inappropriate thought.

"It's my job – the death looks unnatural, besides he was in the prime of his life," Draco continued rationally. "It's an out-of-the-ordinary occurrence; these sorts of things shouldn't be happening, so I must ask you some questions – how can you not see that? If people like me didn't do what we do, then we'd be living in total chaos." His voice was completely calm. "By the way, did you know that we have less violence today than at any time in human history? It's all thanks to the law, and the fact that there are people like me on the planet."

"Please, can't you just go?" Twinka really wasn't in the mood for listening to this horrible little man's musings on life.

"How long has your husband been away in the mountains?"

"For more than three weeks now. He's in the Pamir mountains, he's climbing some sort of a peak, so he won't be home for another two weeks. In the meantime – get out!"

It was enough to make Draco give up. "Okay, fine," he said. "Fine, I'm leaving, I'm leaving already." He got up from the chair. "I don't know who created this world, but what I do know for sure is that their work is far from finished. We're the ones who continue their legacy – we're responsible for the result – we have the power to turn this world into paradise or hell." Draco, now walking towards the door, had sounded a bit hurt and offended.

"Well you can rejoice then, because you've managed to turn my life into living hell." Twinka let her anger rip.

"It's easy to blame me, of course. Very easy, although you already know, deep down, that I'm not the one to blame for your misfortune."

"Go. Just leave already!"

"My condolences. He was close to you after all." Draco, without meaning to, had managed to impart one last insult.

Twinka slammed the door behind him.

As soon as Draco had left, Twinka scrolled to her last conversation with Dimitri.

Don't disappear, don't forget that I love you.

I love you, I didn't mean for anything bad to happen, I was only doing what I thought was best. Forgive me for everything.

Those were the last two messages from Dimitri. She hadn't replied to either of them.

CHAPTER 67

"The cause of death – drowning. Roughly ten days before the body was discovered. His lungs were filled with water, which means that he landed in the water alive. The water is from the canal, so that's where he drowned. There are fractures. The shin on his left leg was broken to such an extent that his foot was practically hanging off. This could point towards several scenarios. Most likely, he tried to get out, and as a result the relatively light fracture, caused by the fall, critically worsened."

"Do suicidal people often try to abandon their plan at the last minute?"

"It's a complex question. We've had cases when people have tried to drown themselves in relatively shallow waters. Or sometimes good swimmers try to drown themselves. Just earlier this year, we had a woman who tried to do so in a river where the deepest water only came up to her chest. She'd filled her pockets with stones and somehow managed to do it. You could say that it requires a strong will and determination, because the body, of course, instinctively tries to fight against death. So, you would have to overcome this resistance from the body by literally forcing yourself to die. But major depression suppresses these natural instincts and – combined with various doses of different anti-anxiety medication, and the likes of ketamine – people manage to do it."

Draco didn't say anything, so the coroner continued.

"But actually, it's pretty common. There must have been a moment when the body resisted. You jump into the water, you hold your breath, you sink, the oxygen starts to run out quickly – usually, considering the stress caused by the situation, no longer than thirty seconds. Then you blow the air out – that takes another couple of seconds – and then there should be a moment when all your instincts, every cell of your body, tries to rise to the surface. We're biologically built to be survival-minded – we're programmed to survive, and to fight for said survival. So, water entering your lungs wouldn't be an easy process: you'd still experience spasms, no matter how serious your depression was. It's not an easy death in any case, at least in my opinion."

"Right, I see. Go on," Draco said.

"There's also a fracture of the left patella; the patellar tendon has suffered a trauma as well; one of the ribs has fractured; there's haematomas on the back. Unfortunately, it's not possible to confirm exactly how these traumas were acquired."

"I'm sorry?" Draco said, sounding both confused and discontent.

"These traumas could point towards a jump into water from a height of eight metres or more," the coroner said, but Draco noticed a lack of conviction in his voice. "But you could also jump from that sort of height without acquiring such traumas. Equally, you could get these kinds of traumas from jumping out of a window from a three-storey building, for instance," he continued. "I would say that, most likely, he's fallen from a height, but not necessarily landed in water. And, if I'm being completely honest, then there could be other options too. For example, he could have fallen down the stairs – that would explain why he's got bruises on his back and a trauma to his kneecap.

"And the weights complicate everything. They open up lots of possibilities. He could have acquired these traumas as a result of the impact as he fell. Or he could have smashed against something as he jumped – banged against something before hitting the water. Like I said, unfortunately right now it's not possible to point to a definite cause of how he acquired these traumas."

"I see, I see, I see..." Draco mumbled to himself, looking satisfied. "So, we don't know exactly where he could have jumped from – or from where he could have been thrown or pushed."

"For now, it's impossible to confirm a single definite cause of how he acquired these traumas," the coroner confirmed. "When we've established where he jumped from, we may be able to draw more conclusions."

"Could he have been attacked? Punched, or beaten up?"

The coroner sighed heavily, making it obvious that he had considered this question himself and hoped that it wouldn't be raised. "There's no signs of resistance or self-defence; no trauma to the head; no haematomas on the hands. If there had been some sort of a violent attack, there should be at least some evidence of this on the body. He has fallen from a height; but, if you ask me whether I can eliminate the option of him being thrown or pushed from it... I cannot."

"Right, I see..." Draco was back talking to himself.

"We didn't find any traces of drugs in his blood," the coroner continued. "There's signs of alcohol and antidepressants, as well as benzodiazepines in amounts that exceed the recommended guidelines – though not enough for me to say that he was so drugged to be completely helpless during his time of death. And we have access to his medical history, which shows that he'd been suffering from depression for quite some time, so this sort of blood count isn't unusual. Alcohol, benzodiazepine, antidepressants – that's your standard cocktail of despair, really."

"And what about his handwriting?" Draco asked.

"Ah. We ran into some issues there."

"Oh?" Draco couldn't disguise his excitement over anything suspicious in relation to Dimitri's death.

"We don't have anything to compare the handwriting on his suicide note to. We have his signature, but that's no use really, as you can't draw any solid conclusions from that. We just don't have any samples of his handwriting. If we did, we could carry out an assessment. But at the moment, we have nothing."

"If he had been in the water for about ten days, how far could the current have carried him from the place where he made impact with the water?" Maintaining formality, Draco continued to question the coroner.

"There is a current, of course." The coroner was very serious again – as though, once more he wasn't quite sure about the answer. "The canal rests on top of an old riverbed. Further up in the north it connects with a lake, from which the river used to flow. Further up still is another lake, and both lakes have rivers flowing into them. The canal does have a current, but it's fairly minor. It couldn't have carried a human body very far, especially not with these heavy weights as well. I'd say, no more than a metre a day, maybe a metre and a half at best. Over the course of ten days that would add up to fifteen, twenty metres – no more than that. Under different circumstances, we could conduct an experiment that would let us determine the exact distance – but there's a problem. The canal has an active water traffic: with boats, motorboats, yachts and jet-skis travelling there and back, from the lake to the sea, and the larger motorboats cause waves in the canal that are capable of moving several heavier objects. As a result, the body could have travelled much further. There are speed limits along the shipyard, though in reality it's been abandoned, so no one really takes any notice of these. Consequently, because of the motorboats, the hydrodynamics of the canal are very difficult to replicate, so I'm not sure our experiment would yield accurate results. We can't replicate the exact movement of the watercraft, as it was on those specific days.

"The only thing we can assume with any degree of certainty is that the waves washed the body from the deepest part of the canal – on its left shore – towards the shallower part, where the body was eventually discovered. Now, if you were to place a perpendicular buoy string to indicate each end section of the canal, then it would look a lot like a swimming pool: where one end is deeper – complete with a steep wall – and the other, the shallower end, is almost flat. At the deeper end, we have landing wharfs and shipyard docks, and at the shallow end we have areas for swimming – with children paddling about, water weeds, fishermen—"

"What are you trying to say?" Draco hadn't let the coroner finish.

"That we cannot say with any degree of certainty, how far the current could have carried the body. Right now, we can't propose a theory that would be based on scientific evidence, but we believe that it couldn't have been that far. Officially we're going to write that it was no more than eight hundred metres."

"So, he got in the water somewhere along the shipyard, or from that railway bridge," Draco clarified.

"Yes, that's a relatively realistic distance, and such an assumption could be corroborated by his phone's GPS data. The last signal it received was from that exact area. The phone is probably still in the water."

"But you said that someone could also get these traumas by jumping from a height of at least eight metres?"

"Yes, I did say that," the coroner confirmed.

"And how tall is the bridge?"

"Five metres thirty."

"Then what are you suggesting?"

"Nothing." The coroner shrugged his shoulders, although it was obvious that he knew what he'd meant. Draco understood it, too.

The coroner wanted to say that he's not an investigator by any means – but if he were an investigator, he would assume that Dimitri suffered the traumas not on impact with the water, but prior to that. And then, after acquiring the traumas, he was pushed off a bridge or thrown into the canal, where he died in agony: desperately fighting for his life; unable to rise to the surface because of his broken leg and the kettlebells attached to his limbs.

Draco was silent for a moment, as though he were considering this scenario. "How come there are no CCTV cameras on the bridge?" he asked.

"It's a pretty deserted place, nothing ever happens there. A while ago, they did install a camera nearby, but the locals broke it on the second night, and they never bothered replacing it."

"And we didn't find any evidence on the bridge?" Draco mused, although he already knew the answer.

"No, we didn't find anything on the bridge."

"I need a boat," commanded Draco. "We need to find out how he got in the water."

"There's another interesting detail," the coroner hurried to add, as Draco was getting up. "We found some acorns in his trouser pocket."

"Acorns?"

"Yeah, acorns. Five acorns from an oak tree – in case that detail ends up having any relevance," the coroner said with a shrug.

CHAPTER 68

Twinka had become attached to Anna. Their meetings were very important to her, and she always anticipated them with great impatience. Anna was the only person Twinka had been completely honest with, and Anna had got her through the most difficult moments of her entire life. And so Anna was the only person Twinka could call after receiving news like that of Dimitri's death.

Anna found a free slot and saw Twinka on the same day, at eight in the evening. Before she left, Twinka decided to change; she wanted to put on different underwear, different clothes. She felt that there was something big bubbling up inside her, although she didn't know what it was.

Twinka stripped naked – she literally tore all her clothes off. Although she didn't fully understand everything, she knew in that moment that everything had changed. The world would never be the same again. Twinka pulled out the black sets of underwear from her drawers and tossed them onto the bed. For a moment she couldn't decide between wearing a lacey La Perla Brazilian-style G-string or very conservative Agent Provocateur panties, and then suddenly she chose not to wear any underwear at all. She didn't feel like she deserved it. It was all just a farce – a pretence, a show – and it disgusted her. Twinka put on a black skirt with a navy blouse. Her nipples were poking through the blouse.

"Were you driving?" Anna asked – Twinka was considerably tipsy upon her arrival at Anna's flat.

This was the first time Anna had seen Twinka in this condition. The situation kind of justified it – it isn't every day you receive a message to say your lover has died – but still, Anna wasn't happy. You couldn't have a therapy session with an intoxicated patient.

"No, I took a taxi," Twinka lied. She could sense Anna's disapproval and tried to pull herself together. "I'm sorry, I'm sorry – I just couldn't... it was all too much. An investigator came. You know, that horrible one. The one who threatened to put Ronia in an orphanage. And when he left, I read through Dimitri's last texts. It's so awful."

"I will get you some water," Anna said.

"Why is God punishing me like this? It's all just horrible."

"Do they know what happened exactly?" Anna asked in a still and formal tone.

"Ha! They have two theories," Twinka said with the full conviction of a drunk. "Either Marat killed him, or he committed suicide. I don't even know which version is better."

"You think that Marat might have killed him?!" Anna's astonishment was palpable.

"That – or he hired someone to do it. Or drove him to suicide. Oh yeah, Marat is more than capable of it. You know, he's spoken about it every now and then. Sort of jokingly, but 'many a true thing said in jest', right?"

"What do the police think?"

"Dunno. Probably the same as me."

Anna felt uncomfortable. Twinka appeared to be quite drunk – they should end this conversation as soon as possible. But she didn't want to be too abrupt about it.

"Marat's been gone for three weeks; he's climbing some mountain in Tajikistan. But who knows where he's really at," Twinka continued. "He had plenty of time to plan it."

"Or maybe you would prefer it if Marat had killed Dimitri? Then you wouldn't have to think about the role you may have played, if it was a suicide?" Anna asked in a cold register that was rather unlike her.

Twinka didn't pick up on the nuance in her tone. "I often wonder, you know, maybe it would have been better if Marat did kill me? For me and everyone else – maybe it would have made things easier..." Twinka said, unexpectedly bursting into tears.

"Nooo, don't talk like that." Anna sat down next to Twinka and embraced her around the shoulders. They were silent for a moment. A large, dark-red butterfly with magnificent, blue-yellow spots flew into the room through a crack in the orangery window. *Can you have butterflies in autumn? Where has he come from? Am I seeing things?* Twinka decided not to look at it.

"I feel just like I did in my first marriage. Like I've been put away in storage again. Nothing's working. I'm the mother of a child, who deserves respect and good care, but that's it." Twinka sniffled. "I'm old and useless, and no one needs me. I wanted to have another child: if we had a baby, things would be so different," she panted.

"You didn't answer my question about Dimitri. Would you prefer it if Marat had killed Dimitri, so you wouldn't have to consider your responsibility, in case it really was suicide?" pushed Anna, without attempting to soothe Twinka.

It worked. All of a sudden, Twinka smiled softly: "I don't understand why people would pay money to be asked questions like these." Tears glistened on her cheeks. "What's my responsibility? That he was in love with me, and I didn't love him back? He's the one who said that the most important thing in a relationship between lovers was not to fall in love. He's the one who warned me against falling in love – and I didn't! How can I possibly be responsible for that?"

"I don't know, I'm just asking."

"Is it even possible to save someone who's depressed to the point where they don't see any hope anymore; any point in going on? If life has become so tough for them that suicide seems like the only way out? Is that really possible?"

"That's a good question. My answer is – yes, of course, it's possible, but I also realise how complicated it is and how many resources it requires. What you need is, essentially, a 24/7 carer, at least at first. Someone who devotes their full attention to you, takes care of you; who is literally next to you, as though you're a small child. That, followed by therapy and drugs – it's all very long-term. So, yes, while it is technically possible, in most cases there's no one available who has such resources – so much time on their hands and so much interest or ability to devote all that attention to us. And it all costs money. In most cases such people are very lonely as it is. No one cares about them – at least, not enough to set their own worries aside and give them their undivided attention. If someone does happen to be nearby, they usually have enough problems of their own to deal with," Anna explained in a tranquil voice, which gave Twinka enough time to calm herself down.

"If I had given my full, undivided attention to Dimitri, he would have interpreted it as me loving him or giving him some hope that we could be together. And that would be so wrong. I'd be lying to him; I'd be cheating him. Either way, it would have come to a bad end. Do you think I should have started a life with him, just to save his life?"

"I don't think anything – I just want to understand whether you're tormented by feelings of guilt and whether you're inventing that Marat is Dimitri's murderer because you're scared to admit that he committed suicide because *you* rejected him."

"Anna, that's crazy! Those questions had never even occurred to me. But now I *will have to* think about them," Twinka hid her astonishment in a jocular tone. "Is this your idea of helping me?"

"There are questions inside all of us, even if we don't realise them." Anna smiled. "You shouldn't be afraid of questions – you should tackle them head-on and talk them through."

"Dunno. You're just living happily in the dark, never ever thinking about such things, until a therapist with their experience and skills makes you wonder about questions you would have never even considered," Twinka said, again seemingly jokingly, though Anna registered the truth in the statement.

"Dimitri was close to you. He essentially saved your life, and he played a very important role in the events that followed. His death is a serious event. So, we must treat it very seriously, which is what we're doing," Anna said solemnly.

"Yeah, that's true, I understand," Twinka agreed. The tension had dissipated. *It would be nice to have a drink now,* Twinka thought to herself, but she wasn't sure if Anna would want to drink with her.

It was time to go home.

CHAPTER 69

Curious, Draco examined Dimitri's tiny flat. He knew that it was the same space Dimitri had previously used to meet Twinka.

It was messy and grimy inside. The kitchen was full of dirty plates, used takeaway boxes and empty bottles of alcohol. He could also make out two dirty saucepans and several unwashed pots. Boxes lined the walls, filled with winter clothes; on top of which a mountain of some other type of clothing rested. There was a laptop on the living-room sofa and a printer on the floor. Every corner of the living room was filled with unopened boxes and more empty bottles. The air was stuffy, so Draco opened a few windows.

He found a torn-off rectangle of paper in the rubbish bin, which said: "The text has finished but the story continues". This sentence had been underlined. There were two other strips torn from the same piece of paper, again their contents underscored: "The mistakes and the suffering of this world can only be ended by death", and "death – it's not the end".

They were written in the uppercase script as the message found in Dimitri's pocket. While this wasn't a suicide note, it still went to show that Dimitri had been contemplating death; perhaps even considering, or even starting to draft, what his would say.

No. This still doesn't prove anything, Draco reasoned. *Someone could have planted it here.*

Draco was searching for prescriptions and medical packaging. He found a supply of the antidepressant Zoloft, but nothing in relation to the benzodiazepines the coroner had mentioned – not even among the empty packaging in the bin. There was nothing else of interest here, and Draco was keen to finish up for the day – tomorrow was Saturday, and Saturdays were promised to Annabella. He was determined to keep up the deal, having no intention of becoming some clichéd police officer from the films: one who has no time for anything except work, and who must frequently renege on his own promises to his children. No, he wasn't going to be like that. Annabella was the only close person he had in his life, and he wouldn't let her down. Nothing would make him give up their time together.

When Annabella was very little, he hadn't felt it quite as much. Annabella's mother had still been alive to start with, and after her death her mother had effectively taken over raising Annabella. Even though Draco tried, he just hadn't felt a deep, genuine connection with the little girl. He didn't know quite how to play with her, and wasn't very good at it when he tried. Nor did he understand how to talk to a child so young, and so spending time together hadn't been easy for them. Back then, even after a few hours, he felt completely drained and exhausted. He was happy to give Annabella back to her grandmother. But as Annabella got older, their bond grew closer. And now, with Annabella being twelve, Draco felt that they could finally share the sort of quality time that enriched them both. Being with Annabella no longer felt like hard work and a matter of duty, but brought them genuine joy. Murders took place every day, and would continue to; but his only daughter could grow up without him during that time...

No, he wouldn't let that happen. If he had a day off, then it would actually be a day off. Draco swore by this.

He had already planned what they were going to do the following day: they would go to the Museum of Art, to see the new Marc Chagall exhibition. Draco had read in the news that this was a rare chance to see so many of the artist's works all in one place: their having been brought together from different museums and private collections, including some works that had never before been exhibited. The exhibition had travelled here from Chicago via Paris and would continue on to Tokyo in six weeks' time. The news portals were full of proclamations to make the most of this unique opportunity. In fairness, Draco didn't understand anything about art, and he fully acknowledged that, but he wanted Annabella to be better than him – more educated and cultured; he wanted her to be raised better and receive a better education than he did, which was why he was trying so hard.

Draco spent the entire evening reading up about Chagall, so that he could explain some things to her, make a few comments and, hopefully, answer Annabella's questions while they were both at the museum. This was much more important than the investigation. The investigation wouldn't be going anywhere.

CHAPTER 70

"I'll make us a breakfast," Annabella said. "How many eggs would you like?"

"Three, please," Draco replied.

"Great, okay!" Excited, Annabella poured a generous dash of oil into the saucepan. "I'll take care of everything here – you just go and rest on the sofa."

"Amazing, thank you," said Draco, though he stayed in the kitchen, discreetly watching his daughter. How could anyone have such a perfect child – how had *he* done it? She was beautiful, intelligent, and kind – she had never once thrown a tantrum or answered back to him. She had never even been noteworthily unwell, at least to the point of calling a doctor or causing him to worry.

All parents probably think that their child is the most amazing person in the world, Draco thought. But even objectively speaking, Annabella really was incredible; and to see her look so happy and be so focused on making breakfast for him, led a fresh wave of love wash over him: stronger than any he'd experienced before. Draco already knew that he'd never loved anyone as much as he loved this wonderful child. He had never felt anything even remotely similar – not towards another woman, not his own parents, not even towards Annabella's mother. He had never loved anyone in the way he loved her now – the way in which loves overflows from your body's every cell.

"Oh!" Annabella exclaimed. Five eggs had turned out to be too much for her tiny hands – one of them had fallen to the floor as she made her way from the fridge to the hob.

"Never mind, I'll clean it up later." Draco laughed. "Don't worry about it."

"I'll be more careful next time," Annabella said.

"It's okay." Draco gently pressed his lips against the top of Annabella's head. "Should we have some tomatoes to go with it?" he asked.

"Yes," Annabella replied, although her entire focus was on the saucepan.

Draco washed some tomatoes, all the while watching his daughter. It looked like she was doing pretty well.

"Did you sprinkle any salt on them?" he asked.

"Where's the salt?" Annabella asked in return.

Draco took a pinch of salt and sprinkled it over the eggs himself.

"It's done," Annabella announced.

"Well done! Should we find some plates?"

There were only four eggs, and Annabella considered what to do for a moment. She decided to put three eggs on Dad's plate and only one on her own.

"No, no, we'll share them equally." Draco moved one of the eggs over to Annabella's plate. He had never felt such a clear sense of happiness before. Right now, right here, in this kitchen, he felt happier than he ever had in his life.

CHAPTER 71

Draco wasn't the only one who'd decided to seize this unique opportunity to see Marc Chagall's works. The long line outside the museum stretched from its main entrance door, snaking across the green square in front of it. Draco felt cross. If Annabella got tired or bored standing in the long queue, then she'd hardly be interested in the paintings, and their day together wouldn't be a success. When it had started so great, with their breakfast together! More than anything right now, Draco didn't want to ruin it.

"We'll stand in the queue for a bit and see how quickly it moves. If it's very slow, we'll come back another day," Draco said.

"Yeah, sure," Annabella agreed.

"Are you following me?" Draco heard a familiar voice say behind him. It was Marat. He was laughing, like he was in an excellent mood.

Draco noticed Marat's Mercedes drive away slowly – it had been parked on the curb, having just let him out. *You can't park there*, he thought to himself.

"Have you brought your child to work again?" Marat continued to joke in the meantime. "Did you think I wouldn't notice you following me?"

"We're here for the exhibition," Draco said, and hated himself immediately – both for the fact that he was explaining himself, and for pointing out the obvious.

Marat was not alone – a woman with cropped black hair stood next to him, dressed all in black. Her trousers, her blouse, the thick frames of her glasses, and her jacket – all black. Black earrings hung in her ears and a black bracelet adorned her left wrist. She was holding an exhibition catalogue and a bundle of papers in her hands. She looked wealthy, confident, and arrogant, which made her seem immediately unattractive to Draco.

"Good afternoon, young lady!" Meanwhile, Marat politely greeted Annabella, stretching out his hand. They shook hands. "Do you want to see the exhibition?" Marat asked her.

"Yes," Annabella replied. She seemed shy all of a sudden.

"Annabella, say hello to Gerda. If you ever want to buy a painting, then you must call Gerda – she owns the best gallery in this entire city."

Annabella carefully examined Gerda. There was a certain distrust in her gaze. "I don't need a painting," she said, very seriously.

"You don't?" Marat repeated.

"No, I don't. I can draw something for you myself," Annabella said. This made the grown-ups laugh – even Gerda.

"No worse than this one, eh?" Marat pointed at the enormous poster of Chagall's exhibition, which covered half of the museum's exterior.

"Yeah, I could," Annabella confirmed knowingly, having overcome her shyness.

"Okay, come with me! Gerda will take us through the back entrance. Let's go and see if there's anything worth seeing, like they say," Marat directed.

Draco didn't know what to say.

"Come on, it will be much easier for you to follow me inside." Marat wasn't about to put up with any objections. Draco submitted, although he felt with utmost clarity that this was very wrong. If he were alone, he'd refuse immediately, but he had to consider Annabella now.

"Are you interested in art?" Draco asked, filling in the silence, as they followed Marat across the square so that they could get around the museum and reach the back entrance.

"The upper castes have always been interested in art. They've supported, collected, and commissioned it. To aid and cherish art by creating museums and sponsoring artists – that's the duty of the highest upper castes, don't you know?" Marat beamed with confidence and haughtiness. "All those people," Marat pointed his head in the direction of the long queue, "they're just imitating the upper castes."

"Right," Draco nodded, smiling to himself. "I see."

"To be fair, I should say that there is an equally small number of those who actually *understand* art, across all castes. That's a real issue. They go and stare stupidly at those paintings, boring a hole in them with their eyes, having waited in line for hours. Meanwhile the wealthier people pay big money, amass and collect, brag and boast, until they're blue in the face, without really understanding anything."

"Well, thank God *you do*." Draco didn't hide his sarcasm.

"I do," Marat replied very seriously, ignoring Draco's tone. "I actually own a few decent Chagalls myself, which is why I came. I wanted to see what they've got here."

"Right."

"I just don't know which Chagalls I personally prefer – the ones on the walls, or the ones on the bottles."

Draco didn't say anything, though he raised his eyes quizzically.

"You see, back in 1924 Château Mouton Rothschild started to appeal to the best artists of the time to help them create the labels for their bottles. Oh, the things they've had on Mouton Rothschild bottles! Picasso, Balthus, Francis Bacon, Lucian Freud, David Hockney, and so on... And, of course, Marc Chagall himself. I have a few of those 1970 vintage bottles. It's a classic. Amazing stuff. It's just absolutely fantastic – but you probably already knew that, right?"

"Yeah, of course." Draco smirked.

"I could offer you some if you like. Then you can taste it for yourself."

"No, thank you, I best not."

"My personal favourite part of the story is that, traditionally, Château Mouton Rothschild didn't pay their artists in money – they paid them in wine. You could negotiate the vintage and the number of boxes, but you were not allowed to bring up the subject of money. It's rather elegant, no?"

Draco didn't respond. They had arrived at a very ignoble, yet almost imperceptible, door. A woman was already expecting them there – she looked like an employee of the museum – and her face blossomed into a warm smile as soon as she saw Marat. She even held open a small metal gate for them to go through and proceed further. After a short walk along some dark, windy corridors that seemed to snake on for ages, they had suddenly arrived at an exhibition hall that beamed with bright light. Draco noticed that Annabella was absolutely taken by what was happening. The day was turning out to be a success after all.

"Thank you." Draco nodded coldly towards Marat and his accomplice, making it clear that he no longer wanted their company.

"You're welcome," Marat said, confirming his words with a generous hand gesture, as though displaying that the exhibition had been delivered and handed over for their enjoyment.

However, Draco's wish to get rid of Marat wasn't meant to come true just yet. After a brief absence, Marat appeared again.

"I'm interested in what *you* think," he said, having turned towards Annabella. "I want to know *your* opinion."

Annabella thought for a moment. "Why are they flying?" she asked, gesturing at the two paintings in front of her: one depicting a bride in a white dress and her groom hovering in the sky above a village; the other painting boasting a flying cow.

"You're an extraordinary girl." Marat's voice resounded with respect. "That's a very good question. They're flying because the most important things are always happening away from the routine of day-to-day life; away from everything that happens in the ever-changing world we live in, which is full of bullshit and idiots. What's actually important always takes place far away from all that daily fuss. Art, love, religion, beauty – if it's real – is stronger than the gravitational pull of the earth. Do you get my meaning?"

Annabella was silent and serious, nodding and squeezing her tiny lips together.

"Chagall's own love – so powerful, mutual, and complete – is a good example of this. No war, revolution, poverty or conflicts could affect it in any way. It's in a completely different reality, in another dimension entirely. Do you know what I mean? There, on the ground, the world has fallen apart – it's in utter chaos. But two people in love – they're completely immune to it all; it doesn't concern them at all; it doesn't affect them – they rise above it. That's why they're flying. But it's not just about love. This is where everything that truly matters, exists – here, in this other dimension. Not only things that are significant, but also everything that is absolute. They're much bigger, and are placed in the foreground; while the rest of the world, with its ever-changing and constantly repeating pattern, and which isn't all that interesting – it stays behind, down there, in the background."

"I think it's a dream," Annabella said, as though she'd considered everything and had arrived at her own conclusion.

"Oh, you're so clever! You're right." Marat's face beamed with genuine respect and gravity. "It's the same in a dream because a dream only contains what's most significant. There's nothing incidental or excessive in a dream: it shows you only that which is most important – the core, the very essence of meaning."

"Do you like this one?" Annabella asked, pointing at another painting.

"I like this artist in general. Actually, it's more than that – I envy and admire him," Marat replied seriously.

"What for?"

"You see, he's like an ideal; like a divine example on how you can remain devoted to your thing, despite the most adverse circumstances. In Chagall's life, everything seemed to be set against him becoming an artist. He was born into an Orthodox Jewish family in provincial Vitebsk; and the Hasids' religion prohibits them from depicting the world created by God. That's why from the very start he was in conflict with his father over his desire to paint. Plus, they lived in harrowing poverty. Then World War I came. Then the Revolution. Then, after a short spree of cooperation with the Bolsheviks, he even became the Commissioner of Fine Arts in Vitebsk. Then his friend's – the world-famous Malevich's – betrayal. Then his flight from the Soviet Union. And just when he thought – *Oh, now I'll be able to live in peace and just paint* – he had to flee from Hitler. He was persecuted relentlessly, he wasn't recognised, and yet he carried on painting all the while. Can you even imagine – Chagall created around 10,000 works of art in his lifetime. That's a lot. It means that – whatever the circumstances, no matter what was going on in his life – he never stopped being immersed in his art, not even for a moment. He continued to work under any circumstances; he carried on doing his thing. And he did it in his characteristic, naïve, bold, childish style the whole time. As though he knew that God had created him to do this, and only this. His own thing, right? His thing. People who have found their thing are very fortunate." Marat spoke passionately – he was ignited – and Annabella listened to him with great interest.

Draco felt how excited his daughter was, so he didn't interrupt them.

"The circumstances were constantly against him. After a short honeymoon period, the communists outlawed his art. The Nazis removed his paintings from the museums, labelling his work degenerate art. The critics were always cruel, but he still managed to rise above it all. He was soaring above it the entire time. I think that's truly enviable."

"You'd like to fly like that, but you can't," Annabella concluded.

"Oh, you clever girl!" Marat was smiling, looking directly into Annabella's eyes. "No woman I've ever met has managed to work me out with such precision and speed."

Draco felt like his last words overstepped a boundary. This murderer – this criminal – was flirting with his daughter.

"Right, then," Draco said, in a firm voice that would entertain no objections – a voice Annabella had never heard her dad use before – "we'll be on our way."

Marat understood everything perfectly. "Yes, of course. It was nice to see you," he replied formally and coolly, but then he broke out into a smile, once more turning towards Annabella. "Next time I'll tell you about two monks. One of them was building a wall, to distance himself from the world, while the other rose in the air, above it all."

"Goodbye." Annabella bid her farewell very politely.

Despite everything, the day was a success, Draco thought to himself as they emerged out onto the street.

CHAPTER 72

"Last time you were saying that nothing is working between you two. Tell me more about that."

Twinka was wearing a thin, bright-green dress with an orange and red pattern. It was a bold, girly and somewhat daring number.

When Twinka removed her sunglasses, Anna realised that her drinking hadn't been limited to that one evening the week prior. Twinka's face was puffy and her eyes were tired and dim – all in stark contrast to her dress.

"Yeah, it's all back to how it was. I'd say it's got even worse."

"And the sex?"

"A few times after he came out of prison, and that's it. He's no longer interested in me, that much is clear. He's only interested in Ronia. I'm just a factor in Ronia's life which he has to take into consideration, but I have no intrinsic value in his eyes. He treats me especially well if Ronia can see it, and when she's not around... it's like I don't even exist. And the worst thing is that I'm playing along with it. Our relationship is a spectacle for Ronia – and a pretty successful one. But she's very withdrawn into her own shell. She's not really talking to me or Marat either."

"And you really thought that things would work out, didn't you?"

"Yeah, I guess I did, although now I know there's no hope."

"And how does that make you feel?"

"Like I'd be better off dead..."

"Have there been any moments when you've contemplated suicide?"

"Sort of, but not really. It's a sin and I couldn't do it – I'd be too afraid. No, I just couldn't. It would be like assuming the role of God, and that's a huge sin."

"You know, there's a song for every moment and emotion." Anna was clearly relieved that she at least didn't have to worry about Twinka having suicidal thoughts. "What sort of music do you like?"

"And he's spoiling Ronia rotten." Twinka pretended not to hear Anna's question. "He's letting her do whatever she likes; he's showering her with presents and stuff. It's not normal. How can I object to anything, if Daddy lets her do everything? He's just raising another spoiled egotist. I can't bear to watch it. He's become totally absurd; he even lets her skip school if she doesn't want to go. She doesn't go to her after-school club either, and he just stands by and watches. And whenever I object I'm then the evil mother, of course."

"Have you talked to him about it?"

"Yeah. He doesn't listen! He says that intelligence has nothing to do with education; that in the end half of the people still can't tell how much a baseball bat and a ball cost; that kids are being tortured with little gain; that he himself is going to teach her everything she needs to know about life; and so on. He indulges her every whim, to such an extent that I am actually grateful for the fact that she is still choosing to attend school!"

"Maybe the positive way we can spin this situation is that it's good news you're still able to talk to him about this. The fact that you're still talking might mean that it's not as bad as you think – talking means that there's still something you can salvage."

"Well, I don't think you can call those 'conversations'. We're communicating about things that concern our daughter. It's like we're exchanging information and opinions and taking them on board."

"Look, this is how I see it." Anna leaned in towards Twinka. She was very serious. "Sex and conversations are two things that characterise a relationship. The more sex and conversations you have, the better and stronger it is; the less you have, the more brittle and weaker it is. It's a simple but accurate marker, which can help you determine what state your marriage is in. When you're in love, you have a lot of sex and conversations. It's the best thing that can happen to us in life. Then you have relationships wherein you have sex but not that many conversations, or you have conversations but no sex. But if you don't have either, then the situation really is quite bad."

"We have a child," Twinka said, as she was suddenly hit by a strong desire to have a drink. She should have taken something with her, so she could excuse herself and go to the toilet, but she hadn't had the forethought to do so. Why were things not going her way anymore? Nothing was working out.

"Are you saying that you're only together because of Ronia?"

"You know, I'm not even sure what's best for Ronia anymore." Twinka tried to get a grip on herself. "Honestly, sometimes I regret not telling her the truth while he was still in prison. I covered for him and saved his image in Ronia's eyes, all so he could repay me like this. By turning me into the evil mother." Twinka's eyes teared up.

"Do you think it was a mistake, your ensuring that Ronia doesn't think badly of him?"

"I could have told Ronia that Daddy was a total egomaniac who's lost the plot, and meticulously planned Mummy's murder because she wouldn't remove corks from the corkscrews! That she was saved by a lucky coincidence. I could tell Ronia that everything they're saying on the internet about Dad is true. I didn't have to play into his story in court: that I had some weird BDSM fantasies, and that he just wanted to surprise me. It's utter bullshit! But I agreed, so I could save him from prison. I didn't have to. I could have demanded a divorce and ensured that he never saw Ronia again. Even with all his money and lawyers, he wouldn't have been able to do much, being in prison. But I didn't do it."

"Do you regret it?"

"I don't know. Back then it seemed like the right thing to do."

"You could still tell Ronia the truth and demand a divorce."

"No, the right moment is gone. Now he's controlling the situation again, and I'll never be able to defeat him." Twinka tried to suppress her tears.

"You'd like to defeat him? Gain the upper hand?"

"I wanted to forgive him, and I did – I thought that's what I should be doing. Marat never forgives anyone, but I thought – *He'll see how beautiful it is to forgive, how good it is to forgive, and he'll fall in love with me again.*"

"And now you realise that you've made a mistake?"

"All he sees in forgiveness is weakness – an opportunity for him to take advantage of."

"And are you angry with him now?"

"It's God's punishment for me. Because it's all my fault. It's my punishment for my sins: I knew that I was sinning, I got pleasure from it. I even went to church afterwards to thank God every time. Oh, I was such an idiot! And now I'm paying for it." Twinka was panting, her make-up smudged by her tears.

"God will forgive you, there's no doubting that," Anna said. "God is good and forgiving, isn't He?" Anna struggled with religious rhetoric – it didn't come naturally to her. She wasn't a priest, she was a therapist. But it felt like that sort of language might help Twinka at this moment.

Twinka was sobbing. On the table in front of her, on the couch, on her lap – every surface was covered in used tissues.

Anna pushed the bottle of mineral water with the heightened pH towards her, and Twinka drank it thirstily.

"Honestly, at this point, getting a divorce would be the right thing to do," Twinka said. "He's ruining my life; he's turning Ronia against me and spoiling her. I don't think he's succeeded yet, but it's Marat we're dealing with – I'm sure he'll be able to get what he wants eventually."

"Don't be hasty. We'll talk about it another time. A divorce is a very serious decision."

"Okay, fine," Twinka agreed obediently, wiping her nose and piling another tissue on her lap.

"But getting back to the topic of music... I want you to find two or three songs for next time which make you feel better. Let's listen to some music next time."

"Okay," uttered Twinka, nodding submissively.

CHAPTER 73

The boys from the maritime police were only too happy to assist the criminal investigation. Draco was dressed in one of his rather worn suits. covered by a thin windbreaker that was shorter than his suit jacket. He left it open as a way of making this less obvious. If it hadn't been raining for several days on end, this trip in a maritime police speedboat would have been rather pleasant. Only a month ago it would have been a nice, refreshing change from the sweltering office environment and his routine; but now, in the humid boat, it felt just like any other work. Draco was forced to zip up his windbreaker after all. Soon enough, they got to the place in the water where Dimitri's body had been discovered.

"We're looking for something that's eight to ten metres above water, or possibly even higher than that – something from which you could jump into water," Draco explained.

"There are several places like that." The commanding officer of the boat began to gesture with his hand. "For starters, we have the floating docks. The mechanism behind them is that they get almost completely submerged in water, then the ship that needs fixing enters them before water gets pumped out again, and they rise above water, complete with the ship. When they're above water – like they are now – the height of the outer wall is more than fifteen metres."

"Would anyone be able to gain access to them?" Draco asked.

"As you know, the shipyard isn't operating at the moment. The territory is being guarded, but it's so huge that anyone willing, who knew the territory, could gain access to it. They're mostly guarding it to stop people from stealing any remaining machinery or things they can turn into scrap metal – as in, they're watching to make sure that nothing is removed and loaded into a car. There's nothing really of value here that you could easily throw over the fence," the commanding officer said, clearly feeling chatty.

"I'll need to have a closer look at those docks," Draco said.

"Of course, we'll take a look."

In the meantime, the police speedboat had slowly arrived alongside an impressive cargo ship that was docked. It had once been dark red. The name plate, although rusty and chipped, read veritas.

"It's a Panamax-type cargo ship," the police officer continued to explain in the tone of a tour guide. "It was left there half-fixed. The owner went bankrupt and, while several creditors are arguing over how much of it belongs to whom, the ship has been sitting here getting rusty. Now it could probably only fetch a scrap-metal price. There's probably about eleven metres between the deck and the surface of the water."

"I need to see how you could get up there..." Draco said. The police boat looked insignificant next to the enormous ship.

"And that's it, I think. Those ships over there –" the police officer pointed with his hand – "are much smaller. And there, further away, is a bridge."

"How deep is it here?"

"It's quite deep." The officer looked at the boat's panel. "Thirteen metres. Further down it gets more shallow. This part of the canal – up to the shipyard – was deepened deliberately, to allow the large ships to enter."

"And how deep is it under the bridge?" Draco asked.

"Let's go over and find out, shall we?" said the commanding officer, and with that the boat accelerated a little.

"Four-fifty," the officer said when they had arrived under the bridge.

"And there's nothing further down there," Draco waved in the direction of the lake, "that could be eight metres or higher above water?"

"No, there's nothing there."

"Okay, let's turn back then," directed Draco. "I need to get into those docks."

They couldn't find a place to dock right away. The wharfs, meant for ships, were too high for them to be able to get out. Finally, the commanding officer of the boat found a suitable place a little further away from the docks. "And while we're at it, let's check how well the security is guarding the place," he said, helping Draco disembark.

It wasn't easy to get to the docks on foot. They were constantly running into dead ends and getting lost; and, when they finally reached their goal, Draco was worn out, his thin windbreaker completely soaked by the cold, drizzling rain. As it turned out, the floating docks had their name for very good reason: they were floating in the water. There was a water barrier of a few metres between them and the shore, which couldn't be seen when looking at them from the canal.

On one side of the dock the police officers found a bridge by which they could enter the docks. Then a narrow, very steep – and, in Draco's opinion, unsafe – ladder led them further towards a narrow platform at the very top, which stretched across the entire dock. Draco wasn't scared of heights per se, but this felt quite uncomfortable. The railing, just like everything else, was rusty: it was just a bit higher than his knees and didn't look safe at all. It was possible to fall in from either side – landing in the water or inside the dock territory. The latter looked likely to cause certain death, compared to a fall or a jump into the water.

Even the chatty commanding officer seemed tired. The dock was about three hundred metres long and Draco had to walk the entire distance there and back, all the while staying at the top. Forcing himself to look only under his own feet, and searching for something that could point towards Dimitri having being here, Draco moved forwards in small, careful steps. Yet there was nothing that could point towards Dimitri having been present. Draco realised that he should have sent the experts rather than tried to make the climb himself, and was annoyed at himself.

On their way back, two men appeared beneath them. Those were the shipyard's security guards, who had finally spotted them. The voices of the guards startled Draco and made him momentarily lose his balance, yet he managed to right himself and complete his walk . Now all that was left for him to conquer was the steep, narrow ladder leading back down.

When Draco was finally back on terra firma, he felt physically and psychologically exhausted. It was only then that he noticed just how soaked he was. Draco wasn't in the mood to question the security guards.

"Let's have a look at that ship," he said.

It seemed to be raining harder. Fortunately, the ship wasn't too far away. The boards of Veritas were tall: you couldn't climb the abandoned ship without a ladder or gangway. They didn't remain there long.

"Okay, let's finish up," Draco commanded.

They went back towards the boat.

From here you could get in by car, Draco thought, but he was too tired to unpick it any further. He didn't have enough energy to sit down with the guards, answer their expectant looks and wait for a police car to collect him. The commanding officer gave him a large, waterproof cloak, though his already wet clothes prevented him from warming up.

Maybe the rain has washed away all traces. It's been two weeks. Maybe Dimitri tossed everything he had in the water,

Draco thought to himself. *Or perhaps he was murdered somewhere completely different and then taken here by boat, to make me climb these rusted, neglected old docks like a complete idiot and get myself killed.*

Suddenly, he was overcome by the foreboding sense that he would never be able to solve this death. There was something hopeless about this autumn, this rain, and this case.

CHAPTER 74

"Did you bring some music with you?"

"No."

"Why not?"

"I don't really listen to music."

"I'd strongly recommend changing that habit. There's a song for every event and emotion."

"Yeah, you said that last time already."

"You must have listened to music in your youth – was there a band that you loved, or a particular song?"

"I don't remember. I used to like some band, but I don't remember what they were called."

"Go on – you must be able to remember them."

"'Diamonds and Rust'. I remember there was a song called 'Diamonds and Rust'."

"Okay, excellent." Anna picked up her phone and looked up the song. "What else?"

"I used to like Victor Jara; we listened to him at university."

"See, you can remember everything perfectly!"

"Jazz. I liked jazz and blues, too. I used to like a lot of things, but I don't really listen to anything anymore."

"Right, Joan Baez..." In the meantime, Anna had found the song and her flat resounded with notes from 'Diamonds and Rust'. "I want you to remember all the songs that ever made you feel good; music that was on when you were very happy."

"I remember the music that was playing when Marat tried to kill me."

"Oh? Go on."

"Leonard Cohen's 'A Thousand Kisses Deep'. You know, that's the music that used to play when I was at my happiest. It was our song. And the rest of the music that I liked – that was also ours. I don't think it's going to help me now though."

"No, Twinka. You can't. We won't let him define who you are. We won't let him steal your identity, your independence, your music. No. You are autonomous, you are with yourself, you shouldn't be afraid of the music you love only because you listened to it when you were with him. No. We won't let him dilute your identity or subsume it into himself, as though there was no distinction between who you are, who he is, and what you are together. No, Twinka, simply no. You are an independent, sovereign, and self-sufficient personality. Everything that's happened is just an episode – life goes on. Your life goes on."

Twinka had never heard Anna talk with such resolution and confidence.

"It's never too late to start a new life – not even the day before death." Twinka smiled.

"Yeah, that's right," Anna agreed.

"It's one of Marat's favourite sayings."

"In that sense he's right. Our entire life is the sum of bigger and smaller misfortunes. I don't know whether you remember, but there used to be this game on the phone called Tetris. And, well, Tetris is just like life: your achievements disappear but your failures accumulate. Life is an amalgamation of failures that have accumulated and achievements that have disappeared. But it's okay, because every morning we can get up and start afresh, and every day we have the opportunity to change our lives. I'm being dead serious."

Twinka examined the label of the water bottle quietly.

"Everything we do in life – it adds up. Every day we can do something small that will improve our lives, and over time it will add up, and after some time we'll start to see results. And it goes both ways: if every day we do something harmful to us it will add up over time, and after a year, or five, it will accumulate into significant damage, which we have brought upon our—"

"So, it's not like Tetris then," Twinka interrupted. "You said that life was full of accomplishments that have disappeared, and failures that have accumulated... But now you're saying that good things accumulate over time, too?"

"Well, maybe Tetris isn't the perfect, all-encompassing metaphor for life, but you understood my meaning."

"I understood that I need to lose about fifteen kilos."

"Well, I wasn't talking about that, but actually it's a pretty good example. Excess weight accumulates. And it's like that with everything." Anna spoke in an educational, didactic tone that she usually tried to avoid.

"I know, I know..." Twinka felt that she preferred Anna's annoying habit of asking her questions.

They both left with the feeling that their session hadn't been particularly successful.

CHAPTER 75

Twinka ignored Draco's phone calls. Which is why, breaking his own personal principle, he sent her a text message.

I don't want to bother you over nothing, to call you into the police station or appear uninvited at your house, so I'd like to arrange a very brief meeting with you, at a time convenient for you. I need to show you something and ask you a few questions about Dimitri's death.

Draco had considered each word carefully. He hoped that his very polite tone would help, and he was also banking on her curiosity being piqued. At the same time, the message contained a hidden threat – that he could call Twinka in, or arrive unannounced, anyway. Draco was hoping that all this would work in combination – and it did! A few minutes later, Twinka called him back and they agreed that she'd come into the police station.

"I don't want Ronia to see us," she had explained.

"I really have only one question," Draco said when Twinka arrived. "I understand that it's a big ask from me, but would you happen to have a letter from Dimitri? Or something that's been written by hand? This really is very important – we need it for the investigation, to determine, whether he really did write his suicide note."

"He left a suicide note?"

"We don't know for sure – maybe." Draco handed over a copy of the missive they had found in Dimitri's pocket.

"I drowned myself in the fragrance of honeysuckle," Twinka read, carefully repeating the sentence out loud.

"Is that Dimitri's handwriting?" Draco asked.

"Hmm, I don't know," Twinka said. "I don't think I've ever seen his handwriting."

"And what about the message? What's all this about the honeysuckle? Does it mean anything to you?" Draco watched Twinka closely.

"It's... hmm... I don't know. Can I keep it?" Twinka asked, holding the copy in her hand.

"Yeah, sure, of course," Draco said, as leniently and politely as he possibly could. His intuition was telling him that it was only with Twinka's help that he could get any further in this case. And that she wouldn't help him, unless he could improve his image in her eyes. Which was why he was now trying so hard.

"Maybe this will mean something to you?" Draco handed Twinka another sheet of paper, which contained an image of the expertly reconstructed torn piece of paper they'd found in Dimitri's flat.

"The text is over but the story continues. The mistakes and suffering of this world can only be ended by death. Death – it's not the end," Twinka read out loud. "That first sentence is from Fernando Pessoa – I wrote a dissertation on him; I didn't know Dimitri had read Pessoa. No one's usually read him..." Twinka seemed lost in thought.

"Is there some sort of context behind it? Does that sentence mean anything?"

"I don't think so, no."

"Well, either way, I'm more interested in his handwriting. It's very important for the investigation. If we can prove that this note was written in Dimitri's hand, then it would tip the scales in favour of suicide. But if it wasn't, then it would point towards the opposite. So, please have a think. Maybe you have a greeting card, a note; maybe a message written in a book somewhere – anything that might have Dimitri's handwriting."

"I understand. Sure, I'll have a think."

"Thank you very much for finding the time to come over." Draco walked Twinka to the door, moulding his face into something that resembled a smile, though he was embarrassed to show his teeth fully. He wasn't used to being smiley and polite, though he was giving it his best go.

CHAPTER 76

"Last time you said you wanted to get a divorce, and you regret that you didn't do it while Marat was still in prison. I think we should talk about it," Anna suggested.

"Okay, let's talk." There was no sprightliness in Twinka's voice. The meeting with Anna at three in the afternoon was a very bad time for her. Twinka used to be able to resist drinking before their meeting. After that she would need to stop by the shop for groceries on her way home, after which she could wholeheartedly say that she'd spent the day well and could open a bottle of wine in clear conscience.

But lately it had become too hard to even get to three p.m. without a drink. She tried to resist, at least on the days when she had a meeting with Anna, and she had even managed to do it today – but she didn't feel well at all. It was hard to focus or think about anything else.

"I want you to be fully aware that what you want is best for you and Ronia. Are you sure you want to get a divorce? Or are there any conditions you'd like to discuss with Marat that would mean that you wouldn't need to get a divorce, if you both followed them? Perhaps it's worth considering couple's counselling? Either way, the first step is working out how you feel and what you want. We need to understand where we are first, before we can work out how to get to where we want to be."

"You think you can just discuss things like that? Okay. My 'condition' is that he loves me again." Twinka was being openly sardonic. "Do you think that if I insist and make it an obligation, he'll fall in love with me again?!"

"Love ebbs and flows; but marriage, in the long-term, is about respecting one another, about being best friends, good partners, it's about being a team – and every team needs a team meeting. You have to be able to define your goals and problems and resolve questions over how you're going to cooperate. What do you think about taking this angle?"

"Things got much worse after he came out of prison. When I first started coming here – sure, we had problems. But looking back now, it feels like we still had a fairly normal family life. Maybe we didn't have sex, but we did have some sort of an understanding between us, respect, I don't know..."

"Expand on that, please."

"It's only now that I realise that back then I was angry at him for not actively trying to make me happy. But things are so much worse now. He is actively trying to make me unhappy."

"And how does he make you unhappy?"

"Listen, sorry, I need to go to the bathroom." Twinka couldn't take it any longer. She had some vodka miniatures in her bag. They sold these next to the petrol station till, and on her way over she had bought two in case they were needed – which they now were. Twinka downed one of the bottles in the toilet and peed. She couldn't make her mind up about the other one. It would be good if Anna couldn't smell it on her. Twinka scanned Anna's bathroom, hoping to find mouthwash. There wasn't any. She decided to hold off from having the second bottle. She fixed her lipstick. *Everything will be okay.*

"Sorry, where were we?" she said to Anna upon her return.

"You said that he used to make an effort to make you happy, but now he's doing everything he can to make you unhappy. Give me an example."

"Oh, yeah." Twinka remembered. She felt a little better. She should have had the other miniature too, because then she'd feel even better. "Well, for starters, I can't say anything to Ronia or tell her off. If I say something, the response I get is like 'Well, Daddy gave his permission', 'Daddy said that I could', 'Daddy thinks that I can'. She doesn't even ask me to consent to anything anymore, because what's the point? If she then goes to

Daddy, then he'll just let her do it. He uses phrases like 'Oh, don't worry about Mum' and 'I'll deal with Mum'. Recently I discovered that they've been planning a holiday together! They've been discussing where they'll go and what they'll get up to. He doesn't spend any time with her day-to-day; he's not interested in anything – school, or what Ronia does outside of school – and then, completely out of the blue, he's planning to take her to the Swiss Alps. They didn't even offer me the choice of going – 'Oh, but you don't like mountains, do you?' He's completely ignoring me as a mother. We're no longer two parents who are raising their daughter together, but two completely separate people: and he is the superior one – because if he wants or decides to do something, it will happen."

"Maybe you're jealous? Are you afraid that he's going to take your daughter, and her love for you, away?"

"I don't think it's just jealousy or worry over him getting closer to Ronia, if that's what you mean. No, it's not jealousy. I really think that what he's doing is wrong, egotistical, and definitely not in the best interests of the child. And he's acting like a proper pig towards me. Like a right ungrateful bastard. I saved him from prison. Yeah, I hate him for it."

"Have you ever tried to talk to him about it?"

"It's pointless."

"Why is it pointless?"

"He always knows exactly what he's doing – he's got a plan, a strategy: he has schemed it all in his head. He's not interested in anything anyone could ever say to him. If he cares about anything, it's what someone can *do*: what IQ, what resources, opportunities, or influence they have. Well, I don't have any influence or resources. Which is why, no matter what I say, it still won't mean shit to him."

"You know, I think you need to consider two things here," Anna said very seriously after a short pause. "Firstly – you are his wife, you are the mother of his child, you have a high IQ, and you know him better than anyone else does: so you do have resources, influence and opportunity – we'll talk more about that and have a think. But, before that even, we need to get clear on something. A toxic home environment is at the root of all mental health problems and even physical ailments. A toxic relationship within a family poisons the well you drink from, the very air you breathe. A toxic relationship can literally kill you. If your family can't help you – as it's, instead, the very thing that is killing you – then that will immediately affect everything else: you then get sick, you then start having problems at work. Absolutely everything in life can be destroyed by a toxic family dynamic. And the longer we tolerate a toxic relationship, the worse the consequences are. It's definitely better to get a divorce than to live locked up in a deep, dark well, breathing in the poisonous fumes. I often see women whose husbands have hammered this belief into them that they can't do anything; that they have no future, no opportunities – that they are literally nothing – and that's why the best thing they can ever hope for is to stay in that toxic environment. But it's not true. It's complete nonsense. Do you understand? It's total bullshit." Anna was talking firmly and certainly, while Twinka sat in her chair listening. "Tyrants and narcissists need to be shown their place, and I can tell you from my own experience that every woman who's ever pulled herself together and managed to free herself from a despot, narcissist, egomaniac, or simply an unloving husband, has come out feeling happy and grateful for attempting it. Yes, it's hard in a number of ways, but it's still better – much better."

Twinka remained silent, but Anna felt like this time she had gotten through to her.

It was time for the second tiny bottle of vodka. Twinka downed it in the car.

CHAPTER 77

When the criminal court forensics lab was ready to return Dimitri's body to his relatives, there was no one who wanted to take the arrangements upon themselves. His parents were dead; his ex-wife didn't want anything to do with it; and his closest relative turned out to be his cousin – a chef by trade – who hadn't maintained any sort of a relationship with Dimitri, and who categorically refused to take on any expenses or inconvenience himself. Which is why, in the end, the council organised Dimitri's funeral.

In fact, it might be a bit of a stretch to call it a funeral – it was more like a burial. They simply buried his coffin, and the act was witnessed by four people: Dimitri's ex-wife's mother who had brought his son with her; some old colleague of his, a mathematician (to everyone's astonishment, since no one present had ever heard of this friend before); and chief inspector Draco. The weather was bleak and humid, and an irritating drizzle dogged the air. There was no ceremony or service. The council workers simply lowered the coffin into a hole they'd dug out earlier, closed it up and fastened a very simple metal cross at the head (the type of which the council had purchased in bulk). The cross had on it Dimitri's full name, as well as his date of birth and death.

A few days after the funeral, Marat came by to visit the humble grave. It was situated in the dingiest corner of a big, remotely located cemetery itself not far from the railway tracks. It wasn't easy to find Dimitri's grave. It had been raining every day for a week straight; but just then the rain had stopped and the sun even was even peeping through the clouds every now and then.

Standing next to the grave, Marat was annoyed. He'd noticed that his perfectly polished, shiny shoes were caked in mud having wandered through the cemetery. He closed his eyes and took a deep breath. You could hear a train go past; a stingy ray of sun flashed from its windows. The drenched pine trees gave off a fragrant odour, along with the cut flowers on the grave mounds further along. Marat thought he could also sense the characteristic smell of the railway tracks.

There was no one around, so he unzipped his trousers. Arranging himself in a more comfortable position, he let the stream of urine wash over the metal cross. He aimed it at the plaque with Dimitri's name on it at first, before covering the rest of the cross.

Walking back to his car, Marat pulled out his phone and called Keiko, the sage.

"I know that this isn't your speciality, mister lawyer, but I also know that you'll be able to do it for me. I want a divorce. Not immediately, but we need to start to slowly restructure my properties, so that there are no complications later down the line. I want her to be fully provided for – but no more than that. No, it's not going to work between us. It's obvious that it won't: resurrection is only the stuff of fairy tales. Of course, I know it's a huge mess, which is why we'll start preparing for it, slowly and carefully. And a trauma for my daughter – yes, I know that, too. But life is a trauma in itself – you can't escape your own traumas, and she's going to be an adult soon. In any case, I'm working on it. And, before you start, there's no need to tell me that I can't forgive her for wanting to kill her – that really isn't the case at all!" Marat laughed.

Marat's S-class Mercedes was parked in the car park of the cemetery. He had gone back to having a limo and a chauffeur: only because he had an exceptional chauffeur now. He was so good that he let him drive him with the same satisfaction he felt when driving the car himself.

411

As Marat approached, the chauffeur got out of the car and opened the door for him. He was dressed in an expensive, tailored suit, with an exquisite black turtleneck under the jacket. On his feet, the chauffeur wore sports shoes with a white sole – his whole outfit was evidently new and flawless. On his forehead, the chauffeur had a tattoo that said NO FEAR.

Theodor wasn't just Marat's new chauffeur – he was Marat's new assistant, his right-hand man, and his new best friend.

"Let's go and eat," Marat directed. "And remind me to visit Mum's grave sometime."

"Yeah, sure," Theodor confirmed, in the tone of a submissive subordinate.

When they arrived at the restaurant, which was favoured by bankers, and where Marat had lunched so many times prior, all eyes were on them. A young man in an excellent suit, with a face covered in scars and NO FEAR written across his forehead. And an elegant gentleman: whose eye was covered with a patch, and whose remaining one showed just how much he was enjoying this situation. It was a striking and impossible-to-ignore sight.

Marat cast his eyes over the room, as though asking whether anyone had any objections or reservations against the two of them being here. No one did. On the contrary, those who knew Marat greeted him in awe; came up to shake his hand; invited him to meet up, have lunch or come by; and shook hands with Theodor. The trial, his arrest, the publications in the press, his new friend – none of that had affected Marat's social standing, at least not at this informal level. Marat wasn't surprised – he was still one of the city's wealthiest people. The mishap with his wife's attempted murder and the presence of the tattooed killer had only made him appear more exotic – perhaps even a touch frightening – but in any case, it hadn't turned him into someone no one wanted to shake hands with. At least that's how Marat interpreted their attitude towards him. And, at the end of the day, if anyone did laugh behind his back – what did it matter? Had the opinions of others ever mattered to Marat?

They had a leisurely lunch and finished a bottle of wine, which had been corked before Theodor was born.

"We'll go for a drink in your Basement, too," Marat suggested, "I want to see that place."

"Definitely," Theodor agreed, full of bravado, playing up to Marat's swaggering tone.

"Let's see who's not afraid of us there."

"The only thing is, I couldn't find any screwdrivers in your garage," Theodor continued to joke around.

"No need. We'll take some guys with us. From now on, we'll always buy violence as an external service, like wealthy and powerful people should."

"As you say, boss," Theodor agreed. "You know, we don't need to go there for my sake. I don't know if I ever want to think about them again, to be honest."

"Yeah, that's probably for the best," Marat said, without his earlier bravado. "You have more brain cells than me. Let's not look back – we have to keep moving forward. It's never too late to start a new life, not even the day before death."

They made a toast and finished the rest of the wine.

CHAPTER 78

That was the autumn when Twinka fell ill.

It all started with some inexplicable nausea and vomiting that came and went. Towards the end of November her condition had greatly worsened. She lost her appetite, and that's when swelling appeared: her legs blowing up so much they hurt. Sometimes it felt like her entire body was aching, and this pain was so overwhelming that Twinka moaned in pain. Her period had become longer, heavier and much more painful, too. It sucked all her remaining energy, and Twinka would only get out of bed to walk a few steps to the bathroom or sometimes to the kitchen. The GP arranged some further examinations, which Twinka didn't attend. She stopped eating almost completely – she had no energy for anything.

During the night, Twinka got up frequently to be sick, go to the bathroom, have a drink of water and take some medication. During this time Twinka discovered that the only thing she could drink was flat champagne. The producer, taste or vintage made no difference anymore – Twinka would take any champagne bottle from the wine cabinet, one after the other. At first, she would have Agrapart of varying vintage, then something from Emmanuel Brochet. But when the champagne from the cabinet was finished – all too soon – she asked the cleaner to bring up a few boxes of Dom Pérignon from the cellar.

Then she started hiding the bottles. The full and the empty ones. She had neither the energy nor the desire to get caught in debates with Marat over how clever her actions were. Perhaps more than those, she was afraid of facing his silent resentment. That look, in which judgement combined with disappointment and pity. Besides, it wasn't like she drank a lot. She drank slowly, taking little sips: no more than a bottle or a bottle and a half a day. This managed to provide her with brief moments of respite; an hour of sleep here and there – and that's exactly what she needed right now.

Every morning, Marat would stick his head through the bedroom door to ask if she needed anything. Twinka would say that she didn't. There was a new housekeeper, who made meals for Ronia and Marat and tried to help Twinka, too, though most of the time Twinka asked to be left alone. The hearty chicken broth, the flaky fish with creamy mashed potatoes, the scrumptious rice with chicken, and other well-intended meals were often left untouched. In the best-case scenario, Twinka would eat a spoonful or two.

Anna would ring her every now and then, but Twinka didn't have the energy to talk. All she wanted nowadays was to sleep and rest. Most of all, she wanted peace. The curtain in her bedroom was drawn closed 24/7, and so she was usually in complete darkness. Twinka didn't let the housekeeper in to tidy her room – it was clear from her attitude that she didn't want to see anyone.

Although, when Twinka had her first panic attack (at least that's what they called it later on), she did wish that someone had been next to her. Her chest felt so heavy, like a concrete block was sat on it; she couldn't breathe; her forehead broke out in a cold sweat; and time, it seemed, stood still. Twinka was completely sure that this was the end, that she was dying – there was no doubt in her mind.

But then she started feeling sick, and threw up. (Or, to be more exact, she started retching until she vomited a half-tablespoon of phlegm, the largest part of which remained stuck to and dangling from the tip of her nose.) Now, at least, she was able to breathe again.

Marat found her the next morning, lying on the floor. Twinka hadn't the energy to get herself back in bed. That's when Marat insisted that she should be taken to hospital. "It can't go on like this – we need to find out exactly what's wrong and get it treated," he said. Twinka couldn't even muster the energy to protest, plus she no longer cared.

That was at the start of December – the same day on which the first, unsteady snowflakes started falling from the sky.

When Twinka's bedroom and bathroom were eventually cleaned, they found countless empty packets of painkillers, anti-anxiety medication, sleeping pills and various tablets for indigestion... alongside forty-two empty bottles of champagne and two empty bottles of cognac. Marat surveyed the haul in complete astonishment. The fact Twinka was drinking was no news to him. But coming to terms with the fact that she'd consumed all of this solely during her spell of illness, which lasted less than a month, was tough.

CHAPTER 79

Draco didn't have the resources to investigate Dimitri's death any further. The prosecution made it very clear that it was suicide and that they didn't see anything suspicious about his death. Draco's direct superior – the Head of Criminal Police, Homicide and Special Investigations Unit – believed the same. As a result, Draco's order for the divers to search a two-kilometre stretch of the canal bed (for which he required his superior's approval) was rejected.

The boss was even angry: *What are you hoping to find? A phone? How is that going to help? We can access the data regarding the phone's coordinates and the call history anyway. What private items? A bag?! How is that going to change anything? We're not going to start a grandiose underwater operation at the start of winter just for that.*

The refusal had been categorical. As far as the investigation into Dimitri's death was concerned, all that was expected of Draco was to formally close the case. Even Draco was forced to admit that he had no leads, except for his own intuition – but that was something they didn't openly mention around here, let alone use it as an argument in an investigation. The boss had already assigned Draco to a different case. The murder of two toddlers – one aged three, the other eighteen months old – wherein the only suspect was their mother, who had suffocated them with a pillow so that they wouldn't get in the way of her relationship with her new partner.

And yet Draco still had a certain degree of leeway. It was always possible to find a bureaucratic reason not to close a case, as to enable one able to continue investigating it. His goal was to understand how Marat had organised everything. Yes, they all believed that physically he hadn't played a physical part in Dimitri's murder – but that didn't mean that Marat hadn't organised or ordered it. And if he had, then there must be a thread somewhere – some existing contacts or connections – connecting Marat with those who had physically carried out the task. And, if such a thread existed, then Draco should be able to uncover it.

Draco relieved his deputy – also known as Muscle – from all other jobs. The man didn't actually look overtly muscular . On the contrary, he was rather skinny (although his athleticism was obvious). He had gained the nickname because of his passion for triathlon. From now on, Muscle would only work on this case, whereas Draco – to appease the management and make sure they didn't get involved – would turn his attention to the murder of the children, just as he'd been asked to do.

CHAPTER 80

Twinka was taken to the same university hospital as Marat had been previously admitted to; only she was placed in the gastroenterology ward, situated in a different wing from where he'd been.

Twinka was clearly very ill. She couldn't walk unaided, so needed a wheelchair to help get from the car to her room. However, the cause of the problem wasn't immediately clear. No one had really mentioned anything about alcohol – and that included Marat and Twinka: neither of whom thought you could arrive at such a state from alcohol consumption alone. Lots of people consumed even more, and worse, kinds of alcohol, and most of the time *they* didn't end up in such a horrible state. Alcohol definitely was a contributing factor, but that couldn't be the only reason why Twinka had taken such a dramatic turn for the worse.

At first, due to the swelling, the doctors suspected her kidneys; then their attention was drawn to the thyroid; then the gallbladder. Then they tried to uncover some obscure allergy. The agony in her legs was explained by a possible case of gout, though they didn't sound too convinced. Every day Twinka was assigned further examinations, had new analysis and tests done. They found significantly heightened levels of progesterone and allergens in her body, a fatty liver and acid reflux – however, none of these conditions on their own, nor taken together, should be enough to cause the serious condition Twinka was clearly in.

Twinka's dad was with her almost the entire time. Occasionally her mum and him swapped over, and once they'd even brought Ronia along with them. But Twinka didn't want Ronia to see her like this, so she asked her parents not to bring her going forward.

Then Marat and Ronia flew to New York. He had told Twinka he wanted to go to the Sotheby's pre-Christmas sale, because this year they had an excellent piece of Chagall's on display and he wanted to buy it, though Twinka knew this was only one of the reasons. Marat loved New York at Christmas: he loved to skate by the Rockefeller Centre, to walk along the decorated shops on 5th Avenue, and just generally adored the city's festive atmosphere. Together, they'd spent numerous Christmases there in the past. He had the audacity to enjoy Christmas while she was in hospital, which would have traditionally riled Twinka up. But he'd taken Ronia along, and the last thing she wanted was for her daughter to visit her. In theory, she had no reason to be angry – Marat had simply arranged a nice Christmas for Ronia – though it didn't make Twinka feel any happier either.

Nonetheless, Marat remained in contact with Twinka's medical team. He called her every day to check how she was feeling, and to inform her of what the doctors had told him.

"Right, so you don't have a brain tumour either," he said that day, full of energetic optimism. "You'll get a visit from a psychiatrist tomorrow, and then, in the evening, they'll take you to the gynaecology ward for further examinations."

"Yes, I know," Twinka responded.

"We need to find out what's wrong. As soon as we have a clear diagnosis, we'll have a clear roadmap with the next steps."

"Yeah," Twinka agreed quietly.

"We'll get you the best specialists on the planet."

"Okay."

"Don't worry about anything – that's the main thing right now. It's important that you rest up."

"Fine" Twinka agreed to that, too.

"Right, well, hope you feel better soon – everything will be okay."

"Yeah, thanks."

Those were the sorts of conversations they were having every day. There was no "I love you" or "love you too", "sending you kisses" or "miss you" – all that had subtly vanished from their conversations.

In contrast to Marat, Dad didn't radiate an "everything will be okay" type of energy. He looked worried and very serious. At times, he looked so miserable that Twinka had to comfort him.

"You know, you don't need to be here all the time. Go home and have a rest. They're taking care of me, I'll be absolutely fine. And if I do need anything, I'll just give you a call." Twinka tried to convince Dad of this, but he remained firmly by her side for most of the day: waiting for the results, talking to the doctors, encouraging her to eat, or simply watching her sleep.

Then Christmas came. Dad got a Christmas tree for her room and decorated it along with some treats; also giving tangerines and gingerbread to the other patients, nurses and doctors. He had brought some speakers, and played a Christmas playlist he himself had curated. Mum came too, and the nurses let them stay with Twinka until eleven p.m. The evening turned out to be lovely and heart-warming. Marat never came. He had a layover in London, as he had to continue onto Dubai from there, so he never returned home. And Twinka didn't miss him either.

After Christmas, Twinka started to demand that she be discharged. She saw no point in being there. They had cross-examined her, using the latest technology; she'd been seen by numerous specialists – and she still hadn't been given a diagnosis. She wasn't receiving any treatment, apart from being hooked up to a system that pumped vitamins and macronutrients into her blood. At the same time, she was doing much better. She was able to walk, eat a few things, and her ongoing nausea had receded too. The swelling remained, but she felt much better.

During the final days of the passing year, the doctors finally agreed to release Twinka, although what happened on her last day at the hospital was very unpleasant. The professor, who'd overseen her stay in the hospital, came into the room, holding a bundle of documents – the findings of her tests and examinations and specialist deductions, including his own conclusion and recommendations.

He sat down in the only chair in the room, which Dad gave up for him. Twinka got the impression that this experienced man, whose hair had already started to turn grey, felt embarrassed.

"I'm here to return all your papers, and I wrote down everything you should do here." He handed the material to Dad.

"I recommend a rehabilitation treatment centre," he said finally, with firm conviction, having mustered the courage. "What we're seeing are very heavy consequences of alcohol intoxication." The doctor stumbled over his words, seeing that the news had caught Twinka's Dad like a punch in the gut. "It's possible that the organism isn't coping well with alcohol, so that's where we should start. Alcohol should be avoided at all costs, even in small doses. Which is why I'm recommending rehabilitation treatment and a narcologist. I wrote down some medications here, and my prognosis is that the symptoms are still reversible at this stage – all effects can be reversed. It's not too late yet, but we are getting close to the mark: the liver has become very fatty, the kidneys are struggling, the entire digestive system has been affected. It certainly wouldn't be a good idea to get yourself back to this condition again. I wrote everything down," he gestured towards the bundle of papers that Dad was holding, "but any rehabilitator will know all that anyway. You definitely need some physical activities and therapy, everything can still be fixed. And that's that," the doctor ended abruptly, standing up. "Best of luck to you, and goodbye."

"Thank you very much. Thank you," echoed behind the doctor.

Twinka felt inexplicably ashamed in front of her father. She was afraid to even look at him.

"Okay then." Dad had managed to compose himself and his tone was collected, warm and pretty ordinary. "We get the picture, now we can go home. We know what to do, eh?"

"Yeah," Twinka replied, still avoiding eye contact.

They didn't exchange another word for the whole journey home.

Marat didn't get home for New Year's Eve either.

CHAPTER 81

"I think I've found the link." Muscle was happy; he knew how much Draco wanted to hear this kind of news.

"There's this guy called Theodor: Marat's cellmate, who was convicted for murder then released from prison almost at the same time as Marat." Muscle placed Theodor's photo on the table in front of Draco.

"Oh wow!" That was Draco's only reaction as he took in Theodor's tattooed face.

"After their time in prison, Marat hired Theodor in an official capacity, as an assistant for one of his companies. As far as I understand, what he's actually doing is working as a chauffeur and being responsible for maintaining the cars, but what's really interesting is that, according to the information held by the National Revenue Office, Theodor receives a salary that is eight times higher than even the salary of the best-paid chauffeur in the country. Let's put it this way – he's incredibly well-paid."

"Disproportionately so," Draco said, after nodding approvingly.

"Exactly. So, that raises a question – what sort of services is this chauffeur actually being paid for?"

"Excellent," Draco's eyes lit up with a gratified spark, "that gives us something. Did Theodor go climbing with Marat, in the mountains?"

"No, according to his phone data he was here, in the city."

"Perfect. Let's find out everything we can about him and get ready to bring him in."

"Yes, boss."

Muscle could feel Draco's elevated mood. The hunt had begun. Every investigation had this delightful moment: that when a good clue had surfaced; the victim didn't suspect anything yet; but the wheels had started turning. The information from countless databases was already flowing to the investigators' computers – bank statements, contacts, purchases, call history, movement data, traffic offences, CCTV recordings – and all this was still just the first, most basic level. The next would involve access to the entire contents of all their electronic devices; their internet search history; a search warrant for their home, their office and any place connected to them; the inspection of private articles; obtaining a DNA and voice sample; and, if necessary, you could even get a warrant to search their body. Their friends, relatives, and anyone associated with them would also be investigated. Investigating a murder offered so many possibilities – and Draco enjoyed, and knew how to use, all of them.

CHAPTER 82

For Twinka, this was a time of slow reflection.

Dad had found her a fine Austrian clinic: one where a world-famous opera tenor had spent some time along with one of Dad's own acquaintances, a violinist from the Berlin Philharmonic. This place was called The Warm Nest and it wasn't quite a clinic – more of a secluded five-star hotel and spa, except for it had doctors and nurses, personalised menus, physiotherapists, psychologists, narcologists, beauty treatments, massage and a host of other procedures. 'Your partner in detox and weight management' – that's how they described their service. They had a chef with at least one Michelin star who prepared a personalised meal for every guest, in which every calorie had been accounted for. Yet even though the food was healthy, it certainly wasn't filling. Not for Twinka, at least.

There were no snacks between mealtimes, only water. There was even a water bar – a beautiful room in which three of the four walls were made of glass, revealing a glorious sight of the Austrian Alps, while the shelves along the fourth wall held countless bottles of mineral water. The room had all different varieties of water, including several bottles with a heightened pH level, which were of course familiar to Twinka. They were all free of charge, and you could either sit there in the room (on glass chairs, at glass tables) and enjoy the water, or else take it to your room.

Had Twinka known how stingy the menu was going to be, she would have smuggled a chocolate bar or two in. But when she first arrived here she still had the opposite issue with her appetite, so had been incapable of imagining that one day she'd feel like she was starving.

The Warm Nest was in a very advantageous spot considering what it was trying to accomplish. It was deep in the mountains, and in order to access it you had to cross a small mountain ridge through a single, narrow road. This meant that, if you did want to get to the nearest village – located some eighteen kilometres away, and where you could buy some chocolate or alcohol – you'd have to go down, then up, then down again. A seasoned athlete might be able to do the thirty-six-kilometre round trip during the winter, on a road like this – but athletes didn't frequent The Warm Nest. You couldn't hitch a ride there, either, because The Warm Nest was located at the very end of a road, in a cluster of houses, with nothing but mountain trails further along, and so any vehicle that drove along the narrow road was connected to the clinic. And so, despite the fact there were no gates and the door was always open, it just wouldn't be possible to sneak out unseen. Mobile phones and laptops weren't exactly prohibited, but it was strongly recommended that they be handed over to a special nurse whose only job was to look after them. If it was absolutely necessary, then you could use the device for an hour after lunch, which was the free-time slot between the morning and evening procedures.

But the stillness, and the kind and compassionate attitude from the rehab personnel, combined with the luxurious and high-brow atmosphere rendered the strict rules almost unnoticeable. Most of the guests acquiesced to them without fight.

(Well, there was this one very angry and morose-looking Russian woman, called Olga, who had categorically refused to give up her phone, and would demonstrate this by talking a lot on it. But over the course of a couple of days, the personnel had managed to convince even her, and after a week spent at The Warm Nest, they had transformed Olga from the aggressive, spiteful and self-entitled sister of a Russian oligarch to a humble, broken woman whom – as it turned out – you could have a rather pleasant conversation with.)

Time passed very slowly here, and the only thing Twinka regretted was that she'd put 'losing weight' down on the application form as one of her goals. In fact, her weight was the least of her worries now, and if she hadn't mentioned it then perhaps she wouldn't have to suffer all these thin root vegetable soups, all these braised vegetables, wheat germs and similar healthy meals, which were served in expensive porcelain dishes. The only thing that helped her to overcome her hunger was that all of The Warm Nest's inhabitants observed a fairly intense schedule. Everyone's program was tailored to their individual needs, yet all of them had regular conversations with the overseeing doctor, as well as physiotherapy and a certain quota of steps they had to walk every day. Since it was winter they amassed these on a treadmill, which was located in a special gallery designed solely for this purpose, facing another all-glass wall overlooking the mountains. The procedures with a beautician were just as mandatory as the physical activities, and you could take your pick from manicure or pedicure to all sorts of saunas, baths and massages, and the most exquisite facials. In the evenings after dinner, it was recommended that everyone go to bed right away. Neither TV nor WiFi were available in the rooms, but you could choose a film from the vast movie collection or take out a book from the library, which, similarly, catered to all tastes, across at least seven different languages.

A central aspect of Twinka's mealtime routine was her taking a handful of pills. They had explained to her at the start what all these tablets were (lots of vitamins, all kinds of supplements, and something else she didn't quite comprehend), although she hadn't been particularly interested. She submitted to all the requirements and demands of The Warm Nest; she consumed everything she was given with the utmost discipline; she did everything that was recommended to her; and she never bemoaned the meagre portion sizes. She didn't even crave alcohol, and was surprised at how easily she could live without it – this being a complete revelation, and one that massively lifted her spirits. She had simply been under too much stress, what with everything that had happened. Yes: she could go without drinking, that much was clear. And she could do it without much effort. Realising this gave her bags of energy and optimism. Twinka felt like she was emerging out of a deep darkness into which she had suddenly fallen. Slowly and carefully, step by step, she would figure everything out, put things in order and get her life sorted, eventually gaining full control over it. She should have done more to find time for this kind of solitude a long time ago; she should have found The Warm Nest much sooner. But, quite possibly, she couldn't have experienced rebirth, or been able to resurrect herself, until she'd hit rock bottom. Twinka was deeply grateful to God for giving her this opportunity, and promised that she wouldn't waste it.

CHAPTER 83

Muscle had been fully immersed in his work, and a couple of weeks later was ready to report on Theodor to Draco.

"I'll start with the bad news. There is no electronic trail that Theodor was ever in touch with Dimitri. They had never called each other, and Theodor's phone coordinates have never come near Dimitri's. We don't have any evidence for any sort of contact between them – at least not for the moment."

"That doesn't mean anything." Draco's hand gesture signalled that this information wasn't particularly significant. "He's an ex-convict, a murderer who's been in jail, so maybe he's learnt how to get around leaving traces like that."

"The good news is that, looking at his electronic data, he most likely won't have an alibi. If we look at the phone coordinates on the respective dates, he's spent all that time at home. In fact, it looks like he never even left home."

"He spent an entire week without setting foot outside his house?"

"That's right. Marat was away, climbing in the mountains, so he didn't need to drive him anywhere or be available, so he's basically spent the whole week lounging around the house and ordering takeaways, judging by his bank statement. He was visited by an escort service three times. By three different girls."

"Prostitutes?"

"Well, in that price range you call them by a different name," Muscle replied, and they exchanged a knowing smile. "Actually, it looks like that's been his only social contact not only during that week but in general. He's clearly very introverted and unsocial. The only other thing he's interested in apart from escorts, is motorbikes. Expensive motorbikes and expensive prostitutes, thanks to his generous salary."

"Right." Draco listened very carefully.

"He took part in a motorbike race. At a racetrack. It's amateur-level racing but still, the standard is fairly good, and he's in the top league. He hasn't quite made the leader board, but he's pretty good."

"And what does he do for Marat – did you manage to find out?"

"I followed him for about a week. Discreetly, of course. I watched the CCTV footage from the office in the house opposite his, and that of the garages, but I didn't really find anything. He's employed as a chauffeur, but Marat seems to drive himself everywhere. Over the course of a week there were no instances where Theodor would actually be driving Marat anywhere. So, I'm not sure what he gets that generous salary for."

"Suspicious, eh?"

"Yeah," Muscle agreed, "there's definitely something we don't know."

"Introverted, unsocial..." Draco repeated, as though to himself. "But maybe it's just a cover – like an image, curated for us." Draco's lips were tightly squeezed, and his eyes once again glistened with the glee of the hunter. "He appears to be at home all the time. But maybe it's just his phone that's left at home. Maybe he's not just a chauffeur. I mean, he actually killed someone – he stabbed them, went through the whole criminal investigation process, then court and prison... It must leave a mark on a person. He could be misleading us."

"From the data at my disposal I can't say any more – we'd need to put him under surveillance."

"Now, surveilling him may not yield much of a result for us... Because, if he really *is* involved in the case, then now is exactly the time when he *would* be staying in." Draco drummed his fingers on the table, his thinking intense. "I think we should intimidate him and see what happens; see who he runs to. He might actually fall for that. Except, if he is that handy on a bike, we probably need to set up some external surveillance that can keep up with him."

"We could only do that with a drone," Muscle said.

"Yeah, a drone..." Marat sighed unconvincingly.

"If we want to put a drone above his head for three days, then we won't be able to hide it from the management," said Muscle, putting voice to what Draco was already thinking.

"Mmm yeah... We'll need to secure all the relevant warrants, and we don't have any basis for acquiring them at the moment."

"We could try attaching some basic surveillance transmitters to his motorbikes. I mean, he does seem to be regularly fiddling with his bikes, but still, I don't think he'd be able to find them right away."

"Yeah, it's worth a try. Let's see if his physical coordinates match those of his phone data, that will give us a lot of intel. We'll find out what kind of animal we're dealing with here and how much we can trust his past phone data."

"Yes, sir." Muscle used the formal language of duty, which he only ever used when he strongly agreed or disagreed with something his superior had said.

"Let's work with him for a bit and then, hopefully, something will crop up." Draco's voice was full of resolve. "We need to examine this thread," he said, confirming his conviction by slapping his hand on the table.

"How are we going to intimidate him?" The contagious mood emanating from his boss had infected Muscle.

"We'll pay him a visit," Draco said, determined and excited. "There's no other way. If we order a summons, Marat will get Keiko for him straightaway, and then we'll get nothing."

CHAPTER 84

Life at The Warm Nest wasn't too bad. Mum and Dad came to visit Twinka; then Dad came by himself twice more. Twinka had evidently lost weight, and it inspired her. She felt much better in herself, too – she still wasn't craving any alcohol, and she had even got used to the food.

Nonetheless, one issue remained: boredom.

The longer Twinka remained here – and she had spent the entire winter and spring here: from January all the way through to the beginning of May – the harder it became to endure the little bubble with its familiar procedures; the well-acquainted employees; the slow, drowsy atmosphere; the boring views of the mountains behind the windows; and the mundane daily routine. In short, she was missing her life on the outside. She missed her home, Ronia, the shops, the cafes, the city life. She wanted to take a drive in her car. She couldn't wait for the first opportunity to see Anna. The only person she didn't miss was Marat.

That was the second significant discovery she'd made during her time here. She didn't need him. Not in the least bit. She actually felt much better without him around. While she was at The Warm Nest, Twinka had also discovered some new music. She remembered what Anna had said: that there's no situation that you couldn't get through by finding the appropriate song. Back then, Twinka hadn't really understood what Anna meant. What music was she talking about? Anything that contained words felt like more pointless information, additional pressure, on top of everything else that was already going on. She couldn't get a grip on all the thoughts and feelings that swirled around in her head, and music had felt like an unnecessary intrusion. But now, she was rediscovering the beauty of music. She remembered all of her favourite songs, artists and concerts; she made her own playlists; and, whenever it felt good to, she would dance in her room by herself.

In her dreams, Twinka saw herself at home, doing ordinary things – frying eggs, making breakfast for Ronia, arguing with her daughter about how you can't walk around with bare ankles in winter. In these dreams she was the caring mother in her own, organised world, and every time Twinka woke up the first thing she felt was disappointment that she wasn't home.

The Warm Nest had given her a lot. For starters, she had quit drinking – and so smoothly at that. And secondly, she had lost nine kilograms! – an amount she had not dared dream possible beforehand. Her blood test wasn't perfect yet, but there had been significant improvement. And the main thing was – she had regained her self-belief, and her confidence along with it. She was ready to return to life.

According to The Warm Nest's open-door policy, the inhabitants could check out whenever they felt like it. And on her final evening, the personnel organised a farewell party for Twinka – one without any alcohol or snacks, of course, but they had balloons, a gorgeous guitar player from Portugal, and lots and lots of well-wishes.

CHAPTER 85

"Pizza!" Draco shouted, after ringing the doorbell next to Theodor's apartment door. "I'm gonna leave it here," he added, then standing aside so he couldn't be seen through the keyhole.

As expected, Theodor, even though he'd not ordered any pizza, opened the door to see what was going on. At that very moment, two uniformed police officers burst into the apartment.

With the words "May we come in?" Draco himself proceeded to march into Theodor's flat, pushing Theodor aside. He was followed by Muscle, who was also in uniform. By law, they could only enter Theodor's apartment with the appropriate warrant. Technically though, he had requested to be let in, and had not received a categorical refusal. And if Keiko did show up, Draco would say that he did ask for permission to enter, and Theodor had agreed.

Theodor looked confused, but not afraid. He didn't say anything and quietly stepped aside, letting everyone barge through.

The flat wasn't substantial – a large, open-plan room housed both the living room and kitchen. The two areas were separated by a hefty, dark-red punchbag, which hung from the ceiling. There was also a small corridor off it, leading to the bedroom and bathroom. And that was it.

Draco paced around, exhibiting his authority. He peered into the bedroom, as though he wanted to check whether anyone else was in the flat, then placed himself down on the sofa in the spot where it looked like Theodor would usually sit. Muscle and the other uniformed officer remained standing.

Theodor stood opposite them, watching everything with a perplexed expression. He still hadn't said a word.

"Sit down, please," Draco commanded.

Leisurely, Theodor took a chair and sat down opposite Draco next to a small coffee table, his back towards the TV screen.

"When did you last see this man?"

Draco tossed a photo of Dimitri onto the coffee table. Theodor lifted and examined it, slowly and carefully, before shaking his head.

"Don't know him."

"Listen, we're not going to get anywhere like this." Draco bent forwards. "We know that you know him well. What I'm asking is – when was the last time you saw him?"

"I don't," Theodor said, sounding surprised.

"Well, if you're going to act like that, then I'm afraid you'll have to come with us." Draco rose to his feet. "Let's go," he said.

Muscle knew that this was a crucial moment. Theodor didn't have to go with them – he hadn't been arrested, and there was no basis for his detainment; he could just ask them to leave or call a lawyer. In fact, he'd make a big mistake by following Draco. Yet Draco was incredibly convincing – acting as though dismissing him were not an option – and Muscle watched his boss with a certain level of awe.

Without saying anything, Theodor started putting on his shoes; submitting without protest. While Theodor was putting on his jacket and while his back was towards them, Draco and Muscle exchanged a knowing look.

So far, so good.

Back at the police station, they walked through the main entrance, continued inside via the metal detector and asked Theodor to leave his phone in a locker by the wall that was meant for visitors. They'd successfully overcome another hurdle: Theodor wouldn't be able to call Keiko quite so easily now. They led Theodor into the interrogation room and left him there to wait. The door was locked, and from here he couldn't physically leave without Draco's permission. Though Theodor hadn't been formally detained, his position was worse than if he had been, because in reality he was a detainee without having the rights typically afforded one.

Content, Draco and Muscle went for a coffee. According to Draco's plan, they would leave Theodor for an hour or an hour and a half. During that time, Theodor would start getting worn down by the stress, the suspense, not to mention the uncomfortable chair. Being trapped in a small, practically empty room that had a single desk and three tattered, uncomfortable office chairs, while being detained and not knowing exactly why he was here – just waiting for something to happen, yet not knowing what would – would be incredibly difficult, on an emotional and psychological level: even for someone who'd been through this sort of experience before.

"I have to say, I was expecting a bit more of a resistance from a convicted murderer," Draco said to Muscle, waiting for the coffee machine to fill his paper cup.

"It's weird," Muscle responded, "that Marat hasn't instructed him to call a lawyer in this sort of situation."

"Yeah, that is a bit weird," Draco agreed.

Time crawled by. The hour's wait – which was designed to weaken the suspect, to suck all of their psychological and physical strength before the interrogation started – was dragging on very slowly, even for Draco. Muscle had been swimming training earlier that morning, and he was opening one of the four plastic tubs containing the food he'd prepared to last him the whole day – three thousand and three hundred calories in total – and starting his breakfast. Draco didn't usually eat breakfast.

When Muscle had finished eating, the two men went over the interrogation plan once more. It was nothing new – they called it "the carousel". They'd start off being friendly and polite, which was all an act, designed to lull the suspect's vigilance; followed by coaxing them, attempting to convince them to cooperate and promising them good terms if they did; and then, if that didn't work, they would go to phase two: false evidence and bluffing ("We already have everything we need", "There's no point denying anything" "You're only making things worse for yourself"). Finally, they would employ threats and intimidation. They'd dealt with plenty of murderers who came into the police station voluntarily one afternoon, absolutely sure of themselves, only to confess by the evening. Maybe with exception of terrorists, whom Draco had never encountered in his role, Draco was convinced the psychological factor led to far more criminals confessing than physical intimidation. He was really hoping they'd get something today that would finally shake up the case.

After an hour and twenty minutes, Muscle went into the interrogation room.

"I'm really sorry we've kept you waiting – we have a bit of a bottleneck today. So much information coming in, through multiple channels. I do apologise. Can I offer you some coffee or tea? Or water maybe?"

"No." Theodor said, shaking his head.

"Are you sure? Maybe coffee? You wouldn't think, but it's actually pretty decent around here."

"No."

"All right, but do let me know as soon as you want something, okay?"

Theodor shook his head for the third time. There was a certain impatience in his gaze, which seemed to be saying "Let's start already".

"Sure, as you wish." Muscle was politeness personified. "We just need to ask you a few questions – don't worry, nothing major – we just need to confirm a few things." Muscle was carrying a folder containing documents. "Do you work as a chauffeur?"

"Yeah," accompanied this time by a nod.

"Could you tell me a bit more about your duties, please?"

"I'm responsible for the cars." As Theodor spoke a whole sentence for the first time Muscle was a bit taken aback by how soft and, seemingly, boyish, his voice still sounded. It jarred with his tough, tattooed face. "Maintenance, MOT, some repairs if needed, car wash, cleaning, winter tyres, summer tyres, changing windscreen-wiper fluids, charging up the battery, that sort of thing. Sometimes just putting in petrol. Basically I do everything, so that Marat can take any car he wants and go for a drive whenever he wants."

"Does Marat usually sit behind the wheel?"

"Yeah, usually; I take him places too sometimes."

"Right. What else?"

"Sometimes I have to take somebody to the office or bring them back home, or other places. Sometimes I have to buy something, take it somewhere, or bring it back. It depends."

The more Theodor spoke, the more it surprised Muscle how clean and simple his language and behaviour were. There was no swearing, no rudeness, no aggressiveness – none of what you might expect, going by his photo and rap sheet.

"Right, I see." Muscle sounded very content with the replies. "A chauffeur, a courier, and an assistant," he clarified.

"Yeah, you could say that," Theodor agreed.

"I see. And when Marat goes abroad – what are your duties then?"

"Then there's less to do."

"Right. We're particularly interested in the period when Marat was in the mountains – if you recall? Especially the first two weeks. Do you remember that time?"

"Yeah, I guess," Theodor said. He sounded surprised.

"Tell me what you remember about those two weeks."

"I remember that I didn't leave the flat during that time."

"You didn't leave the flat?"

"Yeah. There was no work for me, and I was learning the Nürburgring turns."

"I'm sorry?" Muscle didn't understand.

"I want to do to the Nürnburg ring on my bike. It's best to learn the turns ahead of time, so you can drive them faster, once you're there."

"Oh, I see," Muscle nodded. "And how were you learning these turns?"

"On a simulator."

"Right... So, for ten days you were learning these turns and never left the house?"

"Well, almost..." Theodor said, as though he was embarrassed. "I was learning Silverstone and Le Mans, Sepang, and other tracks, too."

"And you never left your apartment at all?"

"Well, maybe I went to get some beers a couple times."

"Tell me, were you learning these turns by yourself?"

"What do you mean?"

"Well, were you alone at home, or did someone come and visit you? Maybe you did it with a friend?"

"No, I was by myself."

"I see. So, then there's no one who could confirm that you really were at home for that week – ten days?"

"I don't know." Theodor seemed baffled.

"That's not good... Not good at all," Muscle said, as though he were gravely worried. "You don't have an alibi – do you understand?"

"No, I don't understand." A tougher note resounded in Theodor's voice for the first time.

"Well, basically, you don't have an alibi."

"What alibi are you talking about?" Theodor was looking at Muscle as if totally perplexed.

"Listen, this is really important." Muscle leaned in towards him, as though he was carefully searching for the right words. He took out Dimitri's photo from his folder and placed it on the table in front of Theodor. "You need to tell me everything you know about this person – the last time you saw him – everything. *Capishe?* You don't need to cover for anyone or take on someone else's blame, it's really not a good idea. Just tell us everything, exactly as it was."

"But I don't know him." There was despair in Theodor's voice. "I don't know him; I don't know who he is."

"Hang on, hang on, slow down," Muscle interrupted, "don't rush into anything. Think it all over first. I understand that you want to cover for Marat, that's what he's hired you to do, but think about it – do you really need all that? Do you want to end up back in prison, just for Marat's sake? Are you ready to go back there because of him?"

"I don't understand what's going on. I'm not covering for anyone – I really don't know that man!"

"Theodor, look me in the eye. I don't want any harm to come to you; I'm not here to 'set you up' or anything like that – just help me out and I'll help you, okay? Don't dig yourself into a hole." Muscle was talking to Theodor almost entreatingly, as if he was imploring a loved one. "Let me help you. Please. Don't make things worse for yourself."

"But I don't understand what you want from me!"

"Right," Muscle's tone had switched to one of disappointment. "Okay," he said abruptly, "you'll need to hold on," and with that he left the room.

CHAPTER 86

The new Chagall, brought over from New York, was the first thing Twinka noticed as she returned home. The painting was hanging above Michelangelo's *Pietà*. The spot was clearly unsuitable for it, and Twinka was baffled by the choice of placement.

"Yeah, it's not right," Marat agreed. "I haven't decided where its rightful place should be – but I wanted it somewhere visible, until I figured out where to put it. Although I think I already know where I'll put it – in the guest toilet."

"The toilet?" Twinka no longer felt attached to Marat.

"Yeah – picture it; you're sitting on the toilet and looking at a masterpiece that's worth half a million. That would be so us."

"So you," Twinka corrected him.

"This way, we'd have just the right dose of scorn for the senselessly overpriced piece of artwork, while at the same time we'd be paying respect to the all-important time we tend to spend in the toilet. The light is pretty good there, too."

Twinka didn't say anything.

"You look really good," Marat said, seemingly genuine.

"Thanks. How's Ronia?"

"She's in school."

"You must have spoiled and pampered her rotten while I've been away."

"Oh, we should stop trying to raise her. She's an adult –" Marat tossed his hand dismissively – "an intelligent, fully grown human being – she's a personality. Spoiling is irrelevant to her now."

"You do realise that teenagers only *say* they want more freedom; when, in reality, if you give them too much freedom, they start believing that no one cares about them and no one loves them."

"There is one snag, of course, and I don't know how to solve it."

"What?" Twinka asked, very firmly and seriously, as though preparing herself for the worst.

"She doesn't know what she wants to do in life. She's drifting around without a firm goal in mind. She doesn't have 'her thing', and there's nothing you can do to help someone like that."

"Didn't she say that she was interested in literature?"

"She only said it because she thought it would make you happy."

"She'll figure it out," Twinka said with a yawn. She had got up very early and her journey had been very long.

"If she knew what she wanted, if she had her own thing, then I could help her in a thousand different ways. And we'd have something to encourage her towards – tell her what to read, what to do, what skills to develop – and what sort of things she shouldn't need to think about. But right now... nothing. She studies for all her subjects, tries to get a good grade in everything, but what is it all for?"

"So that later, when she has figured out what she does want to study, she will have the opportunity to do it at a good university."

"You need more than good grades to get into a good university. There's millions of idiots with good grades." Marat's mood was ruined.

"I'll talk to her," Twinka said, conciliatory. "You said she was an intelligent, fully grown personality, so she'll figure it out herself."

"Of course, she will," Marat agreed. "Me and you have clearly succeeded without the Ivy League."

"'Succeeded'... We'd have to argue over that," responded Twinka, now also annoyed, with an air of contempt. "But I do agree in the sense that I doubt the Ivy League could have protected us." As Twinka finished the sentence, she suddenly felt a strong desire to have something alcoholic. No, she couldn't! She was unpleasantly surprised at how quickly this desire had surfaced, though. She'd been back home for barely an hour, and already she felt an urge to drink.

It was Marat – he was to blame; he made her feel anxious.

"She's a lot like you. You never really had your thing, and she's the same." Marat had felt Twinka's sting, and had become cold.

I did have my thing. My thing was our family, and you were my thing, Twinka thought to herself, though she didn't say it out loud.

"By the way, I don't think my life has turned out to be unsuccessful. At least for now," Marat carried on after a short pause, just as coldly.

"What about my life? Do you think my life has been a success?"

Marat looked at Twinka as though he was examining her. He had never felt such defiant scorn from her. They never even argued. They didn't speak to one another with irritation and resentment. At least they never used to.

"What does it even mean – a successful life? And how can you measure it?" Twinka felt guilty for her tone and tried to take the pressure down a notch.

In the past, she reflected, Marat would have hugged and cuddled her when something like this happened. He would have calmed her down. Instead of looking at her with such judgement, as he was now.

"A successful life means knowing what your thing is and gaining success in it; being good at your thing. That's it." Marat had resumed his typical negligent and superior tone. "That contains everything," he continued, "happiness, content, success, meaning – all these elements are in that. To keep going forward in your thing, to have the sense that things are moving in the right direction. And that's enough – you're happy. And even if you don't become successful from doing your thing, you still feel at peace, because you've done everything you possibly could. That would be fine, too. But if you were good at your thing, then that's a very successful life."

"Interesting... And what is your thing then?" Twinka's anger had suddenly subsided, and she asked this with genuine curiosity.

"Let's focus on Ronia – we have to think about Ronia, encourage her to find her thing, or else—"

"I get it. Or else she'll turn out just like me," Twinka concluded, sarcastically.

CHAPTER 87

Draco had been watching the interrogation on the monitor in his office.

"Let him sit there for forty more minutes," he said to Muscle.

"What if he really doesn't know anything?" The hunter's spark seemed to have gone from Muscle 's eyes.

"Or maybe he's acting? We didn't think he'd just confess at the drop of a hat," Draco objected. "He's got no alibi, he's saying that he didn't leave the house for two weeks. I mean – two weeks, who does that?"

"Well," Muscle shrugged, "his phone data confirms it."

"Phone data is not an alibi," Draco grumbled.

"Yeah..." Muscle didn't want to argue with his superior. "I'll go get some coffee – would you like some too?"

"No, I've had enough to last me until morning," Draco said, disgruntled. The possibility that Theodor may not be connected with Dimitri's death was putting him in a seriously bad mood. It was difficult to bluff if you didn't have anything concrete to go on. There were no other suspects you could say had confessed already; there was no physical evidence that could have had DNA samples or fingerprints on it – they didn't even have a crime scene confirmed or a certain date. What rotten luck!

When Draco re-entered the interrogation room almost forty-five minutes later, he didn't even have to pretend to be angry and bitter.

"Right. We have enough evidence to connect you with Dimitri's murder. You will go back to prison," Draco announced with no introduction, as soon as he'd charged through the door, seemingly filled with energy, urgency and conviction. Draco wanted Theodor to know that he wasn't going to waste any time – that everything was clear, and Theodor's fate was of no concern to him. That was the idea behind the act anyway.

"You'll go back to prison – not for just a bit, but twenty years minimum. I guess you must have really enjoyed it there."

Theodor didn't say anything, his eyes filled with bafflement and nothing else.

"You enjoyed it, did you? Fine, as you wish, what do I care. What did Marat tell you – that everything was safe, that we wouldn't find out about it? Is that how it was?"

Theodor looked at Draco, his eyes wide, but still didn't say anything.

"Speak, for fuck's sake. What did Marat tell you – what did he promise you?" Even though Draco's vocal chords didn't let him speak too loud, he was still, essentially, shouting at Theodor.

"Nothing," Theodor, barely audible, said at last.

"I'm giving you one last chance. If you cooperate with us, I promise it will be taken into account – maybe we'll even relieve you of all responsibility, but you need to tell us absolutely everything. We need to know everything. Names, surnames, and how it all happened exactly."

Theodor said nothing in reply, and Muscle, who was watching it all on the computer screen, thought the man was probably in a state of shock.

"Either you tell us everything now – exactly what happened to Dimitri – or you've only got yourself to blame," Draco continued, firmly and with menace.

"I don't know," Theodor said quietly.

"When will you get it, you tattooed moron, that we're talking about a murder? And it will be your second to date, which is a whole life sentence. That's it. You'll never be able to ride your motorbike for the rest of your life, you'll never see a woman. Ever. Do you get it?"

"I don't know anything," Theodor was almost whispering.

"You don't know anything? You don't know? Do you really hope to get away with it?" Draco spat. "Okay, just remember that I gave you this opportunity. Remember, for the rest of your life, that I gave you a chance. You're the one who refused, so don't blame me for it afterwards: you are the master of your own fate. Remember this moment for the rest of your life, which you'll spend behind bars, when I gave you a chance."

Draco rose to his feet and left the room.

"He should be warmed up now," he said to Muscle, when he returned to the office.

CHAPTER 88

"You look perfect!" Anna was pretty good at pretend delight and admiration. "How much have you lost – must be at least five or six kilos, eh?" she asked.

"Bit more than that," Twinka humbly confirmed.

"Well, you look terrific, that posh nest must have been worth every penny," Anna continued to flatter her. "You can't even imagine how many problems in a relationship and a marriage are caused just by having some excess weight. It's our enemy on so many levels – both physically and psychologically. We sort of feel it and acknowledge it, but not everyone is strong enough to bring themselves to do something about it. I've had clients, you know, where I felt I should just try and get them to lose the extra weight, but in my profession being so direct is rarely possible. We need to get the individual to start wanting it for themselves; get them sincerely working towards that goal, and that's tough."

Twinka's head gestured affirmatively.

"But, really, well done," Anna continued – she could see that these compliments mattered to Twinka.

"Marat has never said anything about me being overweight – he's mad that I haven't found 'my thing'."

"Your thing?" Anna repeated.

"Yeah, and because of me Ronia hasn't found her thing either – she doesn't know what she wants in life, and that's why she won't go to a good university, and she won't be happy in life in general. And it's all my fault."

"By 'your thing', does he mean some sort of a profession?"

"Nah, he got that from Bhagavad Gita or some such place."

"Oh? Tell me more..." Anna was intrigued.

"It's like an understanding of your place in life, in the world. It's a profession, too; but you could, for example, have your own business and some sort of mission in life that is independent from your business or your profession."

"An understanding of your place in life... ?"

"Yeah. It must be derived from the caste system. An understanding of what your caste is, what your mission is, your duty, your place in the world."

"Like karma?"

"Yeah, that too." Twinka spoke with scorn. "All of that – your karma, your caste, your thing."

"And he thinks that you haven't found your 'thing'?"

"Yep."

"But how does that work then, if your thing is something karmic and you're born into a certain caste? Surely, that means everyone has their thing and you or Ronia can't possibly not have it?"

"I don't know, I've never asked him about it in too much detail. He loves talking about castes and 'your thing', whereas I've never really been interested in all that. Maybe it's like: we have it, but we've not realised what it is yet. And you know what's the worst thing about it?"

"Go on." Anna was listening, actively and professionally.

"What if he's right again? Who am I without him? I've never thought about it before. Honestly, the thought couldn't have even surfaced because I couldn't imagine being without him. And why would I? All of me was reserved for him, we were a single entity; and that, to me, was happiness. But now I realise that, outside of him, I don't really exist. I'm just an empty shell. Everyone knows me as 'Marat's wife'. If we get a divorce, I'll be known as 'Marat's ex-wife'. No, I don't have my thing – I don't even have my own identity that's independent of him."

"Hang on, hang on..." Anna spoke soothingly. "It's not all that bad. First of all, you're a mum to Ronia. No one can ever take that away from you, and—"

"And he's trying to undermine that role, too, in any way he can." Twinka hadn't even let Anna finish.

"No, he can't take that away from you: you're her mum, you've raised her, you've been with her since she was born, looking after her in sickness and sharing her joy... No, nothing and no one can take that away from you."

"Well, okay, let's suppose that's true. But is that it then? And Ronia is almost an adult now – just a couple more years and she'll fly the nest, and I'll only see her a few times a year. I'm forty years old – but who am I, and what is my place in the world? My child is an adult, my marriage has collapsed, I don't have my thing, I don't have anything. The only thing I have is alcoholism."

"And how's it going with alcohol?"

"It's not. I mean, I'm controlling the situation, but what's the point? That's not the main issue. If I didn't drink, would anything be different? If I didn't drink, would I suddenly be able to develop an identity and a purpose in life?"

"I understand," Anna said, though she knew that those were not the words Twinka expected or wanted to hear from her. Twinka wanted Anna to say that she was wrong; she wanted to hear something comforting, something inspirational, to be given advice or a roadmap. But Anna didn't have such words.

"We need to find you a hobby, some sort of devotion – it's really important," Anna said, though she didn't believe her own words. "Maybe you could get a pet? Have you ever had a dog or a cat?"

"Marat doesn't like animals," Twinka said, followed by a heavy sigh.

"What about charity? Have you ever thought about it? By helping others, you can really help yourself – you'll gain a different perspective in the process. A new outlook that maybe your problems are not as big as everyone else's, and it will give you pleasure and joy that you're able to help those who need it more."

"So, instead of a family life and love, you're suggesting I take care of a cat or look after sick children. Is that it?" Twinka had voiced her disbelief bluntly.

"I'm saying that you shouldn't give up, and should continue searching for your thing. Find that purpose. Something that takes up your time and occupies your mind."

"You know, all rich wives have a little store, a little cafe, some art gallery, a small hotel, a spa, they do a bit of charity – I always used to laugh at that with Marat, as though it was a compulsory set that comes with a Birkin bag. I always felt like I was above them, but now I see why they do it," Twinka said, sounding bitter.

"Well, there's no harm in having a little cafe or doing a bit of charity, eh? If it makes you happy, gives you something to do, brings joy to others and lets you do something good for them – no harm in that, is there?"

"I don't know, Anna, I really don't... What I do know for sure is that it won't save me. And a cat won't save me either."

CHAPTER 89

They didn't make Theodor wait too long this time. Muscle came into the interrogation room just a few minutes after Draco. He was hoping to capitalise on the shock caused by his boss.

"Would you like some tea now?" Muscle said in a compassionate, kind voice.

"No." Theodor shook his head once again.

Muscle sighed heavily.

"Such a crazy situation," he concluded, in a voice full of understanding.

They sat in silence for a while.

"Listen, you know what we'll do: you tell me everything, off-the-record, without protocol, witnesses, any of that – just tell me what you know, and everything you say will stay between the two of us. And I promise, I'll figure out a way to make you come out clean," Muscle said in a conspiratorial, friendly tone.

Draco nodded approvingly as he watched everything on the screen.

"You're a good lad," muscle continued, "I know your history, I've read it. You're not a criminal, your place definitely isn't around criminals, and you know it, too. Don't worry, I'll help you. We'll sort everything out, but you need to let me help you. Do you understand?"

Suddenly there were tears in Theodor's eyes. Theodor was crying.

"It's going to be okay... Everything will be okay," Muscle said, as comforting as he could.

For a while they sat in silence. Theodor wiped the tears with a quick, abrupt movement – first with his hand, then with his sleeve.

"Tell me everything you know about Dimitri," Muscle said, calm and collected.

"I don't know him," Theodor answered bluntly, having managed to pull himself together.

"Now, now, don't rush – think it over. No one's accusing you of being a criminal. Perhaps you didn't know what was going on, or maybe you were forced – just tell me what happened and I promise I'll figure out a way to help you. If you were forced or tricked into it, then you have nothing to worry about."

Theodor mopped the rest of the moisture from his eyes using his sleeve. Wiped his nose.

"Did they force you to do it? Did they get you involved against your will?" Muscle tried to lead Theodor again. This technique of constructing for them a duress-based explanation of their actions – which could lead towards a confession, or at least a partial admission of guilt – was usually very effective. And when the suspect had partially admitted their guilt, or shared some diluted version of it, then from there obtaining their actual confession often wasn't all that difficult.

"I'm telling you – I don't know what you're talking about." Theodor sounded desperate. "I don't understand."

"Would you like some tea?"

"No."

"Are you trying to say that you've never seen this man before?"

"No." Theodor replied firmly and with conviction.

"And what were you doing at the shipyard?"

"The shipyard? When?" Theodor was baffled.

"When – as you said – you were learning the turns."

"I haven't been to the shipyard, I dunno, probably since my childhood. I haven't set foot there since I came out of prison."

"And if you really thought about it?" Muscle smiled, as though pointing to some shared secret between them.

"No, I've not been there." Theodor shook his head.

"Okay, fine, maybe not inside the shipyard – but somewhere nearby, surely?"

"No, I'm actually avoiding that whole area. I don't want to run into anyone from my old life." Again, Theodor's expression was one of surprised confusion.

"Right. Okay, hold on a moment."

And Muscle left Theodor alone.

Draco was gloomy. "This is a total disaster. We should have realised straightaway that it was too obvious," he said to Muscle.

"What do you mean – too obvious?" Muscle didn't understand.

"Marat's cellmate, a convicted murderer, someone whose photo clearly spells they're a criminal. Just what you want, isn't it? And he gets paid an inadequately high salary by Marat. The perfect suspect."

"You think he's too perfect?"

"Yeah, obviously he's too perfect. It's all done on purpose, so that we put our full focus on this tattooed boyo. He didn't go to the mountains. He doesn't have an alibi. Marat knew that we'd go down this route."

"But, equally, isn't the simplest answer most often correct? Maybe there's no need to complicate things?" Muscle objected, using an argument he'd once heard from Draco.

"He's made a fool of us." Draco crumpled in his chair, disappointed. "I should have seen it sooner – when it was clear that he didn't have a lawyer, and that he hadn't been prepared for this sort of situation. If Theodor was involved, he would have known Keiko's phone number off by heart."

"Mmyeah..." Muscle said thoughtfully.

"And we were ready to follow him with a drone, to waste our time and resources, to become a complete laughing stock. Let him go," Draco ordered.

"Wasn't our plan to see where he's going to go, now that he's been spooked, and who he is going to call?"

"It's obvious who. And Marat will laugh at us," Draco said, angry and disappointed. "Just let him go."

CHAPTER 90

Was that really Twinka calling him? Draco's eyes widened as he looked at his phone. *She* was calling *him*? Twinka? She must have made some mistake.

"Speaking," he said abruptly, so as not to lose face in case it turned out to be some sort of pocket dial.

"Hello," Twinka said, hesitantly. "You said I should call you if I remembered anything."

"Oh yes! Yes, I did – thank you for calling." Draco's tone changed to an accommodating one at lightning speed.

"I have to tell you something," Twinka said.

"Of course, I'm listening, all yours."

"I don't think it's a good idea to say it over the phone."

"Right, yes, of course, I understand – whatever is best for you." Draco was ready to do somersaults for her. "Would you like to come to the police station?"

"Hmm, I don't know... Maybe we could meet somewhere a bit more neutral?"

"Yes, yes, of course, we can meet somewhere a bit more neutral, whatever is more convenient for you."

"Do you know Louie's?"

"Louie's?" Draco didn't get it.

"Louis XVII Boulangerie, at the top of the promenade?"

"Oh, I see – yes, of course, I'll find it."

They agreed to meet an hour later, at three-thirty p.m. By the time Draco arrived, Twinka was already waiting for him. She had ordered a bottle of Coche-Dury.

Twinka had resumed drinking on the fifth day after her returning home, though she didn't beat herself up about it. She had proven that she could go without drinking when she was at The Warm Nest, and she'd made a promise to herself to spend a month there each year going forward. It couldn't do any harm to have a bit of high-quality alcohol in between. The wine was stored inside a fridge next to a small metal table. There were two glasses on the table and when Draco arrived, the waiter offered to fill his too.

Draco hesitated. He could definitely have a drink. It was no big thing, they were here on unofficial business, plus the working day had almost finished. In fact, he would have loved to have a drink. Never in his entire life had he tasted wine as expensive as the one Twinka had ordered; and, most likely, he never would. But today of all days he had to pick up Annabella, and Draco didn't want to be tipsy in front of his daughter, not even a little. Annabella spent most of the week living with her maternal grandma. It was a compromise benefitting both of them – it was the only way they were each able to bear the tragic, painful void that was left by Annabella's mother's death.

"No, just water for me, please," Draco abstained.

It was a particularly warm spring afternoon, and one of the first days of the year when you could sunbathe. The beach was already packed, as if it were summer. Although the weather had only just started to improve, the city dwellers were quick to jump at the opportunity to enjoy the water.

"You were asking me about the fragrance of honeysuckle," Twinka started, without preamble, as soon as the waiter had left.

"Yes." She had Draco's undivided attention.

"Well, it's a reference to Faulkner's *The Sound and the Fury*. The protagonist commits suicide by drowning himself with two flat irons tied to his legs. I mean, not the kind we have these days, but those old, heavy ones."

"Right," Draco said. *The Sound and the Fury*, he jotted down in a small, tattered notebook.

"There's a bridge over the Charles River in Harvard, from which Quentin jumps with those flat irons attached to his legs.

He was a student at Harvard at that time," Twinka carried on. "The other Harvard students have made him a memorial plaque on the bridge, which says: *Quentin Compson III, June 2, 1910. Drowned in the fading of honeysuckle.* And that, I believe, sounds very much like *I drowned myself in the fragrance of honeysuckle.*"

"Right. Yes." Draco excitedly wrote down everything Twinka had said.

"Honeysuckle was Quentin's favourite childhood smell. He associated it with sleepless nights, with restlessness, and an all-encompassing darkness. But there's something else that's even important..." Twinka took a large gulp of wine before she continued. "The main thing is that when I met Marat at the prison gates, he was holding a copy of *The Sound and the Fury* in his hands. He was reading it in prison, he then read it at home; he seemed to be really enjoying it. He was fully immersed in this novel, whereas Dimitri didn't even read books. Dimitri only had a few books, all about maths; maybe one or two on physics or statistics – but he's never read novels. Dimitri would *never* write a sentence like *I drowned myself in the fragrance of honeysuckle.* It's impossible, you know? He just wasn't that kind of a person. He was an excellent mathematician, but he had absolutely no interest in fiction, let alone something as literary as Faulkner. He just didn't have enough interest in or love for literature to warrant writing such a highbrow reference in his suicide note. It's just not possible. It's absolutely out of the question." Twinka emptied her glass and took the bottle to refill it again. "And he believed in God, he was a fervent Christian, so I know that he would never have taken such a sin upon himself."

"But there is someone who could have composed that sentence..." said Draco, taking the baton from Twinka...

"Yes," Twinka said, without listening to Draco. "You know, I've been thinking a lot about it... And I think that suicide note was meant for me. He knew that the police would show me the note, and he also knew that I'd work out the reference to the honeysuckle. In fact I'm wondering whether he was purposefully holding a copy of Faulkner when I met him outside the prison because he'd planned it all already. He took special care to ensure that I could see he'd been reading it. He knew that I would understand – but only me, no one else. He's the one who killed Dimitri ,and I'm the only one who should know about it."

"This is priceless information," Draco said, looking at his notebook.

"Yeah. And that sentence from Pessoa, I explained that to you before. Marat has read Pessoa, he was interested in him, because he was my favourite writer. You asked me what the context of that sentence was. Well, if Marat did write it, then there definitely is a context. He wrote it for me – he knew that I'd know where it came from, and he wanted to tell me that the story continues, even though Dimitri's now dead."

Twinka fell silent, as though she'd said everything. She poured herself more wine. In that short space of time, she'd already consumed half a bottle.

Draco wrote something in his notebook again.

"And you want your husband to face justice for what he's done?" he asked, having stuffed the notebook in the inner pocket of his suit jacket.

Twinka lifted her eyes from the glass and looked directly into the chief inspector's eyes.

"Yes, I do," she said.

"All right. So, this is what I think," Draco started, slowly. "If you're right – and I think it's extremely likely that you are – then Marat will want to make sure that you've understood the message. If he's gone to such lengths, arranged all these references, then he'll want to be sure that you have not only received the message – he'll want to enjoy its effect. He'll want to see your reaction to it. Right?"

"Perhaps," Twinka said, once more with an air of hesitation.

"I think you'll have a conversation about it. You could even initiate it yourself without too much effort." Draco's gaze bore into Twinka. He could see that she didn't quite follow where he was going – yet.

"See, we could then record that conversation. And, if we have a good recording, where Marat confesses to the murder or the part he played in organising it, then we could bring him to justice."

"You want me to tape a conversation, and walk around with a microphone stuck to me?" Twinka finally understood.

"No, no, don't worry. That only happens in films – you won't need to 'wear a mic', if we kit out the rooms in your house. You won't have to worry about anything – all you'd have to do is initiate the conversation."

"No problem," Twinka said firmly, without hesitation, and took another large swig of wine. "I could do it today even."

"No, not today." Draco smiled, content. "If you could give us a heads up over the next few days, as to a time when no one is at home, then we could come over, set up the equipment, and then you could plan to have the conversation afterwards."

"Agreed. Yeah, let's do it. I'll give you a call tomorrow."

Draco watched her carefully, with his lips squeezed tight. *Hopefully she's not just saying that because she's drunk*, he thought.

Twinka didn't want to return home yet. The sea looked alluring. She didn't have a bathing suit, but she removed her sandals and decided to walk along the water. Having reached the water though, she stepped painfully on a stone, which made her change her mind. She decided to walk along the beach, barefoot, but having energetically paced a hundred metres she changed her mind again and returned to Louie's. There was still a bit of wine left in the bottle and she thought it would be best if she finished it while it was still cold. The ice in the bucket had probably melted, the wine was no longer cooling, but white wine should only ever be consumed when it was cold.

CHAPTER 91

"I know it was you. There's just one thing I don't understand: why did you want me to work out that it was you?"

Twinka had been waiting with great impatience for the chance to start this conversation. She was dying to unmask Marat; to say everything she thought about him to his face; and, hopefully, as a result of all this, to put him behind bars again. She wanted to get rid of him, once and for all. The few days that Draco had needed to install the kit had dragged on painfully for her. She had made her decision, and she couldn't wait to start actioning it.

"I'm sorry, dear – what are you talking about?" It looked like Marat really didn't understand.

"You're the one who murdered Dimitri, but why was it so important to you that I work it all out?"

"Oh, Dimitri... Why are we talking about him again? Dimitri is dead and buried, and I don't want to think about him ever again."

"His suicide note – the police showed it to me – was intended for me, wasn't it? Only I could have worked out that the author was you. And how should I interpret it – as a warning that you might kill me, too?"

"Twinka. You're an intelligent woman, but I promise that I'm not trying to murder you. Seriously. I don't have a plan or a desire to do it."

"How sweet," Twinka said sarcastically. "But you wanted me to know that you were capable of it, when you composed the suicide note. So, confess already!"

"Listen, stop flogging that dead horse. I'm not the one who pushed that moral reprobate into water. I was in the Pamirs, even my old friend Draco can't possibly object to that."

"Why can't you just confess, seeing as you wanted me to know?"

"A wise man once told me that the first chapter of *Murder for Dummies* would say: 'If you're planning on killing someone, don't tell anyone'." Marat spoke in his usual superior tone.

"'I drowned myself in the fragrance of honeysuckle' – Dimitri would have never written something like that. He's never read any books, let alone Faulkner." Twinka didn't relent.

"Twinka, just leave me alone – he's dead, he's left the stage, and no one's heard anything about him since.

"'Life's but a walking shadow, a poor playcr,

That struts and frets his hour upon the stage

And then is heard no more; it is a tale

Told by an idiot, full of sound and fury,

Signifying nothing'."

Marat finished quoting from *Macbeth,* clearly pleased with himself.

"But we are still on the stage, our hour hasn't come yet, that's the main thing. And don't look at me like that. I didn't push him in the water. I was in the mountains, summiting a peak, I have a million photos that captured every step of that difficult expedition. There's an expedition diary on Facebook – we brought a photographer and a videographer especially for that. Draco has no chance."

"But you killed him. You're a murderer. And I want a divorce." Twinka had lost her temper.

"Divorce? Oh, really? And what about Ronia? We had an agreement, Twinka, that for Ronia's sake..."

"My daughter could do without a father who's turned into a murderer. I should have done the right thing a long time ago, I don't know what came over me. Everyone considered it as obvious that I'd get a divorce, but my mind was clouded for some reason."

"But Twinka, that will cause a huge trauma for Ronia – do you really think that's the best direction to take?"

"Yeah, she'll have a trauma when she discovers the court materials and the reasons why Daddy was planning to kill Mummy – you should have thought about that when you planned *my* murder."

"Darling, the way you're talking now just makes me want to kill you again." Marat spoke to Twinka like she was a naughty child whose tantrums were rather endearing.

"You'll burn in the fires of hell forever, for everything you've done!"

"My dear, hell doesn't exist – just like the tooth fairy." Marat smirked, clearly showing how he in no way took any of what Twinka had said seriously.

"Go away! I don't want to see you! Maybe Draco won't be able to prove you're a murderer, but I'll prove in a family court that no one can live with a father like you, under no circumstances."

"Twinka, it's best not to go to war with me. That won't be good for anyone, especially not Ronia. We can settle this like civilised people. If you want to get a divorce – fine. But there's no need to turn it into a civil war."

"Good. Excellent," Twinka said. "I totally agree with you. You should just get gone from our lives, in a civilised manner. You can see Ronia once a month for two, maybe three hours, and only in my presence."

"Come on, Twinka, you're being ridiculous now." The arrogant smile had disappeared from Marat's face after all. "I would agree to Ronia spending a week with you and a week with me. That seems fair."

"Ronia is not going to live under the same roof as a murderer. It's impossible, the custody court would never allow it, don't even dream about it. Don't forget that you've been on trial for attempted murder, and you're being held as the main suspect in the plotting of another, successful, murder attempt. And your closest friends, in whose company you parade all over town, are convicted murderers with tattoos plastered across their forehead."

"Hang on, hang on... Not so quick, my dear! I'm not being held as a suspect over the plotting of any murder."

"That's only a matter of time. Draco will drag you into the light and expose you, just like he did last time. Do you really think you're so smart that you can fool everyone? But you couldn't help yourself, and you had to leave your artist's signature. That wasn't particularly clever, my dear."

"Twinka, where's your faith when you need it – where's Christ's love and forgiveness? 'Do not judge, or you too will be judged.' The only thing I'm asking is – let's remain respectful to each other and not raise a ruckus in front of Ronia – let's settle a divorce quietly, like two civilised people."

An anxious solemnity had settled on Marat's face, as he realised that the Twinka he was seeing today was one he'd never seen before. This Twinka was spiteful, determined, aggressive, and ready for a fight – she'd already considered the most painful-to-him angles of approach. Maybe someone was helping her? Either way, it was clear that Twinka wasn't afraid of him, and that she no longer held any respect for him. Marat was taken aback by these sudden changes: when had it happened? He wasn't prepared; he hadn't anticipated anything like this from Twinka. She was the one who'd wanted to save their family, and now she was the first to raise the subject of divorce.

467

"You need to stop spoiling Ronia and pitting her against me," fired Twinka, "and there's going to be no more talk of skipping school, or endless indulgence, or presents. Prove to me that you can be an adequate father to her and I might just think about it," Twinka recalled Anna's suggestion about setting conditions.

"What do you mean – spoiling her? You have to know where I'm coming from – I hadn't seen her for so long, I felt guilty in front of her, so I was trying to redeem my guilt somehow. Naturally, I understand it's pathetic to try and buy my way out, but, darling, I swear I've never wanted to pit her against you. You have to believe me." Marat had completely changed his tone. He was now begging Twinka. "I promise to be a better father to her. From now on, in everything that concerns Ronia, we'll make all the decisions together. I promise. We shouldn't go to war with each other, it would only make things worse."

Marat tried to embrace Twinka, but she evaded him. "Leave me alone! I want to be by myself."

Without giving Marat another glance, Twinka left, grabbing the car keys and sunglasses, which were scattered around *Pietà's* base, and rushing out the door. The outcome of their conversation had been unexpected – so much had been said all of a sudden; so much had happened – and she needed time to come to terms with it all.

Had Marat confessed to Dimitri's murder? Well, he sort of did, but sort of didn't. Twinka was too alarmed to be able to go over any specific details. Had she gained the upper hand? Had she won the war, even before the first battle had commenced? She seemed to have done, and that was completely unexpected. She wanted to call Anna and tell her the news, but she held herself back. Anna probably had more important things to do, and other clients to see.

Without even thinking where she was going, Twinka had arrived at Louie's. A glass of wine would definitely help her now. The Burgundy she chose was expensive and wasn't sold by the glass, so she had to buy the whole bottle.

Oh, if only I had had enough sense to prepare her for this conversation, to train her up for it, Draco thought on the other side of city, removing his headphones. *She wasn't too far off. If only she hadn't digressed from the ultimate goal, if only she'd remained focused on the aim... I should have prepared her better for it.* Draco was rueful.

CHAPTER 92

"We listened to it several times, very carefully," Draco said.

They had met up a few days later, at the same old place – Louie's.

"First, I want to say a huge thank you for trying to help the investigation – you did the right thing. It's very important, and I'm very thankful to you."

"Sometimes you need a bit of time to work out what's right," Twinka said. She looked exhausted, thought Draco – perhaps she hadn't slept too well, or maybe she was hungover.

"However, this recording doesn't quite give us the grounds to accuse him – but it does let us consider him a suspect. It's since been confirmed that Dimitri's death was suspicious, and until it's proved to be suicide it will remain so. We can't prove it was a suicide, we don't even have a place in mind where he could have jumped from, but nor have we identified a crime scene where he could have been murdered. For now, we have nothing... But that's okay, we'll continue working on it."

"But he did confess to me indirectly, didn't he? At least I felt like he did."

"Well, there were several instances that could be interpreted in multiple ways. You're saying that he's the author of the note, to which he replies: you're so clever. You could interpret that as: you've worked it all out. And then there was an instance where he said that confessing would be making the same mistake as telling Dimitri about his murder plot. But these are all just indirect pointers. We'd be laughed out of court if we tried to prosecute him using this alone. We need something else to be able to do that. Besides, he confirmed twice during the recording, and very clearly, that he didn't push Dimitri into the water and that he was in the Pamir mountains at the time of the crime."

"Well, maybe he wasn't the one to push him in," Twinka concluded, resigned.

"Exactly, he probably didn't do it himself," Draco agreed.

"So, what happens now?" Twinka asked.

"I think we should try again. Maybe we can prep better for it. We may have been successful that time too, if the conversation hadn't devolved into a discussion over divorce." Draco didn't want to put any blame on Twinka, which is why he spoke in a soothing tone. "And now we know that he probably won't confess directly. However, having a longer list of indirect elements of confession would really help us. We could then figure out how to set a trap for him."

"But that won't be enough, will it?" Twinka was staring into Draco's eyes so directly and openly, already aware of the answer to her question, that Draco was forced to avert his gaze.

"The investigation continues." He gave a cagey shrug. "We're working in several different directions, and we've got a few clues to go by. Murder cases have no prescriptive period – even if it's in ten years' time, we'll solve the crime. I tend to solve every crime: that's my job. The perpetrators might get caught for something else; or we'll find out that someone knows something, and they'll start blabbing; or we'll come across another clue, and be able to solve it then."

"Right," Twinka said. "And what should I do in the meantime?"

Her direct and intense gaze made the question feel very intimate – it was the sort of question you could only ask a close friend.

"I won't be able to answer that," Draco said, somewhat embarrassed, but Twinka only heard indifference in his voice.

CHAPTER 93

Twinka often went to church these days, spending a lot of time there. She prayed. She helped the lovely old woman Gita with various cleaning jobs. She had asked her dad, as the leader of the congregation, if he knew how else she could be of help. Naturally, there were always things that could be done around the church.

But it was the gift book project that brought Twinka the most joy. Dad had mentioned that they used to have a book gifting desk on Sundays after the service, but the man who'd been in charge of it couldn't carry on any longer due to old age. Twinka latched onto the idea with great enthusiasm. She selected and ordered books herself, and paid for them all too, and then stood behind the desk on Sundays following the service: where she gave recommendations to the members of the congregation, made suggestions, lent and gifted the books, or else gave them away in exchange for a donation to the church.

Twinka was especially keen to recommend Augustine, Dietrich Bonhoeffer, Thomas Aquinas, and the little book she'd started carrying around with her everywhere – Ignatius of Loyola's *Spiritual Exercises*. Alongside it was Donald S. Whitney's *Spiritual Disciplines for the Christian Life*, Timothy Keller's *Prayer*, Bob Kauflin's *Worship Matters*, John Piper's *Desiring God*, and Dostoyevsky's *The Brothers Karamazov*, among many other titles. Twinka's Sunday book desk was very popular. Anna was happy that Twinka had followed her suggestion and found something to immerse herself in; and, with just as much enthusiasm, she encouraged Twinka to carry on.

Twinka truly hoped that all this business with the church would provide her life with a new foundation, on which she could stand firmly and build upon. She was hoping to find the motivation to become a better person, to sort out her problem with alcohol, and work out what to do about her marriage. She was full of hope that this was the right path for her, even though, for now, all she'd succeeded in was making herself busy. But she was trying, from the bottom of her heart.

"Oh, Lord Jesus, hear my prayer! Don't let me be parted from you, and protect me from my enemy. Call me at my hour of death and command me to come to you, so that I could praise you forever and ever, next to all the saints," Twinka prayed, after everyone had finally left following the Sunday service. The book desk was cleared away and she was the last one in the church.

"Lord Jesus, forgive me, a sinner, forgive me for my pride, my lust, my weakness, for being superficial, for my arrogance, forgive me my wrongs... Forgive me, good Lord Jesus, that I lost sight of you, forgive me that I believed you had any responsibilities towards me, forgive me that I acted as though your duty was to help me and I waited until you'd fulfil every small, ego-centred request I made, as soon as I'd uttered them to you; forgive me for my silly, selfish prayers; forgive me that I thought that you didn't know what I needed and what was best for me; forgive me, God, that I lost sight of you. Forgive me that I got entwined so deep inside the labyrinths of sin and desire, that I was sinning even though I remained in denial about it. Forgive me for not appreciating that I had you in my life; forgive me for not cherishing that I could feel your presence, that I could see you; forgive me that I took your presence for granted. Forgive me that I let a sinner take your place in my life while I lost sight of you. Forgive me for my wrongdoings, Lord God; forgive me that I believed you'd sent him in my life, that I thought our love was part of you, God. I truly believed that by serving love I was serving you, God, but by serving this love I actually lost you and went astray. My love

473

was selfish, it all revolved around *me. I* love you, it said; *I* can't live without you, *I* can't imagine *my* life without you. You make *me* happy. You are *my* everything. *Me, me, me...* There's nothing more selfish than that type of love. Forgive me for not seeing it, God.

"Does love even come from you, God, or from the evil one?" Twinka asked, crouched on her knees, her head bowed down. She was pressing her left fist firmly to her heart. "Or maybe love does come from you, but we just don't know how to love? We don't know how to do it without being selfish?"

Twinka put all her hope in God, longing that God would answer her and give her clarity and strength. She was sure of it: she just needed to devote herself to God once more, repent for her sins and ask for forgiveness. She had to truly repent and reignite the lost bond between them. It had been as pure and self-evident as a child's laughter, but now it seemed distant, forgotten and dim, even in her memories.

CHAPTER 94

The summer had gone.

Twinka's demand to not spoil Ronia didn't seem to cause Marat much trouble. He demonstratively let Twinka decide on anything concerning their daughter. "Ask your mum," and "as your mother says", or "only if your mum agrees to it" – even "figure it out together" – those were the only replies he would give. And he was almost never at home. Twinka had no idea where he was or what he was up to, but she wasn't particularly interested. Often she wasn't home herself. The only thing that was obvious was Marat's new passion for motorcycles. Theodor had taught him how to ride and they went on drives together, the garage now having two new motorbikes, complete with helmets and the rest of the kit.

For the entire summer Marat would show up to his meetings – or, rather, his lunches – on a motorcycle. And only now, as autumn approached, he would be seen on rainy days in his G-Wagon or Rolls-Royce. It seemed like he and Theodor had become closer than ever, and Twinka figured that every man must have a deep desire for a son, which Marat was now able to realise through him. It probably helped that Theodor literally adored Marat. Twinka and Marat had not revisited their conversation over getting a divorce, though Twinka knew that it wasn't finished. She had not finished having it with herself.

"I know what your thing is," Twinka said one morning, over breakfast. Her work in the church and her abstinence had led her to once again get up at the same time as Ronia and see her off to school. Marat would usually rise around a similar time as well.

"Oh yeah?" Marat looked interested. He had boiled two eggs for breakfast, which were accompanied by two sliced-open avocados.

"Have you ever read Ignatius of Loyola's *Spiritual Exercises*?

"Hmm, I think I read it a while ago." Marat wasn't sure whether it was the avocado that had ruined his mood, being too firm to be eaten with a spoon.

"Well, there's this one exercise where you need to imagine the chief of all the enemy seated in that great field of Babylon, in a great chair of fire and smoke, in shape most horrible and terrifying. And imagine that he's talking to his innumerable demons and subordinates, whom he's sent all over the world to corrupt people, to catch them in his nets and chains. And do you know what sort of instructions he gives to them?"

"No. What does he say to them?" Marat made no attempt of hiding the self-satisfied smirk that had appeared on his face. He had cut the pieces of avocado with a knife and placed them on a plate next to the two boiled eggs, which he'd sliced in half.

"They have to first tempt people with a longing for riches, then a vain honour, and then with vast pride. And from these three steps he moves on to all their other vices. That's the plan of the chief of all the enemy."

"And what's that got to do with me?" Marat asked, still with the same self-satisfied snigger.

"Well, your thing is these three steps. Your thing is greed and riches, vain honour, and vast pride. You are who you are. You are Satan's victim *and* his billboard."

"Oh, the pathos!" Marat threw the skin of the avocados and their accompanying pits into the rubbish bin. Sprinkled salt over his eggs. Marat's tone was no longer arrogant – he now spoke with despising disgust.

"When will you realise – Christianity is just a power game. Tell the poor not to strive for riches, convince them that there is something bad in it, that you shouldn't envy those who are wealthy, because they will burn in the fires of hell anyway, so you shouldn't even touch them. Christianity protects the rich and the powerful, those who have all the honours, and tells the paupers that they should never rise up against them, because they're doomed to burn in hell's fires forever. On the other hand, they should be happy living their slave lives, enjoy their poverty. It's a genius work of social engineering, which has ensured that the aristocracy and the church have been able to bask in gold and glory for centuries on end. I've always said it: Emperor Constantine was a genius as a politician because he was the first to realise the potential of Christianity. Not to mention how much the Catholic church has benefited from all this nonsense – it's allowed it to become the richest, most powerful and most long-lasting institution in the entire world. It's the perfect religion for ruling over the dark masses," Marat spoke while he ate.

"But you'll agree with me that greed, vain honours and pride is your actual thing?"

"What honours are you talking about? I'm not interested in any honours, fame or the opinions of others. That's why I need money – so I don't need to worry about what the Shudras are thinking about me. Let them think whatever they like, why should I stress myself over it? Vain honours are for those who have nothing else – what use would they be to me?"

"You see, that's pride talking. Every word you've said is pure pride."

"And have you noticed that your Christianity doesn't even support education or striving for knowledge? They preach 'poverty of the spirit' because the only wisdom is apparently to pray and praise Jesus Christ, and the only book that should ever be read by anyone is *The Bible*. I'm telling you, it's the perfect tool for suppressing the masses: 'Enjoy your suffering, it's actually good for you, even though you may have thought it was bad at first. And don't read any books, remain stupid, it will be safer for all of us, if you continue to believe in our nonsense'. If the Reformation hadn't loosened the reins of the church, we'd still be living like they were in the early Middle Ages.

Marat had finished his eggs and avocado.

"Oh, you're just one of those demons who are being sent around the world by the chief of all the enemy, in order to sow disbelief and sin, to make people fall in love with pride, greed, all kinds of sins and vices, to murder and spite others." Twinka said all of this jokingly and playfully, but Marat's examining gaze bore into her.

"Listen, you need to put the brakes on all the church stuff, otherwise I'm starting to get concerned about your mental health. You realise that it's a completely alternative reality where there are devils and demons, and the chief of all the enemy, and probably angels, the Holy Ghost and whatnot. It's a realm of fairy tales."

"Quite the opposite – the church is the only thing that's helping me," Twinka said spitefully.

"Okay, fine. It's time for me to go and spread my greed and pride." Marat was being ironic now. He washed up his plate and mug in the sink.

Twinka opened the window to let some fresh air into the room. *Where did the summer go? Why is time moving faster with every passing year? So frighteningly fast. Is there anything I can do to make it slow down? I'm halfway through life, and everything is such a mess. What am I saying – it's not even halfway, because all the good things are behind me. I feel like I only just turned thirty; if it carries on like this, I'll blink and I'll be fifty, then sixty. And then what?*

CHAPTER 95

Ronia was the first to discover Marat's still body, lying in a pool of blood.

"Dad is dead," she said, seeing Twinka approach.

Twinka got out of the car, not quite comprehending what Ronia had said. The sharp December wind was blowing, but they hadn't had any snow so far.

Ronia was standing on the steps outside their house, next to the main door. She was shaking.

"Dad is what?" Twinka said, only now properly realising what was happening from Ronia's demeanour. "What's happened to Dad?" she asked, rushing towards her daughter.

"There." Ronia pointed at the door.

Twinka charged inside. Ronia didn't follow her in – she remained stood in the doorway.

Marat was still alive. Twinka couldn't explain how she knew, but she could feel that he was.

It's not one of our knives, she figured, throwing a quick glance at the blade that had been tossed next to the body. She frantically looked for her phone before calling an ambulance.

Twinka could see the wound on his right side. She grabbed the first piece of clothing she could find – Marat's sports jacket was hanging on a clothing rail nearby – and started applying pressure on the wound. She realised there were two wounds – one lower down, in the abdominal area, and one higher up. She could feel Marat breathing. His pulse felt very weak, but she could sense that his heart was still beating, plus his blood was warm.

Marat suddenly opened his eyes and their eyes met.

"Solon..." Marat said, barely audibly. There was no sign of fear in his eyes – all she could see was a sneer.

Tears burst forth from Twinka's eyes.

"Please, don't talk right now," she begged.

The ambulance arrived quickly; followed by the police, who got there a few minutes later. By that time Twinka was completely covered in blood. The paramedics, rushing to help Marat, pushed Twinka aside – at least that's how she felt. She remained sat on the floor, with her back against the cabinet unit, which was supporting Michelangelo's *Pietà*. Twinka's pose looked a bit like the Virgin Mary's in the sculpture, except Twinka was drenched in blood and her face most definitely didn't look calm or spirited.

Twinka beheld the medics working on Marat. She realised that a police officer had photographed her several times. The stretcher appeared, then more paramedics and policemen came – Twinka watching the scene unfold, as though she were a distant observer.

Marat was taken away. Some policewoman tried to ask Twinka a few questions, and she answered some of them. And then, that familiar, rat-like shit with the tiny voice and tight lips appeared. *Oh, what would we do without you!* Twinka thought. Draco's arrival seemed to bring her back to reality. *What a repulsive little man,* she thought. Her watch was showing 13.13.

"Your house has become the epicentre of our city's criminal life. I have no other work besides investigating all your murders," Draco scolded, as opposed to offering a greeting.

Twinka responded with a wry smile – she wasn't sure what she was feeling. It was so unexpected. The only thing she knew for sure was that she desperately wanted a drink. She had to have one. Immediately.

She grabbed a bottle of cognac. It was a Delamain Vesper XO – one of Twinka's favourites. Her hands were covered in blood, so there was blood on the bottle too. While Draco chatted to the other police officers, Twinka took a good big gulp, then poured some more out for herself. The hefty crystal glass with its luxurious, engraved patterns was also smeared in blood.

The forensic experts appeared.

"Examine her first," Twinka heard Draco ordering them.

One of the experts was a young girl. She came up to Twinka and took samples from the inside of her nails with a delicate instrument. She proceeded to examine and take photos of her arms and neck. "We'll also need to take your clothes, if you don't mind."

Twinka didn't mind. She would never wear them again anyway, not even if she was able to remove all the bloodstains.

The girl walked Twinka to her dressing room, tossed Twinka's clothes inside a cellophane bag and took photos of Twinka in her underwear, capturing her front and her back. Twinka thought that she could probably object to all these demands or give Keiko a call, but she didn't have the energy for that, and she didn't really care either.

"We'll need your statement, too. I think it's best if we go to the police station; it's a bit crowded here," Draco said after she'd changed her clothes. His voice held none of the ingratiation from last time.

"Okay, fine," she said, disinterested. "Let me just call my dad, so he can take Ronia for a few days."

"That's a good idea," Draco agreed. "You can call him on the way." He urged her towards the car.

Suddenly Twinka felt completely exhausted. She had no more energy left and was overcome by an all-encompassing ennui. It was all too much. Far too much. What was even going on here? Twinka's mind felt completely void – there were no thoughts or feelings swirling around. She wanted to go back to the kitchen and take another glug of the cognac, but Draco wouldn't let her.

"Later, later," he said, stealing the glass from her.

Twinka obeyed, although she really didn't have much to tell him. It was her mum's birthday today. She had just turned sixty-seven and it was a tradition for Twinka to see her on the morning of her birthday. She had given her mother the complete works of Sigrid Undset as a present. It was an exquisite edition from the thirties. Her mother adored this author – she'd read a lot of her writing, but she didn't own a copy of her complete works. Twinka had gone over to her mum's early in the morning – she'd got up, had a coffee, seen Ronia off to school and then headed over there. She'd stayed there for a few hours, they had some coffee and cake, and then Twinka went home again. Ronia had a short day at school and was finished by twelve, so Twinka had wanted to get home around the same time as her daughter. That was all. No, she didn't notice anything suspicious.

"Did you lock the door when you left?" Draco asked.

"It's on a latch, but you can't open it from the outside."

"And that's how you left it this morning? The door shut and you couldn't open it from the outside?"

"Yeah, that's right."

"How did the murderer manage to get inside the house then?"

"Why are you asking me? I don't have a clue."

"Okay, good," Draco said as he finished writing everything down. "I won't detain you today, but I'll be honest – you're our main suspect right now. Not only did you have a good motive – you had a whole entourage of reasons to kill your husband. You wanted to get rid of him. You were hoping that he'd get arrested for Dimitri's murder. You even tried to encourage the process, but nothing happened. And, as we all know by now, your family considers divorce to be a huge mess. So, all eyes are on you. And you'll inherit an absolute fortune."

"I was at Mum's," Twinka objected. A scarcely audible laugh escaped her lips as she remembered Marat saying: "I've got a million photographs from this complex expedition" and realised that her tone of voice sounded just like his.

"We'll make sure to check that, don't you worry. Obviously, an alibi from relatives isn't exactly enough to mitigate our suspicions, but we'll see. This will be a massive investigation. Marat was a pretty famous and influential man in several circles, so I've been granted all the necessary resources for this investigation – unlike with Dimitri's death – so I'm sure we'll get to the bottom of this very soon."

"A bird crashed into my windshield today," Twinka said, ignoring Draco.

"Excuse me?" Draco didn't understand.

"Yesterday a bird crashed into my windshield. I think it was a jackdaw or maybe a crow, I'm not sure. I got so scared. I almost drove off the road. I had to stop. I was literally shaking, it was awful."

"It's just a coincidence," Draco said. "Birds dying has nothing to do with people dying."

"It's weird though, right?" Twinka was talking to Draco, but she seemed very distant, lost in her thoughts. "Mum used to say that on the day my gran died, a bird smashed into her windshield, too. It almost broke the glass."

"It's just a coincidence," Draco repeated. He seemed bored with the conversation, writing something down energetically. "There is absolutely no connection between a person's death and the behaviour of a bird. It is simply our mind looking back and searching for some sort of sign that could have signalled something or warned us. We want to believe that these sorts of signs exist, so that we can look out for them next time, but it's still just a coincidence," Draco rattled out, not once lifting his eyes from the papers.

"Or maybe, the soul isn't something that's trapped inside the body alone – maybe it's much more expansive," said Twinka. "What if there's a little bird out there somewhere who's only alive because he's part of my soul? And if I die, then it means he must die, too. Maybe that's why we have all these intuitions and hunches, like we know what's going on somewhere else, because our soul can actually see it through the bird's eyes. Perhaps that's why we sometimes have a feeling that we've been in some place before, that we know everything about it, even though it's the first time we're there."

Draco lifted his eyes at last and sent her an exhausted and condemning look. "I mean, you're an educated person – and I gather you're Christian too, since you go to church. So how can you possibly believe all this nonsense?"

"And you're an investigator, so how can you possibly ignore all these things, these coincidences?"

"Well, as an investigator I'm telling you: facts don't corroborate all these theories. Witnesses can give accurate testimonies over facts. For instance, they can testify true facts that a bird smashed into their windshield, but then they go on to draw the wrong conclusions from these facts."

Draco returned to writing.

"I guess you're right." Twinka let out a heavy sigh. "Anyway, those mics that you installed to record my conversation with Marat – are they still working?"

Draco jolted into the back of his chair, as though he'd been given an electric shock. "You really are an incredibly intelligent woman." He was shaking his head, unable to tell what had shocked him more – the fact that he'd completely forgotten about the microphones or the fact that Twinka, even in this condition, was able to forge this key connection. "Yeah, I think they're still on."

"That will probably help the investigation then," Twinka concluded, with indifference in her voice. "I really am very tired, so can I go now?"

The only thing that Twinka wanted was to be left alone, so she could fall asleep and not think about anything.

"Yes, you're free to go for now. But don't leave the city, okay?"

Twinka's phone was ringing. An unfamiliar but compassionate voice said that Marat was conscious and that it would be better if she came by. Twinka wished she'd brought the bottle of cognac with her. This was all so hard.

"I'll take you, it'll be faster that way," Draco said.

They got into the car and Twinka saw the blue police lights reflecting in shop windows and bouncing off the walls of the buildings they passed. She watched other cars let them pass, and everything felt so surreal: as though she were watching a movie she should be participating in, but was incapable of doing so. She didn't know what her part was; or who her protagonist was, having all these emotions. What was she even feeling? Was she relieved that Marat was alive? And what did they mean by "it would be better if you came"? Was he dying? Was she worried? Upset? Scared? Could she even feel anything anymore? And what should she be feeling?

Cognac might have helped her. Pity she didn't have any.

CHAPTER 96

Draco knew exactly where to go. Twinka obediently followed him, somewhat grateful that he'd come along with her. She couldn't even imagine how she'd find a place to park while in this condition, or which entrance to use, or what corridors or lifts to take. She was freezing. In all the shock and confusion, she'd only put on a very thin second layer.

Marat was in intensive care. The ward looked different – there was a lot more equipment compared to the last time – but Twinka nevertheless felt like she'd gone back in time. As they approached Marat's room, Draco rushed ahead and went in first.

"Who did this to you?" he asked Marat, without any kind of greeting or introduction.

"Twinka. I only want to speak with Twinka." Marat's voice sounded very weak.

"Just tell me who did this. What did they look like?" Draco stood between Marat's bed and Twinka, blocking her way.

"Please, just go. Just leave, please." Marat was speaking with his good eye half-shut.

"Leave us, please!" Twinka was trying to squeeze between Draco and the bed.

"All I need is a few words. Just one sentence. Who attacked you and what did they look like?"

"Go! Just leave us, you can do this afterwards!" Twinka succeeded in pushing Draco away from the bed. "Go! We can talk later."

Draco finally gave in and left the room, angry and annoyed.

"Oh, my poor pirate." Twinka smiled softly. "What happened to you?"

Marat was looking at his wife with loving eyes. He looked very peaceful.

"Do you remember the story about Solon?" Marat's voice seemed to have perked up a little.

"Solon?"

"Remember, Croesus was living in luxury and comfort, unlike anything anyone had seen before. The most beautiful women, the most exquisite possessions, the most trustworthy servants: all revolved around him. He had unlimited power and he could carry out any whim that came to his mind."

"Darling, what are you talking about?" Twinka gripped Marat's hand.

Draco came back into the room. He was carrying a chair this time.

"Here, have a seat," Draco said to Twinka, and once more left the room, though he left the door half-open. He pressed himself against the wall and stood there, eavesdropping. Twinka didn't seem to have noticed, but even if she had, she didn't have enough energy to pick a fight with him – all her attention was focused on Marat.

"Solon had come to visit him," Marat continued. Although he was speaking quietly, he sounded just like himself. "Croesus was showing off his new palace – no other mansion in the whole world was as marvellous as this. And then he asked Solon, without giving it much thought: 'Wouldn't you say I'm the happiest man alive?'"

The sight of Marat's body terrified Twinka. He looked so pale, so still and lifeless. The only thing that seemed truly alive was his one remaining eye and his weak voice.

"Croesus wasn't even expecting an answer. It was obvious. But Solon replied: 'I don't know, I guess we'll see on our dying day'. Croesus didn't understand what he meant by that, they had a big fight, and Solon left. Do you remember that story? You must do."

"No, Marat, I don't remember any of it. And why are you telling me all this now?"

"And so," Marat continued – his lips were barely moving, "soon after their conversation, Croesus' son died in a hunt – Croesus might have even killed him by accident. Then later on, his kingdom was seized by the Persians, they arrested him and decided to burn him alive. They tied Croesus to a stake and started lighting the firewood. And that's when Croesus cried out: 'Solon, Solon, you were right!'"

"Oh, I remember now," Twinka said. "But he didn't get burned in the end."

"He didn't in the end." Marat fell silent.

"And why are we talking about this?"

"Because my dying day has arrived."

"Nonsense, Marat, don't say that! You'll pull through, just like you always do!" Twinka's voice was desperate, and tears poured from her eyes.

"Only when you're dying can you truly say if your life was successful – that's when you can tell if it was a good and happy life. Do you understand? Only on your deathbed. While we're alive, we can never know for sure because circumstances and events are constantly changing. Nothing ever stays the same, even if some things appear to be stable. Nothing is guaranteed or set in stone. Nothing is here to stay. And nothing is finished until it really is finished."

"Marat, nothing's finished. Even the day before your death it's not too late to start a new life, remember? You're scaring me."

Marat didn't paid no attention to what Twinka was saying. "The question now is –" he said, – "what can I say about my life on my dying day?"

Twinka realised there was no point in arguing. She simply held Marat's hand with both of hers.

"I have to admit, I kind of fucked everything up towards the end," Marat concluded, sounding matter-of-fact, as though he were commenting on an unlucky game of chess or set of tennis. "I screwed up the final scene, and now I'm Croesus. That's how things turned out."

"Marat, stop talking about dying. No one is dying, you're in good hands, no one in this hospital is going to let you die. Don't you dare even think about it."

"Of course, that wasn't supposed to be the final scene. I was planning on living until I was a hundred years old. But I'm only fifty-two."

"Marat, what even happened to you? Who attacked you?"

"I'm glad that I've taken care of Ronia, at least. She'll never have to worry about money."

"Answer me, Marat – what happened? Who did this to you?" Twinka tried to divert his attention.

"Definitely say hi to your dad, tell him that I'm sorry we didn't get to know each other better. I think he's a good person. A decent man. Of course, all he ever saw in me was a repulsive example of how far libertarianism can lead you, but I still respect him. He could have been a Brahman. He's a proper man. I should have made more of an effort with him."

"Marat, what are you talking about now? Tell me what happened."

"Although it's not all that simple. With the story of Croesus." It was clear that Marat was starting to get tired. He had to take a break and rest in between his sentences. Nonetheless, he continued, as though he was determined to say something.

"If Croesus had turned down all the perversion that comes with luxury, would it have really saved him from losing his son, and everything that happened after that? Bad luck can visit anyone, at any time. And does Croesus' final tragic scene cancel out the fact that he lived happily for many years before that? No way. And it's the same with me. If I look back on it now, was there anything wrong with my life? I've been in love and I've been loved; we've had a wonderful marriage. I've been able to do whatever I wanted almost without exception. I've been able to get and achieve anything I wanted. I've had my fair share of love, success, wealth and admiration. Truly. So I, of all people, shouldn't be moaning."

"Love, you're scaring me."

"But there is a point to life – make sure you tell Ronia! Don't let her believe anyone who says that life is pointless. They say it because they don't know, and they don't know death. It's all just bosh. In reality, they all want to live. They instinctively feel that it's better to be alive than dead. Everyone is fighting death, even if they don't know it."

"Marat, I think you should rest. Get some sleep, eh? We'll chat tomorrow."

"Death is endless. Death means that all hope is gone. And without hope, we have nothing."

"You'll tell her yourself when you're ready." Twinka was speaking as quietly as Marat. Maybe she was just tired. Perhaps she finally felt what Marat was feeling. Or maybe she just didn't want to argue anymore. She had no idea what she felt.

"Tell her that you shouldn't be afraid of death and you shouldn't regret anything, if you've done everything you could. As long as you haven't wasted your time, aimlessly cruising through life. If you've done everything you possibly could, if you've filled your cup to the brim, if you've pushed your boundaries to their utmost limit, then that's enough."

"Everything will be okay. Just hang in there, my pirate."

"I'm not afraid but I do have my regrets. I screwed up the end, I wasn't as clever as I should have been. If only there was more time..."

"Marat!"

"Tell Ronia to use her time wisely. The biggest worry, the biggest fear of anyone who's dying is whether they wasted their time. Did they waste the majority of their time? How much of the time I've been given have I wasted? Time. That's what I regret."

"Marat, don't."

"Forgive me..."

One of the machines let out a quiet but sharp beep. A nurse and two doctors appeared in the room, kindly asking Twinka to step aside. They performed some sort of procedure, while a moment later another doctor asked Twinka to leave the room.

Suddenly Twinka was consumed by weakness and indifference. She walked into the corridor and stopped by the closest window.

A huge, striking seagull landed on the outside windowsill. The cold wind ruffled the bird's feathers, threatening to blow it off of its perch.

The seagull, with its head turned sideways, was staring at Twinka, without blinking, through its black and curious but cold and vacuous eye.

CHAPTER 97

"He's in a coma."

"And what are the doctors saying? What's his prognosis?" Anna asked compassionately, trying to sense Twinka's mood and adapt to it.

"Nothing for sure. They're saying that he might wake up or he might die. Or I might even have to decide whether to switch off his life support. His condition might stabilise and, in theory, there's a hope that he might come round. But they won't be able to keep him in intensive care forever, and then I'll have to figure out how best to equip our home. I'll need to hire the personnel myself or move him to some institution where he would be looked after while he was in a coma."

"That's horrible." Anna gave an understanding nod.

"I don't even know which of these options is worse. I mean, of course, it would be best if he woke up."

Anna didn't say anything, just continued to nod.

"Or that he died. But to picture him nearby, lying in some care home like a vegetable, because there's apparently hope that he might wake up one day, as if by miracle. Or that they'll come up with a new treatment over the years – stem cell therapy, or something that could help... It's incredibly tough."

"And they can't say anything for sure at the moment?"

"One of the doctors – if I read him correctly, of course – hinted that if I didn't want to bring him home and look after him in such a condition for years, then they could arrange for him to die. Apparently, they do it quite a lot in these sorts of cases."

"What?! But that's not allowed..." Anna was astonished.

"Apparently all they need to do is tweak the ingredients, remove some sort of feeding substance and something else, and a person can die without anyone thinking it was suspicious or wrong."

"And he was asking you to give him permission to do it?!"

"I didn't understand him fully. He said that in these sorts of cases people often make the decision to stop fighting and just let 'nature take its course'. Most people can't even afford to keep a relative in a coma for years. It costs a lot of money."

"And what did you say?"

"Nothing. I got confused. I think I said that Marat definitely wasn't the type of person who would be happy if nature was taking its course – he always had to have everything go according to his will. Something like that."

"But if you had the option, would you make the decision to 'let nature take its course'?"

"I'm scared to even consider it. I don't want to think about it. If I start thinking about it, my only reaction is that I need to get pissed."

"Does that help you switch off from thinking?"

"Yeah, it does."

"But maybe the right thing right now would be to think? To try, at least?"

Twinka didn't say anything. She was fiddling with the decorative braid that was attached to the zip of her leather jacket.

"You're drinking because life is asking you too many tough questions, all of which are impossible to ignore. But at the same time it's too hard to think, it's too uncomfortable. You have to have a drink in order to stop thinking, to forget all those questions. But that doesn't solve anything. In reality it just makes things worse. Maybe, if you weren't afraid to think, to call things out for what they are, to talk through it, you might find it easier to abstain from alcohol."

You've already told me all this – you've just forgotten. Or maybe you've confused me with another client, Twinka thought to herself, though said nothing. "Are you saying that all alcoholics are basically just people who are afraid to think?" Twinka tried to keep up the conversation, although alcoholism didn't feel like her biggest problem right now.

"Life is tough, often unbearably so, and alcohol allows us to set life aside for a moment, to press pause on it and, yes, to stop thinking."

"I think it would be the same as committing murder." Twinka had decided to go back and address the main question.

"Okay. But maybe it's like compassionate homicide? A murder that ends someone's suffering?"

"Whose suffering? His or mine? He's in a coma: he doesn't suffer anything, as far as I know."

"If you knew that he was suffering, would you do it then?"

"I don't know if I still love him like I used to. If I knew that the suffering was ceaseless, and nothing could be done about it, then yeah; I could probably do it if I really loved him."

"But wouldn't you say that if you really loved him, you'd take him home to care for him in a vegetative condition, hoping that one day he'd wake up? But since you don't love him as much, you're saying that you'd rather he died in the hospital."

"No, I don't want to think about it." Twinka gave up after all. "Am I even supposed to love him? He wanted to kill me and he almost succeeded. I shouldn't even be worrying about him."

"Yes, of course, no one could judge you for not loving him. You could have left him while he was in prison, or even before that."

"You know, I've already planned his funeral in my head. I had a dream where I saw it in full detail, what it would look like. That statue Dimitri gave us, Michelangelo's *Pietà* – that would be his gravestone. I'll make them screw it into some sort of pedestal and add an engraving: *My poor pirate.* I saw that in my dream, but then I woke up, remembered everything and realised that it wasn't a good plan. I hate that statue, I need to get it out of the house."

"You probably feel guilty for having all these thoughts, considering that he is still alive?"

"I don't know if I do. Don't you think that in those moments, when really big life events happen, with real emotional trials, you stop feeling anything that's nuanced? It just disappears. Intense pain, massive success, a big misfortune, intense experiences – all of that just makes you numb. It's like an incredibly loud noise that stops you hearing more subtle sounds. That's how I feel. I feel like I've gone numb. I'm like an alky who no longer gets tipsy from drinking beer. Do I feel guilty for having these thoughts? No. I just don't feel anything anymore."

"Would you like to feel again though?"

"I don't know. Yeah. I guess so. I would love to have my old life back – where I was a wealthy mother and housewife with a degree in Portuguese language and literature, living in peace."

"And you'll definitely have all that again. You still have a long life ahead of you, you'll have all that for sure." Anna smiled, and Twinka felt like she believed in what Anna was saying.

"I hope so," Twinka agreed.

Anna had really succeeded in calming her down a bit today and cheering her up.

CHAPTER 98

"Have you heard any more news on what happened that night? Anna asked Twinka a week later. "What are the police saying?" Anna's face wore a worried expression.

"Well, I'm the main suspect." Twinka, with a look of resignation on hers, laughed. "They know that Marat's death was advantageous to me, and I will inherit a large sum of money. Huge. And all of that makes me the prime suspect, of course."

"We have never talked about the money before. How important is it that you'll inherit all of it now?"

"Honestly? It would be a huge burden. It's the only thing that could make things even worse."

"How do you mean?"

"Well, I wasn't short of money before all this, so I don't need any more. Until now it was like I didn't even have to think about it. I just had it. But now I'm going to have to take care of all that money. It's an enormous sum – it needs managing and protecting; someone will always try to steal it, everyone will want to get their hands on it, snatch a little piece for themselves; it's invested somewhere or needs investing; there are properties that need managing, businesses, shares, stocks and funds, buildings, land, employees – and I haven't got the first idea about any of it. My area is Portuguese literature! I mean, I'll get swindled and used by everyone who's not too timid to try their luck. I already had a call the other day from some director from Marat's bank. He said we should meet. I mean, he was very kind, but I'm sure they've already come up with a thousand different ways to do me over, and probably in a way that will make me feel like they've actually done me a favour. Marat's not even dead yet, but they've already started to plot. I saw them at the hospital."

"Who?" Anna didn't understand.

"All those directors and partners. They were gathering information and talking to doctors. It was obvious from their faces that all they could think about was how to take advantage of this situation. So, I'm sure the inheritance will only give me a massive headache."

"You don't think you'll be up to the task?"

"No. I mean, I'm not thinking about anything. For now, at least. I don't even know what I should be doing or thinking about. Actually, I do. I need to think about Ronia. Yes, I need to think about her, that's the main thing right now."

"And how is she taking all this?"

"I don't really know... I've been living in a kind of a fog these last few days. It feels like someone has stuffed my head with cotton wool. I can't connect to anything properly or focus on anything. I haven't even discussed it all with Ronia yet. I just can't face it. And I wouldn't know what to tell her anyway. I'm just dazed and disoriented. Fortunately, she's been staying with my parents: I hope they managed to talk it all over while she was there."

"You've been through some massive changes in a very short space of time. Marat's attack on you, then his imprisonment, the trial, then Dimitri's death, and now Marat in a coma. It's only natural that you feel as though your head is stuffed with cotton wool. It's the body's defence mechanism. There's been too many emotions, too much has happened, too many important things, so your body is just making sure that you don't burn out. It's important to process everything that's happened, and all the emotions, properly. You need to slowly start sorting through and putting them in the right places, and everything will be okay. It will take some time, but everything's going to be okay."

"Unless Draco puts me behind bars," Twinka added.

"Are you afraid that might happen?"

"Yeah, I'm a little scared of him. I mean, he threatened to take Ronia away from me that time."

"Did he interrogate you? How was it?"

"It seems to be okay for now, I have an alibi: I was at my mum's.

"Good." Anna nodded as she said this.

"Marat was in the mountains, and I was at my mum's." Twinka laughed.

"How do you mean?"

"Marat told me that the book *Murder for Dummies* would say: 'If you've killed someone, the main thing is not to tell anyone'."

"I don't quite follow – could you explain in a bit more detail, please?"

"Never mind. It just came into my head. You know: whether you think that, if I *had* really stabbed Marat, I *wouldn't* be confessing. And so I'm thinking to myself – if you know *that*, then what do you think about everything I'm telling you?"

"Well, clients often lie, especially at the start of the therapy," Anna said with a smile. "Of course, in order to get results, honesty, openness and trust are vital. But what's even more important is that you don't lie to yourself. It's important that you know, and are able to tell the difference between when you're lying or not. So that you know what's true. But it's not always that simple, of course."

"I'm sorry, just ignore what I said. I didn't stab Marat, and I'm not lying to you. I think I'm just recalling all sorts of things connected to Marat – what he said, how he said it; just about everything reminds me of him, his thinking and the phrases he used to use."

"I understand."

"I don't know how I should behave. People think that everything was good between the two of us. Marat wanted everyone to think that I was on his side and believed him; that Dimitri had made this whole story up about Marat wanting to kill me because Marat had grown sick of me and divorce would be too messy. Which means that there was no attempted murder. There was only ever a love triangle, just a trivial act of jealousy, which the police turned into this huge thing, making an elephant out of a fly. That was his strategy."

"And did you play along, for his sake?"

"Yeah, I did. Well, for Ronia's sake, really. And if I really think about it, in that version he was the good guy and I was the villain, who basically deserved being hit over the head with a bottle."

"And how did that make you feel?"

"It was complicated. I mean, I did deserve some of it. I was just confused by it all."

"And what's changed?"

"Well, now I know for sure that he's an egotistical narcissist and a murderer who didn't give a shit about anyone other than himself. And he was a killer to his core."

"In one of our last sessions you said that you thought it was a mistake to protect his image in Ronia's eye while he was in prison."

"Yeah, I did say that. And yes, it probably was a mistake. But everything's different again."

"What is it like now?"

"If he died then that would probably be for the best. Then Ronia wouldn't have to live with the burden of knowing that her father was a very bad man."

"I think it's important to understand what Ronia is making of all this. How does she perceive the situation?" Anna said.

"I just can't seem to be able to grasp the fact that everything can change so quickly in life, and then it can change again, and again. One day, everything seems so stable and solid, like it's all hopelessly doomed. And then suddenly something happens and turns everything upside down – and nothing's like it used to be."

"Yes, and going through all these changes can take its toll psychologically." Anna looked very focused. Everything about her – her attitude, her body language – signalled that she believed this conversation was incredibly important. "You're holding up really well though, considering the huge and dramatic changes you've had to live through in such a short space of time."

"'Changes'... That's a beautiful, clever word to describe the fact that nothing in life goes according to plan. The fact that nothing ever happens like we hoped or expected it would. Changes – when actually it's just shit that's constantly gushing over us."

"Well, there can also be good changes," Anna objected delicately.

"When there's good changes in life, no one ever says – 'Oh, you're just going through changes; it's always tough, but you're holding up really well'."

"I guess you're right." Anna laughed. "But, in any case, it's best to look at life as a series of constant changes, rather than shit that's constantly gushing over us."

"Do you think two or three bottles of wine a day is a testament to how well I'm holding up?"

"Oh, I thought you said that after staying at that posh nest you'd learned how to control your relationship with alcohol?"

"Yeah. I sort of did. And then Loyola's *Spiritual Exercises* helped me a lot. He teaches how to search your conscience and focus your thoughts; how to set your thoughts in the morning and then carefully monitor them, so that whenever an unwelcome thought comes into your mind you can spot it and destroy it right away. That's how I was monitoring whenever the desire to drink came up. And it helped me."

"And why did you stop doing that?"

"Why did I stop?" Twinka sighed. "Why do you think?"

Anna didn't say anything.

"I feel like I hate changes. Why couldn't everything just stay exactly as it was during the first ten years of our marriage? Why couldn't we just carry on living like that until we reached old age?"

"Do you have any answers to that question?" Anna had once again adopted her uber-professional tone.

"Have you any idea how much that annoys me? The fact that you ask me another question just when I want to hear an answer from you."

"But you do know why I do that." Anna smiled. "I don't want to teach you how to live your life, or lecture you about anything – I want you to find the answers for yourself."

"Yeah, yeah... I know," Twinka submitted, grumpily.

Anna said nothing further, and Twinka felt guilty for saying that Anna's questions and general attitude often annoyed her.

If only you, of all people, could be a bit less complicated, she thought to herself.

CHAPTER 99

Listening to the audio recordings took Draco a lot longer than he'd expected. The listening device was only activated whenever there was noise in the room, so that it only captured whatever could be deemed of interest to the investigators. But Twinka had put some music on in the morning, meaning the passage of audio containing that which was of interest to Draco was in itself over five hours long.

In the house on Button Street, the morning got going at seven a.m., with Marat being the first to rise, followed by Ronia, and, around seven-thirty, Twinka. Despite the music playing in the background, it was clearly audible that Twinka wished Ronia a good day at school at exactly seven fifty-two a.m.

Then Marat was swimming or maybe exercising, or busying himself around the house until nine-twenty a.m. At nine twenty-nine , Twinka left the house and Marat remained at home, drinking coffee and doing something inaudible, most likely reading a newspaper or using his laptop.

At eleven fifty-six , he suddenly exclaimed: "What's happened?!"

Four seconds later, he screamed. To Draco, it sounded like a scream of pain and surprise.

At twelve-twenty p.m., Ronia came home and herself screamed. You could hear the door bang as she ran out of the house.

Three minutes later, Twinka appeared.

"What's happened?!" Draco replayed this particular audio several times. Draco didn't quite understand what Marat had heard, or what had happened. All he knew was that Twinka had an alibi.

Draco had checked it out, too, of course. The traffic cameras, the CCTV at her parents' house, and the phone data – everything corroborated that she was with her parents at the time of the attack, plus her parents themselves would likely confirm that.

Dimitri was dead and Twinka had an alibi. Suddenly, Draco realised that he actually didn't actually know anyone outside of their love triangle, and he didn't know much about Marat either. Who was he again? Some sort of banker, an investor – what did he even do for work? Draco was annoyed, realising that he'd been hoping Twinka would turn out to be the murderer. It was only logical – so predictable and simple. But no, it wasn't her. Despite this, he vowed to check everything just one more time. What if she'd done something similar to what Marat did when he tried to kill her? What if she was supposed to be at her parents' house, but had actually managed to get home unnoticed? Draco had to check everything one more time; talk to her parents; examine every step, minute-by-minute.

It was a Thursday evening. The year's least-bearable season was upon them: during which the temperatures fluctuated between zero and sub-zero, and you could get just about anything coming down from the heavens (from freezing-cold rain to a wet snowy drizzle).

The pressure of the previous few days and the significant uncertainty of the work that lay ahead weighed heavily on Draco. Although he didn't do it very often, he pulled out an open bottle of whiskey that was stashed away in the bottom drawer of his desk. *Even machines need a restart every once in a while,* he thought to himself, justifying his actions. There were no glasses, so he poured the whiskey straight into a coffee mug.

The first few sips made him wince, but after that it went down pretty smoothly.

He pinned Twinka's picture to a blackboard, put his feet up on the desk and poured himself some more whiskey. She was stunning. She was so beautiful. Draco finally admitted something he'd been constantly thinking about in secret: that she was a fascinating woman. That smile, those eyes – plus she was so kind, and so strong. A truly remarkable woman.

The alcohol angel had descended onto Draco's shoulder, caressing him with its glistening silver wings, stroking him from its lofty perch. This soothed, relaxed and healed Draco, flooding him with warmth, calm and confidence. Oh, yes, Draco had really needed this.

"What are you worried about? Everything's okay," it addressed Draco. "Things are just fine. You'll solve the mystery of Dimitri's death, and Marat's too. There's no need to rush anywhere, everything will unfold in its own time. You're always setting such high expectations for yourself, that's your biggest problem, always demanding too much from yourself."

I wonder if a woman like Twinka would ever be with someone like me? Even in his mind, Draco said "someone like me" – he wasn't ready to use the words "with me", not even in his private thoughts. *I wonder if she even considers me to be human: I'm probably some sort of a lower-level being to her. I wonder what she thinks of me? Probably nothing good. That time, I just had to pressure her to encourage her a bit – but it wasn't personal, I was only doing my job. I wonder if that's how she sees it, though. Probably not.*

The angel's wings were starting to grow heavy. The bottle was almost empty, and the fairy had started to resemble a dying bird, with the sheen of its wings fading.

A worm; I'm just a worm to her. A pathetic being; nothing. I'm even worse than empty space. I'm like some sort of a gnat that attaches itself to your skin when you walk through a forest.

Something you can flick away with a single stroke and forget about it.

The man who'd conquered Everest had a whole room filled with suits. A whole room: dedicated to just suits, with a row of identical white shirts – some fifty or sixty of them – all the same! And a room, twice the size of that, in the basement... just for sports clothes! Then a separate room solely for mountaineering equipment. When did they even meet? How did Twinka meet him? And where did they meet? How do women like her find men like him?!

Draco only owned two suits: one of which was tattered and old, so you couldn't even really count that.

The dying bird had turned into a thick, slimy, dark cloud of fog, and he had to fight his way through it.

No, don't even think about it! You're not driving anywhere in your car. You're an officer of the law. You don't do stuff like that, you don't drive when you're drunk.

Drunk or not, I'm a cop. I know what I'm doing. I can control myself. I can control the situation perfectly.

Draco bought a further two bottles in a shop: another whiskey and a cheap bottle of cognac. There was no way he'd be able to drink both of these today. And it's not like he wanted to, anyway. If he finished both, he wouldn't be able to go into work tomorrow. If he finished both, he would surely die. Fine, it didn't matter anyway, so he'd just have both. It made no difference anyway.

He mustn't forget about Dimitri. Perhaps, and this was very likely, Marat's and Dimitri's deaths were connected. Yes: it was a very important thought; it was really important that he remembered it. Their deaths were most likely connected. Either way, as long as the circumstances of Dimitri's death remained unclear, the theory couldn't be ruled out. Ha, it wasn't a bad thought, was it? That was his thirty years of experience talking.

It wasn't like those years had been spent in vain; it wasn't like he'd lived for nothing. No, it wasn't all for nothing, and he wasn't a worm or some sort of a bug. No. And anyone who believed otherwise was making a serious mistake. Fatal. A f-a-t-a-l mistake, fatal. Very fatal. He was who he was – he was Draco, the chief inspector of particularly difficult cases, the city's best. He was no gnat; and anyway, someone's worth couldn't be measured by their suit.

Okay, maybe he hadn't climbed Everest: but not because he *wasn't capable* of the feat. He couldn't be treated like some sort of a secondary citizen purely on account of having not done so. Climbing Everest wasn't the be all and end all. If he didn't have more important things do with his life, and if he could hire fifty people to carry him up Everest – to supply him with oxygen like they do for deep-sea divers; to assist him in having a piss, so that, God forbid, his expensive little dick wouldn't freeze – then there was nothing to it.

If I had that life, I'd be climbing Everest too. Without any problem. But in the meantime, I'm catching paedophiles; mothers who suffocate their own children because their new boyfriend wasn't ecstatic about them; murderers and pimps. I'm cleansing our city of all sorts of garbage, so that your daughter and my daughter wouldn't need to be afraid to walk to school by themselves. But no one appreciates that. No one, ever. But if I wasn't sat here, in my one pathetic suit, without a family, without a wife, without any friends, working morning till night without taking a break, without any private life, then soon enough none of you would be climbing Everest; you wouldn't be able to leave the house without an entire army protecting you and all your fancy businesses and restaurants, your golf and horse racing courses, and your tennis courts – you could forget about it, because you wouldn't be able to feel safe anywhere, if it wasn't for gnats like me, who enforce the law. The law! What a arbitrary activity it is to climb Everest anyway. How much strength, money, effort and risk it takes – and all of that for nothing but vanity: so you can show off and appear unique. For that kind of money you could have bought thousands of hearing aids for disabled children, or saved a cancer patient. But no, the pompous prick wanted to show off; to show that he's excellent, all-powerful, that nothing is too difficult for him, nothing is impossible for him! And where are you now? You're lying with your chest open on a coroner's slab. Something went wrong, didn't it, Superman! Something went awry, not everything played out exactly as you assumed it would...

The cognac felt sweetish, like the smell of a corpse. He should have bought vodka, he thought, examining the bottle. He shouldn't have had any in the first place. What a stupid idea that was.

CHAPTER 100

"Did I tell you we had sex next to his mother's coffin?"

"No. No, you didn't."

"It was back when he was still in prison. He'd been released to attend his mother's funeral, and we had sex literally in front of his dead mother."

"Seriously?" Anna didn't mask her astonishment. "And did you... enjoy it?"

"You know, if he dies – and from what I understand, his doctors are saying there's almost no chance that he'll ever come out of the coma – then I'd like someone to fuck me hard next to his coffin. I literally get butterflies in my stomach just from thinking about it. Except, there's no one who would. Ha! I had one too many suitors, and now I have none."

"Why do you think this idea turns you on?"

"I don't know – you tell me. I mean, I'm fantasising about having sex with a stranger at my own husband's funeral, even though he's still technically alive. Would you call that normal?"

"Tell me a bit more about it." Anna was wearing her professionally indifferent face.

Once again, Anna's reluctance to express her actual opinion irritated Twinka, though she accepted the rules and continued. "I have fantasies about Marat's funeral where someone takes me from behind by force, while I'm still standing, holding onto the coffin and staring at him. My tits and my stomach hit against the coffin – *bam, bam, bam* – and Marat is pinballing around inside. Me and the man's faces might even touch, or I might kiss him, and I come *so hard*, like I never have with Marat. I can picture it all so vividly: I'm almost scared that, if he dies, I'll end up grabbing a random staff member at the cemetery."

"But why does it arouse you? Why does it appeal to you? Should we have a think?"

"I don't know."

"So, you've planned his funeral, you're having fantasies over what might happen during it – are you hoping that he will die, and this will all be over?"

"Hmm, maybe..."

"Have a think."

"I don't know... You know what makes it so complicated? Yes, if he died, that should be good news for me on the one hand. If you were to consider it from a rational point of view, then that's how it should feel. But I don't feel any relief or joy, now that he's essentially dead. I don't feel anything anymore," Twinka said, collapsing into Anna's comfortable office chair. Her eyes bore into Anna's almost expectantly, as though waiting for Anna to bring the relief she longed for.

"I opened a bottle of Dom Pérignon P2 today. Do you know what that is?" Twinka asked.

"No, not really," said Anna, faking her interest.

"It's a type of champagne that's been aged considerably longer – I would say a generation longer – than the regular Dom Pérignon. Basically, the standard Dom Pérignon is kept in cellars for up to eight years aging on lees in the bottle. Then it gets disgorged: they open it, remove the lees and add a secret mixture based on the cellar master's all-important recipe to fill the bottle up. Then it gets its cork and is laid to rest, so that all the ingredients merge together for another year or so, before it gets released to the market."

It's one of the finest champagnes in the whole world. But, unlike the rest, about ten percent of Dom Pérignon's yield is left unopened even after those eight years have gone by, and left to age for another five or six years, which, of course, leaves a massive impact on the taste and texture of the champagne.

These Dom Pérignon wines are called Plénitude 2. I absolutely *adore* them! The difference is relatively small, but definitely noticeable. You can feel the maturity, aristocracy, experience and wisdom – but it's still fairly fresh and almost without any bubbles, with that characteristic aftertaste of a cheesecake. It's really good, you should try it sometime," Twinka said, knowing full well that Anna would never be able to afford such an expensive champagne. For some reason, today she wanted to play the role of the shameless rich wife. "And then there's P3, which is even rarer," she continued. "Those bottles are set aside from the P2 yield and left to mature for another generation. If things carry on like this, life will drive me to having P3 for breakfast. I mean, I'm as rich as Croesus now! But it's sheer opulence, excess, if you know what I mean? Drinking P2 first thing in the morning, all by myself, wearing a black dress. It's so... there's a bit of everything in that. It's incredibly beautiful and sad at the same time. And not because Marat is in a coma, but because even P2 can't make me happy anymore. It's never going to feel special again. And the only reason I'm telling you all this is to remind myself how special it is, even though I can't feel it anymore. It doesn't mean anything to me."

"It's just your way of reacting to all these traumatic experiences. It will pass," Anna said comfortingly, having allowed Twinka to get things off her chest.

"Marat's death would solve a lot of problems for me. There's no point in denying that. It would allow me to have a fresh start, and, hopefully, set things right with Ronia. No one will get in the way, we won't have to suffer through a suffocating co-habitation process, or too many compromises, or divorce. Ronia won't be torn between two households, tormented by all sorts of revelations or things that we've bottled up. His death would be very convenient for me, but I don't wish him to die, as much as I'd like to, after everything he's done to me. It wouldn't be a sin if I did, but I don't feel like I can. I don't know why."

"And how do you feel?" Anna asked.

"I don't know. I want someone to fuck me by his coffin. That would one hundred percent be in his style. I think he deserves seeing that I've become just like him on so many levels. In a way, that would be the greatest show of respect to him. If I had someone, I'd definitely do it," Twinka sighed.

"Are things really that bad that you have to prepare for the worst?"

"Yeah, it looks that way."

CHAPTER 101

Draco didn't have any regrets. He knew what the morning would be like when he started yesterday – he knew what he was doing. He'd needed it, and it couldn't be helped. There was a half-empty bottle of whiskey and an open bottle of cognac on the floor next to the sofa. *Plus, I had some whiskey at work.* Draco tried to calculate how much he'd drank. It could have been worse. He sealed the bottles and put them in his bag. Their place was not at home. They belonged at work, stashed away in the bottom drawer of his desk.

He stood in the shower for longer than usual, intermittently splashing himself with cold water. Then he opened the cabinet where he kept all his medicines, looking for a Saridon tablet for his headache. Then he tossed some dissolvable aspirin in a glass of water. Made some coffee. Thankfully, it was a Friday. He'd be able to get through the day and have a lie in tomorrow and sort himself out. All he needed to do today was chair the investigation group's team meeting – that was all that needed to be done, and he was sure he could get through it.

At the meeting, the forensics expert was the first to speak. They hadn't found anything at Marat's murder crime scene. The nearby shop's only CCTV camera – the same one that had captured Dimitri last time – hadn't recorded anything. They had no clues.

"This is what we'll do," Draco said, standing up.

He walked up to the blackboard and attached Twinka's picture with a magnet. Underneath it, he pinned Dimitri and Marat's photographs.

"We have two bodies. Two men, connected to this woman. One of them was her lover, the other one her husband. One of the two cases is definitely a murder, and the other is very likely a murder, too. Until we're able to rule it out, we'll consider these two cases as linked to one another. I don't know in what way exactly, but they're all too close together. It looks to me like different chapters of the same story. So, first, let's focus all our efforts on finding out the exact circumstances of Dimitri's death."

"You five," he pointed at some of the police officers in the room, "your task is to go to the shipyard. Check every corner: we need to find out exactly what happened to Dimitri. Did he jump in the water? If so – where was it? If he didn't do it himself, then where was he attacked? How did they push him in, and where? We don't have any clear answers at the moment. Everyone else needs to go to Button Street. The murderer was definitely covered in blood. If we can't find any fingerprints, it means they were wearing gloves, and the gloves themselves must have been soaked in it. I doubt they'd then be walking the streets, dripping with the stuff. They could have taken only one possible route of retreat where there are no cameras, so we need to search that again, to make sure nothing was ditched around there. We need to check the side streets, maybe there is something further down. We need to talk to all the neighbours. And the data forensics people need to keep going – checking his laptop, phone, bank records – we're looking for a motive. Who else could have had a motive to kill him, besides his wife? Who else would have benefitted from his death? And we need to find out everything about Twinka. Who is she seeing? Who is she calling? We've got her under twenty-four-hour surveillance. She's got an alibi, but that's not enough to rule her out. She is her husband's equal – a very intelligent, strong woman. If we assume that Marat arranged Dimitri's murder, then we need to also assume that Twinka could have been able to organise her husband's – one with a very lucrative outcome for her. That's it. I want the results on Monday."

Draco had a rule to never carry on drinking the next day. It was an important rule. If he had any alcohol today then he'd be drinking tomorrow too, and the day after, and the day after that – and he definitely didn't want that. He was over it now. He bought an apple-flavoured vape. That would help get him through the day.

Marat's alibi was just too good. Everything pointed to him having secured a bulletproof alibi on purpose. And he'd loved it; boasting about the fact his alibi was so strong, and how he didn't necessarily know the exact moment of Dimitri's death. It looked to be the perfect crime.

Equally, Twinka's alibi sounded too good to be true. Was it just a coincidence, or had she learned all that from Marat?

Husband and wife. Two perfect crimes.

No, surely not... That sort of thing never happened. Or could it?

Never mind, I'll get to the bottom of it. I always do, Draco pepped himself up. *But not today; that's enough for today. It's been a tough day.*

CHAPTER 102

Twinka went to the hospital once a week to visit Marat. Seeing Anna had taught her to ask herself more questions. But for now, she couldn't find the answer as to why she was visiting him. Marat was being looked after, so she couldn't help him anyway. If there were any changes to his condition, she'd be notified right away. Twinka had asked the doctor who was overseeing Marat's care, if it's true that you should talk to someone who's in a coma, because they may be able to hear you, and the familiar sound of your voice might aid their waking up. The doctor, albeit reluctantly, had made it clear that Marat definitely couldn't hear anything, and the rest belonged to the field of esoterism, not medicine. But if she wanted to, she could definitely talk to Marat. It certainly wouldn't do any harm.

Twinka didn't have any particular desire to talk to Marat, and yet she still came to visit. Most likely, she thought of it as her duty. You had to visit family members in hospital, even if they were in a coma. And she did. No one else would come and see him. She had brought a large vase with her and put it next to Marat's bed, replacing its contents with fresh flowers each time she came. Even if this made no difference to Marat, at least it made it more pleasant for the nurses. She would usually sit by his bed for about ten minutes, then leave.

One side of the corridor had windows looking out at the hospital's forecourt. As Twinka's gaze slowly slid across the dull, snowless winter scene, her eyes suddenly collided with Marat's car – one of his cars. It was the black S-class Mercedes. She couldn't see the numberplate from here, so maybe it wasn't Marat's one – after all, the city was full of black Mercedes just like his. Despite that, Twinka still felt it was Marat's car. It was the vehicle Marat had always used whenever he wanted to be discreet. But why was it here? She went outside to check.

As she'd suspected, it turned out to be Marat's Mercedes. Seeing Twinka approach, the door opened on the driver's side and Theodor got out.

"What are you doing here?" Twinka asked, embarrassed by her stern, bossy tone. Without a greeting or an introduction, she'd spoken like a true rich bitch.

"I don't know, madam," Theodor said quietly. There was something submissive and deeply wistful about Theodor. Twinka felt sorry for him. She walked around the car, opened the passenger door, and gestured for Theodor to get in, too.

"Don't stand outside in the cold," she said, speaking to him like he was her equal, her voice devoid of any attack. They both sat in the car.

"What are you doing here?" Twinka repeated the question, much calmer than the first time.

"I wanted to find out some news, but they're not letting me in. They're not telling me anything."

"Then why are you hanging around?"

"I don't know," Theodor spoke very quietly. "I don't know what to do. All the cars are clean, the tanks are full, the tires have been checked." He spoke softly, with his head hanging low, and Twinka realised he was close to tears.

"Right," Twinka said, completely confused. It was so bizarre and unexpected that someone in the world could be more affected by Marat's condition than her. She knew Theodor's story, Marat had told her. But she had no idea that Theodor – this tattooed murderer and criminal – had grown so attached to Marat.

"My car is parked just around the corner. Follow me and let's meet at Button Street," Twinka said in a voice that brooked no objection. She felt sorry for this boy whose closest person was Marat, and who was sat on his own in the car, staring at the windows of Marat's room.

"What are you drinking?" Twinka asked when they had arrived at Button Street.

"Madam, I can't. I'm behind the wheel." Theodor had managed to pull himself together. He sounded formal and reserved.

"You're not behind the wheel anymore, you'll leave the car here," Twinka said, having switched back to her bossy tone. She was surprised to hear it herself – she couldn't remember ever speaking in that voice before.

She poured Theodor a glass of cognac – she felt that cognac would suit him best. He didn't argue back and took the glass. She felt that they'd get along just fine.

"I'm afraid Marat probably isn't going to pull through," she said. "The doctors say there's almost no hope for him."

Theodor didn't say anything. He downed the cognac in one gulp, and held the glass out to Twinka again.

"We need to prepare ourselves for the worst," Twinka said, re-filling Theodor's drink.

"And nothing can be done?" Theodor asked gloomily.

"They're already doing everything they can," Twinka replied, examining Theodor carefully. There was something appealing about him – the paradox of his stern appearance and his sensitive, gentle personality made him attractive. The incongruity between his hard life, his readiness to bear the worst news, and his utter vulnerability – there was something about it that made Twinka feel a tingling in her stomach. She also realised that she had absolute power over the boy.

"I want you to know that I'll find him and kill him. I swear – I'll kill him!" Theodor was speaking with absolute determination, which surprised Twinka.

"Who are you going to kill?" She didn't understand.

"The bastard who killed Marat. I'm going to kill him."

"Oh, I see!"

"Marat was the only person who'd ever been kind to me."

"It's going to be okay," Twinka said.

"He was such a good man, and then some scumbag just killed him."

"Everything will be okay," Twinka repeated, and embraced Theodor tightly. She could feel his body clinging to hers in absolute dependence. There was genuine, real intimacy in the embrace, which Twinka enjoyed

CHAPTER 103

"Really? You had a strange dream?" Anna rubbed her hands together in a playful, exaggerated manner. "Go on! I love analysing dreams."

"Well, I often see Marat in my dreams, but until now they were pretty standard dreams. And after having them I usually don't remember much. Like, I remember that Marat doesn't usually have his pirate's patch in my dreams. He's young – like he used to be when we first met. I've had sex dreams where I see him naked, he's lying in bed on his back, we're talking about something, teasing each other, we're just about to have sex, I'm so turned on – but we never quite get to the sex. In the best-case scenario, I see him touch my tits or some other area with his tongue. But this time it was different."

"Oh?" Anna had frozen in her 'professional, active-listener' pose.

"I don't remember how it started, but the idea was that Marat now could enter anyone's dreams. Well, not anyone's, but people he used to know. Somehow we'd met each other in the dream, and so we could enter other people's dreams together – including people I knew."

"Oh, that's interesting." Anna said, nodding to signal that she had understood everything so far.

"And he was asking me whose dreams I'd like to enter, and suddenly we saw you."

"Me?!" Anna exclaimed with a laugh.

Up until today Anna's mannerisms hadn't struck Twinka as being exaggerated. But now, to Twinka, they seemed markedly, and increasingly, so.

"Yeah, we saw you in a swimsuit by a pool, in a small house, which looked like Southern France. It could have been

Provence. And there was a man there too, and we were stood behind a hedge, so you couldn't see us, though the dogs were barking. You had two Labradors, light in colour and still very young. They weren't quite puppies, but not fully grown either. They didn't bark in a vicious way – they seemed curious more than anything. They were separated from us by a metal fence, which was covered by a hedge."

"Seriously?" Anna was unable to hide her surprise.

"You looked in our direction, but you didn't really see us, and we were leaving anyway – we were suddenly in Draco's dream."

"Who's Draco?" Anna's question interrupted Twinka's flow.

"The police officer: our investigator who was assigned to the first case, then Dimitri's death, and now he's investigating Marat's murder. He was in some sort of office – sitting by a computer screen, wearing headphones – and we could hear what he was listening to in there. And do you know what that was?" Twinka was looking directly into Anna's eyes.

"Ohh, what was it?"

"He was listening to our conversations."

"Ours? How do you mean?" Anna didn't understand.

"The conversations we're having here."

"Here?"

"Yeah, our conversations here."

"He was listening to us?" This time Anna looked truly perplexed.

"Yeah."

"Oh my God, that's awful."

"Yeah, I must admit, it wasn't a very pleasant feeling."

"I have two corgis, I've never owned any Labradors," Anna said.

Twinka didn't reply – she was looking at her fingers.

"Are you afraid that the police may be listening in on our conversations?" Anna seemed to have gathered her thoughts, and had reacquired her formal, professional tone.

"I don't know. So much has happened lately that all my feelings have been blunted. I don't care if they listen. I've got nothing to hide anyway."

"Okay, let's not forget that it was just a dream. You just feel persecuted, that's all. Like the police are paying attention to you, watching and surveilling. It's perfectly normal to have this sort of a dream, given the circumstances. It wouldn't surprise me if you've developed a subconscious fear that the investigators may be listening in on our conversations, and that's what the dream revealed."

"Yeah, you're probably right." Twinka shrugged.

"When did you have it?" Anna asked, getting out of her chair. Their time was up.

"The day before yesterday."

"I have to say it's quite an unusual dream," Anna said, arranging something on her table. She didn't raise her eyes at Twinka.

Twinka felt like her story had left a bigger impression on Anna than Anna wanted Twinka to know, and that seemed to boost Twinka's mood.

"Have a nice weekend," Twinka said to her, cheerfully.

"You too." Anna looked into Twinka's eyes. It was the formal gaze of a busy and tired person, which wasn't in her usual character.

There's something going on with the Labradors and that man, Twinka concluded.

CHAPTER 104

The evening turned to night, and the night became the early morning. Twinka was surprised at how good she felt in Theodor's presence. It was like gentleness and pointed rebelliousness were uniquely intertwined in Theodor. Behind his tattooed and scarred face, behind the tough lifestyle, she could glimpse a sensitive and kind soul. One minute he was ready to cry like a child, the next he was telling her how he'd find and dispose of Marat's killer. There was a vulnerable and gentle boy inside him, in equal measure to the experienced murderer who wouldn't stop no matter what. Twinka questioned how congenial he ultimately was. The thought was a bit scary, yet incredibly attractive. Likewise, she wanted to embrace his inner child and tame his inner killer, and she felt that she may be able to accomplish both. Theodor would let her. It was another exciting thought.

"He's such a good person, he could have lived for many more years to come, he shouldn't be dying," Theodor repeated, over and over.

Twinka re-filled Theodor's glass, then put the bottle down. She had another, larger gulp herself and placed her hand on the back of Theodor's neck. She pulled him in and pressed her lips against his. Theodor didn't resist her, though he didn't answer the kiss either. When she let him go, Theodor's eyes looked so confused that it made Twinka burst out laughing.

"No fear," she said, grinning and searching for her glass. "I understand that Marat may have been like a father figure, but I'll tell you now – I'm not going to be a mother to you," she said. Again, she was astonished at how foreign her voice felt. What had she even said? What did she mean by it – where was all this cynicism and arrogance coming from? It was the rich bitch talking, whom Twinka had always feared, though she could sometimes sense her inside. At times, she had even wanted to hand over full control to her, and just enjoy it. Somehow Theodor had managed to tap into this hidden part of herself. Like he'd given her free rein.

Or was it something to do with Marat's dying? The fact that it would make her the boss over so many things?

Theodor didn't say anything. Twinka reached for her glass and they toasted.

"You know, I was just thinking how each year goes by faster than the rest. It's like, as you get older, you start paying attention to the fact that you're aging. And as soon as you do that, you start to age faster. The more precious your time seems, the quicker it starts to go by. The more you want to stop its passing, the harder it becomes. Have you ever thought about that?" Twinka asked.

Theodor shook his head in denial.

"Albert Camus had this idea – I believe it was in *The Outsider* – that the best way to stop time is to do something unpleasant or very boring. For example, sitting in the waiting room at the dentist's without any intention of being seen. Time must have dragged on in prison, eh?" Twinka was looking at Theodor with quizzing eyes.

"I guess," Theodor replied, though it was obvious that he didn't know quite what to say.

"It's absurd though..." Twinka didn't seem to be expecting an answer from him. She topped up the cognac again. "What's the point of doing it, if time is only slowing down when you're doing something unpleasant? I'd like for time to drag while I'm doing something pleasant, right? But how do you achieve that?"

"I don't know," Theodor said quietly.

"One idea does come to mind... Do you know the only pleasant thing that can make time go slowly?"

"I dunno." Theodor wasn't even trying.

"Sex, of course! Sex is the only enjoyable thing that can make time go slowly. It literally stops when you do it. How long does it even go on for normally? Ten minutes? Fifteen? It takes me longer to put makeup on in the mornings. Cooking takes a lot more time, and I probably spend as much time on the toilet over the course of a day, although all that time feels like it's completely flown by. But sex – those ten minutes – that stays with me. I remember it, I feel it on my skin and my entire body, sometimes for years."

Theodor was completely lost. He had no idea what to say. Which seemed to amuse Twinka even more.

"Do you know what I mean?"

"I guess." Theodor was averting his gaze.

"Do you know what it's like to anticipate a message or a text from your lover? It's the best way to make the seconds go very slowly. Does that make sense? It's exciting and painfully slow, all at the same time."

"Yeah, that makes sense," Theodor said, although Twinka wasn't sure if he'd understood.

"Basically, everyone should be fucking a lot more. We all need to fuck," she said.

Theodor felt like Twinka was wasted, and he was right. The cognac had made his cheeks flush, too. If Marat was dead, he reasoned, then it probably wasn't a massive deal to let his wife kiss him. But what if he wasn't?

She's not bad for a MILF, he thought to himself, finally considering Twinka in that way. *She's definitely a crazy MILF, but then again, she's Marat's wife and there's no way that someone like her could be a simple housewife, that's for sure.*

Twinka had clocked Theodor's appraisal of her, and it tickled her somewhere in the lower region of her belly. She couldn't even recall when she'd last felt a tingling down there.

"Stay there and don't move," she said, coming up very close to him. She knelt down and started to undo Theodor's trousers. The belt, the button, the zip – it felt slower and harder than it might seem. An uncomfortable silence ensued, charged with a level of awkwardness for both of them. Theodor didn't assist her. Finally though, Twinka had reached her goal.

His dick wasn't hard. Not even a little. *Surely I'm not that old – that he can't even get hard over me,* Twinka thought in shock and horror. *Someone as young as him shouldn't be so soft, should they?!*

If Marat was alive, Theodor wasn't allowed to do it. But now, with Twinka taking Marat's place, would it be wrong to push her away?

With Theodor still frozen by doubt and uncertainty, Twinka started stroking his balls. With three fingers of her other hand, she was holding his pride, though its shape remained undetermined. She looked up at him playfully and their eyes met. Twinka stuck out her tongue and licked his dick, still holding it in her fingers. She was still looking into Theodor's eyes. And it worked. A moment later, Theodor was hard and he'd turned beautifully crimson.

Not bad, Twinka thought, assessing the end result with satisfaction. It was fatter and larger than she'd expected, based on Theodor's delicate build. She took it in her mouth, continuing to stroke his balls with one hand, while stroking his ass with the other.

Suddenly, and completely unexpectedly, she realised that Theodor was coming. She barely managed to pull herself away. A large jet of semen shot into Twinka's eye, before several others landed on her face. There was a lot of it, and Twinka was surprised at the force by which it had collided with her face. They weren't too familiar with each other, and their relationship definitely wasn't one where Twinka felt comfortable swallowing, not to mention she'd been caught utterly off-guard by such a quick climax. She tore herself away, by now covered in Theodor's cum.

"Oh," was the only thing she managed at first, wiping her eyes and face.

Meanwhile, Theodor had got himself dressed at lightning speed.

"See! That's everything anyone needs to know in relation to stopping time," Twinka said, followed by the loud, self-satisfied laughter of a drunkard.

CHAPTER 105

"I don't know if it matters, but Ronia wasn't at school on the day of the murder," said one of the assistants assigned to Draco for the case. She was a young police officer, a recent graduate of the academy. Her name was Lara – or Larissa in full. Her very serious but childish-looking face was covered in freckles. Draco had instructed Lara to keep an eye on Twinka's electronic communications, namely her outgoing messages and phone conversations.

"Ronia?" Draco repeated.

"Yeah. The evening before, Twinka had sent the school administrator an email, explaining that Ronia wouldn't be coming in due to family circumstances, so that the schoolbus driver would know how many kids to collect that day."

"But how? We heard on the recording that she left for school that morning." Draco was surprised. "I mean, Twinka saw her off and wished her a good day."

"I don't know. All I know is that she wasn't at school that day." Though Lara always spoke in the accustomed formal and professional tone, there was always a note of annoyance or maybe even sadness to her voice. Draco never quite knew which it was.

"And it's been a bit of a pattern lately," Lara continued. "Last month, she skipped nine days – she would miss almost every other day. The school have sent Twinka an email to ask if they could discuss it, but Twinka had never replied to it."

"If her mum knows that her daughter isn't going to school, then she probably also knows where she is going. Maybe it's something they didn't want Marat to know?" said Draco, thinking out loud, now fully engrossed.

"It was her grandma's birthday that day, so maybe Ronia wanted to wish her a happy birthday too?" said Lara, offering her version. "And Marat didn't believe you should skip school for that, but Mum let her?"

"Then they would have returned together, surely. But we only saw Twinka on the cameras outside the house." Draco shook his head, deep in thought. "And it wouldn't explain her missing school so often."

"True," Lara agreed.

"Please, find out as much as you can."

"Yes, sir," Lara obeyed, and there was something sad in her voice again. She was hardworking, so it didn't look like it had anything to do with work. Draco watched her thoughtfully.

"And Ronia was the one who found the body?"

"Yes," Lara confirmed, believing that Draco's examining gaze was linked to his thoughts on Ronia.

"Have the forensic experts checked her over? Did she have any blood on her clothes or anything like that?"

"No. No one checked her – only her mother." Lara let out a sigh.

"Well, do we have her witness statement at least?"

"It hasn't been signed and she's underage. But even so, there's only a few sentences there. *I came back from school, I saw Dad lying there, it looked like he was dead. I ran outside and saw Mum arrive. I didn't see, hear, or spot anything else.*"

"That's it?"

"Yeah. I mean she's still just a child. The doctors paid more attention to her than our lot did."

"Interesting, very interesting..." Draco repeated to himself. "Ronia is sixteen, she'll soon be seventeen. Could Ronia have killed her dad? Stabbing her own father twice? To be honest, nothing surprises me about this family anymore." Although he was unsure as to his line of thinking, Draco felt the pleasant hunter's instinct and excitement return. This would be an interesting case.

"I want to know everything about Ronia," Draco ordered. "Check her social media, her friends, her internet search history – go to the school and find out what sort of a child she is and what they make of her skipping so many classes. It's a private school, so they probably know all their pupils really well. Just be careful and make sure that her mother doesn't find out, or she'll deploy Keiko's entire army on us, and we won't be able to get anywhere near that child."

"Yes, sir. Thank you."

CHAPTER 106

Twinka was being driven everywhere by a chauffeur now. She couldn't understand why she'd never done so before. It was *so* convenient. Especially going to the shops. Theodor would push the shopping cart behind her, pack the bags at the checkout and then take them to the car. While they were driving, Twinka could do stuff on her phone. She didn't need to worry about where to park the car and, most importantly – she didn't have to think about how much alcohol was in her system. It was super convenient. Up until this point, her subconscious fear about turning into the typical rich bitch was probably what had stopped her from considering the idea. Yet now, Twinka submitted herself fully to enjoying the feel of the black Mercedes, to Theodor's subservience, and to the attitude she felt from others due to this symbol of her elevated status.

It makes no difference to me – let them think whatever they want, Twinka thought to herself. *I'm not thinking about them at all. I've got enough to worry about as it is, who cares what some strangers think of me.*

"I have another dream to tell you," Twinka announced, as soon as she'd stepped over the threshold of Anna's flat. She was in a buoyant spirits.

"Oh, really? That's interesting – you didn't use to have dreams like these before, and now you're seeing them almost every night."

"Yeah, that's true," Twinka said. She wasn't ready to discuss Theodor yet. She wanted to talk about it, but she'd get to it some other time. For now, she felt too ashamed to broach the subject, not even with herself. She was sleeping with her chauffeur. A young boy and her employee. She was using him. How could she? How could she stoop so low? What had she turned into? It was all Marat's fault. Actually, no, she wouldn't talk about it with Anna. No one would ever find out about this.

Nor would she worry about it either. She would simply go with the flow.

"So, listen. This one's even more bizarre than the one I told you about last time." Twinka settled into the chair.

"Go on," Anna tilted her head towards Twinka and once more assumed her static, active listener's pose.

"I don't remember exactly how it started, and I can't tell you where it was set. Probably at home, but all I remember is him saying to me: 'Tell her, make sure you tell her'. He sounded nervous and quite demanding, but I couldn't understand what it is I needed to tell, and to who. Then I realised that I have to tell Ronia something, though I didn't know what. The only thing I understood was that it was very important. Marat just kept repeating: 'Tell her, make sure you tell her'. I was crying, I told him I didn't understand. Then he said: 'Get up and go into my office'. And I got up and went."

"In the dream or in reality?" Anna asked.

"In the dream. But listen to this. I got up, went in there, and he told me where to look. There was a blue notebook on the bookshelf, stashed somewhere in between two spines. I'd never seen it before, but it turned out it was a notebook where he'd scribbled down all his thoughts. I opened the notebook, and it said in large letters:

To Ronia.

And then it said:

Life has a purpose. We are all organisms whose every cell is programmed to resist death. That's the basis of everything, that's the main thing. Everything that's meaningful in life is essentially resistance to death, in one way or another. Art, architecture, science, kids – everyone has their own way of going against death. Everything that people find to be meaningful, it's all just an act of resisting death, to reach somewhere beyond it, to extend themselves beyond death, outside of death, maybe even to make themselves immortal.

"'Of course, that's not possible, but we all strive towards it anyway, whichever way we can,' Marat said to me, once I'd read that far. 'Evolution has programmed us to disseminate ourselves as far and as wide as possible, including beyond the boundaries of our own death. That's our biological essence and the purpose of our lives. There is only one way to live a meaningful and happy life: to find your thing – namely, your own way of resisting death – and then strive to attain this thing in fulness. Not only would it give your life a meaning, but lots of happy moments too, because happiness means getting closer to your goal. But how can you get any closer to your goal, if you don't have your thing? Your thing brings you not only meaning, but happiness too.'

"And I said that I was very happy while he was still in love with me, with or without having my thing. He probably didn't hear me because he went on: 'I started considering the meaning of life too late. It just seemed like a daft concept to me before. Pleasure was the only thing we can attain, at least that's what I thought at the time. I was sure that meaning was just pleasure – one of the forms of pleasure. I thought that doing something meaningful is the same as drinking a good, vintage wine – just one of the ways you can give pleasure to yourself.'

"And then I calmed down, stopped crying, because now I knew what I had to tell Ronia. Then, Marat rose up into the air and we went on a flight together. 'Do you like speed?' he asked me. 'Tell me that you like speed and being naked.' I replied something. Then he said: 'Pleasure is utter crap. Because no amount of the best vintage wine, no amount of sex or the most exquisite food, can make an unhappy person happy again, whereas a meaningful life can. In fact, it's the only thing that can. A meaningful life is the only thing that matters. Pleasure is just decor, a lovely detail, one of those little joys in life, it makes us different to beasts who like to eat, to shit, fart, sleep, and then everything again from the top. It's a beastly life, anyone can do that, it's the state of the lowest castes; but we're not like that, so tell that to Ronia. Of course, she'll already know it – blood ties have a huge effect, but tell her anyway. And tell her that if something doesn't work out in life, she shouldn't throw in the towel, because even the day before death, it's not too late to start everything new.'

"Then we started flying somewhere. 'Where are we flying?' I asked him. I saw the house on Button Street from above; it was night and there was an unusually large moon shining in the sky. Marat was wearing black clothes now. He was on a black horse and the moonlight illuminated his silhouette. It looked scary, but I didn't feel any fear. 'I'm going further,' he said. 'Kiss me, please.' I kissed Marat on the forehead and said to him: 'Don't think you'll get rid of me so easily, I'll come visit you in your dreams.' 'I know. I'll come and see you too,' Marat replied."

CHAPTER 107

Twinka's dad opened the door to her parents' apartment, and Draco immediately noticed his striking resemblance to Twinka. The old man's face had the same static grimace of a smile as hers, except his appeared to be more genuine and kinder. In the first few seconds of their meeting, the greying old man had already managed to charm Draco with his polite manners, his warm smile and his kindly attitude.

"Police?" he asked. "Well, come on in! Come on in, police," he said with good-hearted humour.

Everything in the flat testified to the occupations of its inhabitants. It was crammed with books, concert posters, and string-quartet photographs taken at what looked like prestigious concert halls and events.

Anderson led Draco inside a small living room that had a massive, old-fashioned oval table in its middle, and invited him to sit down.

"Should I call the missis?" he asked.

"Yeah, that would be great. And I'm very sorry that I've come unannounced, but I only have a few quick questions for you." Draco realised that people like them must have thought his impromptu visit tactless and rude, so he tried to soften the impression by any means he could.

"Of course, just a moment." The old man didn't show any signs of discontent or annoyance. Rather, he acted as though Draco's arrival brought some sudden promise of entertainment, which he was now greatly anticipating.

"Excuse me, I'll just go and get her," he said and disappeared into another room.

Meanwhile, Draco continued to examine the flat – at least the part that he could see. It was so different, compared to

Marat and Twinka's house. Everything was smaller, cosier and more personal around here. You could tell that every item had a story. The massive dining table had one; or the vase that was placed on top of it; or that small landscape, painted in bright colours – each object felt deeply personal, full of memories that were important to its masters. The longer Draco remained there, the more taken he felt by the flat's inhabitants.

"She's coming, she's just coming." Old Anderson re-appeared in the door, still smiling. "You know what women are like." He shrugged jokingly, and Draco felt embarrassed again. "I'll go and fetch us some tea or coffee in the meantime – what would you like?"

"Oh, no, thank you, there's really no need," said Draco, trying to talk the old man out of it. But he wasn't listening, clamouring around the part of the kitchen that Draco could see from the living room.

"It's too late for a coffee, it's no good to have it after five," Anderson said. "But we have a really nice Chinese green tea. It's jasmine, I'll fetch you some."

"Okay, sure, if you don't mind." Draco realised that Anderson wouldn't take no for an answer.

While the water was boiling, Anderson brought a small plate with chocolate biscuits into the living room and placed it on the table. Then he carried in the cups, making Draco feel more and more embarrassed with his every move. He was ready to get up and leave; he really didn't need anything, and if he did then he'd already learned everything he needed to learn. But it was too late to leave now.

The tea was ready, but Mrs Anderson still hadn't made an appearance. Draco's awkwardness was palpable.

"How's the investigation going? Have you come across any tracks yet?" Anderson asked, to maintain a conversation.

"We're working on it. We have a few clues, but it's too early to say at this point."

"Of course, of course," Anderson nodded. "By the way, did you know that you have some competition?" he asked with a cunning expression that appeared in his smile.

"What do you mean: competition?"

"Do you know that chauffeur Marat has? The one who was with him in prison at the same time?"

"Theodor. Yes, I do," Draco didn't hide his surprise.

"Well, he's sworn to find and dispose of whoever killed Marat."

"Oh yeah? It doesn't really surprise me, to be honest. It seems like Marat was the only person who'd ever taken care of that boy. I mean, not just taken care of him – he was very generous."

"Yes, yes, yes, that's what I figured, too." Anderson nodded.

"But how did you know that?" Draco asked.

"He swore to Twinka that he would kill Marat's murderer, that's what she told me."

"Oh, I didn't know that. Thank you for the information."

"You're welcome, very welcome." Anderson pushed the little plate with the biscuits towards Draco.

"I wanted to ask you some questions about that morning – you know, the morning of your wife's birthday," Draco started.

"Yes, yes, of course." Producing a shadow of seriousness and worry on his face seemed to require some effort from the old man. "Twinka was here – but you already knew that, didn't you?" he said, achieving said seriousness.

"Yes, that's what I wanted to confirm. What time did she arrive?"

At last, Twinka's mother appeared in the door. A small white dog, only a touch bigger than a cat, ran into the living room with her.

"Don't worry, she's friendly," Twinka's dad rushed to clarify. "Her name is Banga."

Twinka's mum looked much older than her husband, even though they were the same age. She was thin, crooked and tiny. There was no zest for life about her. She'd obviously spent all this time arranging her hair – it was carefully combed, pinned and arranged to give her thinning grey top a bit of volume and curl. She had tried to make herself presentable, and Draco again felt the rudeness of his sudden interruption.

"The police are interested in your birthday." Anderson had resumed his warm humorous tone, greeting his wife by making an exaggerated announcement of Draco's arrival.

"Good afternoon." Mrs Anderson reached out her hand. Draco clumsily, at the last moment, made to get up and squeeze it, but it was too late for him to do so. Twinka's mum had already come too close towards him, so he didn't quite manage to stand. He half-pulled his butt away from the chair, while holding onto the chair with his free hand, and, with the other, very gently squeezed Mrs Anderson's fragile, offered-out palm.

"Yeah, I wanted to ask you some questions about that morning," Draco said, rushing to get it over with. "Do you remember what time Twinka arrived?"

Each Anderson looked at the other, as though expecting help.

"Around ten o'clock, I think," the father said.

"Yeah, probably around then," his wife confirmed.

"Was she alone?" Draco asked.

The question seemed to surprise both Andersons.

"Alone. Yes, she was by herself," the husband replied, his wife nodding.

"Did Ronia come by at all?" Draco continued.

"No, she was in school. Twinka brought us a card from her. Ronia had drawn it herself," Mrs Anderson looked around, searching for the card with her eyes. It had to be around here somewhere...

"Right. And how long did Twinka stay with you?"

The elderly Andersons exchanged a look again, as though seeking the answer to this in the other's eyes.

"Not too long – until twelve o'clock I'd say," Mrs Anderson replied.

"Yes, around twelve," Twinka's father confirmed.

"Did she pop out at any point during that time?"

"No, she didn't," the father replied in a stern tone, as if in judgment of such a silly question.

"Great, that's all from me," Draco said, truly relieved. "I won't keep you or cause you any more inconvenience. Sorry for barging in like this."

"It's okay, don't worry," the elderly couple consoled him, getting up from their chairs. "If there's any way we can help, just say." Twinka's father was smiling a warm and glowing smile.

"Thanks for the tea," Draco said, rushing to leave.

CHAPTER 108

You can't tell she's only sixteen, Draco inferred, examining some of Ronia's photos while he waited to hear back from Lara, who'd gone to visit her school.

Dressed in everyday clothes, Lara resembled a schoolgirl herself. Her build was small and insignificant, and her face was covered in tiny freckles, which meant that she wouldn't cut a conspicuous figure. Ronia's social media channels presented the image of an earnest young woman. She was about one metre seventy, with short, cropped hair. She'd definitely inherited Twinka's slender build and attractive facial features, even though she didn't have her mum and grandad's characteristic quiet smile.

I'd think she was eighteen or nineteen, at least, Draco concluded. The most striking thing about Ronia were the girl's eyes. They were so serious, calm and wise. There wasn't an ounce of childishness about them. She didn't have too many photos online. In fact, her behaviour on social media seemed responsible, slightly guarded and reserved, compared to most adults he'd seen on there. As such, you couldn't tell a lot about her from that alone. She trained in Taekwondo, she loved nature and reading books – those were the only things you could elicit from her profile, although of course there was no guarantee that this itself was a true reflection.

Muscle interrupted Draco's train of thought. "Have you got a minute, boss?" he asked, sticking his head inside Draco's office.

"Yes, sure," Draco said, gesturing for him to take a seat. But Muscle remained standing.

"No news on Dimitri's case, but I've got a witness on Marat's. We found this woman; she's not quite homeless, as she has a room, but she's a bit of a hoarder. She spends her days walking around the area we're interested in, looking for things – that's my understanding, anyway. She checks the rubbish bins, in case anyone has disposed of something useful, and that sort of thing. Anyway, she remembers that day very clearly because there was lots of police around, and the ambulance. And she remembers seeing a priest leave the house on Button Street just before."

"A priest?" Draco repeated.

"Yeah, a priest. A grey-haired man of a medium build, around sixty, with glasses. She's trying to help with his physical likeness at the moment, but she says she doesn't remember his face – all she can remember is that he was a priest, dressed in a priest's clothing, grey-haired and with glasses."

"Is she a reliable witness? I mean, what's the state of her mental health? You said she was a hoarder. They might say she's a schizophrenic in court; that she's made it all up."

"I don't know for sure, but she seems pretty coherent to me. At least she left me with a sane impression. I don't think she's got any serious mental health issues. You could talk to her yourself."

"Yeah, I'd like to see her."

"Her name is Greta, she's with the artist – they're working on a Photofit."

"Is there anything else?" Draco asked while they were walking towards the artist's office.

"We checked Twinka's GPS data from the past month. There doesn't seem to be anything suspicious there. She went to see a psychotherapist once a week, but otherwise she'd go to the shops, take her daughter to school and sometimes collect her after and take her either back home or to Taekwondo – though not every day, as her daughter usually gets the bus from school. Twinka has also been to see her parents a few times, though she's mostly been at home. It doesn't look like she's got a lot of friends. Oh, and she goes to church."

"To church?" Draco repeated.

"Yeah, always on Sundays, though often during the week as well."

"Did you say the priest was grey, with glasses?"

"I don't know. Should we find out?"

"Please," Draco said in a tone that inferred it was of the utmost urgency.

"Hello, Greta," Draco greeted the woman. "How are we doing here?" He looked at the computer. Nothing had come of the Photofit yet.

"We're working on the shape of his glasses and hairstyle at the moment," the police artist explained.

"Why don't you tell me about the priest, Greta?"

"I already told you everything I know," the woman replied, tetchily. "I saw that a priest had been there that morning."

"Have you ever seen him before?"

"No, that was the first time."

"Was he carrying anything?"

"Hmm... I don't think he was."

"Are you sure? A bag or a parcel, or maybe a briefcase?"

"Yeah, actually, I think he had a bag or a briefcase on him. And an umbrella."

"An umbrella?"

"Yeah, he had an umbrella. They forecast slushy snow that day."

"What else can you tell me about him?"

"I don't know..."

"Was he in a hurry? Did he seem anxious to you?"

"Yeah, he was walking quite fast. It was supposed to snow, so he probably wanted to get home quick."

"And you didn't notice anything unusual?"

"No, he looked like you'd expect any priest to look like."

"And where was he going?"

"Towards the railway tracks, but I didn't follow him."

"And when was it – do you remember the time?"

"It was in the morning. I'm not sure when though, probably around eleven."

"Right. Thank you, Greta. You really helped us. If I can steal just a bit more of your time, please be so kind as to help us construct the Photofit. It's really important," Draco squeezed the woman's hand, forcing a smile.

"I'm trying already," the woman growled.

"Right. Let's look for a priest then, shall we?" said Draco as they were walking back. "I'm inclined to believe her. She didn't have any reason to make it up."

CHAPTER 109

Ronia was having some issues in school.

Lara found out that some girl from school had started saying that Ronia wasn't a thief's daughter – she was a killer's daughter, and the tag had stuck:

"Ronia, the killer's daughter."

A fight even broke out, wherein Ronia hit the girl – in the face, and quite hard – though this had only made things worse.

"Ronia, the killer's daughter."

"Ronia, the killer's daughter. She's a killer herself."

"Ronia, are you going to kill me too?"

And so on.

The press and other media outlets had now started publishing extracts from Marat 's trial – both from what was said in court and the judge's final ruling. There was that photo accompanying the headline about how Ronia's mum had miraculously survived.

Ronia's peers had basically started bullying her – in person and on social media. They were quite cruel, and that's what had made Ronia's start missing classes, and which in turn led to her grades declining. The school had reached out to Ronia's parents a few times, but until now they still hadn't managed to organise a meeting because her mother wasn't replying to their emails.

Draco thought of Annabella. What would possibly need to occur for a daughter to decide to kill her own father?

Attempting to murder her mother?

Making her a laughing stock at school?

That might do it, though Draco still couldn't recall a similar case in all his experience. And so he wasn't sure whether he could accept this version.

"How's her mental health?" he asked. "Has she ever had any problems?"

"No, there's nothing about anything like that," said Lara. "She's a perfectly normal child; she studies well, she's into sports, she's not really had any problems until now. They're saying at school that she's inherited the best qualities of her parents. She's smart, beautiful, ambitious, and she loves to compete and prove herself. She's always been an excellent pupil and she's had considerable success in sports to boot. In fact, she's one of the best young Taekwondo athletes in the country. She competes internationally. And she's been able to balance it all. Until now, she's never had any issues. In fact, quite the opposite – any school would be proud to have her."

"I see," Draco said thoughtfully.

"They've known her since kindergarten. They have their own associated kindergarten."

"Right," Draco repeated, almost to himself.

"You know, while I was at the police academy I had this assignment on sexual abuse in children. I can't see any signs here. I spoke to everyone, even the kindergarten teacher. We even dug out some of her old drawings, and there were no signs that Ronia might have ever had any problems. Children who are sexually abused tend to become very withdrawn; they want to remain unseen, and certain characteristic elements appear in their drawings. But Ronia doesn't seem to match that profile. I can't imagine what reasons you could have for wanting to kill someone – I mean, your own father – but I haven't seen anything suspicious that could support it."

"Right. Okay. Let's work out where she was that day, and why Twinka was covering for her – maybe everything will unravel from there. We need to meet with both of them." Draco was resolved. "It's probably best if you try and meet Ronia outside her home. After school, or at school, or... you have a think. If there is any hope that she'll talk, then she'll only talk to you, not me or Muscle. As for Twinka – we need to call her in. I'll talk to her... No. You know what, let's do it at home," Draco said, changing his mind. "I want to see her when Ronia is with her."

"Right," Lara confirmed with a little sigh, as though she was taking in some bad news.

"Well done by the way. Keep it up," Draco said, attempting to gee her up.

"Thank you," she replied politely, though her eyes retained their sadness.

I wonder what's wrong with her? Draco thought to himself. Lara seemed so lonely, so unbecoming and unhappy. Draco felt a desire to help her but chased it away. He didn't believe in the idea of interfering in his colleagues' private lives.

CHAPTER 110

"I'm really sorry, but I need to trouble you again. We need to talk about Ronia." Draco pressed send on the message to Twinka.

She called him back immediately.

"Ronia? What do we need to talk about?" Her tone was a mixture of anger and worry.

"Don't worry, it's nothing major, though I do have a few questions. When could I come over?"

"Come over now if you like." Twinka didn't want to put off meeting the little rat to a later time – she'd only fret over what he wanted.

"Great," Draco said as politely as he could. "I'll be there within the hour."

Twinka let Draco and the freckled Lara into the small guest room, making no attempt to mask her impatience. She was holding a glass of white wine.

"Don't worry, we won't stay long," said Draco. "So, tell me, why wasn't Ronia at school on the day of Marat's murder?"

"What do you mean – she wasn't at school?" Twinka didn't understand.

"Come on, you know that she wasn't at school. We want to know why, and where was she at the time." Although it hadn't been Draco's intention, he heard his tone growing stern.

"Hold on. I don't understand. Why would you think she wasn't at school?"

"What do you mean? You gave the school prior notice that Ronia wouldn't be in due to family reasons. What reasons were these?" Draco was looking Twinka straight in the eye.

"*I* gave them notice? What are you talking about?!" Twinka stared back with wide, confused eyes.

"You sent an email to her school to let them know Ronia wasn't coming in."

Draco searched for the printout in his backpack, so he could show the message to Twinka.

"I didn't send any emails."

"What do you mean? You did." Draco handed the printout to Twinka. "Here."

As Twinka examined the email, her face registered nothing but incomprehension.

"What sort of family reasons? Why wasn't Ronia at school?" Draco repeated, squeezing his lips tight.

"I don't know. I didn't send this message, and Ronia was at school." Twinka took a gulp of the white wine, handing the paper back to Draco. "I don't understand."

"But Ronia wasn't at school." Draco's tone sounded almost strict.

"She wasn't?" Twinka looked genuinely surprised.

"No, she wasn't," Draco confirmed once more.

"And I sent an email message to the school, saying that she wasn't going to be in?"

"Yes, you sent a message. And more than once."

"I don't even use that email. I open it maybe once a month."

"Could Ronia have gained access to your email?" Lara interjected.

There was an expression of disbelief and astonishment on Twinka's face. "I don't know. I wouldn't think so."

"Then you have no idea where Ronia was on that day?" Draco asked.

"No, I don't."

"Okay, in that case – with your permission, would you let us pose the same question to Ronia?" Draco tried to sound compassionate again.

"Sure, go ahead. Roniaaaa!" Twinka shouted. "She might not hear me. I'll give her a bell." Twinka started looking for her phone, though she didn't need to because Ronia had heard her. The girl's footsteps resounded on the stairs.

CHAPTER 111

"Hello, Ronia." Draco greeted the girl as friendly as he possibly could.

"Sit down," Twinka commanded her daughter. She was now the one sounding strict.

"Hi," Lara tried to act casually, treating Ronia like her equal. Her and Draco had agreed beforehand that she'd be the one talking to the girl.

"The police have some questions for you." Twinka sounded angry.

"Dad said that if the police ever ask me anything, I don't have to answer." Ronia remained standing.

"Sit. Down." Twinka's voice was so rigid that what she said sounded like shouting even though she didn't say it loudly.

Her daughter sat down.

"Ronia, we need your help. Will you help us out?" Lara was trying to sound calm, almost matter-of-fact.

Ronia let out an almost imperceptible shrug.

"Tell me, where were you on that day when your dad was attacked?"

Ronia was looking down at the floor without saying anything.

Twinka topped up the wine in her glass.

"We know that you weren't at school – but what were you doing?"

"Nothing. I was cruising around."

"Cruising around?" Lara repeated. "Could you give us a bit more detail, please?"

Ronia shrugged again.

"Are you sending emails to school in my name?" Twinka's question sounded like a threat.

Ronia didn't reply.

"You may not have to answer the police, but you will answer to me!" Twinka was unable to control her anger.

"I was cruising around on my bike," Ronia said, raising her eyes to Lara.

"Now, in winter, on a bike?" Twinka was looking at her daughter, seemingly unsure as to whether she should be angry or surprised.

"All morning?" Lara asked, remaining calm.

Ronia shrugged again, though this time it was meant to convey an affirmative answer – as though she was saying: 'Yeah, all morning, what about it?'

"Did you send a message to school from my email?" Twinka repeated.

"Yeah I did," Ronia snapped back. "You should come up with a password you can actually remember without having stick a note saying "Beaujolais" to the computer."

"Oh, my God." Twinka had a large sip of wine.

"I was following Dad and his lover," Ronia said to Lara quietly.

"What?" Twinka wasn't sure if she'd heard correctly.

"Dad has a lover, one of the older girls in our Taekwondo club." Ronia was addressing Lara, ignoring Twinka.

"A schoolgirl?!" Twinka exclaimed, full of shock and anger. "Oh, my God!"

Although, did it really come as a surprise? Twinka caught herself thinking. *It's obvious that he had a lover. It would be astonishing if he didn't – but right in front of his daughter, with a girl from her club? That head injury must have removed any last behavioural boundaries.*

"She's turning eighteen this year. She doesn't go to school, she just goes to training," Ronia said quietly, still with her eyes cast down.

"But your dad didn't leave the house that day, did he?" Lara asked, maintaining her calm disposition.

"No, he didn't on that day." Ronia shrugged. "But Theodor takes her everywhere in Dad's car. I was on my bike while she was in Dad's car." The anger of a helpless child had crept into Ronia's voice – she was on the verge of tears, though she didn't cry.

"Oh, my God!" Twinka re-exclaimed, this time quietly, before embracing Ronia, having suddenly realised that she was not the one who needed consoling right now.

For a moment nobody spoke.

Twinka needed another drink, so she let Ronia go.

"Ronia, look at me – did you stab your dad?" Lara asked, very seriously.

Ronia shook her head in denial.

"Ronia, do you know who did it?"

"No," Ronia said, almost a whisper.

"Ronia, it's really important. Do you know who did it?"

"No."

The relief in the room was palpable – the questions had been asked and answered.

"Ronia, here's my last question for you: tell me, did your dad ever make you do anything you didn't think was appropriate, or anything that felt weird?"

"No."

Twinka hugged Ronia again.

"Has Dad ever touched you in a way that you felt was wrong? Has he ever made you touch him?"

"Come on! That's crossing the line! You've lost your minds!" exploded Twinka.

"No," Ronia said quietly.

"Ronia, you really helped us today," Lara said. "I'm very sorry, but we had to ask," Lara said, trying to indirectly explain to Twinka.

"Everything is going to be okay, darling." Twinka squeezed her daughter towards her.

Draco gestured to Twinka that they'd let themselves out.

CHAPTER 112

"Did Marat make you drive around that girl from Taekwondo club?" Twinka wasn't sure if she should be angry at Theodor, because it wasn't really his fault. He just did whatever Marat told him to. Even so, she could hear anger in her own voice.

"Sometimes," Theodor gave a reluctant reply.

"How often?"

"Oh, I don't know..." Theodor was clearly feeling embarrassed.

"Go on – how often?"

"A few times a week maybe? Once I took her and her mum to her parents' house in the countryside."

"Marat knew her family?"

"I don't know."

"Where else did you take her?"

"Well, sometimes we'd go to some hotel or a restaurant. Marat used to drive everywhere himself, so I don't know too much."

"Did Marat go to restaurants with her openly?"

"Yeah, I guess. I don't know."

"That one-eyed bastard!" Twinka let out a heavy sigh. "And when did this start?"

"I really don't know. Sometime this year, after we got out."

"Right." Twinka sighed again. She had managed to calm down a little.

"You should ask your father – he saw them together."

"What?!"

"It was in the evening; one of the first times I drove them home. They were saying that your father had seen them somewhere. I don't know – in the hotel or maybe the hotel's restaurant. Marat was worried."

"Fuck." Twinka sat down.

"Some friends of your father's – musicians – were giving a concert, and they were staying at that hotel. Marat was worried you'd find out."

"For fuck's sake!" Twinka used her elbows to balance herself on the table, and dropped her head into her hands.

Sounds like Marat lived by the same principle: that everyone should be fucking more, Theodor thought to himself, but he didn't say it aloud.

"Want some wine?" Twinka asked.

"No, I'm driving."

"Fuck! Then open it at least." Twinka found a bottle of Frantz Chagnoleau Les Raspillères in the cupboard – lately, it had become one of her favourite Burgundy wines – and handed the bottle to Theodor. He took it, removed the cork, placed it on the table, then filled a glass carefully and handed it to Twinka.

"Thank you," Twinka said, collapsing into the chair. "If you ever decide to cheat on your wife, please never do it in a public place where everyone can see. It's a matter of respect. It's just ugly. Why couldn't he allow me that one shred of dignity? Just enough to keep it from my parents." Twinka took a generous gulp, failing to register any trace of the full-bodied composition of the wine.

"Of course. I won't." Theodor sounded like a submissive servant, and Twinka enjoyed it. In fact, with every passing day she fancied him more.

"That bastard! That one-eyed son of a bitch, I'll disconnect him as soon as I get a chance. I'm going to go see that doctor tomorrow, the one who said that I could let things take their natural course."

CHAPTER 113

Twinka didn't tell Keiko about her dream. She simply asked him whether there was a way to check if her therapist's office was tapped, and Keiko had replied straightaway – with no deliberation, and without any hint of astonishment – that he knew some experts who were ninety percent accurate in finding such devices, but he would only be able to organise it if the owner of the property consented. Twinka was sure that Anna wouldn't object, and her and Keiko agreed that next time she went to see her, she'd bring Keiko's boys along. Keiko offered to join, too – just in case.

"It's best if we don't say anything to Anna ahead of our visit," he said.

"Why not?" Twinka didn't understand.

"Best not to." Keiko remained mysterious.

"Okay, fine. If it's so important then I won't say anything," Twinka agreed.

Keiko also suggested that they check the house on Button Street, to make sure that Draco hadn't "forgotten anything". Twinka had noticed that Keiko's attitude towards her had changed, ever since Marat was in a coma. It wasn't obvious – in fact, the difference was barely noticeable – but still she clearly felt the shift.

Now she was the one paying the bills, she had all the power; and the world had started reacting to this before she'd even had the chance to come to terms with it. Someone would pay her more compliments; someone else had become more attentive; and others were still rushing to pledge their allegiance, openly and bluntly. Every day Marat's partners, subordinates and associate entrepreneurs made themselves known to her – whether through email (now checked more frequently, since Ronia's school incident), phone, or via other people. She didn't want to meet any of them; she felt no desire to get involved, or to sort things out. She didn't even want to think about it. But she had started to notice these changes happening all around her.

As Anna opened the door to find Twinka, Keiko (dressed in an expensive suit and sporting a silk pocket square, as usual) and two quiet young men with briefcases, Anna looked properly taken aback. As if she were afraid.

Keiko introduced himself as Twinka's lawyer with the utmost courtesy.

"My client told me that you wouldn't have anything against us checking these rooms, just to make sure there are no illegal listening devices or video recording equipment hidden away." Though he spoke very politely, there was something in his voice that clearly indicated that only an affirmative answer would do.

"Yeah, sure. Of course. Although I must have checked..." she said, still confused.

"I'm sure you did, but you can't be too careful about these things," Keiko said, with a consoling smile. Meanwhile the two young men had opened their briefcases and were busying themselves with their devices. One of them held something on a long telescopic stick that looked like a metal detector, while the other seemed to have set up a miniature radio station. Anna and Twinka watched them work with awe and curiosity.

The two men hadn't even looked at them or said a single word, acting as though the two women weren't even here.

"Tell me, do you often get visits from police representatives?" Keiko asked, turning towards Anna. Twinka smiled. Sometimes Keiko reminded her of Draco. By now, she was experienced enough to understand what he was doing. Just like the police, he was using the effect of surprise – capitalising on Anna's confusion and bafflement to elicit information, without giving her any time to think it over.

"No... No one's been here," Anna said.

"Good, very good," Keiko said in a kind voice, as though he was consoling her. "And they haven't called you in either?"

"No... They haven't." Anna's voice sounded increasingly surprised.

"The attempt on Marat's life is a scandalous, high-profile case and they need a result fast. In such instances, the police are willing to take a rather loose interpretation of their rights." Keiko's tone was soothing.

"I understand," Anna said. It seemed to Twinka like Anna was consumed with anxiety as she watched the specialists at work.

"What a marvellous winter garden," Keiko said, pointing at the window.

"Yeah," Anna replied.

A rather awkward silence descended upon the room, before one of the boys broke it by announcing: "We found a device".

He stretched his hand out towards Keiko, and in it was something that reminded Twinka of a small, black beetle, with shiny whiskers, a few millimetres long.

"We've got one more," the other guy said, holding another tiny device. This one was a small, dark rectangle.

"Do these belong to you?" Keiko asked Anna.

"No!" Anna replied, and her astonishment felt genuine to Twinka.

"Would you object if we borrowed them for a couple of days to run some tests and investigate this further?" Keiko's tone had become very serious.

"No. Of course not."

Another awkward silence hung over the room. Twinka realised that she was enjoying the situation. Maybe it was the power that she felt, or the fact that her dream had turned out to be true, or maybe some completely unknown reason – but she was enjoying seeing Anna look so scared and confused. It would be perfect if she had a glass of champagne now.

The silence seemed to last forever, until finally one of the boys nodded to Keiko, signalling that they were finished.

"Excellent. It looks like we're all done here! Thank you very much, and please accept my apologies for the intrusion," Keiko said politely, smiling again.

Twinka admired the speed at which both specialists packed their equipment back into the briefcases. They managed to collect their stuff and leave all in a matter of minutes, and without saying another word.

Keiko stayed behind in the front room. "Are you coming with us?" he asked Twinka.

"I'll stay here a little longer," Twinka said; and, moments later, Keiko too was gone.

"Dreams are so fascinating," she said to dispel the uncomfortable atmosphere that had settled in the room after Keiko and his specialists had left.

"Yeah, they sure are," Anna agreed, but her eyes were wandering around the room, as though looking for something to latch on to.

"Well, I guess there's no point in us talking about anything else today," Twinka said, looking at her watch theatrically. In fact, she would have liked nothing more than to talk all this through with Anna, but she could see that Anna wasn't ready.

"Yes." Anna forced a laugh. "That's enough for today."

CHAPTER 114

"Thoughts?" Draco asked Lara when they were in the car.

"It's tough on the girl, that much is clear. They bully her at school because she's a murderer's daughter, and in her afterschool club because her father is sleeping with one of the girls. It's horrible when your peers laugh at you, haunting you at school and outside too." Lara spoke with understanding and compassion, making Draco wonder whether she knew this situation all too well.

"But was she so desperate and angry that she was capable of murder?"

"I don't know. Not everyone can kill somebody – but to kill your own father? I don't know. I highly doubt it, if I'm honest. She's unhappy, desperate and lonely. She's bullied and humiliated by friends while her mother drinks and doesn't notice what's going on around her. That's incredibly tough at that age, of course. She probably blames her dad for everything – but to go so far as to kill him?"

"Often though it's teenagers who are the most ruthless," Draco said, as though trying to convince himself. "They don't know fear and they don't know the consequences of their actions."

"Hmm, I'm not sure... To stab someone? Twice, with a knife? Your own father? There'd have to be some extreme history of abuse, and even then it would be hard to believe. And nothing speaks to that here."

"In the recording Marat asks what's happened. So, most likely, it was someone who knew him, whose presence in the house didn't come as a surprise. I don't think he'd say that if he suddenly saw a complete stranger in his house."

"True," Lara agreed.

"And it's very strange that at the hospital Marat didn't want to tell me anything about the murderer while he was still conscious. He could have said something, but he didn't want me to catch the killer. He was protecting his own assassin." Draco was driving slowly, like he wanted their journey to last longer.

"No fingerprint marks were found on the blade, which means that it wasn't a spontaneous act of rage, but something pre-planned and pre-prepared," Lara said. "Can we picture Ronia doing it?"

"Maybe... She knew that her mum was going to Nan's that day. And she had sent an email to her school from her mum's account, saying she wouldn't be in," Draco said, though he sounded unconvinced.

"I don't know..." Lara too remained sceptical.

"At the end of the day, she takes after her father. It wouldn't surprise me if Marat has managed to raise someone with the same beliefs he has. There are the 'little people' – slaves, sheep, the crowd – and then there are the upper castes, the chosen ones, people with a capital 'P', and for them murder is always an option, often the best one. Morality – and ethics, with its notions of good and evil – that's all just a control mechanism for the crowd, the slaves, the sheep. Real warriors and aristocrats do what they have to do in order to reach their goals. Maybe her father was causing too much chaos in her life. What more could he give her? What else was left for him in life? He'd already accomplished everything; he'd done everything he possibly could in his life. What more could he do – climb Mount Everest again? Make some more millions? What's the point? There isn't one. He'd spend the rest of his life seeking out trite experiences and sleeping with her girlfriends. He'd be better off if he was dead, before he ended up a pathetic old sugar daddy. Right?"

"And she knows that she won't have to talk to the police. Plus she's underage, so she won't have to face a real punishment for it," Lara added, her voice now bursting with respect and admiration for Draco. She was really pleased that her first experience of working under a police superior was him. *I'll learn so much from him,* Lara thought.

"Like father, like daughter. The apple never falls far from the tree. It wouldn't surprise me," continued Draco in the meantime. "And what about Taekwondo? Not a very girly choice, is it?"

"But she did talk to us."

"Yeah, but maybe it's all just a setup. Maybe Ronia wanted to tell us and her mum about her dad's lover. As soon as she'd said it, no one was angry at her for hacking some stupid email account. She's just manipulating us. Well, at least with her mum. And let's not forget that she's the one who actually found Marat. He was still alive when Twinka got there. The assault had only just happened, and Ronia was sat on the stairs. If she wasn't sixteen, if she was an adult, then she'd be our main suspect, based on these two factors alone."

"Very true," Lara agreed, though reluctantly. "So, what's our plan now?"

"To do absolutely nothing." Draco laughed. "I have another version of events – probably a more likely one."

"Really? Who?" Lara was baffled. Draco had only just managed to convince her that the culprit was Ronia.

"I need to do a bit more work on it." For the time being, Draco didn't want to disclose anything further.

CHAPTER 115

"Now, my love. I hope you can hear me, so listen up," Twinka said, sitting at Marat's bedside. She had brought a fresh bunch of flowers for his room, cut the stems and placed them in a vase.

"Listen to me very carefully. Your situation is very grim. I went over everything and thought about it long and hard, and I'm sure that you'll understand and support my decision. Ronia and I, we don't need a Schumacher in our house. To keep you going in this state for years – that's a huge burden. It's a terrible mess. You understand that, don't you? Financially, psychologically, and emotionally. A father who's just lying there for years – that's such bad energy, it will only get in the way of us living our lives. Even if you did emerge from the coma, you'll likely be disabled, so unfortunately there just isn't a good outcome for you either way. A pathetic existence, stretching on for years. There's practically no joy in that. Besides, I'm going to divorce you anyway. I'll most likely start a new family: you know how I've always wanted to have another child. This is my last chance to make it happen. I still have so many options left; I can start all over again if I want to, it's not too late for me. As for you though... I'm afraid there's nothing good left ahead of you. Of course, none of it is your fault – I'm just relaying the facts. Life is so cruel towards old, decrepit, incapable men. On the other hand, if you were to die, we'd arrange a spectacular funeral for you. We'd grieve for a bit and remember all the good things. But life would continue its course, maybe flowing even stronger than before. It will be best for everyone. It's nature's law – I'm sure you understand that better than anyone, don't you? So, that's it really." Twinka exhaled audibly and got up from the seat. She grasped Marat's hand and stood by his bed, looking down at him. "It's a real pity you can't say anything back. I'd be very interested in hearing your thoughts on all this. Euthanasia, you know. Relieving the suffering of a doomed, irreparable patient. It's a good death – it's the last thing I can still do for you. You'll always be the love of my life, and we have a wonderful daughter together. Thank you for giving me all that." Twinka kissed Marat on the forehead. "Goodbye." Her own speech had moved her, and she rushed out of the ward, worried the sentimentality of it might make her burst into tears or – worse still – change her mind.

Twinka couldn't remember the name of the doctor who'd mentioned the option of *letting nature take its course,* so she asked the nurse if she could speak to one of Marat's team. It turned out to be the very same man Twinka had been looking for.

She examined him carefully. He wore glasses and he looked tired. He was a skinny man of indeterminable age who didn't leave any distinct impression.

"I'm so glad I can speak to you, Doctor. Has anything changed?" Twinka asked in a friendly manner, unable to completely conceal her nerves.

"No." The doctor sighed. "His condition hasn't changed. There's little hope I'm afraid."

"I wanted to tell you that I'm not a supporter of stubbornly going against God's plans. I don't know how things work around here – in terms of the law and whatnot – but if I need to sign somewhere or explain my will in some other way, or if you need my permission..." Twinka was struggling to say what she wanted to say.

"I understand," the doctor came to her aid, nodding energetically.

"I'm ready for everything. If you need anything from me, if..." As they so often were, Twinka's eyes were cast down. "I just want everything to take its natural course, and for all of this to end."

"Of course. I understand, madam. That's usually how these sorts of cases go. You can't help him," the doctor tried to soothe her.

"Then you understand what I mean." Twinka didn't want to drag the conversation out – for some reason she was embarrassed to look the doctor in the eye. "Just give me a call or let me know if you need anything from me," she added, before leaving with hurried steps. She didn't want to return here. Ever.

"Yes, madam, I will," she heard the doctor say behind her.

CHAPTER 116

This swing was bigger than the one she'd fallen out of in childhood, though its construction looked the same. Twinka was swinging up, Marat pushing her higher and higher. They were laughing and she felt that pleasant tingling in her stomach that usually signalled a powerful arousal – the kind that radiates through your entire body and makes you shut your eyes, so that nothing can distract from it. Twinka surrendered to the flow of the swing. She was holding on tight; she wasn't going to fall. The swing was safe, and Marat was beside her, so the sensation of fear felt pleasant. Every time the swing reached its apogee, it froze momentarily before then crushing back down at speed. Up she went, catching her breath, her heart skipping a beat – and then back down again. Up and down, and up again. It felt like she was flying through space, and time stood still – there was nothing except the flight itself, a barely noticeable pause at the highest point, and then she was off again. There was no fear; only pure, unadulterated joy...

Marat was inside her, squeezing her towards him – they were tumbling through a bed filled with endless sheets and pillows – then Twinka was on top of him, pressing herself against him just as tightly as he had, then he was back on top again. They soared over cities, houses and church spires, going up and back down again. Twinka's heart would skip a beat intermittently, just as it had at the swing's zenith. They were flying over fields and hamlets now – Twinka was wearing a white wedding dress, which flowed like a white billow as she flew.

Suddenly, she was falling.

Something was wrong. She couldn't fly anymore and she was falling out of the sky, the white wedding dress flapping around her like an unopened parachute. Terror seized her; she was about to die... Just then, the swing hit her hard in the face. Her white wedding dress was covered in blood and Marat was standing next to the swing, laughing. It wasn't an evil laugh – he was laughing as though he'd witnessed something funny, something that resembled a joke. Then, out of the blue, a volleyball came flying towards Twinka and hit her on the head.

Luckily, that's when her dad showed up. He kicked the horrid ball away from her and helped Twinka to get up again. He pressed her tightly towards him, and she was happy once more. She was a small child in a cosy room. Winter raged behind the window, and there were pots simmering away on the stove. Two little lambs were hiding in one of the corners of the room, and Dad was sat in another, tuning his violin. Twinka didn't linger here – she left, flying out through the window. She could still make out the tiny house with Mum and Dad for a long time, but she was still leaving. A bright, unnaturally large moon was shining in the sky. It didn't feel familiar. It felt foreign, cold and scary. Twinka felt so lonely and vulnerable. She was cold, very cold...

Then she woke up. A freezing winter gale had pushed the window wide open. It was still nighttime, but Twinka didn't feel like going back to sleep. *There's no moon tonight,* she managed to observe, shutting the window.

"My thing" was to love you. That was the whole purpose of my life. Is it possible to start your life all over again, a day before death, if the only real thing you ever felt in your life was love towards that one person? It's not possible to re-live that, from the beginning. What am I going to do all by myself, with Ronia being almost an adult now? Maybe I could still have another child? Will that give me answers to all my questions? Is that even ethical – to desire a child only to imbue your own life with some sort of meaning? Do I even truly want to have it – and with whom? Should I get pregnant from the chauffeur? Surely not...

566

She got up and put some music on. 'Diamonds and Rust'. Her watch was displaying 04.44. She decided to have a snack. She took some paté out of the fridge and found a crusty but edible nugget of bread, pausing to decide on what beverage would best compliment her meal. She decided in favour of a glass of dessert wine. Sauternes and foie gras – what could be better than that? She remembered Marat's law: if the wine is thirty years old, then it's impossible to make a mistake. It was worth going down to the cellar to look for one – she was sure they had an old bottle of Sauternes somewhere.

"No amount of pleasure can make a desperate person happy again." *That's the sort of thing Marat used to preach. It's probably true; but still, it's a bit more bearable to be in despair if you have some vintage Sauternes to have with your foie gras,* Twinka replied to him in her thoughts.

CHAPTER 117

"Those listening devices weren't planted by the police," Keiko said. He had rung Twinka to tell her the news. "The experts are sure this isn't police equipment. Police don't use such devices. They're too expensive; and, at the same time, not as good as the ones the police use."

"What are you saying?"

"Well, the only thing we know for certain is that someone had been listening in on your conversations with the therapist, as well as the other conversations she was having in her office, but we can rule out the police. It was a private third party. We also know that the devices we removed haven't been active for some time – the batteries were flat, and would have been for a while. They can work for two, three weeks tops, depending on the length of the recording, before they need changing."

"A private third party?" Twinka repeated. "I don't understand."

"There are numerous possibilities, but if you were to ask my opinion then, candidly speaking, I sincerely hope that this third party was related to you, rather than being a complete stranger. And I believe such a possibility exists."

"Marat?!" exclaimed Twinka, when she realised what Keiko was trying to tell her.

"Of course, we don't know for certain, but we can't exclude the possibility." Twinka felt Keiko carefully choose each word. "But anyway, since we know it definitely wasn't the police, we need to work out who it could be. Whose resources and psychological profile matched the action? Let's just say that I wouldn't rule out that option."

"Marat? He wanted to know what we were talking about?"

"Of course, it would have been easier to ask him directly. As I say, we don't know for certain. We don't have any hard evidence, but from the information we do have, it wouldn't be – how should I put it – the first case in history whereby a spouse has displayed a desire to control their partner."

"I don't believe it," Twinka said instinctively, though her tone suggested quite the opposite.

"I'm telling you all this because we need to be careful in terms of next steps and how we process this information. I don't think it's worth causing a scandal, in case that only makes things worse for ourselves."

"Interesting..." Twinka said, suddenly conscious that she was parroting one of Anna's expressions. "Do you think Anna knew about it?"

"I don't know, but I think we can't exclude that possibility. But, as I say, I don't know."

"Interesting," Twinka repeated, having managed to fully calm herself. "Thank you for the information."

"It's best not to tell the police for now. They don't need to know everything."

"Yes, of course. Thanks again." Twinka wanted to end their conversation. She needed time to digest the news.

And there were two pieces of news. One – Marat had been listening in on her conversations with Anna. This itself wasn't easy to comprehend, and she needed more time to process it. But the second piece of news that Twinka had picked up on during their conversation was much easier to digest. Even though it was only a small detail, and it wasn't spelled out, she noticed that Keiko had seen and heard her. He had always been very polite and respectful towards Twinka, but he never left any doubt over the fact that his client was Marat and his job was to represent Marat's interests, and those alone. Something about Keiko's tone of voice and attitude towards Twinka had definitely shifted. Even though it was elusive, it was clear that he was now representing her interests. He was her lawyer now, which in turn meant Keiko was no longer considering Marat's return as a realistic possibility. Everyone had recognised her, Twinka, as the leader of the kingdom henceforth. The king was dead – long live the queen. This was the exact moment it had shifted. Marat's team was now working for her.

Twinka hadn't expected for the changes to happen so soon, let alone so smoothly and so blatantly. Marat hadn't even been buried yet – he wasn't even dead! – yet they'd already written him off. Despite encountering this huge shift, Twinka didn't feel anything different to how she'd feel if she were, say, witnessing a cow birthing a calf. It was simply nothing special: this sort of thing took place every single day, and had done so for thousands of years. The only difference was that she'd never witnessed it first-hand before now.

Alright then, she thought to herself. She decided she wasn't going to worry about it.

Anna was a different matter, however. On what level was Anna involved in all of this? Had she been hiding something this entire time? And who should she talk all this over with, if she could no longer talk to Anna? Oh God, it was all just horrid...

Alcohol helps to stop thinking – wasn't that what Anna had said?

That's wonderful – I don't want to think about it either. For the moment at least, I want to stop thinking about it all.

CHAPTER 118

"Did you really think you could buy a friend with money?" Twinka couldn't see Marat, but she recognised his voice. "I used to think you could, but it turns out you can't. You can buy almost anything with money, except all the things that matter. Real friendship, genuine respect, actual success. The only thing I'm not sure about is love – you might be able to buy that with money." Marat laughed. They were drinking *Cristal*.

"You can't buy happiness with money either. Only something short-term. And you can only feel the effect if you used to be poor. Then it's fun, at first – for a year, maybe two at most... And then now you'd have had your fill of P2 or P3 and it no longer makes you happy. And you thought you could buy yourself a friend? How naïve!"

Twinka was amazed that Marat seemed so chirpy and well. *But you're dead! Are dead people supposed to be so smug?* she thought to herself.

"So: you thought that somebody, who gets paid by the hour, was your friend? It's like falling in love with a prostitute. She's just doing her job. You're nothing more than a client to her, and clients come and go. It's nothing personal, and yet you thought she was your friend," Marat repeated.

"Why did you have to listen in on my conversations with Anna?" Twinka asked.

"You used to cheat on me. Or have you forgotten already?"

"No, I remember..." A wave of guilt washed over her as she said it.

"I knew you were cheating on me. I felt it right away. It was written all over your face, it came out in your behaviour – everything. I instantly knew what was going on."

"But you didn't know it was Dimitri."

"Yes. That I didn't know. At first, I wanted to spy on you, but then I thought I'd only gain some superficial information that way. I wanted more – I wanted *everything*. I wanted to know every single detail, which is why I came up with the whole Anna scheme. I wanted to know all your reasons and emotions. I wanted to understand."

"And did you?" Twinka asked.

"Anna believed that it's best to wait until you're ready to start talking about the cheating part yourself – she didn't want to rush you. Still, it was very interesting."

"What you did was horrid. It's so bad, it makes me feel sick." Twinka's face twisted. "It's worse than reading someone's diary – it makes me want to wash and scrub myself all over, like I'm covered in dirty handprints."

"Now, now." Marat laughed, making faces at her. "Should I remind you that you're the one who invited the police to kit out our home with listening devices? That you made every attempt to send me back to prison? How many dirty handprints are on me? Or should I remind you about your conversation with the doctor and how you're against resisting God's divine plan? Don't you think that by resisting God's plans you've taken on the role of God yourself? You practically commissioned my murder. How are you any different from me?"

How does he know all this?! Twinka thought intensely, trying to figure it out. *There's no way he could possibly know!*

"So, in the end, as to who's the bigger bastard of the two of us – we could have a nice long debate over that." Marat smiled smugly.

"You, of course. You're to blame for everything," Twinka said, though her voice sounded warm, rather than aggressive. Even in her sleep she suddenly felt the desire to drink. "How did this happen? We had such a good start, and now we're arguing over who's the biggest bastard and who can produce the longest rap sheet?" Twinka was asking. Or was she hearing her own thoughts?

"At least our lists are pretty impressive." Marat laughed. "Not every couple could boast something like that."

"How can you be *so* bad?" Twinka asked. "How could you even come up with the idea to kill a person?! I just don't get it. How could you even imagine setting someone up with a psychotherapist and then listening in on what they were talking about? You're a bad, evil person."

"At least you can't say it's been boring being with me." Again, Marat laughed. "There's no greater evil in this world than living an unfulfilling, boring and tedious life. Yet so many people do! They're dead, empty, they're nothing but the shell of their bodies. To eat, shit and fuck – that's all they're living for, like they're a cross between a pig and a rabbit."

Twinka wanted to drink, so she decided to wake up. Her desire for alcohol was much stronger than that of continuing her conversation with Marat. She opened her eyes and got out of bed. She threw on her dressing gown and went into the kitchen. She popped a bottle of champagne and poured it straight into a basic Bordeaux glass.

I'm not miserable. I'm not! she realised suddenly. *Things aren't that bad. I have a brilliant life. Maybe it's not exactly as I'd imagined it, and not quite the glittering existence we had for the first ten years of our marriage, but you can't say it's been boring. It's been exciting, full of all sorts of intense experiences and events. And I'm only forty. I can survive without any of them. I'll get by without Marat, if I have to. Maybe I'll do even better than I have done until now.*

The glass was empty, so she poured herself another one. For the first time in her life, Twinka suddenly realised herself as an adult: a separate, autonomous being, independent from everyone.

I'm fine, and everything's going to be fine. Thank you, my poor pirate! Thank you for everything. In just a few large sips, Twinka had emptied the second glass. A tiny burp escaped her lips. The time was nine forty-seven a.m. *It's fine. I'm fine. And I still have a whole lifetime ahead of me. Everything is going to be fine.*

CHAPTER 119

"Oh, hi! How have you been?" Anna was all smiles as she greeted Twinka. She seemed a bit too friendly.

"I'm fine," Twinka said coldly, taking her time to settle into the chair. Anna had picked up on Twinka's strange energy, but she didn't say anything. "I've got lots of news to share," Twinka continued, as frigid as before.

"Go on – start from the beginning." Anna was keeping up her friendly tone.

"Actually, you could really help me with some advice," Twinka started, slowly. "You probably know all about these sorts of things."

"Of course! How can I help?" Anna's tone and body language signalled a sincere readiness to rush to Twinka's aid and do whatever it took to help.

"Tell me what happens if, say... I don't know... A therapist tapes all her private conversations with a client or a patient against their will and hands them over to a third party? Surely, there must be a law against that sort of thing – or is it purely a question of professional ethics? Where do people usually go to seek help when this happens – do you take them straight to court, or is there a professional organisation you can submit your grievances to? Or a government institution that certifies people like you? What's the standard process? I don't really know much about these things. What's the process for taking away your professional licence or getting some sort of compensation – how do these things normally work?"

"Oh, Twinka..." Anna sighed heavily. For the last fortnight she'd lived in fear of this conversation. "I really didn't know about it – it's been a shock for me too."

"I don't believe you." Courageously, Twinka was looking Anna straight in the eye. She'd come prepared for this conversation. "I don't believe that Marat had installed listening devices without your consent."

"Are you sure it was Marat?" Anna asked. Any trace of a smile had disappeared from her face, and she looked gravely serious.

"Yeah, it's a fact," Twinka answered confidently.

"Right," Anna said, almost to herself.

"You haven't answered me – where should I turn to report this serious offence?"

"Twinka, I understand that you're angry. It's absolutely normal, given the circumstances, but you have to believe me – I had no idea."

"There must be some institution that can investigate offences committed by a psychotherapist. Or I could just go straight to the press. I recently found out that Marat had an entire PR department. They've been coming to me for work, so this would be a great story to give them."

"Twinka, believe me, I'm not your enemy. I've never done anything to harm you."

"What do you mean? To let my husband listen in on our conversations – did you think that was in my best interests? How much did he pay you? I'd say pretty well, judging by that brand new Porsche Macan you have."

"You have to believe me that this situation is very distressing, probably more for me than you. I have other patients too, and... Well, let's just say that our conversations wouldn't be half as interesting for other people's ears as theirs."

"Oh yeah?"

"Twinka, you have to know that you're a very strong woman with very good mental health. Everything is okay and you're dealing with the sort of problems and hardships we all encounter in life pretty well. But I have other clients who don't. I have patients whose thoughts, fantasies and anxieties go well beyond anything that people who have never come across such things could even imagine. If this came out in the media, their lives would be destroyed. Literally, their lives would be in danger. Do you understand how serious it is? They're struggling to find any reason to live as it is; they wouldn't be able to cope with the fact that their deepest darkest secrets have come to light. It could break up their marriage for some of them, yet the consequences would be catastrophic for *all* of them. Trust me, it's not me I'm worried about," Anna pleaded, in a desperate voice.

"Fine. Then you better explain to me how Marat was able to set up these listening devices here?"

"I didn't know they existed." Anna collapsed in the chair. Her energy was spent.

This was the perfect moment to launch a full-scale attack on Anna, so Twinka asked her the most important question: "How do you know Marat?" She realised that Anna didn't know how much Twinka knew, which undoubtedly gave her the upper hand.

"I'll tell you everything I know, if you promise to help me." Anna looked like a wreck. Twinka didn't reply, and it didn't look like Anna was expecting an answer from her. "Marat was my client before you," Anna said.

"Your client? But he doesn't even believe in psychotherapy!"

"And that's why he didn't want anyone to know. He didn't fully believe in it, but he had decided to try it, in case he found something that did work for him. You know how obsessed he was with self-improvement. Education, sports, well-being... The constant drive to be better than everyone at everything. Naturally, he wanted to explore every method and avenue that might help him."

"Right," Twinka sounded surprised.

"He didn't come very often, and it was before we met. We had a good connection."

"Okay, and what happened next?" Twinka was becoming impatient.

"We talked about your marriage. We talked about you, of course, and he came up with the suggestion for you to come and see me. He thought it could help you – he was worried about your dependency on alcohol; he thought you were depressed, and that alcohol was your cure. And yes, he thought you had a lover."

"And you agreed to discover everything for him? To gain my trust and then tell him everything he wanted to know?"

"No. It wasn't like that."

"Oh yeah? How was it then?"

"He didn't want you to know that he'd been my client. I objected – I said that it wouldn't be proper, but he said he'll just stop coming, that he didn't need it anyway. He preferred me working with you. And that's when you called. That's how it all started."

"And you didn't feel it appropriate to tell me?"

"I shouldn't have agreed to have you as a patient in the first place, but officially Marat was no longer my client and I'm not allowed to disclose information about one client to another. And it seemed like there would be no harm done to anyone. I really didn't mean to cause anyone any harm."

"Right. And what happened next?"

Anna sighed and paused for a moment. She was trying to get hold of herself. "Marat would show up sometimes. Well, you know him – he loves to show up, out of the blue. I wouldn't call it therapy. We were just chatting."

"Did you have sex?" Twinka was astonished and excited at how brave and direct her question had come out. Had she learned that from Draco?

"No, we didn't," Anna answered, though her tone didn't sound particularly convincing.

"Okay, whatever, I'm not interested in that – I want the recordings," Twinka said with a certain forgiveness in her voice.

"I did have my suspicions at first, but I didn't pay much attention to them. It felt odd that he wasn't asking me much about you. He did show an interest, but it was always quite casual – he didn't try to find everything out. That felt suspicious to me. This behaviour felt neither natural nor characteristic of him. Once I even asked him – 'Are you not going to ask me anything about Twinka?' And he said something like – 'No, I already know everything I need to know'. Something felt wrong, but I thought he was just acting that way so I wouldn't feel like I was caught in the middle. I remember thinking he was being very genteel."

"So genteel that you decided to sleep with your ex-patient who was also your current patient's husband?" Twinka felt a foreign and cruel pleasure from having so much power over Anna. "To ask me all about sex, to lecture me that a good relationship is characterised by conversations and sex while you're the one having all the sex and the conversations with my husband?" Twinka continued to launch her attack.

"That's not how it was," Anna said, her voice barely audible. She didn't resist, as though she was letting Twinka enjoy her moment. But then she managed to pull herself together. "Twinka, I have one request. I'm begging you – could you have a look through Marat's stuff? If these recordings do exist, then they should be destroyed. Not the ones from your sessions – you can do whatever you like with them – but there must be other recordings with the rest of my patients, and they need to be destroyed. Do you understand? It's really important."

"I'll have a look," Twinka said, her tone cold and careless, as she rose from the chair.

Anna didn't walk her to the door.

CHAPTER 120

Twinka was woken early by a call from the hospital. Her watch was showing five fifty-five a.m.

Having recognised the hospital's number and spotted the symmetrical numbers on her watch display, Twinka's heart filled her chest with a single, powerful beat. Or maybe two. She had been expecting and fearing this phone call, and finally it was here.

"Good morning, I'm sorry to call you so early," a tired but professional voice of a woman said down the receiver.

Twinka didn't recognise it.

"I'm listening," Twinka said, almost inaudibly, after the woman had introduced herself.

"I wanted to tell you that your husband woke up from his coma during the night. His condition is stable and he's able to communicate, so you can come and visit him."

"Marat?"

"There's a long road of recovery ahead of him still; but, besides that, our prognosis is quite positive."

Whether it was the effect of sleep or the unexpected news, Twinka found it hard to gather her thoughts. She knew that she wanted to ask questions and find out more, but she didn't know what she should ask. "Many thanks," was the only thing she managed to say.

"You're welcome." The woman had put the phone down before her words had properly resounded through the receiver.

His prognosis is positive? He's going to live?

Oh, you bloody pirate! A smile broke out on Twinka's face. *How many lives do you have?!*

Her tiredness had gone completely. She wanted to share the news with Ronia as soon as possible, but she decided to let her sleep.

You bloody old pirate. Such news!

CHAPTER 121

The Easter weekend was windy, cold and overcast this year. The sun didn't show its face. The winter was retreating unwillingly: as though it had only just realised that it hadn't done enough while it still had the chance, and, now that it was no longer capable of doing much, had become stubborn, refusing to leave completely.

Banga, the white West Highland terrier that belonged to Twinka's parents, didn't seem too bothered by it though. Anderson had taken the dog out for a walk, following it along the park trails; patiently stopping every few metres to let Banga sniff around and mark yet another tree, shrub, bench, stone, or some other inanimate object.

Draco had purposefully come to the park to see Anderson. He couldn't fully explain it to himself, but he wanted to talk to Anderson one-on-one, on unofficial business. He caught up with him on a trail next to the pond.

"For a dog," he addressed Anderson, gesturing towards Banga, "the park is like social media."

"Yes, it's the internet of dogs – so much information, and it changes every day," answered Anderson in the same tone of voice.

"Do you walk her every day?"

"You must be joking. Of course! Sometimes even twice a day. I usually take her out in the morning, then my wife walks her in the evening – she prefers the dark. And it's healthy for us oldies to get out for a walk too – maybe it's even more important for us than the dog."

"Yeah, I know what you mean," Draco agreed. He hated this kind of mindless small talk. He didn't enjoy it and he didn't know how to have it.

"I'm counting my steps. I try to walk at least seven thousand a day; I think that should do it. We usually do about five thousand a day with Banga."

"I know who murdered Marat," Draco said, interrupting Anderson.

"You do?" Thomas Anderson was now looking straight into Draco's eyes with a quizzical gaze. That same, erasable smile that Draco had so often seen on Twinka's now adorned her father's. They were very similar, although Thomas's eyes were kinder and energetic, and they had more lustre than Twinka's. He was looking at Draco without any hate or fear, as though he was getting ready to give him praise.

"Why, how did you manage to work that one out?" Anderson didn't disguise his curiosity.

"I guess it started with a witness we found. From there it was pretty simple."

"I see," Anderson said, turning his attention back to the dog.

"You know, I have this rule – it's really important to me that the criminal confesses his crime."

"Oh, how interesting. And do you often succeed?"

"Sometimes." Draco was evasive. "I think it's really important that the murderer understands that what they did was wrong and regrets what they did. Because if they don't they'll still remain a murderer, no matter how long they spend in prison. But, as a true believer, you probably understand all this better than me. Their soul will remain broken, they'll never be able to regain inner peace, and they'll never receive forgiveness."

"You sound like a sage," Anderson said. Draco couldn't detect any irony in his voice. "You must come to our church sometime and speak to the youth at the Sunday school."

Draco didn't reply.

"I'm being serious," Anderson insisted.

"And I'm saying, very seriously, that I know who did it," Draco answered. There was impatience in his voice.

"I understand." Anderson changed his tone, worried that Draco had interpreted his invitation to come to Sunday school as a sign of disrespect and arrogance. "You know what I'm going to say in response to that?" This time, Anderson chose his words carefully. "That there are some murderers who will never regret what they did."

Banga marked a small tree for the third time.

"I wouldn't have believed it myself, but now I'm wondering whether there are murders that can be considered as good work," Anderson said solemnly.

"A murder cannot be good work by definition. But you already know that. Committing a murder is in breach of the law," Draco objected, albeit not too passionately.

"Do you have children, sir?" Anderson asked.

"I do, but they've got nothing to do with this conversation."

"Well, the reason I ask is because if you do, then you may be able to understand how people are capable of anything for their children's sake. And you know what? I think it's only right."

"There's nothing wrong with parents protecting their children, but there are certain boundaries that no one should be allowed to cross." Draco was irritated and made no attempt to hide it. He didn't like it when people mentioned Annabella. No one was allowed to touch her – not even in their thoughts or words.

"You think such boundaries exist?" A sad but warm smile adorned Anderson's face.

"Of course! You're crossing a boundary, if it involves taking another person's life."

"Then let me ask you this. If your underaged daughter was raped and kidnapped by a paedophile, wouldn't you be prepared to kill him to set your daughter free? Wouldn't you?"

"Stop with all this demagogy – your daughter is forty years old and she hasn't been kidnapped by a paedophile."

"Of course... Still, indulge me with this thought experiment. In a hypothetical situation, wouldn't you be ready to murder that paedophile?"

"The law is the only thing that protects us from chaos. The law must be upheld because it's the law. That's just how it is."

"If I may, you didn't answer my question. Let's pretend, just for a moment, that your underaged daughter was kidnapped by a paedophile who had – God forbid – hurt her in some way. Wouldn't you kill him?"

"I wouldn't want to get into that situation," Draco succumbed, entering into Anderson's thought experiment.

"Of course – nobody would, but unfortunately, we do get sucked into these situations. Very unfortunate situations."

"The law is the only thing that can protect us. If the law has no authority, then we're doomed – all of us. Not only our daughters but everyone. Without the law we'd devolve to being wild beasts: where only the strongest have rights, and where everyone wages war on everyone else. It's the worst possible thing that could happen to a society," Draco said firmly, as though repeating, for the umpteenth time, some text he'd learned off by heart.

"I'm not arguing against it – the law is the best thing that we have – but life is so complicated that, unfortunately, the law doesn't always protect us. For instance, the law failed to protect Dimitri. Or are you going to tell me that he committed suicide?"

"Mmm." This barely audible moan escaped Draco's lips.

"And you can't... I mean, *the law* isn't able to bring Dimitri's murderer to justice. And we're talking about a murderer who's committing his second crime, undoubtedly getting better with every attempt. With all due respect, sir, he's better than you. He wasn't punished for attempting to murder my daughter either. Sounds like your law isn't up to the job."

"Well, anyway, you can't go around and lynch people. You have to understand that, the moment you do, everyone will start dishing out judgement according to their personal beliefs, because they think they know who the culprit is, what actually happened, and what's the right thing to do. Can you imagine the chaos that would unleash? Do you realise that you're no different to Marat?"

"Oh? How so?" Anderson looked genuinely surprised. "Is there really no difference between me and a murderer who almost also succeeded in killing his wife, simply because he'd got bored of her? And then went after his own best friend, because he had given him over to the police? Is that what you're saying?"

"I'm afraid murder is still murder. And the law is the law," Draco said, almost compassionately. "Vigilantism just isn't acceptable – it ruins all basis of court justice and procedure. A convicted murderer has already sworn to avenge Marat's death – you know that, right? Marat was like a father to him – the only person who'd ever helped him. He has sworn to kill the culprit, and if I were you I'd take his words seriously. Do you think he's got the right to lynch?"

"Just for the record, I'm not motivated by revenge. All I did was stop evil in its tracks. I took a stand against it. I wasn't going to let it dominate any longer."

"I don't see any difference."

"I didn't crave for some satisfaction – I don't want to see someone suffer over what they've done to me or anyone else. Nothing of the sort."

"Call it whatever you like, it's still a lynching." Draco kicked a clump of earth with his foot.

"Okay. I understand your position, and I agree with everything." Anderson remained calm as he spoke. "And I'm not an advocate of lynching – I condemn them. But saving my own child... That I cannot condemn. Frankly speaking, I don't understand how anyone could fail to act if their child was in need. Anyone who has a heart can't just sit there and do nothing – they get up and do whatever is in their power to rescue their child, even at the cost of their own life. That's all I can say to you." Anderson was looking straight into Draco's eyes. His gaze was so sad and solemn that it had erased all the smile lines from his face.

The two men were silent for a while.

"I genuinely believe it's impossible not to save your child, even if that means going into fire or jumping into deep water – whatever it takes," Anderson resumed after a long pause. "It's necessary for a father or a mother to sacrifice themselves to allow their child to live – I think it's only natural. It's proper and it's good."

"I still don't get it... I mean, what about the ten commandments?" Draco asked. "You're a Christian man, the leader of a congregation; how do you join these two things together?"

"*Put away your sword. Those who use the sword will die by the sword.* I guess no one mentioned that to Marat." Anderson was smiling again. "I know that killing is a sin; it's a serious one, a cardinal sin – but sometimes one must stop evil in its tracks. It just needs to be done, because we cannot allow evil to triumph in this world."

"But it's not our call to make, is it? To dish out God's or people's justice," Draco objected. "Surely, you know that."

"I disagree. God allowed us to experience evil, so that we could take a stand against it. That's the only reason God allows evil to exist – to put us through a test. To give us the opportunity to triumph over evil. God is almighty, so he could defeat all evil, if he wanted to – to strike evil in its core, to never let it fester. But for some reason God has left it up to us. Why does He do it? Why does God allow evil to exist? Why does he leave us with evil? Surely, not to make us observe it passively, waiting for someone else to do something. No, he does it so that we can take a stand. Because taking a stand against evil is like actualising the desire to strive towards goodness and truth. Giving into evil is the same as cooperating with it. It's a way of supporting evil – and it's not what God wants from us. God gave us the ability to tell evil from good, so that we would fight the good fight."

They stopped again, in accordance with Banga's latest whim.

How can such a small dog carry so much liquid, Draco caught himself thinking.

"We kill terrorists, don't we? And usually without a trial – we just fly over there, kill them, and everyone agrees that it was the right thing to do, that this was us standing up against evil. Sometimes we might kill the wrong target; say, blow up a wedding by accident – and everything is very tragic, and yet everyone still understands that there's a war between good and evil, and, as with any war, there are victims. The war between good and evil is ongoing, it happens every day, and it's just a question of conscience, whether we get involved in the fight or become passive observers."

"Mister Anderson, I'm going to remind you that you're speaking to a police officer. I've spent my whole life fighting for the law."

"You keep saying the law is the law. But ask yourself – by seeing nothing but the law, haven't you lost your ability to tell good from evil? Oh, don't get me wrong, I'm not criticising you. I'm not accusing you of anything – I've no doubt that you fight against evil. But your fight is formal and bureaucratic. Bureaucracy and formality can kill goodness."

"But the fight against evil should never be led by emotions or become subjective," Draco objected. "If everyone just started killing whoever *they* thought was the bad guy, our streets would be littered with corpses. The corpses of innocent people."

"I understand." Anderson stopped again, letting Banga have a good sniff around a bin. "However, you have to realise where I'm coming from. If we want to give evil a real push-back, sometimes we have to resort to using its weapons. What we do isn't always some banal, shallow act of evil as it may appear to someone looking in – sometimes we have to remove a tumour. We must destroy a malignant virus."

"That's all well and good, except you should leave that sort of thing to the government. The government is authorised to do that sort of thing, and you're not."

"You're right, of course. And I agree. There is a certain bureaucratic difference, although there's no difference in terms of morality."

"You think that it's a tiny bureaucratic difference whether the government kills a terrorist or whether you're the one killing someone? There's a *huge* difference!"

"Is there?" Anderson stopped again, only to look directly into Draco's eyes.

Without saying anything, Draco carried on walking. They had circled the park and were now onto their second lap.

"I don't know how to explain it, but I think we're both right. The truth is very complicated," Anderson said, smiling, as though offering the officer the chance for a truce.

"There is only one truth. There can't be two mutually exclusive realities," Draco objected grumpily.

"Perhaps I'm wrong – in fact, that's very likely. But I want you to know that my conscience really is clear. If you see a burning house with your child trapped inside, you have to enter, no matter how little hope there is. You just go in, without thinking what will happen to you, correct? Because it doesn't matter what happens to you. I may not have done everything I've ever been capable of or wanted to do, but I have acted at times. Simply doing what had to be done."

They walked in silence again for a while.

"I do have one question. And it's a very important one," Draco said after a pause. "Did Twinka know about it?"

"Are you mad?" Anderson was smiling. "Come on – who would put their own child in danger?! Who would get their child involved in something like this?"

"I understand."

Silence descended once again, as they followed the white, happy Westie, patiently stopping every time it decided to sniff around a tree or a shrub.

"Did you know that the house was tapped?"

"Yes, I did – Twinka told me. If he'd said my name, he would have at least remained alive *that* day."

"And what about dressing up as a priest?"

"Oh," Anderson tossed his hand dismissively. "I just thought, in case I get splattered in blood, it would be handy to throw on some overalls, so it doesn't soak through, that's all."

"Very sensible," Draco acknowledged. "The only thing we can hear in the recording is Marat saying: 'What's happened? What's happened?'"

"I put on a bit of an act. I pretended to be unwell, doubled myself over, to make sure he came up to me."

"Solid plan," Draco concluded.

Again they walked on in silence.

"Did you know," Draco said, breaking it, "that Marat refused to tell me who attacked him?"

"Did you manage to speak to him?"

"He was conscious for a bit before he fell into a coma. He was talking to Twinka. I was there too, and I asked him who'd stabbed him, but he didn't answer me."

Anderson didn't reply – he was watching Banga sniff around a twig that had fallen on the ground.

"Hopefully he will do now. Hopefully he'll make a statement – I'm definitely going to pop in to see him in the coming days," Draco continued.

"Let him do whatever he thinks is right," Anderson replied with indifference. "The only thing I care about is that he stops hurting Twinka and Ronia. I want him to stop ruining their lives. I'm not worried about anything else."

"The fact that he survived somewhat softens the sentence; but still, you're looking at a good few years in prison for an attempted murder with grievous bodily harm."

Bitterness slid across Anderson's face like a subtle shadow. "You have to realise that there are things we can influence and there are things that are in God's hands alone. Over the years I've learned not to stress over those I cannot influence. Do what you must, and let everything else unfold – that's my life's motto. I rely on God completely, and I recommend that you do, too." The bitterness disappeared as quickly as it had appeared, and, once again, Anderson was smiling warmly at Draco. "The minute you start trusting in God completely, you no longer have any fear. It's a very good feeling."

"I'll agree with the fact that if we want to protect them, people need to know they'll pay the highest price if they as much as lay a finger on our daughters, sisters and wives," Draco changed the topic. "But we can't guarantee it in practice, you're right about that. That's why they try. That's why they dare to attack, rape and murder," Draco was speaking like someone who'd recognised the upper hand of their opponent's argument. "We'd be living in a much better society if everyone who committed rape and everyone who dared to lay a finger on a woman knew it would be followed by revenge and punishment. Unavoidable and ruthless."

"You see," Anderson was smiling. "Our positions are not that far apart."

They had arrived at the central feature of the park – a huge, majestic oak tree.

"You're probably right: revenge can be preventative. At the same time, it's wrong and shouldn't be allowed," Draco said.

"That's exactly what I've been saying – it's right and wrong, all at the same time." Anderson sighed. "Unfortunately, that's the world we live in. Things can be both right and wrong simultaneously, and God still wants us to find a path through it."

"Maybe I should retire." Draco himself sighed.

They watched in silence as the dog had a poo.

"We've come to a dead end in Dimitri's case. We don't have a single clue. I'm losing my touch. I just can't find anything, no matter how much I search."

Anderson pulled a poo bag from his pocket and carefully cleaned up after the dog, who seemed happy and sprightly again, having completed such an important task.

"I need to start thinking about retirement. Based on my years in service, I probably could."

"Do you have anything to occupy yourself with in retirement?" Anderson asked.

"I have a daughter. That's probably plenty."

"Oh, yes, I know that all too well..."

Their eyes met briefly and they looked deep into one another's eyes.

"Thank you," Anderson said, stretching his hand out to Draco.

They shook hands firmly. The handshake felt longer and tighter than a simple goodbye.

"God be with you," Draco said and briskly walked away.

"Christ has risen," Anderson said as Draco departed. "Truly risen," he replied to himself quietly.

CHAPTER 122

"Dad, can I come see you and Mum?" Twinka had called her father immediately after leaving Anna's office.

"Darling, of course! Come anytime. We're in the park with Banga, we were just setting off for home. We did quite a distance today."

"Can you wait for me there? I'm not too far. I think I could do with a walk and some fresh air."

"Yes, of course, come on over! I'm sure you'll spot us right away."

Unbeknownst to Twinka, she happened to cross paths with Draco, who was just leaving the park.

"What's happened, darling?" Anderson asked her, having immediately picked up that something was wrong.

"Well, nothing, compared to what's happened over the last two years." Twinka smiled sadly. The presence of her dad and Banga soothed her.

"Did anyone hurt you?" Worry crept into Anderson's voice.

"No, it's all good, except for the fact that my therapist was sleeping with my husband and they'd recorded all our conversations, so that Marat could listen back to what I'd been telling her."

"Oh my God! Seriously? How did you find out?"

"Dad, is there really no one I can trust in this world?"

"You can always trust in me, darling." Anderson hugged his daughter, squeezing her tightly towards him with one hand while holding the dog leash in the other. "Always. You know that, don't you?"

"I do."

"That's what dads are for – so they can take care of their children."

"I know," Twinka said, snuggling up to her father.

Banga ran up to them and, rising on her hind legs, scratched Twinka's legs with her little paws, demanding attention.

"Ouch," Twinka shrunk away from the dog.

Anderson picked her up. Now he was embracing his daughter with one hand and holding Banga in the other.

"We'll go to church tomorrow, eh? Everything will be okay. You know you can always trust Banga and me, don't you?" he repeated.

"I know, I know." Though teary-eyed, Twinka was smiling.

Made in the USA
Las Vegas, NV
19 February 2024

85997594R00331